CW01457727

HAUNTINGS
AN ANTHOLOGY

Edited By
HANNAH KATE

HAUNTINGS
AN ANTHOLOGY

EDITED BY HANNAH KATE

TWENTY-ONE NEW TALES OF THE UNCANNY, BY:

RACHEL HALSALL

BRANDY SCHILLACE

ALLEN ASHLEY

HANNAH KATE

AUDREY WILLIAMS

JAMES EVERINGTON

DAVID WEBB

SARAH PEPLOE

MICHAEL HITCHINS

PATRICK LACEY

TRACY FAHEY

RUE KARNEY

KERIS MCDONALD

GUY BURTENSHAW

B.E. SCULLY

MARK FORSHAW

STEWART PRINGLE

DAISY BLACK

MERE JOYCE

JEANETTE GREAVES

ELISABETH BRANDER

HIC DRAGONES

HIC DRAGONES

First published 2014 by Hic Dragones
PO Box 377, Manchester M8 2DE
www.hic-dragones.co.uk

ISBN 978-0-9576790-7-8

Cover by Rob Shedwick

A CIP catalogue record of this book is available from the British Library.

Designed and typeset by Hic Dragones.

Printed and bound by CPI Group (UK) Ltd, Croydon CR0 4YY

CONTENTS

THE CONCH

RACHEL HALSALL

MY AUNT ONCE TOLD ME that when you cup a seashell to your ear the sound you hear is not, as most believe, the echo of the ocean but the last breath of someone who has drowned. As far as she was concerned this was no mere folktale or forgotten strand of sailors' mythology; it was the simple truth and that was all there was to the matter. She kept proof of the legend on the mantelpiece in the form of a large conch shell the colour of a cloud at noon—pinkish orange, inside and out, and rubbed smooth by the fingers of waves. According to my aunt this particular specimen was very special, for it contained the soul of her husband who had died when I was six years old.

She had found the shell washed up on a beach mere miles from the cove in which his boat had been dashed upon the rocks, its shattered planks afloat in a scum of blood and white algae. Three weeks had passed since the event and grief, still in its strongest swell, made my aunt so restless that the only thing that soothed her was taking long walks along the shoreline which often lasted several hours at a time. She would drift up and down along the lip of the sea until her bare feet were rubbed raw and bleeding by the rocks and pebbles there, for she always left her shoes on the steps that led down to the cove so that they weren't spoiled by the salt water. The habit persisted for several days—nights too, for it had gotten to the point that my aunt couldn't sleep without answering the wordless call of her obsession. Sometimes she would walk until evening flowed into day, the sun seeming to melt the moon into a puddle of darkness. These late excursions exhausted her, but she couldn't help herself. Sorrow had become her addiction.

It only ended when she came upon the shell.

"I don't even know why I picked it up," my aunt said, shaking her head. She had her arms plunged to the elbows in the washing bowl, and as she leaned forward to rinse I sensed the agitation in her, every inch of her body as tense as a violin string beneath the veil of her dowdy house dress. "My mother used to say that shells were dirty because nasty things like slugs and crabs crawled into them to die. If she ever caught me with one she'd always make me throw it back again, and then the minute we got home she'd scrub my fingers with this awful nail brush to get rid of all the germs. I hated that brush. Its bristles were frazzled and yellow 'cause we'd had it that long, but she still used it, bloodily scouring away. And kept on about what I'd done—you know, 'you'll catch diseases, you'll die of salmonella', and all of that. I always kept away from shells after that, even when I was grown up and she couldn't nag me anymore. Every time I bent down for a pretty one I'd remember what she said and stopped. But then, this one afternoon, I forgot."

On a whim or perhaps out of some subconscious instinct my aunt bent down to dislodge a large conch lying half-submerged in the sand at her feet. It was almost as big as her head and looked like the kind one only ever saw displayed amongst the snorkels and plastic spades in tourist shops, for it wasn't cracked or fragmented like most seashells are. This shell was flawless, even abnormal in its perfection, and yet it was real.

My aunt ended up squatting on her haunches with the conch balanced in her lap, looking at it with an interest she had been unable to muster since my uncle's death. Then, scarcely thinking about what she was doing, she had lifted the shell and held it to her ear so as to listen to the sound of the sea, just as if she were a little child still young enough to believe in such fantasies.

"But it wasn't the sea," my aunt insisted. "It wasn't the sea at all. I knew that straightaway—God, how couldn't I? It was my husband's voice, his breathing, just as if he was alive and standing there right there beside me with his mouth up against my ear."

"How did you know it was Uncle Henry?" I demanded. My voice was shrill with a child's precocious scepticism, causing my aunt to wince and turn away. "It could have been anyone, if it was anybody. My teacher said the noise you get in seashells is just rushing blood and air echoing around inside your head, and you just imagine it's something else because you want to."

"Ah, well, usually that's true," said my aunt, somewhat reluctantly. "But only if the shell's properly empty, and it hasn't got a soul trapped inside it. I suppose most of them don't, but… I think they're all open to one, sort of like a house with unlocked doors. Maybe the shells remember, in a way, that they used to be a home for a living thing, and they yearn for it, so a human soul is always welcome. I don't know that for sure, of course, but it's what I like to think."

She paused for a moment, appearing to gather her thoughts. Then she blinked and said, "Oh, I'm sorry, darling—what was it you asked? How did I know it was Uncle Henry?"

I nodded.

"I was with that man every single day for the last ten years of his life," said my aunt. "I knew all the different little sounds he made. That's what happens when you've lived with someone for a very long time. You can tell if it's them coming up the stairs just from the way they make the floorboards creak. Anyway, he'd been smoking since he was sixteen and it gave him a terrible chest; you could hear it before he'd even entered the room. You must remember that, surely. It used to frighten you when you were little. And that was what I heard when I listened to that shell. That was how I knew it was him. You know, when I lifted that thing up I could even smell the nicotine on his breath."

My aunt's eyes were closed, remembering, and as they moved beneath the lids I realised that she was seeing a face that wasn't there, a man I had barely known but she had loved. Unnerved, I glanced towards the living room door. It had been shut to keep the cat out of the kitchen, but had it been open I would have been able to see the shell sitting there on the mantelpiece where it had always been.

"I brought the shell home with me, of course," my aunt continued. "And I still smell that smell whenever I pick up the conch, and sometimes even when I don't. It seems to follow me around the house as if your Uncle Henry was walking behind me. You do remember Uncle Henry, don't you? What he looked like?"

I nodded, somewhat uncertainly. I had been so young when he died that what I recalled of his features was hazy and unreliable. However, it occurred to me that I had been frightened of him, this big, lean young man like a gangling wolf, cursed with hair turned prematurely grey and hands worn coarse by the ropes of fishing boats. It was those hands and his pale eyes that I knew best, for he would sail out with me alone sometimes and those grey-blue irises would be all I could make out through the mist of the low-hanging clouds. There were callouses on the pads of his fingers and his lips were just as rough, though soft on the inside. Over time I came to associate my Uncle Henry with the sobbing call of white Cornish gulls, winding in endless circles overhead. Although I knew that we must have spoken often about many things during these small ventures, only one conversation we'd ever had stayed firm in my mind. I recall looking out at the blurred specks of boats bobbing in the distance, most of them tourist vessels crawling with children. Watching them glide to and fro I asked if their passengers could see us as clearly as we did them. The idea, I remember, distressed me.

"No," said Henry, following my gaze. He smiled at me, the soft inner line of his lips pink and shining. "They're too far away."

I did not tell my aunt any of this, not back then and certainly not now, but I affirmed that I did indeed know what he'd looked like, and this appeared to satisfy her. Humming, my aunt pulled the plug out of the sink and began to dry the plates, forgetting all at once that I was there. I took the chance to slope off into the living room and stood there staring at the seashell that allegedly held my uncle's soul. I don't quite know what I expected to see there; some sign of occupation, perhaps, or a cloud of his infamous smoke. If so I was disappointed, for it looked disarmingly ordinary settled alongside the dainty ornaments.

But this was not enough to quell my curiosity. After checking that my aunt was still distracted by her kitchen duties I dragged a chair up to the mantelpiece and clambered onto it so that I was made tall enough to reach the shell. It was surprisingly heavy, and I struggled to get it down without letting it slip from my hands. Yet somehow I managed and settled cross-legged on the chair with the shell balanced on one knee where I gazed at it in silence.

I don't know how long it was until I mustered enough courage to lift it to my ear, but I know that it must have been a fair while because the muscles in my thighs and bottom went numb, forcing me to shift about to bring the feeling back into them. It wasn't that I was particularly frightened; in fact I was certain that it was only my aunt's grief that had made her hear her husband's voice in the shell, and I pitied her for it. Rather, I wanted to suspend the eerie fantasy, if only for a little while. My annual visits to see my aunt were pleasant but, ultimately, monotonous, so I was glad of a mystery to keep me entertained. But my curiosity bettered me and eventually I raised the cumbersome object, swivelling its blushing aperture to the side of my face.

Minutes passed. I listened, first intently, then with a thwarted disgust, for there was nothing to be heard but the expected hollow rush of my own blood bounced back at me. My aunt's story hadn't held true as I'd known in my heart it wouldn't, yet I was disappointed all the same. Sighing, I began to push the shell up back up into its spot on the mantelpiece. Then abruptly I stopped and brought it down again, my small fingers fumbling with shock. I wasn't sure whether I had imagined it or not, but for a split-second I could have sworn that there was a break in the rushing noise in which a harsh rasp slipped through.

Anticipation crackled on the surface of my skin, hair sharply upending as if I was bristling with needles. The room seemed to grow very quiet around me, although in truth there had been no sound before. And then, as I pressed the shell's hard rim against my ear, I began to hear the noise just as my aunt had described it. That slow smoker's breath, coarse and rattling, was unmistakable, and I recognised it instantly. I listened, transfixed with a horrified awe; its familiarity after so many years shocked me into stillness.

The sound began quietly, scarcely more than a papery crackle at first but soon it grew louder, louder, its hoarse, phlegmatic undertone strained into a roar. I cowered in the thrall of that sound, overwhelmed by the oppressive terror it imposed upon me. My spine was a frozen rod within me. It held me so upright that my back didn't even touch the cushion of the chair although I was pressed right against it. The breaths gradually became seized up with coughing, great hacking snarls full of phlegm and spittle that told of a promise of a cancerous death that had wrestled with the ocean and lost to it, one fate consuming the other.

Suddenly the choking ceased. The slightly more even pattern of breathing I had first heard resumed its course, though tainted now with a sly intimacy. I shuddered. It was, as my aunt had said, as if the living form of Uncle Henry was leaning over my shoulder, pushing his face up to mine. The sensation made me feel soiled and panicky. All I wanted was to cast the shell away from me but before I could do so something awful happened, something so sickeningly real and corporeal that, for all its hideous physicality, it was more frightening than anything that had come before.

Two cold, wet fingers reached out from the mouth of the shell and touched the whorl of my ear. The skin was shrivelled from years of rotting in the sea, but the callouses I knew so well remained. I felt them, as coarse and chafing as they had ever been, and they caressed me tenderly, and with love.

The shell shot out of my hands and skidded across the carpet. At once I was on my feet and staring down at where it lay, hot bile rising up in the back of my throat. Pale human fingers were writhing in the aperture of the shell like the limbs of an overturned crab, groping blindly for me. Then they withdrew inside with an audible slither, and that was as much as

The Conch

I could take. I turned and bolted for the kitchen, one hand clapped over my open mouth. In hindsight I'm sure that I was screaming, but either my palm smothered the sounds or my aunt chose not to hear them, for when I burst into the room she was still stooped over the plates with her back towards me. Whatever the case, she didn't ask what the matter was, nor did she ever enquire as to why her husband-shell was on the living room floor. I think she preferred not to know, so in love was she with the memory of my uncle that she couldn't bear to think that he might have frightened me.

Deeply shaken by what had occurred I left the house and decided to take a walk down into the centre of town. It was little more than a large fishing village and I was trusted to go there alone, for the locals knew me by sight and would keep an eye on me to make sure I didn't stray too far. Although rarely busy there were always three or four people milling about, but in spite of this there was a tranquil quality to the atmosphere that appealed to me. Yet today there was a veritable crowd, crammed into narrow streets already congested by lobster pots and café signs. They were all were very grave, talking in such hollow, sombre tones that I knew that there was something amiss.

I lingered amongst them unnoticed, shamelessly eavesdropping on the conversation. It didn't take long to get the gist of it, for all present intoned the tragedy in tones of melancholic revelry. That morning there had been an accident at sea which had involved a local ferry in the process of chivvying tourists back to the mainland. Some spontaneous fault in the engine had triggered an explosion that disembowelled the vessel and set the deck aflame. All this had happened in a matter of minutes so there had been no time for anyone to intervene, only for them to bear witness as its blackened hulk succumbed to the waves.

Later, the ferry was winched up from the depths so that the charred wreck could be trawled for remains, of which there had been many. All of the passengers and staff on board were lost that day, their bodies so severely burned that one blackened husk could not be distinguished from the other. Disturbed by the image, I slipped away under someone's arm and took up my restless walk again.

One way or another, my direction turned to the hidden cove that lay behind my aunt's house. It was barely used, being a great deal smaller than the other beaches on the island and sheltered by a labyrinth of shining black rock. I weaved my way around it, knowing the way from years of experience, and headed for the steps leading down to the sand. I shed my shoes at the topmost stair, a habit I'd picked up from my aunt. Unlike her toughened soles, my own feet, spoiled and city-soft, were hurt by the smallest of stones and soon began to bleed. At one point I grazed my heel on a sharp edge and bent to check the damage. Whilst doing so I bent my head and glanced down at the beach below.

There was no beach to be seen. None left uncovered, that was, for every inch of the sand from the cliffs to the sea was heaving with conch shells, the near endless spread of them gleaming silvery-white under the sun like a mass of pale flesh. Each was of an abnormal size and smoothness and quite empty of the creatures they had once housed, but the mouths of those turned towards me appeared to drip with something thick and pink-red, like bloodied sea-water. Flies crawled ceaselessly in and out of their apertures. Besides the waves, they were the only thing in the cove that moved.

I looked at the shells, wondering where they could have possibly come from in such a number, and why, on an unrelated note, I could hear the wind on a day that I could feel had none. The sea was so calm that the waves came in slow and languorous, their torpid strokes unprovoked by breeze. Yet I could hear it whispering, soft but insistent.

Then I realised my mistake. It wasn't the wind after all. What I was hearing was the hopeless breaths of all the people who had died on the ferry that morning. Their souls were trapped within the shells spread out below me, and having caught my attention their voices echoed across the beach, sobbing, gasping, choked upon their own death. Some were not quite breaths at all but screams of agony, but somehow the breathing was worse.

Petrified tears streamed down my face, and as I stumbled away from the beach I turned my ankle on the stairs and almost fell back onto the shore below. In the corner of my eye the mound of shells appeared to heave, and in the gaps between them I made out something charred and oozing. In my delirious horror I imagined that whatever it was rose up with shells sticking like burs to its shapeless mass and crawled up the stairs in pursuit of me, and I ran to my aunt's house barefoot and screaming, for in my panic I'd forgotten my shoes.

I stood on my aunt's porch and hammered the door in a speechless frenzy, doubling up to retch in the front garden three times before she let me in. By this time I was crying too hard for my aunt to comprehend a word I was saying; alarmed, she assumed that I was ill and put me to bed. Once tucked beneath the safety of my coverlet I tried to explain what had happened, but I was too tired to make much sense even to myself. It would have been difficult to express in words the full extent of what I'd seen on the beach, although I was certain that she wouldn't have disbelieved me had I tried. The mere idea of relating the trauma was physically exhausting, and I was asleep before my aunt had even left the room.

That night, there was a storm. I had never experienced one at my aunt's house before, although the island's geographical positioning and temporal climate meant that they were a fairly common phenomenon. The residents had purposely built their houses squat and low in order to withstand the frequent squalls unlike some of the tourist buildings, whose flimsy structures were damaged on a regular basis. But I was in no condition to take much notice of the hell-winds stirring outside. The events of the previous day had left me with a fever that made my head throb as if my skull had swelled. I sprawled in a tangle of sweat-soaked sheets, gripping either side of the mattress to prevent myself rolling off onto the floor. It felt as if I was spinning in circles, the walls and ceiling rotating like parts of a puzzle box. Ripples of sheet lightning, distorted by the storm, undulated in queer waves overhead and, with a drunken fascination, I watched them dance.

These shapes created the bizarre effect of being underwater and as the fever ebbed in and out I thought I must be drowning. Eventually the hallucination intensified to the extent that I couldn't breathe and, terrified, bellowed for my aunt to save me. She never came.

Gradually the delusions faded, and I huddled there in the dark with both arms hugging my torso. Never had I known such loneliness or abandonment; my aunt had always come when I wanted her before, whatever the reason might be. Snivelling, I grew tired of waiting and got out of bed to seek her out. I was surprised to see her bedroom door half-open. Switching on the light I found her bed was empty. The bathroom which I had passed on the way had also been unoccupied, I noticed, leaving only the spare room and the stairs unsearched.

Barefoot I crossed the landing and descended the stairs wide-legged, avoiding the boards I knew to creak, and after shuffling through the hallway went directly into the living room. The curtains at the window stood open. Clearly they been parted in a hurry, for the left hung askew on its rail and the other had been torn down completely. A sheen of condensation glistened on the inner windows; the room was sweltering with a humid, storm-birthed heat, sticky and intimate in a way I'd only ever known abroad. However, I was already so warm from my fever that it made little difference to me. Peeling the collar of my nightdress from the back of my neck, I squinted about the room for any sign of my aunt's presence. In an instant I saw her and drew back into the shadows of the doorway so that I was not glimpsed in return.

My aunt was sprawling in the armchair, her head, thrown back against it, cowled in a hood of dampened hair. Her eyes were squeezed shut, her face and body soaking with sweat. The salty tang of it was so potent that it rolled off her in pungent waves. Her long pale legs were splayed and hooked over the arms of the chair, the sticky tangle of her nightdress rucked up around the upper thighs. Its lace-rimmed hemline had become embedded in her skin and beneath it, clasped in her naked lap, was Uncle Henry's shell. Its curling point, like a wicked eye, glared at me from across the room.

My aunt was clutching the conch's white body as if it could never be close enough to satisfy her. I could see how its jagged rim cut into the flesh of her stomach and yet she was smiling, her teeth and lips bared in a too-wide grin. But she was weeping, too. Her tears were silent, awful, rolling over cheeks swollen with misery. Watching them fall felt like a dirty voyeurism, the observation of some private act which I should not see. Although I didn't understand what I'd witnessed I withdrew from the room and returned to my bed feeling even sicker than before. My mind kept straying to the ugly shell, that thing that had touched me, and I marvelled that my aunt could love such a thing as if it were a man.

The following morning was a kind of anti-climax, cool and mild, as if the night's rain had worn itself out in the violence of the storm and retired to recover its strength. I crawled to the foot of my bed to look out at the garden and the line of the sea beyond it, etched at the horizon as if in ink. After looking at it for a long time I decided with childish simplicity that I must help my aunt, and there was only one way that I could think to do so. I washed and dressed in under five minutes and went straight to the living room with my travelling bag, now empty, dragging on the floor behind me. Uncle Henry's shell was on the mantelpiece as usual, the very image of innocuousness. But my aunt's greasy fingerprints still gleamed upon its flank, and seeing them my stomach clenched at the reminder of the pain the thing had caused.

With one hand I held the top of the bag open and used the other to gingerly tip the shell inside. It was a relief to tug the zip down over it, and I scarcely believed I had managed it. The bag, as I hauled its straps over my scrawny shoulders, had grown heavy with the unnatural weight of the thing it contained. Its canvas sides had actually stretched taut at the seams which alarmed me, for I feared it would split and spill the captive object onto the floor with a clatter that would wake my aunt.

Keeping both hands clenched over the strained stitches I edged into the kitchen and opened the nearest drawer with my elbow. There was a spool of sticky tape amongst the cutlery, the thick brown variety my aunt used to seal parcels or wrap around pan handles. Twisting my head at an obscure angle I was able to tear off several long clumsy strips with my teeth which I wrapped around the bag in the places it was weakest. Smears of saliva and crumpled ends made it tricky to apply, but I forced myself to persevere until I was satisfied that it held strong.

I left the house with the bag strapped to my back, walking in a hunched, unnatural fashion so as to avoid the shell touching my back even between layers of material. As if this weren't difficult enough I quickly became aware of something cold and wet dribbling onto my bare legs. From a skywards glance I knew that it couldn't possibly be rain, yet drop after drop rolled down my thighs and seeped into my socks. I paused in bewilderment, sliding the bag off one shoulder, and it was there I found the source. The canvas was drenched through and still dripping; somehow the shell was leaking, and from the salty fug I knew it was seawater.

I gave a disgusted moan and peeled the travelling bag from my body, holding it away at arm's length. The strain of its weight upon my wrist was secondary to my revulsion, and besides, I didn't have far to go. Ahead of me, the steps leading down to the cove jutted from the cliff like a broken ribcage. As I drew up to them my apprehension grew, my mind flitting back to the death mound of molluscs heaped upon the shoreline. I needn't have worried. The squall of the previous night had washed them all away, leaving the sand pale and naked in its wake. I was reassured by the sight, but regretted that I had to spoil the smoothness of the virgin sand.

After slipping off my trainers I stepped down onto beach. Even now foul water pulsed from the bag, running down the lengths of my upper arms. Holding my breath, I hoisted it over to the sea's edge and stood, ankle-deep, in the churning spray. The water was unusually dirty, the tide afloat with algae scum and tattered jellyfish. A dead shark, filmy-eyed and desiccated, lay belly up in the shallows. Gulls patrolled in the air around it, cawing piteously, yet not quite daring to swoop with me standing in such close proximity. I'd always been told never to throw stones at the birds, but then I felt that nothing would have given me more pleasure than the thick thud of rock against flesh and an agonised caw as I sent the whole the flock scattering.

The Conch

With shaking hands I opened the travelling bag and let it fall to my feet, lifting the shell out into the open air. Ignoring the ghastly whoop of my own nervous breath I turned the conch's black mouth towards me. Glistening dabs of seawater quaked on the pinked curl of the aperture, drawing my gaze down into it. I was glad that I'd looked before putting it to my ear, for the shell began to foam a glutinous lather like a threatened snail. The gnawing dread this provoked in me was dizzying. I let out a weak cry and peeled my palms from its surface, but this wasn't enough to stop it. Without even having to put it to my ear I could hear that hideous breathing again, and this time it formed words.

"They're too far away," it said. "They'll never see us. Never see us. They're too far away."

It broke off with a thick, gargling snarl that sprayed rank foam up into my screaming face. As it dripped from my eyes and mouth I realised in a near-aggressive burst of shame that I had wet myself. It was humiliation, not fear, that gave strength to my arm as I crooked my elbow back and lobbed the shell out into the sea as far as I possibly could.

There was such clumsy force behind the throw that the entire limb from wrist to shoulder was set alight with a roaring ache that I knew would last for days. Yet it was worth the effort, for the shell travelled several feet before it landed, knocking a garish orange buoy aside and sinking with a ripe sucking noise that was almost greedy. In the place where it had been, the water churned and rippled, unsettled by the monstrous thing it had taken, and I clenched my fists in anticipation of it being expelled again. But it didn't come back.

23

The waves settled back into their usual motion and I stood so still, watching them, that the seagulls grew brave and dived for the body of the shark.

Their quarrelling squawks as they scrabbled at the fish disoriented me, or else drew me back into a reality that was alien to me in the absence of horrors. Shaking my head, I took several steps back and sat down heavily in the sand. Somehow I didn't know how to feel. Getting at my emotions was like trying to prise one's fingers beneath the lid of a box that has rusted shut; I only felt numb and listless, too drained for tears. When planning this jettison I'd expected relief and exultation, wild with liberty, but in the wake of the event I felt nothing, perhaps because I wasn't free.

For now I understood that I wasn't rid of my uncle despite what I'd done. The mind is a shell that remains inhabited long after the death of its occupant. I couldn't cast out my memories as I could their physical manifestation; without a solid medium for their projection I was constantly trapped with that presence, no longer able to leave it behind on the mantelpiece. Now I was haunted by the clarity of my own recollections, and they were a ghost that I could not exorcise, and the sea could not bear away.

Squatting quietly in the sand, I cupped my hands over my ears and listened to the breathing.

GHOST PINE LAKE

BRANDY SCHILLACE

I T WAS A FUNNY OLD place, he'd always said so.

In the dockhouse of Ghost Pine Lake, Arthur McGhee stubbed out his cigar. Then, he carefully tucked the stump (barely distinguishable from his tobacco-stained fingers) into the folds of his coat.

"Fer later, ye understand," he croaked apologetically at a slim young man.

The man—hair slicked back in the popular way, black suit, fetching hat—was only one of two standing on the dock, but the other wore sunglasses. McGhee didn't like talking to folks who wore sunglasses. Great big holes in their face; you never knew what they were looking at.

"Take your time," the slim man said, though he clearly didn't mean it. They had come without calling ahead at the end of the season. Most of the vacationers were gone and the weather was changeable. McGhee didn't get many boat-renters this time of year and didn't like to hurry.

"Fifteen-horse. That alright with ye?" McGhee pushed a piece of carbon paper at him. "Sign fer it. It takes just gas, none o' the oil. Easier to run it, don't make such a foul smoke."

The slim man did not reach for a pen.

Behind him, Sunglasses smiled, all teeth. "We'll pay in cash," he said, and Slim nodded agreement. "We only need it for a short spell, anyway."

"Ye pay by the day round here," McGhee reminded him. "Twenty-four hours. Rules o' the lake."

Slim opened a sleek leather wallet. Crisp and clean it was; the sort you never saw for sale on Father's Day. He folded a bill and placed it on the counter. Then he pushed it forward until its papery edge slid beneath McGhee's thick fingernail. A hundred. Three times what it cost to rent the boat for the whole damned weekend.

"Ain't got change."

"Then keep it."

McGhee's watery blue eyes wandered upward, peering out of grizzled hair and faded denim cap like distant stars. Sunglasses was still smiling, teeth like gate pickets. Slim smiled too. Both of them oily as the water snaking round the bilge pump. *Them* kind of fellas.

"You ever been to Ghost Pine before?" McGhee asked, digging out the cigar stub and lighting it again.

"We're new to the place," said Slim.

McGhee nodded from his cloud of blue-gray smoke.

"I reckon, then, you ain't never seen the light on the water, layin' soft as lovers? Never seen it go fuzzy round the edges, twistin' like smoke and fog?"

Slim exchanged a look with Sunglasses.

"We just want to see the lake. Just tonight."

"Sure." McGhee left the bill on the counter and ambled around the side. "Fog an' all that light playing out there. An' this time of night—sundown comin'."

He snatched a shapeless mass of wool from the door-hook—a greatcoat that had seen better centuries. His bowed body shrugged it on, and his gnarled fingers found the deep familiar pockets. If they were going out this time of night, he may as well go ready.

"The boat's jest here," he muttered over the cigar stub. "This 'un."

"A wooden boat." Sunglasses said his questions without question marks. It saved time in his line of work.

"Aye. Can't trust aluminum."

McGhee uncoiled the ropes, taking what seemed to be unnecessary amounts of time and happily chattering to himself.

"Can't trust batteries, neither. Always best to have yer oar in. The light, she goes pink at the edge with the sundown. All white like a will-o-wisp candle. Ye ain't never seen a lake dance like that—here…" He handed Slim a kerosene lantern. "When she get dark 'round here, she get dark."

"We don't plan to be out long," Slim reminded him.

"We don't, but we never know, do we?" McGhee asked, eyes twinkling.

"We," asked Sunglasses. McGhee just smiled, more yellow stumps clutched round the red-cinder cigar.

"We. But I bet you 'ave somethin' you wanna get out your car, don't you?" he asked. "That long black car. Somethin' big an' lumpy you don't want no more."

A pause. Sunglasses knew when Slim was thinking. He could tell by the way his spine turned rigid, and how his face got the look of brittle plastic, sharp around the edges. Slim tugged his fedora into place. He knew his work.

"Does that happen often?" he asked. "People here in black cars."

"Oh, now and then. I know *them* kind of fellas," McGhee said, and Sunglasses nodded. He knew *his* work too.

"You ought to come out with us then."

McGhee puffed, watching the sun slide down the golden treetops of Ghost Pine Lake. A fog was rising, strange and white and menacing.

"Oh aye," he said. "I always do."

Water lapped the boat's wooden sides to the sound of an idling engine. McGhee kept his hand steady on the throttle. Years of use had taught him the sweet-spot—that is, fish-trolling speed—of every motor at the dock.

"Ye got to love it a bit, see," he muttered, chewing the cigar (which had gone out). "Got to jest ease her in place, like."

Sunglasses and Slim were perched awkwardly on the slat seats—one on either side of a troublesome looking plastic bag. It had been, at least, troublesome to get it in the boat; their leather shoes and spats were damp, and Slim's sleek pant leg wet to the knee. He'd lost the fedora, too. His slick blond hair reflected the sun's last rays almost as well as his partner's reflective lenses.

"It does go faster than this, doesn't it?" Slim asked.

"When it want to, sure enough," McGhee said, but without the least indication of changing speed.

"It's getting dark," Sunglasses said.

McGhee's face was creased like an overused map, but it was still possible to discern the occasional spasm of mirth.

"Well, you got them glasses on," he said, simply, and then turned back to the serious business of setting their course.

Ghost Pine Lake was crescent-shaped, long and lean at the edges, wide and flat in the middle. It was an old lake too, covering ancient canyons and unnumbered centuries with deep, cold water. It was McGhee's specialty, carving through and leaving scarcely a ripple, no sound but the quiet hum of low speed.

"Somethin' special about wood boats," McGhee said. "They know water. They used to be trees."

Slim ignored this aside like he'd ignored the other ones, in vain hopes that the old man would stop talking. The sun was nearly gone, just a red stain leaking through the pine boughs.

"The middle," he said, pointing to the empty center.

"Sure? It's funny out there," McGhee went on, now appearing to address the roughly man-sized plastic bag at their feet. "Rises up. You know the curve o' the earth?"

"It's round, yeah," said Sunglasses. He'd learned a few things in his schooldays, after all.

"Aye, it's round. An' the lake, she be like that."

29

Slim reflected back an empty expression he'd perfected with the boys in Chicago. But McGhee went on anyway.

"Like the earth, I always said so. Water piled up on itself out here. Standing on the shoulders o' all them years below it."

"Are we there yet?" Slim asked.

"We're always *there*."

McGhee slowed the engine until it idled. The water eddied strangely and there was a white mist rising, floating on the water, dancing with soft light. Sunglasses reached for one end of the plastic bag.

"You dropping that over the edge, then?" McGhee asked. He was leaning back, hands in his pockets, squinting at the two men as though seeing them through a glass darkly.

"You said so yourself, old man."

"I says people do it. I didn't say you was gonna. It's pollutin' like."

"Well." Sunglasses hefted the man-shaped object (which had gone rather stiff). "We's gonna."

McGhee kept his post, looking for all the world like he was carved out of wood himself: a knotty old pine, badly hewn into the likeness of a codger chewing a cigar. They ignored him, Slim and Sunglasses, and wrestled instead with the plastic bag. It went over with a splash, light end first, heavy concrete end last, and sank quickly out of sight.

Then again, *everything* was sinking out of sight. The light had gone, and McGhee was right: when she got dark, she got dark. The mist was curling up around them too. It rolled in like a low cloud over a plain, hiding the distant shore.

"Now, you," said Sunglasses, turning toward McGhee. It might have been menacing. But McGhee only plucked the cigar from his teeth and held it between his yellow fingers.

"I wouldn't think you boys could make it back by yerselves," McGhee said, examining the tobacco stump. "What with the fog and that."

Sunglasses had been lumbering slightly forward, digging about in his coat for a purposefully heavy object. Now he looked around.

"It is getting thick."

There was pea-soup thick: cloggy and yellow. Then there was this. Wispy tendrils filleted the water like a hovering squid: ghost-white, lit up with moonlight, diffuse and dancing.

"She wouldn't like you callin' her thick," McGhee said, speaking as a matter of fact. Then, he killed the engine.

"What are you doing?" Slim demanded, a faint edge of panic to his voice.

"Now you look jest like the rest," McGhee grinned in the dark.

The fog was starting to spin on a sudden breeze. It whirled like a vortex, getting whiter, brighter, more compact. Sunglasses finally took his off his shades.

"Like—the rest—of *what?*" He stuttered over the words, but he was full of inflection.

"Fellas that come always look jest as scared as you when they first sees her."

Her.

"Whatisthat?" Slim choked suddenly, but he wasn't waiting for answers. He was a man of action, after all, and he had about six rounds of action on his person.

"Oh, she won't like that, neither," McGhee whispered. "She won't bear with bein' threatened."

But it was too late. Slim was already firing, and—not to be left out—Sunglasses was firing too. The blasts echoed on the water, ricocheted off the tree-line. The bullets themselves passed harmlessly over the waves, lodging themselves in dirt and deadwood.

THAT WAS HOW IT usually went.

The white light pulsed, drew itself in like a breath, and waited. In the sudden quiet, the world went still, and Slim and Sunglasses had twenty seconds to see her, as she really was: ice and cold and steel, teeth and claw and scale, the lady of the lake.

BUT ONLY ARTHUR understood her.

Suddenly, the silence burst—like hurricanes and gales, saved over centuries, it rolled over the boat in a banshee squall. It spun the little vessel; it zapped the engine; it sucked the battery; it charged the craft with electrical pulses that would have turned a metal boat into a fiery conductor.

McGhee tucked himself into his greatcoat and nestled like a hibernating ground squirrel into the prow. Waiting. And when the lake grew quiet, he was alone.

That was how it usually went too.

McGhee unfolded himself, straightened his cap, and dug about in deep pockets for a light. He puffed, pulling on the cigar until the tip glowed red and smoke (real smoke) mingled in the air. They never understood… them kind of fellas.

He put his oar in the water. It would take an hour or so to make it back, but the fog was lifting. It played along the edge of the waves, diffuse in the moonlight. The old man smoked in the silence, humming to himself.

It was a funny old place, Ghost Pine Lake.

He'd always said so.

HAUNTING MELODY

ALLEN ASHLEY

WE AGREE TO MAKE A temporary base at this house in the blasted countryside. The horse needs the respite from the violent weather. Bricks and timber have survived thus far and can shelter us and our working animal for a while at least. Nobody ever said reclamation was going to be a walk in the park.

Derek is the first to comment upon the music just at the edge of hearing.

"I wonder where it's coming from," he says. "Doesn't it remind you of something?"

"Yes, something classical," I say, busy lugging supplies into where I judge to be the central—and therefore the most secure—portion of the building.

"No," he continues, "it was a popular hit when I was a child. It even had words. One of the divas used to sing it.

Something about when the world was young and love was new… You must remember it, Adam."

He hums a little of it, complete with his trite words. I wish he would divert this energy into necessary labour. The tune nags away in the background like morning bells or the lost song of the nightingale, but it's not as he describes it. The first few notes are similar—perhaps transposed a semitone or two—but then Derek's nostalgic ditty goes into a major fifth associated with uplifting music; the piece I keep hearing descends into minor keys, unresolved sevenths and ninths. Unable to be resolved. The emotional effect is quite, quite different.

"Maybe we can locate the source," I say as I take a brief break to flex my fingers. "Once we've finished our tasks here. I'm sure that the tune will become tiresome and downright irritating after a while."

"It reminds me of better days," he says.

He is stuck with the wrongly ascribed lyrics and they've coloured his emotions. Then again, we're both old enough to recall those long lost, better days. Which is no excuse for shirking in the here and now.

IT'S JUST A TUNE BUT it nags into my brain and I can't get rid of it. It reminds me of the Beethoven melody 'Für Elise'. I always wondered who the real Elise was and how special she must have been to inspire such music. She would certainly have been beautiful or charming or striking or coy or possessing

35

other traditionally feminine qualities. I wish she were here with us now. I could wish for almost any woman, so mono-sexual is our environment.

"One of you," I say, "has deceived us and brought along some sort of still-functioning electronic device. A phone, an MP3, whatever."

We submit ourselves again to bag searches. Nothing is recovered.

Perhaps there is something wrong with our recording and monitoring apparatus. It has never been subject to trilling or tinkling the ivories, not ever, but that was back in the lab. In field conditions, who knows what might happen? I nervously ponder a ghost in the machine.

We don't really believe in ghosts, we survivors. We are rationalists and cynics. We eat our rations and know that the blander the taste the better they are for our health. We hear the wind whipping round the outer walls and don't fancy that there are spirits and ghouls abroad.

Anthony speaks of ancient hauntings, perhaps a famous musician who met an untimely end but whose piano still broadcasts his final composition to an uncaring, barely perceptive world.

There is no piano or evidence of one ever having been in this habitation.

Besides which, Anthony is an idiot. Qualifications, courses and abbreviations after your name count for nothing in his case. Maybe he swallowed a global tracking device and that's what's playing up. He can keep his lost souls to himself.

Haunting Melody

In traditional plotlines from the old DVD age, Anthony would either be the first to go or the last. First because he had the knowledge and the phantom wants to leave us increasingly powerless. Last because he would need and relish the opportunity to crow 'I told you so' a few times before being bumped off.

There are no ghosts, no supernatural beings. But I hear the music far too often.

I'M THE OLDEST IN OUR group by some distance but I'm not the leader. Our new world vision has attempted to dispense with such titles. It's all about relevant skills: What can you carry? How far can you walk? Can you read and rewire?

The compound that we left two days ago is not the first semi-permanent home that I've known these past few years since the climate changed. It's all about finding stores of food and fuel to keep us going from one day to the next. I used to work in financial services and before that I was in car insurance. Not an easily transferable skill set but I have done what I can in this world without the internet, mobile phones, electricity and, in most places, mains water. The next task is to encourage plants to grow again. Even if we are to be reduced to living off mushrooms and root vegetables, we need to replenish. My stomach never coped that well with beetroot and carrots before but these are different days…

"Adam," John interrupts my thoughts, "what do you think this building used to be?"

I shake my torch, demanding another few minutes of life from the nearly spent batteries as I sweep the beam into the shaded recesses of the damp and musty cellar. "My information is that it was a divinity college or a monastery, something of that sort," I answer. "A place for retreat and silent contemplation."

"Not going to get much silence around here," he says. "What with the wind and that tune. It's driving me crazy. It's worse than some of those old ringtones from the time before. It's doing my head in."

"I'd say it was more like... a music box that's got stuck."

"Christ, you might be right! I hadn't thought of that. We should search the place thoroughly, put it out of action."

I mumble agreement even though I'm thinking that we have more pressing concerns than shutting off an annoying sound source.

BACK AT THE COMPOUND, I hardly ever dreamed. Now that we're trapped with each other for the foreseeable, I sleep fitfully, plagued by visions called forth by that annoying ostinato. Maybe it's an effect of our water supply. Sure, we strain it through gravel and break up wood to boil every drop that we drink, but I still suspect that it contains mercuric toxins which will affect our brains as if we were Bronze Age shamans.

The cunning drip-drip of its silent, quicksilver fingers will rot away our intellects first. Death will be slow, agonising and inevitable.

Isn't it always inevitable?

In my most recent dream, I had traced the source of the sound to an attic warren. A hooded figure raced ahead of me and I knew that he was responsible for the irritating music. I raced after, careless in pursuit. The wooden joists wobbled beneath my weight. I ducked under some eaves and then I was in a cellar, no longer above our sleeping quarters but below them. Dream logic; I didn't question it.

Dust and fibres were falling off my cloaked prey. One desperate lunge and I had hold.

He turned to face me and the shocking thing was that he looked so ordinary. Just an average Joe, eminently forgettable. Maybe that was the point.

Until he smiled. Teeth whiter than starlight reflected on new-fallen snow.

With grubby fingers, he began playing these bright molars and incisors like they were piano keys. That annoying melody, over and over—until the walls collapsed around us and there was nothing in the world except wind-blown desolation and those notes in D minor.

I don't remember waking. Perhaps I haven't... No, that's too fanciful.

I'm sure he was a *he*. The more I analyse the dream, the more I think he was a facet of the Earth Mother, Gaia, and I was being shown an image of what we have done to the once beautiful world. As if I didn't know already.

All set to moody music like it was some pop video from the old days.

~~~

YEARS AGO I NEEDED A soft mattress and comfy duvet in order to sleep but nowadays I'm more used to stretching out on cold hard floors wrapped up in a mud-stained coat or scrap of tarpaulin. Slumber is often fitful.

And is broken suddenly by raised voices and urgent commotion. Anthony, close by, already has one hand on a torch and another on his rifle. It seems likely that we are being raided by a gang from a rival compound. We've had to fight such battles before.

The door to the room crashes open. I am up on my feet but have yet to locate my sturdy boots. In the flickering light there is an initial confusion of movement, aggressive gestures and shouted expletives.

The intruder is revealed as our colleague John, but his eyes are unnaturally wild. He wields a knife in his left hand and I instinctively take a couple of steps backwards, locking into a defensive position. He waves the blade—

—and slashes at his ears like a crazed Van Gogh.

"Make it stop! Make the music stop!" he yells.

Anthony edges towards him, urging calm. John's actions are angular, unpredictable. Blood runs down the side of his neck, soaking stains into the collar of his pale blue sweater, as if the clouds in the sky were bleeding.

A sudden flurry of motion, dragging me into its whirlpool. Hands pummelling, grabbing, grappling, the three of us fighting with what little strength we can muster from our strict rations. Joined by others into the fray, alerted by our nocturnal cacophony—pulling us apart, restraining, tending to wounds with inadequate first aid kits.

I'm bruised and scratched but otherwise unharmed. Anthony has an incision on his right arm; Derek endeavours to staunch the flow. John, however, lies dead on the floor, his weapon discarded next to him. We are not medics nor pathologists. He has sustained deep lacerations but could just as easily have perished from a blow to the head as he crashed to the ground.

The annoying, omnipresent tune is a mockery of a funeral dirge.

"Rest in peace, friend," I whisper, wondering how culpable Anthony and I will be judged in our colleague's demise. "Rest in peace. Peace at last."

I'M CONCERNED FOR White Star, our horse. We have cooped up this gelding in an unsuitable outhouse for two days now as the weather worsens. He's been a trusty servant but is now confined to an unlit, airless space stinking of his own manure. If he doesn't get regular exercise he'll go lame and be rendered useless to us, except as an emergency meat source. I lead him slowly round the edge of the house, holding tightly to the reins against his nervous skitters. He needs a proper ride but I can't offer more than ten minutes sedate pacing in this wild wind and acidic rainfall. Thousands of years ago a few species from the animal kingdom made a pact with humankind to be our servants or beasts of burden and, with the changed world order, we are glad of their continued compliance. But this is how we currently repay them—scraps from our food table and solitary confinement as we ponder our next move.

TREVOR HAS BEEN BUSY with our stash of semi-functioning electrical equipment. There are those within the Institute for Renewed Progress who believe we should dispense with such hangovers from the old days and develop a lifestyle more in tune with the new climactic conditions. The new conditions are: nothing will grow; vegetation will wash away in the near-incessant rains; wildlife has been decimated and only a small selection of domesticated creatures survives under our weakening umbrella. Scientists predict another month, another half year, another decade… take your pick when it comes to the misery of surviving.

Of course, I suspect that Trevor has somehow set off the music that is driving us all crazy. Some sort of electronic conjunction that I don't understand, an alarm system or sympathetic vibration from some buried electronic instrument. If only we could locate it and shut it up.

Haunting Melody

I'm clinging to rational possibilities here and refusing to go along with the more lurid supernatural suppositions that have been spouted by my erstwhile colleagues. Spooks and hauntings are old-fashioned nonsense; we have enough to deal with in the real world without resorting to irrational fireside tales of ghosts playing invisible pianos.

Anthony has heard enough, however, and declares his intention to follow the course of the flooding river a little further to the west in search of somewhere else that might offer food supplies and, more importantly in his eyes, be further away from the tinkling that never stops. Derek, Trevor and I agree that he can take White Star with him.

I think that's a silent admission that we've reached this far and will go no further.

Anthony intends to leave in the morning. The sky has been grey or black for three days now; only Anthony's digital wristwatch tells us the difference between day and night. Further reliance on the old technology that no longer seems quite so relevant to our current condition.

JUST THE THREE OF US now. Just the same trio of choices on the metaphorical table: to push ahead with our mission of reclamation; to hold fast here and consolidate what we have; or to admit defeat and head back to the compound. Options one and three both involve braving the meteorological conditions which today are as wild as I've ever seen them. Who could last a minute in that maelstrom? Staying put, however, can only be a temporary solution, one which involves hearing the irritating tune over and over.

Derek is pacing up and down with his gloved hands over his ears. It's a disconcerting dance in response to, but not in time with, the ever-present music.

"Shit, guys, I can't stand it anymore!" he says. "Are you sure you looked everywhere?"

"You were with us, Derek," I answer. "If there's a stone you think we've left unturned—"

"This place is haunted. You know that. They play this music and it drives you mad and then they play it again when they come to kill you. I know that sounds like some crappy old horror film, but that's the way I see it."

Trevor quietly: "And just who are 'they', Derek?"

"Christ, I don't know! The enemy of some sort. The people or the supernatural beings who are behind this whole catastrophe. The aliens or the future race that wants us out of the way." A brief pause in his ravings before he bends down to where I'm sitting and I look into his brown eyes and see not an unhinged mind but considered decision. Like the calm in the eye of a hurricane. "Adam," he whispers, "you know we're wasting our time here. You can set up as many glasshouses and polytunnels as your strength will manage but nothing's gonna grow. This place is cursed. Maybe the whole world is cursed. What if this tune is now playing all across the face of the Earth? It's the death rattle of mankind."

"Very droll," Trevor says. "I've got chores to attend to, so how about *you* give *me* some peace?"

"Peace? If only—"

An hour later, Derek is beyond the wall without further goodbyes and with only a day's supplies to sustain him. Neither of us who remain gives chase.

I wonder whether my disturbed friend is right, that the incessant music has now become ever-present across the ravaged planet and whether it serves as some sort of precursor to further travails and tribulations. Or perhaps Derek will get lucky and find a distant spot where the maddening melody is rendered inaudible.

Either way, I don't expect to ever see him again.

THEN IT CAME TO ME in a strange mash-up of observer theory and solipsism: we had all been hearing either a different tune or differing versions of that ostinato. There was common ground, certainly, but we weren't all on the same plane. Any attempt to combat the effects of the nagging melody was doomed to fail.

TREVOR'S HAD ENOUGH of being cooped in here. "I'm going out," he says.

"Into that?" I say. "It's certain death."

"Maybe so, but what a good way to go, eh, Adam? I want to see the new purple river at close hand. We are living in incredible times for our Earth, most likely the final days. As much as we might be seen as the perpetrators of this disaster, it behoves us to also be the witnesses. Don't hold me back."

I could take him down in a fistfight—he's scraggly, unkempt, well out of condition. Even more than I am… In a thriving economy, the institute would've pensioned him off. Violence isn't going to solve anything, though. Besides, I like the guy.

I help him to prepare his equipment. His green eyes twinkle behind the goggles and I'm sure he's smiling behind his mouth filter. Little good it's going to do him. We'd already detected excess amounts of argon, sulphurous oxides and methane in the local atmosphere two weeks ago; conditions have surely worsened since.

He seems such a small, insignificant figure as he treks across the battered landscape. Representative of humankind in general. And yet we have over-achieved as a species… with disastrous consequences.

The river has expanded and changed its course over the past few days, cutting off our retreat should we ever seek to try to return to base. It rolls and swirls now like the extended claw of some monstrous beast. A bright purple liquid, pleasing to the eye, emitting splashes of yellow and puffs of vapour that are surely noxious clouds rather than mere water vapour. Even a gas mask wouldn't protect your lungs for very long against those deadly emissions. Trevor has described it as a roiling dragon and I could see the appeal now.

He steps forward slowly, a hypnotised victim of the mighty surge.

Haunting Melody

Our walkie-talkies have been intermittent at best but now mine sputters back into crackly life with Trevor's awed voice offering an awed commentary.

"That tune we keep hearing," he says. "I know what it is now: it's the sound the river makes. Oh, Adam, it's so beautiful. I'm going to stop talking and just listen a little closer—"

I ALONE AM LEFT HERE to tell the tale.

C, Dm, Em, F, Gm, F, Em, Dm—is that right?

I hear the tune all my waking hours and throughout much of what passes for sleep. One by one the music has called and taken each of us, and so I know for certain that these must be my final moments.

F, Gm, Am, Bm, B, Bm, Am, Gm, F?

Amongst Trevor's discarded belongings I've found a recording device—some type of Dictaphone running onto a mini disc. For a while, I suspected that he'd rigged up the whole supernatural melody business as a bizarre, backfiring prank. Brief investigations prove otherwise. Besides which, I have now listened to that infernal ostinato so long that I can no longer recall a time before and without it.

Perhaps that is the key. The melody was already there, calling us to this place, and we heard it subliminally throughout the wretched journey. Mere automata, unable to resist its spell.

I'm not sure how receptive the microphone is on this machine. Can you hear the melody? Now can you hear it?

Maybe it's too faint to fully register. Let me hum it for you. It goes like this…

LEVER'S ROW

HANNAH KATE

THERE'S A BRANCH OF Superdrug in town that sells the weirdest things. I don't mean the one in the Arndale—though that branch has a bit of weirdness all of its own. Do you ever stand in that bit of the Arndale, near where Superdrug is, and try to remember what it was like before the bomb? It's weird—like you can sort of picture the way the Arndale used to look, but not quite. You think you can remember where each of the shops were, and how things were laid out. You can almost put your finger on where you had to stand to catch the first smell of the fish stall in the old Arndale market, or where you'd go out to the bus stops on Cannon Street, but then it's not there—all you can see is Nando's and those big glass lifts to the car park.

What do you mean, what bomb? Oh, I forget you only moved here a couple of years ago. But you must know about the bomb? It was in—I think—1996. A bomb went off outside

Marks and Spencer's. The big one near the Corn Exchange—that's the Triangle now. The centre of town was pretty badly destroyed. It took them years to rebuild the Arndale and Marks and Spencer's—well, that building's partly Selfridges now. It was scary when it happened—I was a teenager and a lot of my friends had Saturday jobs in town. They were all okay, but they had to be evacuated by the police. Up Market Street and into Piccadilly Gardens.

But speaking of Piccadilly Gardens, I wanted to tell you about that other branch of Superdrug—the one that sells the weird things. It's the branch in Piccadilly Gardens that I mean. Just up from Debenhams. It's not like any other Superdrug that I've been in before.

I first noticed something wasn't right when I went in a couple of months ago—I was looking for a nice aftershave for my brother's birthday. I went to the perfume counter, sniffed at a couple of samples, got asked all the usual questions about whether he likes musky or fruity scents, that sort of thing. I was waiting for the girl to make another recommendation—she had her back to me, looking at the shelves—my eyes sort of wandered over to the other side of the shop. And you'll never guess what they were selling—records. Actual vinyl records. They had a whole wall of them, in those display shelves everywhere used to have—though you're probably a little bit too young to remember that, since I'm only just old enough myself—and there was even a customer flicking through them.

Apparently there's a couple of second-hand vinyl shops round the corner, on Oldham Street, so I guess it's not too strange to see someone shopping for records in Piccadilly Gardens. But I didn't really expect to see it in Superdrug.

"When did you start selling second-hand records?" I said to the perfume girl.

"Oh, we don't sell second-hand here. You'd have to go up Oldham Street for that."

"But I can see them over there," I said, pointing at the man who was engrossed in the back of a sleeve he'd pulled out of the rack.

"They aren't second-hand records," she said, and she sounded like she was a bit amused by my mistake. "We only sell new stuff here."

"New records?"

"Oh yes," she said. "All the new releases."

Well, I didn't know how to answer that, so I just bought my aftershave and left. I didn't think too much about it—just that it seemed an odd thing for a branch of Superdrug to do. It surprised me that they still release anything on vinyl, to be honest.

NO, YOU'RE RIGHT. That new road layout is a pain in the neck. I used to just cut along the side of the Printworks, down Dantzic Street and past the Ragged School—now you get taken all round the houses. It's not really much of a short-cut any more—you might as well just go up Cheetham Hill.

The Ragged School? I don't know too much about that. I think it was built when all that area was slums. Do you not remember that story about what the archaeologists found when they were getting ready to build the new Co-op building? You know, that big glass building that looks a bit like a boat. They found the site of a Victorian house and fishmonger's shop. The papers said it would have been a horrible, cramped little place, because Dantzic Street—it was called Charter Street back then—was part of the filthiest slum in Manchester. They found a privy that they reckon was shared by nearly a hundred people. So, I guess that's why there was a Ragged School on Charter Street—sounds like they needed it, from what I read. Angel Meadow—that was the name of the slum. Bit of an ironic name, when you think about how horrible it must've been. I think there's a park on Rochdale Road called Angel Meadow now—must be to remind people, or to make the area seem nice again. It's probably something to do with Regeneration. We seem to have quite a bit of that.

But I've gone off on a tangent. I was telling you about Superdrug, wasn't I? About what happened the next time I went in.

It was a couple of weeks later, and this time I wanted to pick up some bits and pieces like shampoo and that. I didn't see any records this time, but when I got close to the back of the shop—where the pharmacy counter used to be—it was all laid out like a café. I was a bit surprised, because I didn't think branches of Superdrug had cafés in them. And I didn't think there would be much point putting one in the Piccadilly branch, when you've got Starbucks, Caffè Nero and Costa all on the doorstep.

But this wasn't like those coffee shops—it was more like a restaurant really. There were waiters and waitresses going around, and menus on all of the tables. I thought—I might as well have a coffee while I'm here, so I went and sat down. I actually wondered if I was going to get told to move, because they had this stern-looking man in a uniform watching all the tables. He didn't come over though—I got the impression he was really there to keep an eye on the waiters.

I've never seen a menu like the one on that table. It was a full dinner menu, but it said if you wanted something called the 'general bill of fare', you had to ask a waiter for a pink card. I can't remember everything on it, but I know it included lemon sole and grilled mutton cutlet. In a Superdrug café! I also noticed that it had a warning not to tip the waiters—it said the staff were 'not permitted to benefit by any breach of the regulations'. Have you ever seen anything like that before?

Suddenly, out of nowhere, a string quartet started playing. I kid you not. A string quartet in a café—I was that taken aback, I didn't even notice the waitress standing next to me. Mind you, the waitresses were nipping about the tables so fast, it's not surprising I didn't spot her.

"Can I just have a latte?" I said to her.

"What's that then?" She was all smiles, but she sounded confused.

"Oh, just a coffee then." I didn't really know what to say.

"Certainly. And would you like any cakes with that?"

"No thank you. Can I just ask," I said, "if you always have a string quartet playing in here?"

"In the afternoons we do. We have other entertainment in the evenings." She nodded at a bright poster in a frame on the wall. "You should come to one of our supper dances. We're known for them, you know."

And with that, she'd rushed off again. When she brought my coffee, I drank it faster than I normally would, left some money on the table (without a tip), and hurried out into the main part of the shop.

As I was bustling my way out, trying to avoid drawing any attention from the café supervisor, I nearly bumped into a woman refilling the make-up section.

"Sorry," I started to say, but I could see the shop doors over her shoulder, and something struck me as being a bit off.

"No, my fault," the woman said. "I'll get out of your way." She could obviously see that I was staring out across Piccadilly Gardens, and she looked across as if she was trying to see what I was looking at. "Are you alright?" she said.

"What's that over there?" I said. I think I must've sounded a bit mad.

"Over where? On Parker Street?"

"Parker Street?"

"Other side of Piccadilly Gardens—Parker Street. That's just the warehouses."

"Where's the M&S food shop gone? I could've sworn it was still open."

"M&S? Not sure what you mean—that's Templeton's over there."

I know it sounds rude, but she'd really confused me. So I just put my head down and left the shop. I hardly looked up again until I was back at the Arndale car park.

I bet you think I've started hallucinating or something, don't you? But there's a perfectly logical explanation for it all. I found out afterwards that Parker Street was the old name for that side of Piccadilly Gardens—it used to be called Piccadilly Plaza, but that's probably before your time. I guess the woman in the shop just called it by its old name—you know the way some people still call the MEN Arena the NYNEX? What do you mean it's not called the MEN Arena anymore? When did they change that?

Anyway, I suppose this woman just called Piccadilly Plaza by its old name. Well, it's older name, since it's not even called Piccadilly Plaza anymore. And I think I must have been looking out at a weird angle, and seeing the side of Primark, instead of the corner of M&S. That used to be a warehouse, I think. Or at least some of the buildings on Mosley Street did. Did you know that Primark used to be Lewis's? Before the bomb, I mean. Apparently that branch of Lewis's used to have a ballroom on the fifth floor when it was first built. I read that on Wikipedia—a full-sized ballroom in a branch of Lewis's. That makes the café in Superdrug seem pretty normal, to be honest.

I wouldn't blame you if you did think I was hallucinating though. That was my first thought. So I went back into Superdrug a couple of days later—just to check I hadn't completely lost my mind. Well, you'd do the same, wouldn't you? You wouldn't just pretend it hadn't happened.

It was the same thing—the shop looked just like a normal branch of Superdrug, but the back half of it was a café. Only this time, the café looked a bit different. This time, it was a bit darker, a bit more—how can I put this—plush. The string quartet was gone, and there was a small jazz band playing. It seemed more like something you'd get in the Northern Quarter than on Piccadilly Gardens, but I guess everywhere in the city is trying to be a little more stylish these days.

The menu was different as well. There was no mutton cutlet this time, but they were serving herring roe on toast. I have no idea what that is—but it didn't sound like my cup of tea. Not one bit.

The place was full of waiters again, so I didn't have to wait long to get served. I asked for tea this time, as the coffee hadn't been that good. He seemed to be expecting me to say that, and he brought me a pot (and not one of those metal ones) and a cup (not a mug) in no time at all.

To be honest, I quite liked the changes they'd made to the place. It was a bit less stuffy than it had been the first time I went in. I overheard a couple of people chatting about art—which is not really what you expect on Piccadilly Gardens, but I guess the art gallery isn't that far away. One of the waiters joined in, and I'm sure he said that they'd once served L.S. Lowry in there. Some story about him being a regular customer. I must've misheard them, as the café hasn't been open more than five minutes and Lowry's been dead since the seventies. Maybe they were talking about a show at the Lowry—do they do art exhibitions there? I've only ever been to plays and concerts.

Anyway, I quite enjoyed my little visit to the café that second time. I could've stayed longer, but I was meeting someone at the Cornerhouse so I had to run. Did you know the Cornerhouse building started out as a furniture store? The main building, I mean. The cinema building on the other side of the road has always been a cinema, from what I've heard. Even in the days of silent films there was a cinema on the same site—I think I heard it was originally called the Manchester Electric Theatre. Isn't that an amazing name for a cinema?

DID YOU HAVE A GOOD time last night? Where did you go? Oh, Opus One—I've heard it's nice there. What was the food like?

Always a hotel? No—it's not always been a hotel. Up until the 90s, that was the Free Trade Hall. They used to have concerts there—I think it was the home of the Hallé Orchestra until they built the Bridgewater Hall. Have you ever heard that Bob Dylan concert where he plays electric guitar instead of acoustic, and someone shouts 'Judas' from the audience? That was recorded at the Free Trade Hall.

No—it wasn't built as a concert venue. I think they only started doing concerts there after it was renovated in the 50s. It got bombed during the Blitz, as far as I know. Or maybe the Hallé had been there for longer—yes, that's right, I think the Hallé had been there since the 1850s, but in the twentieth century they moved a Wurlitzer organ in for more popular concerts.

But it was first built as a public meeting hall, on the site of the Peterloo Massacre—you know about the Peterloo Massacre, don't you? Of course you do, sorry. Well, the Free Trade Hall was built on the site to hold public meetings. That's where the letter to Abraham Lincoln was written, during the American Civil War. Have you never wondered why there's a statue of Abraham Lincoln on Brazennoze Street? There's a couple of websites that have looked into the history. During the American Civil War, there was a blockade put on cotton exports to Britain. This meant that all the cotton weavers in Lancashire were effectively out of work—people in the mills lost their jobs too. It was pretty bad, and people were starving and dying. They call it the Cotton Famine.

But the thing is, a lot of people in Manchester—and in the rest of Lancashire too—were against slavery. They didn't like that the cotton that came in was being grown and picked by slaves. So they supported the North against the South in the Civil War. A group of them met in the Free Trade Hall to discuss making a public statement of their support for Abraham Lincoln—although some of them didn't believe that he would really abolish slavery; they thought he just wanted the South to join the Union, and that he'd sacrifice the issue of slavery to get a united country. So they wrote him a letter, basically telling him that the people of Lancashire supported him, even though it meant many of them were starving. Typical Mancunians though, they told him he'd done alright so far, but he had to roll his sleeves up and get ready for a bit more work.

He wrote back and praised the heroism of the people of Lancashire—I think a bit of his letter is inscribed on the statue, but it's a bit hard to read now.

How do I know this stuff? I don't know really. You just sort of absorb it when you're growing up and living here. It's like— you go on a school trip to the Manchester Museum and you see the elephant skeleton—Maharajah, I think he was called. And the card tells you that this elephant's owner walked it all the way from Scotland to Bellevue Zoo in Manchester—and now, without even trying, you know there used to be a zoo at Bellevue. That little fact just goes in, and you can never go past Gala Bingo at Bellevue again without remembering that it's on the site of the old zoo and pleasure gardens.

Or when you go on the tram or the train to Deansgate, and you see the station sign that says 'Deansgate'—the same as any other station—but above that is the older sign, and it says 'Knott Mill Station'. It's like the new sign and the old sign are trying to elbow each other out of the way. And so you just file that little fact away—that Deansgate used to be Knott Mill— with all the others. You don't even realize you're doing it.

I'm waffling now—I know I am. Sorry. I'm not really feeling myself at the moment. I had a bit of a scare—well, not a scare, not really. But something happened, and I'm feeling a bit—unsettled.

Do you remember I told you about that branch of Superdrug on Piccadilly Gardens? The one with the café? Well, I went back again. Only this time it was all a bit confusing.

You probably think I'm making this up—but it'd changed again. This time, there was hardly any of the proper shop left.

There were a couple of aisles of the usual stuff—shower gels and deodorants, that sort of thing—but more than half of the shop was taken up with the café. Only, it didn't look anything like it had before. It wasn't all plush and decorative, and there wasn't any music. It looked a bit more like one of those 'ye olde taverne'-type pubs—all varnished wooden tables and chairs.

While I was standing staring, a man came in, looked around the tables and then walked through a door in the far right-hand corner. I hadn't noticed that before—and I couldn't work out where it might lead to—it was dark wood, with a sort of coloured glass panel and a brass sign on it. Nothing like you'd expect in a shop café.

"Excuse me," I said to the nearest shop assistant—she only looked about twelve, so I think she must've just started there. "What's through that door?"

"That's the smoke-room. But would you not be happier with a seat in the commercial-room? It's the men who normally want the smoke."

"Smoke-room?" I didn't want to mention the smoking ban, in case I'd misunderstood what she meant. "Yeah—I guess I want the commercial-room then. Is it just meals, or do you serve drinks as well?"

"We do breakfasts and teas—meat and fish is extra. Or we've got chops and steaks, with chips and tea included. Is it just your tea you're after, or are you travelling?"

"Travelling?"

"Yes—will you want a room for the night?"

"I don't understand."

"Have a look at our tariff, if you want to make up your mind." She handed me a small stiff card from one of the tables. It declared: 'BEDROOMS AND ATTENDANCE… 3/6.' And: 'NIGHT PORTER.'

I must've still looked a bit bemused, as the girl added, "And all our rooms have excellent sanitary arrangements—they're ventilated too."

"I don't understand—I thought this was Superdrug?

"Oh yes," the girl said. And she sort of waved at a table near the window for me to sit down.

That's when things got really weird. I looked out of the window, expecting to see the tramlines and the Wheel of Manchester—you know, the big wheel that they moved up from Exchange Square or wherever it was before—but none of that was there. There were some tramlines, sure, but the Metrolink stops were gone. All of Piccadilly Gardens was gone—and this time I knew I was looking in the right direction. I should have been looking diagonally across the Gardens to Kro Piccadilly, and I should've just been able to see the hotels on Portland Street behind that. Instead, all I could see was a huge brick building that looked a bit like a mansion, with grand pillars on the entrance and a huge clock tower. In front of it was a wide paved area with statues. At least that was something familiar—I could see the big bronze statue of Robert Peel— that's the one with the two figures sitting on the granite plinth underneath him—I think I read they're meant to be allegorical—I think they're meant to represent Manchester and the Arts and Sciences. But seeing the statue of Robert Peel in its right place just made things worse in a way, because I should've been able to see those new fountains and walkways behind it—and then the bus stops and tram stops behind that. Instead all I could see was this huge imposing building with its dramatic entrance and its metal railings.

The shop assistant was still standing next to me—waiting to see if I wanted a chop or a steak, I assume—and I think she could tell I was getting a bit agitated.

"What's that building?" I said. I don't even know how I got the words out, because it's not the sort of situation you expect yourself to be in. Do you know what I mean? You don't really have a response prepared when something like that happens. So I just blurted it out really—what's that building?

"That's the infirmary," she said. She was very polite—maybe she thought I was a tourist or something, because she was very patient. "And the lunatic asylum."

"The what?"

"The asylum."

"Are you being funny?"

"No—" She looked quite taken aback. I think I sounded angrier than I meant to. "—of course not. I'm sorry. I know it's not really the asylum anymore. Since they got rid of the lake and built that new esplanade. But I still think of it as the infirmary and the lunatic asylum. It's what we always called it."

"So what is it really called?"

"Well, it's just called the Manchester Royal Infirmary now."

I suddenly had this feeling that everyone was watching me—like they were all waiting to see how I'd react. It wasn't so much as I thought they were playing some big joke on me—

more that I felt I'd missed something and I was making a fool of myself.

"But the MRI is on Oxford Road," I said.

"The MRI?"

"The Manchester Royal Infirmary. It's on Oxford Road—opposite the Whitworth Art Gallery."

"I'm sorry. I've never heard of the Whitworth Art Gallery."

"You know—the one near the university."

"Do you mean Owens College? But that's on Quay Street—Cobden's House. Perhaps you mean the new buildings they're doing in Chorlton on Medlock—I hear they're going to be very grand. A bit of a change from Quay Street, that's for sure."

I couldn't process anything she was saying. It didn't make a bit of sense. I could still feel the eyes of the other customers on me, so I just got up and left the shop. I know, I know—they were probably just winding me up. Or she'd got things all muddled up—she was only young after all. But I couldn't deny what I'd seen, could I?

Only when I got out of the shop, Piccadilly Gardens was back to normal. I could still see Robert Peel, but I could see Kro behind him. And the Metrolink stop. And the fountains. And the little white market stalls that sell organic food and crafts. In front of the market stalls was a band with two men breakdancing to their music—quite a big crowd had circled them. The music was really loud—even the trams that were going past didn't drown it out. I'm not a huge fan of all these buskers that play with amplifiers now. Have you heard the racket on Market Street on a Saturday? You can't hear yourself think. There's always been buskers on Market Street, but it used to be an awful lot quieter. When I was a kid, there was this brilliant pair of buskers—two old guys—one used to play the spoons and the other one played the banjo. They used to sit on a bench at the top of Market Street every weekend. If they were there now, they'd be drowned out by all the electric guitars and people hawking those flashing headbands and whistles.

I'm digressing again—I'm just still so shaken up. Do you think it's a sign? That the girl said I was looking at a lunatic asylum? Do you think that's a hint there's something wrong with me? Maybe I imagined the whole thing, and that was my subconscious's way of telling me I need to get my head checked. I don't know.

Can I ask you a favour? Would you come to the shop with me? To Superdrug? It would help if I knew how someone else saw it all. Maybe you'll be able to come up with a logical explanation for it. Thanks—I really appreciate it.

THANKS FOR MEETING me here. Do you want to have a look around any shops before we go to Superdrug? Yeah—the Arndale is quite big—there are two branches of Eat, so I had a bit of a panic you might have gone to the wrong one.

I think the Arndale's one of the biggest shopping centres in Europe now. It's even bigger than it was before the bomb. Do you know, when I was a kid, there used to be an aviary in the Arndale. And there was this weird little exhibition place—I think it was called The Light Fantastic—where they had optical illusions and light shows and stuff—I used to go with my friends if we'd come into town on a Saturday—I can't actually remember when it closed down though. Or we'd go to the Market Centre—no, not the Arndale Market, the underground market that you used to get to down an escalator on Brown Street. I think it's H&M now—it never reopened as a market after the bomb—but it used to be a bit like the Corn Exchange or Affleck's Palace. But then, you won't remember the Corn Exchange, will you?

There used to be flats on the roof of the Arndale. I only found that out quite recently. I think someone tweeted a link to an article about it. There were about sixty of them—just council flats and bedsits—and it was called Cromford Courts— there was a little entrance on Shudehill. I've seen pictures of it, but I never noticed it when it was there. Why was it called that? Oh, I think that was what that part of town was called before the Arndale was built. That's right—it was Cromford Court—a shabby, cobbled part of town that used to have loads of nightclubs. I think one of them was called The Magic Village or something. Anyway, it was the place to go for music and partying and stuff, so it had a bit of a dodgy reputation. Most of the clubs were shut down by the 1960s, and then everything was knocked down to build the Arndale. The council built the flats about ten years later to try and encourage people to live in the city centre. From what I read, it was a little community and one of the old nightclub owners ended up living in one of the flats. What? No—the flats survived the bomb—strangely enough—but they didn't last much longer after that. All the development work meant that they had to go.

Anyway, we should go to Superdrug and get it over with. I want to know that it's not just me. Or if it is, I want to know how crazy I'm going.

Debenhams? That's been there for ages. The building's called the Rylands Building—or at least, that's its official name. It was built as a warehouse for the Rylands textile company. You know the John Rylands library on Deansgate? The one that looks like a church from the outside? That was built by the widow of John Rylands in his memory. He was Manchester's first multi-millionaire, and he made all that money in textiles. During his lifetime, his company had huge warehouses all along High Street. Some of them were seven storeys high. He died in the 1880s, I think. But the company he founded kept on going, and they built the Rylands Building in the 1930s. But it's been Debenhams for as long as I can remember.

Superdrug's just a bit further along, past Tib Street and Starbucks. Tib Street is that little street that goes up the side of Debenhams and into the Northern Quarter. The name? Oh, it's called that because that's where the River Tib flows. You haven't heard of the River Tib? Well, you wouldn't have done, I suppose. Most people haven't. It's only a little stream, really, and it's been completely culverted since the nineteenth century. Now it quietly flows along underneath the city centre until it joins the River Medlock near Knott Mill Station—I mean Deansgate Station—I'm getting all muddled up now, aren't I?

I know it's only a stream and it's underground now, but I sometimes think that I can hear the River Tib. You know—if I stand here, with my back to Piccadilly Gardens, and I block out all the noise of the trams and the buskers and the shoppers—I can just about hear the sound of the river. Can you? Listen—can you hear it? I'm pretty sure I can hear it.

But anyway, here's the shop I mean. Look—it's all changed again. It doesn't even look like a branch of Superdrug anymore—they've even taken the sign down. Have you ever seen something like this in the middle of Manchester city centre? The wood frame on the outside looks like it's been put up by hand, and the windows are a bit lopsided. And who would put windows like that on a shop anyway? Those tiny little panes with the lead lattice? No one can even see in.

Do you see what I meant about it being weird? What have they done with all the stock? Oh yes—I can see a few shelves here and there now you've pointed them out. But most of the shelves seem to be covered with seashells—there are seashells everywhere. And why would you put so many stuffed animals in a branch of Superdrug?

What have you found? A sitting room? Are you sure it's not just the café? No—you're right—this is more like an old parlour than a café. There's even some bookshelves on the wall. It does seem quite homely though.

Can you see out of the window? Can you see Piccadilly Gardens? Or can you see the infirmary building I thought I saw last time?

A pit? What do you mean you can see a pit? Ask that girl at the till if she knows what it is. Well, tell her that we don't know what daub-holes are. Okay—so that's where people used to get clay for repairing their houses, but now it's just a big pit? Is she winding us up?

67

Ah—I can see the clay pit now. But I can see other things too. A lunatic asylum, a textile warehouse, a Wurtlizer organ being taken to Peter Street, a multi-millionaire and a fishmonger from the slums, an elephant on its way from Scotland, eighty thousand protestors heading towards Mount Street, Saturday girls being evacuated by the police, a New Romantic going down a broken escalator to buy skinny jeans, Friedrich Engels shaking his head, a light show in a nightclub off Market Street, a banjo-player and a man on the spoons, L.S. Lowry running for a tram, a man with a collection of seashells and stuffed animals—

Look—there's windows at the back of the shop as well. Through this area that looks like—I'm not imagining it, am I? —that looks a bit like an old kitchen from a stately home. Now, from these windows we should be able to see out to Tib Street and Sachas Hotel. We should be looking onto Back Piccadilly. And—no? Let me have a look.

I don't know what to say.

There aren't any buildings. Where are the buildings?

All I can see are fields. I think they're cornfields. Cornfields stretching right across where the Northern Quarter should be.

And do you know what?

They're absolutely beautiful.

Lever's Row

The site now known as 7-9 Piccadilly, Manchester is currently occupied by a branch of Superdrug, which was built in the 1990s. Prior to this, 7-9 Piccadilly was the address of an early twentieth-century building in a pseudo-Mughal architectural style, which housed a branch of Our Price records. Earlier still, these premises—complete with dramatic onion-shaped dome—were the Lyon's Popular State Café and, before that, a Kardomah Café (one of at least three in Manchester, and reputedly the branch favoured by the painter L.S. Lowry). Before this, the site was home to the White Bear Hotel, a coaching inn built in the first half of the nineteenth century. The White Bear Hotel was built on the site of the home of Ashton Lever (1729-1788)—a somewhat eccentric collector of natural objects, who was born at Alkrington Hall (near Middleton) and who owned the land between Ancoats Lane, the daub-holes (later flooded to form an ornamental lake, now Piccadilly Gardens) and the River Tib. Lever began by collecting seashells, but soon amassed a collection of natural curiosities and specimens, which he exhibited at Alkrington Hall and then in London. The Manchester street now known as Piccadilly was originally called Lever's Row, after its owner, but today only the name of Lever Street (one of roads leading from Piccadilly to Great Ancoats Street) remains as an echo of this history.

CRYING FOR MY FATHER

AUDREY WILLIAMS

MOMMA AND I STEP OFF the bus early morning in front of Johnson's Funeral Home. The brick building looks like a combined house and bank with a small driveway with a black hearse in front. I feel strange in front of the funeral home because I know that my father's body is inside.

Momma grabs my hand and we walk up the pathway with nice, trimmed grass; the yellow flowers look pretty. The glass doors automatically slide open when we reach them. Inside the lighting is soft and dim. It takes several minutes before my eyes adjust from the bright sunlight outside to the dim lighting inside. There's a soft stillness to the room; that's comforting. We stand in a reception area with a small couch, a tiny table with flowers in a vase on top, and several chairs. We're looking for my father's service. That fact is not upsetting. I'm relieved that my father is dead.

Crying for my Father

"Evan Small," Momma says to the woman sitting behind a desk. The woman's real pretty with curly black hair. She's lighter than Momma's brown skin and I'm darker than both with my black skin. She glances at the paper in front of her. On it is a list of names, dates, and times.

"Are you Mrs Small?" the woman asks in a hushed voice that matches the quietness of the room.

"Yes. And this is Louise, our daughter," Momma says.

"I'm so sorry about your loss. Come this way," the receptionist says. "Already some family has arrived."

She walks us down a hallway and into a room. It's a large room with two aisles, each with eight pew rows. The pews are the kinds that are in most churches. The usher, who was standing just inside the doorway, leads us to the front of the room by my father's casket. The usher looks young to be doing this. She's younger than Momma, who's forty, but a lot older than me. Maybe she's twenty-five. She wears more makeup and jewelry than Momma and spike-heeled boots.

Momma and I sit. I look at no one. I feel nothing towards my father's body and everything towards this strange experience. Finally I shift slightly in my seat without actually turning around which allows me to see the people behind us. Some people are crying. They're dabbing and wiping at their eyes with tissue. I sit not knowing what I should be doing. Finally I look over at Momma. She's crying too, though it's hard to tell because she keeps her head down. Still, I see the silent tears slide down her face in a steady stream. I think she's crying because she's happy that my father won't hurt us anymore.

71

It wasn't new to see people crying in my father's presence since Momma and I did it all the time. What is new now is that I'm not crying. The beatings have dried my tears. When I was five, he beat me with a belt and I thought I would never stop crying. What had I done? That was like asking why the sky was blue. It just was blue and my father just beat Momma and me whenever the alcohol affected him, which was always because he always would drink. Later, I think the beatings were more habit than alcohol and they occurred if my father was drunk or not.

"HATTIE, WHERE'S MY damn coffee?" my father hollered. He drank coffee because he'd heard that it took the effects of alcohol off quicker. He drank lots of coffee, sometimes four cups before he left. Momma always made his coffee as soon as she rose. Only once did he complain about it. Spitting the coffee out across the kitchen table, my father yelled, "This is bitter, dammit." The coffee splattered the table and the wall. I could tell from the snap in his voice that he was close to punching Momma. "Wash the damn pot out!" My father glared at her. Momma rushed to wipe up the coffee.

He turned and looked at me. I froze and tried not to look frightened. Please don't know, please don't know. Fear squeezed me, making my stomach twist into a knot. I felt like throwing up, but I managed to hold everything in. "Get my jacket," he snarled. I jumped and then took a deep breath in order not to run to get away from him. Running was never allowed. Glancing back I saw Momma pour my father another cup of coffee. Then I saw her put some drops into the coffee from a small dark bottle. This wasn't the first time I'd seen it. Then Momma quickly stuck the bottle into a pocket under her apron. Stretching so that she was on her toes, she grabbed the sugar from the top shelf in the cabinet and added it to his coffee. No one but I knew that Momma was poisoning my father. Our eyes met, and I saw a tiny sparkle in them that touched me. I realized that Momma was alive on the inside and that she wouldn't let the endless abuse defeat us.

"Here, exactly how you like it," she said, talking to the floor. She wasn't allowed to look my father in the eye.

LOOKING AROUND THE funeral parlor I wonder whose idea it is to put my father in a white casket with a bunch of too-sweet smelling red flowers. He almost looks like nice and caring. Since I know otherwise, I don't think he should be made to look that way. I think he should look the way he's looked in my dreams. In them he's dressed in black, and his casket is a rotten box with bugs crawling through it. Maggots are eating at his flesh. That's how it ought to be for him.

I look around. There're no bugs, no insects, and no rotting body. The only thing similar to my dream is that the funeral parlor is dim. There are tiny lights going up both sides of the walls just beyond the pews which give off a small glow. Up front is a dark podium, probably where the preacher will stand and talk. An organ is in the corner.

Momma glances up. Then she bows her head again and her mouth moves silently. I guess she's praying. I want to say that it's alright now because he's dead, but I don't, because she doesn't look my way.

Family members walk up and I'm introduced to Uncle Ray-Ray, Aunt Suzie, Uncle Mack, and Aunt Babs. All are family from my father's side. I don't remember seeing any of them before now. Aunt Babs is Uncle Mack's wife. Both Uncle Ray-Ray and Uncle Mack have wide noses that flare out when they talk. My father's nose is small like a button.

Momma smiles softly at everyone but doesn't say more than, "Nice to see you." It dawns on me suddenly that Momma doesn't look directly at anyone. Have I ever seen her look my father in the eye? No, that could get a smack across her face. She's so used to keeping her head tilted down. When she looks at him now, she turns her head away quickly, and then sneaks glances from the corner of her eyes.

Another thing that's different from my dreams is that everyone is dressed in different colors. Momma has on a black dress that stops just above her knees, black shoes with a two-inch heel, and she has on lipstick and eye shadow, things my father would never let her wear. Aunt Suzie is wearing a black suit and black pumps. She has a gold watch on one wrist and a gold bracelet on the other along with small gold hoop earrings. She looks very professional. I wonder what she does.

Aunt Babs is wearing a light grey pantsuit that doesn't fit well. The jacket seems too tight, or her breasts are too big. She must've had this jacket for a long time because there's a dark, round stain that stands out against the rest of the grey jacket. She also has on a grey skirt that's only an inch out from under her jacket. Her red lipstick matches her red fingernail polish. On top of that she has large hoop earrings that could probably be worn on her arms they are so gigantic. She wears a suit but she doesn't look professional at all. Uncle Mack has on a brown suit and tie, and Uncle Ray-Ray has on a blue suit with no tie. In my dreams everyone wears festive white, except my father of course.

I have on a new ivory dress with a silk belt. Momma bought it for me for the funeral. I don't get new clothes often. Both Momma's clothes and mine usually come in plastic bags from the Hands-On Thrift store and the Salvation Army, places like that. My father's clothes come in nice shopping bags from Carson Pirie Scott. Momma bought my dress from there too. It has a pleated skirt that spread out like a fan, and it feels real soft and good next to my skin. I don't remember ever having anything this pretty in my life before.

AT THE ALA-TEEN meeting every Wednesday I was supposed to say, "I'm Louise Small and I live in a dysfunctional family." Sometimes I said it. Other times I didn't say much of anything. Mrs Jared said that the meetings were for teens with alcoholic family members, a place where we could vent and learn to deal with the injured member of the family. There were six kids in the Ala-teen group: two blacks, three whites, and one Hispanic. Mrs Jared ran the meetings. I think she used to be a nun because she was always in white. White gym shoes, white skirt and top, and white hair. Sometimes her eyes would tear up and she would pray whenever anyone told her sad things. I didn't like making Mrs Jared's eyes tear up. She told me to love my father but hate his drinking. But how could I separate the two? My father was his drinking. She also said that the abuse wasn't truly him. I couldn't see that difference either.

I'm really not looking forward to Mrs Jared's questions next week. It's not that I don't like her; it's just that I don't trust most outsiders. I've learned from Momma to tell them only what I want them to know. I've also learned from Momma that what goes on behind our closed doors are too dangerous to share.

Miss Cooper suggested the Ala-teen meetings a week before my thirteenth birthday. She sent home several notes and then she visited to get my parents' consent for me to go to the meetings.

"These Ala-teen meetings will help Louise deal with her feelings," Miss Cooper said.

My father wasn't buying it. "I know how you people think. My daughter is fine and she doesn't need any meetings," he said.

"Going to them will help her deal with many different issues," Miss Cooper continued, trying to persuade my father.

"Don't tell me how to raise my family," he said. These were the same words he'd used a year earlier when another teacher,

Ms Lichtenstein, recommended that I attend the Gayle Sayres Academy for gifted students.

"Louise is a very precocious child, alert, bright; this will help her greatly," Ms Lichtenstein said.

Needless to say, I wasn't allowed to go. "The public schools are just fine for Louise. I went there and look how I turned out," my father said, closing that argument.

"Think about it," Miss Cooper said. Then she gave me a hug on her way out.

As soon as she left, my father said, "Louise's not going to no damn group." Then he turned on me. "What the hell've you been telling those people in that school?" I shook, watching my father's eyes. They were pure black and pure evil without a bottom to them. Momma spoke up, "If you let her go, you won't have to be bothered with Louise for that hour. She won't say anything at the meetings." Momma talked quietly and calmly, never raising her voice or her head. Maybe that got him to agree. My father's only rule was: "Don't ever say anything about me. Talk about anything, but don't put my name in your damn mouth."

LOOKING AROUND THE funeral parlor everyone is sitting about halfway back. Only Momma and I are in front. It's as if they don't want to get too close to us. Or is it him? A woman sticks her head in. Then she steps in, pausing in the doorway. The first thing I notice about her is her nappy, black hair sticking straight up on her head, on one side. On the other side of her head it's matted down and clinging to her scalp. Just looking at her gives me the creeps, so I turn around in my seat and stare at Jesus instead. I think Jesus knows that my father was too bad to live for a long time.

The woman catches my eye as she walks past the pews right up to my father's casket. She has large holes in both of her shoes. Her little toe hangs out of the right side of one shoe and her clothes are filthy. She stands there looking and then her lips turn up as if she doesn't like what she sees. The next thing she does surprises me. She drapes one arm across the casket and cries. Not the silent kind, with tears running down her face, but saying loudly, "Oh Lawd… Lawd… Lawd…" She's crying as if she's lost everything that's ever mattered to her. Who is she? She slowly walks away, heaving with every step. She walks past Momma and me to the back of the parlor where she stands quietly, still crying. Could she have known my father? Momma said once that some people who have nothing else go to funerals, even if they don't know the deceased.

Two people, a man and a woman, walk in. The man has a bald head on top with black hair around the sides and back. It reminds me of a clown's head. The woman, who is super skinny, is dressed in a black suit skirt and white blouse with two layers of ruffles circling it. They walk in and up to the front, looking at my father. The man turns to face us and says, "Hattie, I'm so sorry about your loss." The same line that everyone has said so far. I think someone is handing out a script. Too bad they all have the same line. Momma smiles a tiny bit, but doesn't say anything. Then the man turns to the skinny woman. "This is my new wife, Regina," he says. Momma smiles again and shakes Regina's hand, and the man looks at me. "I'm your Uncle Norman," he says. Then Uncle Norman and Regina go and sit midway back in one of the pews. Everyone is letting us grieve in private. We've been grieving in private for years.

I look around and count the people. There are eleven including Momma and me. Everyone is sniffling or talking quietly amongst themselves. Everyone, that is, except the nappy haired lady. She keeps walking halfway up the aisle and back again, wringing her hands and looking over at me. Her face is twisted like she's trying to hold back her tears. I can hear her breath catching in her throat.

"They wandered blind in the streets. They have defiled themselves with blood. So that no one would touch their garments," she says. Is she quoting the Bible? I'm not exactly sure what she's telling me. Does she know how my father died?

WHEN THE CALL CAME from the morgue, Momma answered the phone. She slumped forward and cried. This cry was different than her shrill cries at the hand of my father. This time she seemed to be releasing something... I'm not sure how to explain it but to say it was different. Then she took a tissue and wiped her eyes.

"Evan is dead," she said. And then, "I have to identify his body." We went right away.

"What happened?" Momma asked after identifying my father. She'd come out of the morgue and into the waiting room where I'd been instructed to wait. A doctor in a white lab coat with the words 'Medical Examiner' on it walked with her. His eyes were pushed back into his head, and he slumped forward as he walked. He looked tired. This was probably a hard job, seeing so many dead people.

"No one told you?" the medical examiner asked. Momma shook her head.

The examiner whispered, "It seems that your husband was killed in an accident. He appears to have been sitting in a car that was marked for demolition." Then he added, "I'm sorry for your loss." He heaved and slumped even more and turned and left.

Momma said nothing for a long time. She just stared and then I saw her lip tremble.

"Momma, are you alright?" I asked.

She walked over to the couch and sat. I followed. "He wasn't always terrible," she finally said, but it wasn't directed towards me. She was like someone waking up from a bad dream. "Before that damn Desert Storm he was a much better person. He came back a dead man. A combat veteran... and the VA Hospital, not providing treatment—" Momma stopped suddenly, as if remembering where she was. "Let's go," she said. It was hard to imagine, but could Momma have once loved my father?

We walked around the corner. Two men were looking around, not knowing which way to go. I recognized one of them. Mr Middling was my father's boss.

"Mrs Small, I'm so sorry for your loss," Mr Middling said.

"Thank you," Momma said.

"How could a man get so drunk and sleep in a car marked for demolition?" the other man asked. Then he looked at Momma. "Sorry 'bout my outburst," he said.

"This is Mr Peterson, Evan's coworker," Mr Middling said introducing the other man.

"A terrible accident, my con-dol-sense," Mr Peterson said. Everyone nodded in agreement. Momma looked down at the floor. "No one could have guessed he was asleep in a marked car." Momma gripped her hands together and looked at me, then back to Mr Peterson.

"I understand," Momma said.

"Well, let me know if there's anything we can do," Mr Middling said. Momma nodded a little, and she grabbed my hand and we left.

THE STRANGE WOMAN walks towards the front of the funeral parlor again. I keep staring at her. She stops at my pew, but she's standing off to the side. She's not jumpy like she was at first. Now, she's looking sad, with teardrops clinging to the corners of her eyes. What does she want? I look at Momma to see if she sees the strange-looking woman. But Momma is not paying attention to anyone. The woman inches closer towards me, but her eyes stay on my father. I slide closer to Momma.

"I am precision. I am balancing the world on my fingertip," she says.

I jerk my head towards her and then she's crying again.

"Tears cleanse," she says, not looking at anyone. Then she walks to the back of the parlor again.

What will the reverend say when he talks about my father? I wonder if the people here will cry when they hear how horrible he was. Just thinking a tiny bit about the things he's done makes me sad. What will everyone think when they hear how my father choked Momma after he smacked her, knocking her against the wall? I flinched when I saw Momma's throat bulging out between his tightening fingers pressing against her neck. Just thinking this makes me feel glad, again, that my father has no more power.

The usher who led us in comes and tells Momma, "Reverend Jones was delayed. He had an emergency and had to rush to the hospital. He's on his way now."

"I hope everything is okay," Momma says.

"He should be here in about five or ten minutes. I'll be at the back directing any more family that arrives," she says.

A much older woman with a long white robe on walks into the funeral parlor from a different door. She reminds me of a grandmother. I think it's her gentle spirit. Her hair is more white than black. I like her. She walks up to the organ bench, turns a key, and begins playing soft music. It sounds nice, like church music. She finishes that song then starts another melody. I wonder when Reverend Jones is coming. I want my father's funeral to be over.

Crying for my Father

Ten minutes turn into thirty, and finally Reverend Jones appears. He's dressed in a flowing black robe that sweeps the floor as he strides in. In his hand he's carrying a small red Bible that almost looks lost inside it. He's well over six feet tall and makes me think of a basketball player. I wonder if he was one once. His smooth face doesn't betray that he was rushing. He looks like nothing would ever cause him to hurry.

Reverend Jones looks at Momma the way a starving man looks at a juicy steak, licking his lips, as if he wants to eat her up right on the spot. He looks over her entire body. Instantly I don't like him. Taking both of Momma's hands into his grasp he says, "Sorry, I was running late." Momma lets him continue to hold her hands. I can't tell what she's thinking, and all of a sudden I look away because I don't know how I'm supposed to feel. Reverend Jones looks over my head and doesn't say a word.

Everyone sits as he makes his way to the podium. He sets his book down, turns some pages as if he's thinking. He seems to be a man who's used to commanding attention with his presence alone. Like my father wanted to be. When Reverend Jones is done with that, he picks up a glass trimmed in gold and takes a sip of water. He's in no hurry although he was already late. "It's so nice to see all of you here," he finally begins. "To celebrate Evan Small's passing on to a better place."

My father isn't going to a better place. He's going down below. Not even God would want him.

"Although I didn't personally know the deceased, I can see he was loved," Reverend Jones goes on in a strong, sure voice.

"He was a good man," the reverend continues.

Looking around I check to see if everyone else is agreeing with Reverend Jones. Most of them have their eyes fixed on him, so I can't tell if they agree or not. The odd woman is now in the same pew as Momma and me, but she's over a ways. She's bent over trying to cover her toe that's slipped out of the hole in her shoe. She pushes it in and wraps her sock over it, but the sock has a hole too, so the toe keeps peeking out.

I pinch myself. I have to be dreaming. Tilting my head forward I look into Momma's eyes. Immediately I remember a time when I looked into her eyes and saw my father in them as he walked into our kitchen. He walked up to Momma, grabbed her hand and twisted it backwards, breaking her finger. Momma dropped to the floor. Her scream didn't stop him, because at that exact moment his fist smashed into her face making Momma gurgle her scream and the extra air in her mouth gushed out. She had stayed out longer than he'd told her to when she went to help Grandma right before she died. Momma set her finger by herself. She used Epsom salts on all our aches, swellings and bruises, which were almost always brought on by my father.

"Don't you need to go to a doctor," I whispered to her.

"Too many questions," was Momma's reply. She'd learned the hard way not to let the authorities interfere. Once, she had called the police on my father. He stayed a night in jail, and then came home the next day and beat her. As if that wasn't enough, he turned as if on second thought and then smacked her so hard, leaving his hand print on her cheek. In domestic violence cases the procedure is to let the bad spouse sleep off his stupor, pay a fine, about $75, for causing the police trouble, and then go back home and make up. Momma knew that wasn't going to happen. My father was too evil for a night in jail to change his ways. Momma never called the police again.

I LOOK INTO MOMMA'S eyes again trying to see if she is thinking, like me, that Reverend Jones is lying.

"Death is reality," Reverend Jones shouts, waving his arms for emphasis and moving his body as he talks, as if certain swoops, dips, and bends go with his words. He paces to and fro past the podium. Standing in front of it and raising his arms, then standing behind it and making one of his body swoops.

I WOKE IN A COLD sweat and pain stabbed me in my stomach, but I caught my breath before it escaped. I couldn't let myself scream. Instead, I pulled my cover over my head, crying into it. No way could I let a bad dream of any kind make me run into my parents' room. Instead, Momma came running into mine. I didn't know if it was because my father was hitting her or because I'd screamed anyway.

"Stupid... bitch!" My father hurled the words towards me. I was six years old. I didn't react to the words as much as I reacted to my mother's reaction. Her eyes widened, and when she looked at me, her tears showed the pain she felt. As I got

85

older I realized that my father's rage, like his slaps and kicks, were forever slicing through me leaving a trail of unseen scars.

"THIS IS A CELEBRATION. Let your hearts be glad," the reverend continues waving his arms. "He made it to forty-five years of age. There are many who don't make it that far… Louise—" Reverend Jones shocks me by calling my name. "You're Evan's child. Do you wish to say anything to those of us who loved him?"

Reverend Jones holds his outstretched arm towards me, motioning me with his fingers to come up to the pulpit. I freeze. Can I really tell them what I think?

I look at Momma and she's staring at the floor. I realize that I'm on my own. Momma seems to have used up whatever strength she had. "No, thank you," I say.

"Let not your hearts be troubled," Reverend Jones says, looking at me. All eyes except Momma's are staring at me. Don't look at me. Even with my new dress I feel ugly and shameful. I want to get out of there. I want to run from the funeral parlor and from all of this, but I stand there looking helplessly at Reverend Jones. Then I feel tears filling up in my eyes and I quickly brush them away. I wish I was anywhere but here.

Crying for my Father

"LOUISE! LOUISE!" my mom called. I hurried and got out of bed, because if I took too long a swift openhanded smack across my face could follow. I had morning chores before my father left for work.

"Is he up?"

Momma nodded yes.

"Sleep well?" she asked quietly.

"I dreamt it again—poisoning," I whispered. I could never dodge my dreams, although I told myself, every night, this night I wouldn't dream about killing my father.

"Sometimes dreams are all you've got," Momma said.

"Mine scare me," I whispered.

"They're only dreams," Momma said.

I know they gave my Momma strength because in them my father was always dead or near death, and my Momma would slowly rise up and become very big. Poison was often the cause. Other times I used medicines he was allergic to and put them in his coffee, so when he drank it he died. Another time a large boulder fell down a mountain crushing him.

"IT'S OKAY, CHILD," Reverend Jones says, bringing me back to the funeral parlor. "Brother Small has gone on to higher grounds." I don't bother to think about his words and sit back down next to Momma.

"Know that you did all that you could," Reverend Jones says, addressing everyone.

I wonder if the preacher knows who he's talking about. His words slide out too freely.

Then Reverend Jones says, "We give praise for the time we've been granted. We return from whence we came."

The usher walks over and Momma stands, grabs my hand, and I stand with her. We walk up to my father's casket and look at him a last time. I can't believe he will never again terrorize us. All he'll do now is lie there. That's reassuring in a strange way. We stand there for a second longer and then turn and walk towards the back of the parlor.

The funeral is over. Everyone is still sitting, waiting for Momma and me to pass. The weird lady must've moved seats again. She's sitting on the last pew, crying. I look at her and quickly turn away, but not before I see her walking towards us. "You've both got stained coats," the woman says, and then, "Take care of that son you're carrying now."

Momma looks at her strangely but nods politely. I just look but don't say anything. We don't have coats on, and Momma isn't pregnant. Is she?

THE MAN IN BLUE BOOTS

JAMES EVERINGTON

ROB AWOKE FROM A DREAM he'd known was unreal as he dreamt it, to a feeling of dampness and chill seeping through his clothes.

Groaning, he sat up and pressed his hands against the base of his spine to try and massage away the ache. His senses were still fuzzy and he was slow to register his surroundings—he was in a field of dew-soaked grass, and in front of him was a black row of trees which marked the perimeter of some woods. *The Woods*, he thought, still too asleep to disbelieve.

The rising sun was behind the treeline and Rob shivered in his damp clothes.

'The Woods' was what they'd always called them as children; there were other areas of woodland around the outskirts of the village but all the kids had instinctively known which were *the* woods. At the end of a cul-de-sac was this field of grass and beyond that the shadows under the trees began. As a child Rob had played in The Woods so often he'd known every hiding place, every line of sight.

He hadn't seen The Woods for over fifteen years and he had no idea how he had come to be on their perimeter now. Still befuddled, he looked around half-expecting to see his brother there too. But he was alone.

He stood, beating his arms against himself to try and warm up. He looked behind him, not quite believing, and the old housing estate was there, the houses and fences still forming a pattern he recognised.

Footsteps, still just visible in the dewy grass, led away from where he'd woken up and towards The Woods. They were bigger than a kid's footsteps, bigger than Rob's now. As he stared at them they were almost visibly fading as the grass dried in the morning air, as if wilting under his disbelieving gaze.

Tom, he thought.

The Man in Blue Boots, he thought.

FOR ROB AND TOM'S parents and extended family, The Man in Blue Boots had been nothing more than an amusing family anecdote, retold with added embellishment at reunions and to embarrass Rob in front of any girls he might bring home. (He remembered one girlfriend letting go of his hand with a gasp as the story was told, because he'd suddenly gripped hers so tightly.) The family story went like this:

The Man in Blue Boots

They'd been on a camping holiday to France and the hot beaches and campsite had been like a new world for the two boys, who hadn't been abroad before. Rob had been ten and Tom eight. They'd shared a tent, a flimsy thing that was all they needed to protect them from the hot but placid night. They'd lain awake, feeling the heat slowly drain from the interior of the tent, talking boy talk and swatting at the mosquitoes that had made their way inside. Along the bottom of each side of their cheap tent had been a strip of gauze-like, semi-transparent material, so when lying down they could turn their heads and see out at ground level, a few hazy inches through the mesh.

One early dawn, Rob had been woken up by his brother shaking him, whispering in his ear that there was someone outside. Sleepily, not really believing, Rob had turned to look outside through the material and seen a pair of blue boots, pressed together as if the person wearing them was standing to attention, right outside their tent.

Of course, their parents would say laughing to his politely smiling girlfriends, of course it was just some Frenchman, drunk probably, lost on his way back to his own tent. And certainly the fear the boys had felt had been partly a put-on, the same disbelieving excitement that made kids shriek on rollercoasters or at the end of ghost stories. They'd remained silent despite this excitement as they'd looked out at the person's boots, and the odd thing was that it had seemed like hours and whoever it was had just remained standing there.

Looking back, Rob didn't believe that, and he supposed that in reality he must have fallen straight back asleep, and so not seen the man leave.

The next day Tom, the younger, had seemed quieter and somewhat unnerved, and so to show the boys that there was nothing to fear their parents had forged a note from the stranger, apologising for waking them and containing a series of cryptic clues—a treasure hunt leading to a jar of sweets they'd buried beneath a rock on the beach. They'd signed the note The Man in Blue Boots.

The name had become a family joke, and the notes and buried sweets had been repeated on subsequent family holidays, as though The Man in Blue Boots was some kindly, avuncular figure following them around. As the years had progressed the boys had become noticeably cooler about the notes and clues. Their parents had assumed this was due to them getting older and ceasing to believe in The Man in Blue Boots just like they had with Santa Claus. With some regret (for they'd enjoyed composing the clues each holiday over a bottle of French wine) they'd written one final farewell note, and killed off their creation.

But the real reason for the brothers' unease had not been because they got too old and stopped believing, but because of what had happened the second time they'd seen The Man in Blue Boots, when they'd camped out near The Woods.

ROB FELT HIS UNEASE grow as his dream faded; the sun still wasn't above the trees and he felt cold. How had he got *here*, of all places? Nothing seemed to have changed. From where he stood he could see a huge toppled tree trunk dead centre on the perimeter of The Woods. He remembered climbing over it as a child—even though you could just walk round it, to the kids like Rob and Tom there had been an unspoken understanding that the *correct* way to enter The Woods was to climb over that tree trunk.

The layout of The Woods was coming back to him now: over on the right-hand side was a small, weak stream that ran through a straggle of silver birch before disappearing underground again. Moving away from the stream the trees became oak and ash, surrounded by dense bramble patches and mysterious growths of mushrooms. Then on the far left there was a short but steep slope, the trees thinning out until at the far corner there was a deep depression, a huge, obviously artificial hole in the ground like an empty lake—they used to ride their BMXs up and down its slopes, after laboriously dragging them through the trees.

Rob remembered standing in the bottom of that depression, unable to believe what was happening, whilst Tom had screamed and gathered sharp rocks from the dusty ground.

But that, surely, hadn't really happened.

He looked round again, at the familiar houses behind him. Too familiar, as if they hadn't changed at all in the last fifteen years (or as if fifteen years hadn't passed at all). Rob looked for obvious signs of change, of the twenty-first century: a satellite dish maybe, a new car parked outside, someone on the street talking on a mobile phone. But there was nothing, no people or movement, no sounds except the birdcalls from the opposite direction...

It doesn't really matter how you got here, Rob thought. *You know you've been drinking since Tom disappeared. So you got drunk and you ended up in one of the places you played together. It's horrible but it's not mysterious. Your car is probably parked just round the corner; the sensible thing is to walk to those houses, find it, and go home—your real home, not this place that used to be.*

But then why was he even considering the idea of going into The Woods? Why wasn't he walking back already?

He looked again at the footprints in the grass, almost vanished now, leading away from the odd, tent-like depression and towards the trees.

Tom, he thought. Tom was missing and despite the frustrations his younger brother had caused him, he did love him, very much.

Rob had never believed in The Man in Blue Boots and what had happened, but *Tom* had.

Telling himself it was a waste of time, and not admitting to any deeper misgivings, Rob followed the footprints towards the edge of The Woods.

THE BOYS HAD PERSUADED their parents to let them sleep overnight alone in their tent, pitched on the grassy area in front of The Woods. It was just round the corner from their house, Rob had said to his sceptical parents, and other kids had done it and been alright. Looking back, he suspected they had only agreed because they'd planned to secretly check up on the boys throughout the night. Another reason why what he remembered happening couldn't, in fact, have happened.

What Rob remembered was this: waking in the middle of the night to see, through the gauze-like material at the side of the tent, two blue boots in a familiar at-attention pose.

Tom was already awake and whispering frantically in his ear, and Rob flapped his arm angrily at his brother like someone waving off a dream. His eyes felt thick with sleep and he shut his heavy lids, then reopened them deliberately slowly, convinced the sight of The Man in Blue Boots would be gone. It wasn't.

Even in the darkness of the tent he could see Tom's eyes were wide and panicked; Rob was scared his younger brother would cry out or do something else to make the stranger outside aware they were awake (he wasn't sure why he didn't want to man to know this). He didn't speak but tried to meet Tom's gaze and hold it, to communicate a calm he didn't really feel himself. *Just a drunk man on his way back...* he thought, a garbled version of his parents' comforting invention.

Suddenly the shadows outside moved and the man slapped a splayed hand against the side of the tent. From the inside it looked bigger than a normal person's hand; the fat fingers clenched slightly so that they pushed the fabric of the tent inwards.

Tom stuck his fingers in his mouth and whimpered audibly.

The man roughly slapped his palm against the tent again and dragged it down with a squeak; the whole tent moved on its frame slightly. Rob peered through the mesh and saw the blue boots stagger as if the man were off balance. Other than those boots all that could be seen was the huge shadow of the man through the tent's flimsy material and his hand flailing against the side like a fly against glass, with as little purpose. When he struck again it was with more force than before, and the tent swayed with the blow, pulling up one peg from the ground outside.

It was then that Tom cried out: "Go away! Oh go away!"

Something about the sound, about the fact that Tom was so accepting of the impossible person outside, chilled Rob although he couldn't have said why. There was an immediate effect though—the hand stopped swiping against the side of the tent.

Cautiously, Rob bent down and looked through the material at the bottom of the tent; Tom did the same on his side. There were no boots, no signs of anyone out there.

"Has he gone?" Tom whispered. Rob was still struggling to believe it had actually happened, and he shook his head in lieu of a sensible answer.

Cautiously, they pulled down the zip at the front of the tent, wincing at the loud noise it made in the night. They'd both slept with their clothes on, but even so the summer air still seemed overly cold. There was a fuzziness to their vision, as if there were unseasonal fog or as if they were still looking at the world through gauze. Hurriedly the boys got out the tent and started to run across the field to the houses and safety.

A figure was standing at the far end of the field, blocking their escape. It stood still and ramrod straight, as if deliberately trying to keep its stocky, heavy body from slouching forward. It didn't move and its colour was just a deeper black than the night, but Rob knew it was the same person who had been outside their tent.

The boys stopped some twenty metres from it and paused, both of them breathing raggedly. The figure remained silent and motionless, like a statue marking the perimeter of the black and lifeless housing estate behind it. Although all adults seem large to children, this figure seemed even heavier and out of proportion than normal.

"What do we do?" Tom whispered. "Shall we run into The Woods?" And Rob felt momentarily angry with his brother again, that Tom was acknowledging this was even happening. Surely the best thing, as long as it didn't move, was just to stand there and wait the figure out? Surely when the sun rose and the lights flickered on in the houses behind and the adults looked sleepily out, surely then the figure would be gone because it just couldn't be true?

But Tom was pulling at his arm and speaking loudly about how they, the kids, knew The Woods so well and how even at night they'd know all the hiding places and dead ends. Reluctantly, Rob let himself be pulled along, and then suddenly he turned and both boys were running full-pelt towards The Woods. Just before they entered Rob took one confused look over his shoulder, and The Man in Blue Boots' dark and faceless shadow was coming with long, stumbling strides after them.

ROB ENTERED THE WOODS, climbing over the tree trunk that marked the perimeter just like he had as a kid. He turned right and started walking, listening out for the trickle of the stream— he and Tom had always competed to hear it first, and Tom had always won.

Although it was summer the earth in this part of The Woods was always slightly spongy; the smell of soil and damp moss was close and ridiculously familiar to his nostrils. The sun had risen somewhat, although Rob was still not sure what time it was. Light filtered down through the leaves and made patterns like someone moving stealthily between the tree trunks. Just a game of hide and seek, Rob said to himself, trying to pretend he wasn't looking for a real figure in amongst the hunched shadows of the brambles, the arm-like branches and torso-like trunks of the trees.

"Tom?" he called out and immediately felt stupid. But was it so stupid after all, that Tom should be here?

His younger brother had grown up to be a timid, unworldly young man, who had recently finished years of studying theology at some remote college that specialised in the subject. He had seemed to pick the course on a whim, surprising both Rob and his parents. He had lived at home all his life and they'd given up thinking he would ever move out. He'd studied monk-like in his rented room, and everyone had known he'd get a First, but as he neared the end of his course his family had been increasingly worried about what he was going to do afterwards; his studies seemed to have left him even more unsuited to the real world than before.

The Man in Blue Boots

On the day he got the letter confirming his First Tom laid it out on his bedside table for anyone to see, left his flat, and had not been heard from since.

That had been weeks ago and miles away; *so why*, Rob thought, *are you looking for him here in these woods where you played as a child?* But he knew the answer—because Tom *had* believed in what had happened here years ago, believed in it enough to let it shape his beliefs in adulthood: that Evil, as an abstract thing outside human activity, did exist.

Rob gasped as a pheasant clumsily clattered away from him on heavy wings. He stood still and looked around, but even motionless as he was The Woods seemed full of hallucinatory movements of things between trunks, tricks of light and shade forming bodies and faces. *The proper thought to have now*, he said to himself, *would be to marvel at how* small *these woods seem compared to how you remember them*... But they didn't. The Woods still felt as large and as full of hiding places as fifteen years ago.

Suddenly he realised why he'd stopped where he had: he could hear the stream.

Walking towards the sound, he called out his brother's name again.

AS THE TWO BOYS climbed over the trunk and ran into The Woods they realised how dark it was under the trees at night. At first they had to stick to the paths, stumbling over depressions in the ground they wouldn't have been able to see even if they had dared look down. But as their eyes adjusted slightly they left the paths, to dart between tree trunks and around bramble patches, the layout of which they knew from countless games of catch and hide and seek. Yet The Woods seemed bigger in the dark; the black tree trunks and undergrowth seemed to conspire to form impenetrable barriers in places they knew to be passable in daylight.

Behind them, The Man in Blue Boots crashed and stumbled through the undergrowth, tripping over roots and ricocheting off trees, but never letting this stop his dogged and voiceless pursuit. They couldn't even hear his breathing and Rob hated the thought that this was not because of the ragged noise of their own, but because there was nothing to hear.

Rob risked a backward glance: the heavy bulk of The Man in Blue Boots was clattering off balance towards them, but despite the ungainliness of his pursuit he never fell or stopped, and his strides were long. It seemed impossible that such a clumsy, awkward pursuer could be gaining on them, but he was.

The two brothers knew exactly where they were heading without the need to speak to each other—a huge thicket of brambles with a small crawlspace down in one corner, and a hollow space inside just big enough for the two of them to hide in. It was their secret; they'd never told any of their friends and no other child had ever found it as far as they knew. They couldn't outrun the pursuing figure but they would be practically invisible in there.

Rob glanced at Tom and his younger brother looked back— Tom was scared but no longer seemed on the edge of panic.

The Man in Blue Boots

They were both tired but could manage one last sprint at the right time, to dart round a heavy, thick-trunked tree that would hide them from view as they got down on their hands and knees and crawled through the scratching brambles to the safe space inside. Neither needed to speak, they both picked up the pace at the same time, and then they were round the tree and crawling in darkness towards where their memory told them the hidden entrance to the bramble thicket was. Rob felt cobwebs brush against his blind face, felt barbs tugging and ripping at his clothes as he crawled sightlessly after his brother. And then they were both in the middle of the bramble patch, hugging each other and burying their faces in each other's shoulders to stifle the sound of their hoarse breathing.

Now they weren't running themselves the sounds of the crashing and staggering thing coming after them seemed even more unbelievable—how could something so clumsy and uncoordinated have kept pace with them? And the man didn't seem tired or slowing; it wasn't fair, Rob thought. The man hadn't even come over the tree trunk at the perimeter of The Woods but *around* it, and that wasn't fair either.

It's a joke, he thought, some practical joke, but even that thought seemed trite and unbelievable.

On the other side of the wall of brambles, the man crashed straight into the tree the boys had swerved around to sneak into their hiding place. There was no muffled curse or reaction, just a thrashing sound as he was thrown by the impact against one side of the thicket the boys were sheltering in; the whole thing shook like their tent had earlier. The man didn't cry out at stumbling into the sharp thorns, didn't make a sound or pause in righting himself, blundering around the tree trunk, and then stopping, right outside the entrance to the crawlspace, as if he knew exactly where they were.

The two boys held their breath, but there was no further movement from outside, no stumbling pursuit off in the wrong direction like they'd expected. Although Rob could barely see Tom in the darkness, he felt his younger brother tense.

Reluctantly, Rob turned and crawled partially back down the entrance of the tunnelled brambles; he moved cautiously and very slowly, giving himself enough time to convince himself that this was all a dream or somehow not real. About halfway down the crawlspace he stopped—the shape he could see was indistinct through the darkness and brambles. It was two blue boots, pressed against each other and at attention, as their owner stood as if waiting, silent and motionless and right outside their only escape route.

This isn't happening, Rob thought, *I don't believe this can be happening*. The Woods were very quiet now in the darkness, and he realised he could hear the trickle of the stream.

ROB WALKED TOWARDS the sound of the stream. He wondered if he'd been drinking the previous night, for his vision kept wavering and doubling. But he had none of the other symptoms of a hangover.

He swore as he tripped over an exposed root, and the ungainly, off balance steps that followed reminded him of the thing that had chased them through The Woods fifteen years ago. He'd kept the memory buried all this time and hoped it would fade, but re-examined it was as clear as before.

"Except it never happened," he muttered to himself. He didn't believe in The Man in Blue Boots.

There was another dull, heavy clattering as somewhere another pheasant made its clumsy escape. It must be the season for them, Rob supposed, for the whole wood felt full of their noise. He stopped near a large tree to get his bearings and realised it was the oak near the bramble thicket in which they'd hid that night. He turned around quickly to look at the brambles; too quickly, for his vision blurred and made figures stand watching him between the trees.

"Tom?" he called out; his voice sounded uncertain and was swallowed by The Woods.

He walked up to the brambles, which snagged at his clothes when he got too close. Was that secret hiding space still inside? And could anyone be hiding in it now? The thick, twisted brambles were impenetrable to his gaze, and he couldn't remember where the opening to the crawlspace was. Feeling foolish, he got down on his hands and knees roughly where he thought it should be—nothing but a solid wall of thorns inches from his face. He felt oddly vulnerable on all fours, as if something could sneak up on him—but the one thing The Man in Blue Boots couldn't do was *sneak*. Nevertheless Rob got up quickly and the blood rushed to his head.

He wanted to leave The Woods but he couldn't forget his brother's face, never seemingly happy or relaxed in adulthood. But he also remembered that night when it had been clear with purpose whilst Rob had dithered. Even if that night was imaginary his debts from it weren't: he owed it to his brother to check one more place. The pit, where they'd fled after they'd somehow escaped from the tangled briars they'd trapped themselves in.

I CAN'T BELIEVE THIS is happening, Rob thought, staring at the two blue boots stood to attention right outside the exit. He crawled back to where Tom was still crouched in the centre.

"We can't get out can we?" Tom whispered, his face very pale in the darkness.

"*He* can't get in," Rob surprised himself by saying.

"Shhh!" Tom said. "It doesn't matter, he—"

"It *does* matter!" Rob said loudly, angrily. "*You can't get in!*" he shouted to the figure outside.

"What are you doing?" Tom said, horrified.

"He's just a man, he can't get through that narrow space, he's too big," Rob said. "You can't get in you fat bastard!" He felt more confident now and protective of his younger brother. "He's just a man, he'll have to go away at some point, we can just wait him out," he said to Tom, who was shaking his head. "He's just a man, he's not—"

Suddenly the whole bramble patch seemed to shake to its roots as The Man in Blue Boots reached out two hands and shook it. From the force the boys could tell he must be gripping the thorny branches tightly. *Has he got blue gloves on too?*

Rob thought with a touch of hysteria. The brambles to the side and overhead shook with the same kind of clumsy, pawing attack that the tent had earlier, and they heard and felt branches snapping around them. Rob and Tom both scrambled back until they felt spines press into their backs against the wall of their shelter.

There was a pause, and then the sound of slow, manoeuvring footsteps outside. The two boys had time to glance at each other before the footsteps charged and thudded towards them, and then the whole bulk of The Man in Blue Boots was bursting through the bramble thicket to get at them; he'd run right in as far as he could and then dived, like a fat man determinedly striding into the cold sea as quickly as possible. The whole structure of the thicket buckled and sagged under the weight; brambles bent and snapped and the ceiling overhead bowed down to just above the boys' heads but didn't break through. One huge, trunk-like arm managed to find a route through and reach down, the hand a big, bloody paw.

The two boys screamed and instinctively held each other, but the wildly grasping hand didn't find them. It withdrew and their hiding place seemed to lighten slightly as the man levered his bulk up from the brambles. He wasn't panting or even audibly breathing; he'd not said a word the whole time or showed any signs of pain or fatigue.

Like something still half-made he staggered awkwardly away from the brambles and there was a pause. He was lining himself up for another charge.

This time as he came lurching and crashing through the sagging brambles the two boys were already on their hands and knees crawling towards the way out. The Man in Blue Boots stumbled and tore through the main structure—Rob risked a look behind him and there was just a big, black shape of a man, but too big for any normal man surely, his face hidden in darkness, his long, thick arms flailing through the brambles, swiping at the air trying to find them. If he had come crashing through in such a way as to block the exit he would have been upon them by now, but his clumsy, staggering manoeuvring outside had saved them.

Tom was in front and already out, and Rob felt a swipe of air as the man's paddle-like hand swung inches from his neck. But then he was up and out and running too, in the night woods that seemed lit up in his vision after the darkness of the bramble thicket.

ROB REACHED INTO HIS jacket pocket for his mobile, to see if he had a signal in The Woods. But his phone wasn't there. Something about this unnerved him, as if all proof that he wasn't back in the past had been removed. *Your memories are proof*, he thought, angry with himself.

He could no longer hear the sound of the stream and the ground was getting less spongy as he headed up the shallow incline to the top corner of The Woods where the hollowed out pit was. Or presumably still was. What had it *been* anyway? Rob wondered—as kids they'd not thought much about it, other than it being a cool place to ride their BMXs up and down. Or that, when he and Tom reached down, there would be sharp rocks at the bottom of it.

Rob assumed he was taking the same route from the bramble thicket to the pit as they had that night, although he wasn't sure. He wanted to get there as quickly as possible in order to prove to himself how foolish searching these woods was, just as they'd wanted to get there quickly in order to escape the blundering thing behind them. He shook his head, annoyed at the memories crowding it. At the memories of a hallucination, at that.

He passed a single silver birch—he remembered it, the only one in The Woods not near the stream, oddly isolated and out of place. He remembered it seeming almost ghostly that night. Here, he thought, here's where you looked back and realised *why* The Man in Blue Boots might be so clumsy.

"It wasn't real!" he said out loud in exasperation. His voice scattered pigeons noisily overhead, their wheeling shapes sending shadows across and between the tree trunks. He turned around, but of course there was nothing there. He could hear the wind shaking the trees and the rustle of animals and birds in the undergrowth, no doubt sounding larger than they actually could be. Any other sounds were drowned out.

He suddenly understood he was afraid, in a way he hadn't been for years, and which made him almost nostalgic.

"Tom?" he called out uncertainly.

He looked to his left; he could just turn that way and walk out these damn woods—they weren't as large as they seemed and he could be out in five minutes, less if he ran.

He remembered how, as they'd ran, it had been *he* who'd hurt his ankle, and he remembered the shame he'd felt that his little brother, who he was supposed to protect, had had to help him instead. He'd felt the same shame on and off throughout his life, the last time being when he'd heard Tom had gone missing.

Deep down, he knew his younger brother had probably killed himself—since that night in The Woods it had always seemed a possibility, and there had been odd little 'episodes' resulting in hospital visits before. Since that night when Rob had failed to protect him.

There was a crashing sound, as if somewhere in The Woods behind him something bigger than a man had just run full force into an impenetrable wall of brambles and undergrowth. Rob almost reached down to finger through the dusty ground for stones—after all, what could it hurt if he didn't believe?—but stopped himself. It wasn't healthy to give in to the logic of childish fantasies. And besides…

"You believed in him, you stupid sod," he said sadly to his absent brother. "You believed in him and it might have worked that one time, but look where it got you in the end."

The sound didn't reoccur and Rob resumed walking towards the far corner of The Woods. He no longer knew if he was looking for his brother, or his brother's body. He felt clouded with grief by this, and it made the nagging thought that he could hear faint sounds of something coming after him seem even more ridiculous and unimportant.

The Man in Blue Boots

THE TWO BOYS RAN AS fast as they could towards the corner of The Woods. From the noise behind them they could tell The Man in Blue Boots was still keeping pace by just blundering through all the undergrowth that they had to dodge around. They didn't know quite why they were running to the pit in the top corner of The Woods—maybe it was inconceivable that anything so large and clumsy could make it up out of the pit if they made him run down into it.

Rob saw something white and ghostly ahead and it took him a second to work out what it was—that single silver birch away from the water where it should have been. As he passed it, he risked a look over his shoulder.

The Man in Blue Boots was mostly a *noise* rather than anything that could be seen, a thrashing, snapping presence coming through the brambles and trees. But Rob could just make out the dark shape of their pursuer, bigger and stockier than he had seemed before.

I don't believe this, Rob thought, a thought he had been having since waking…

… simultaneously, the figure stumbled again, thrashing amid a briar patch.

How can he be so clumsy? Rob started to think, but then he lost his own footing and tripped over an exposed root. He stumbled and as he righted himself he felt a sharp pain in his ankle. He cried out, tried to carry on running but the pain made him hobble. The sound of The Man in Blue Boots already seemed closer behind him.

Tom turned back to his brother, holding him up and giving him a skinny shoulder to lean on. They stumbled together and Rob almost felt like laughing because it was like when they had done the three-legged race at school. Just as hopeless.

You're slowing Tom down, he thought sickly.

Staggering and out of breath, the two boys reached the pit at the top corner of The Woods; they could see the moonlit and open fields through the trees, but the local farmer, fed up with kids damaging his crops, had planted thick hedges all around the border and ran them through with barbed wire, almost invisible in the tangled branches even in daylight.

Without pausing the two boys ran down the side of the pit, Rob knowing even as he did so that his ankle would never take it. He pushed Tom aside before he fell so that he didn't drag his brother down with him. He tumbled and rolled the last few metres down to the bottom.

"I'm alright, I'm alright," he said, getting quickly up and standing with his weight on his good leg. No longer directly under the trees there was some extra light and he could see the expression on Tom's face more clearly—the childish features grimly set. It frightened Rob and it took him a few seconds to realise why—*he believes in all this*, he thought. *He believes it can all be happening, and I think The Man in Blue Boots needs us to believe in him or…* But he didn't quite know what he was thinking, or if it was quite right.

Then it seemed to darken again, and both boys looked up to see The Man in Blue Boots' bulk on the edge of the pit. He stood sentry-like for a few seconds, and then started to pace around the rim.

I'M NOT RUNNING, ROB thought to himself, *I'm just walking quickly so I can get out of this place and back to my life*. His hands were thrust stubbornly in his pockets and he tried to stop the odd little bursts of speed as he walked, as if he wanted to break into a run.

Because there was definitely someone following him through The Woods. Someone maybe zigzagging somewhat erratically a ways behind him. The sounds were muffled by the wind in the trees, the flustered flights of birds, and Rob's own footsteps, but he could no longer pretend he didn't hear them.

But whatever it was it didn't seem to be catching up with him.

Obviously, Rob told himself, *because it isn't The Man in Blue Boots; The Man in Blue Boots doesn't even exist! Hasn't ever!* The 'thing' behind him was a combination of other sounds—another walker, maybe, on the same path and keeping equidistant behind him. A walker with a *dog* perhaps, running through the undergrowth and back again to his master... And an auditory illusion was causing Rob to combine these sounds with other, unrelated ones: branches snapping in the wind as the trees shook, pheasants beating clumsily through the air.

Another part of Rob's mind, a younger part perhaps, told him that the reason The Man in Blue Boots wasn't catching up was that his disbelief was keeping him weak and clumsy, that without his younger brother's credulity he couldn't grow stronger. It didn't make sense, for how could disbelief be used as a weapon against something unless you believed in it? But he was still reluctant to examine the paradox too closely. If he could just ignore all the memories and emotions The Woods had stirred up inside, then surely whatever was behind him would fade into silence.

Rob was still heading towards the pit, the place where they'd defeated The Man in Blue Boots before (one way or another). Was that a good idea? Wasn't that partially admitting to himself that what he remembered happening was true, and so might be again? Rob stopped indecisively, hands clenching and unclenching in his pockets. His vision must have blurred, for the trees seemed to move in front of him.

And suddenly he thought, what if there was someone following him, clumsy and staggering because they were injured? Or befuddled in some way? Having seen their brother walk past and been unable to cry out for some reason? What if the person coming after him was Tom?

He turned around, and as he did so he realised two things. Firstly, that the sharp pang of hope he felt at thinking his brother was still alive made his childish fears seem silly.

And second, that whoever or whatever was following him was closer than he'd thought, and almost upon him.

The Man in Blue Boots

THE MAN IN BLUE BOOTS paced the lip of the pit the boys were trapped in, a black silhouette looking too large and ponderous to be a real person. Rob felt a distant fear but that was all; his mind was hazy with his inability to believe in any of what was happening. He told himself it was a joke or a dream or somehow not real even as he heard the trickle of dirt sliding down the pit's side as The Man in Blue Boots' tread dislodged small amounts of earth from the rim.

"Tom," he said. "Tom, you have to not believe in him."

"What?" his brother said; Tom was bent down gathering sharp rocks in his small hands.

"If you don't believe he... well, it—" Rob struggled to express what he meant. He knew his thinking made no sense—if the thing didn't exist how could his belief or otherwise affect it?

Tom looked up at the bulky shadow blocking out the moonlight above them. "Of course he exists," he said. "And the more real he is, the more we can hurt him." Tom looked afraid but not visibly panicked, like he knew he had a plan that would work as long as he kept his head.

"But—" Rob started to say.

Above, The Man in Blue Boots backed up, off balance slightly, and the boys knew that he was about to charge.

"Get ready!" Tom yelled.

"Close your eyes!" Rob yelled. He shut his own, and heard pounding, staggering footsteps. He could sense the vibrations in the earth. He tried not to think about what Tom was shouting or if it made any sense even as he felt his brother press a rock into his hand.

He was never sure if he threw the rock or not, but he knew he never opened his eyes. The darkness he was sheltering in trembled like the flimsy tent had before, as the thudding sound of something vast and bulky came closer. He tried not to picture it at all—tried not to picture its arms outspread as if to crush him dead. Rob screwed his eyes up tighter.

He could hear it was almost upon them, and then Tom cried out, a vicious sound of triumph. Everything suddenly seemed very quiet and still, but it was a long time before Rob opened his eyes.

"I killed it," Tom said, breathing heavily. "I hit it with a rock right between its eyes and it disappeared. I *killed* it."

No, Rob thought, I *killed it. By closing my eyes, by not letting it be true. That's why it disappeared.* I *killed it.*

But even then he wasn't quite sure if that was true. Either he'd saved his brother or almost killed him, and the doubtful voices that started in his head that day never quite quit.

IT WAS DAYLIGHT IN The Woods the second time, and as the figure came blundering out of the trees towards him the only things stopping Rob seeing it clearly were the tears in his eyes. They seemed to magnify and darken the figure in his sight, but he refused to blink them away because that would be closing his eyes if only for a second, and he wasn't going to do that this time. *Tom*, he thought at the last instant, and the figure rushing towards him and blocking out the light had its arms outstretched, as if to sweep him into a great hug or crush him where he stood.

A HANDFUL OF DUST

DAVID WEBB

"**N**OW I'VE FOUND YOU, I won't let go."
It's been three years now and I don't think she ever will.

Porthzennan's a pretty little place. From the steps outside Gerry Bateman's office at the top of the hill square houses of grey stone tumble down to Trewardan beach, their rooftops dappled burnt ochre with lichen. There's a church tower away to the left of the strand and beyond it lies Torknow Point, where Proserpina died.

According to Gerry, he'd called me in because I was 'edgy'. The council had got themselves pumped up by the tourist board, who were worried Porthzennan was losing out to package tours. A contemporary sculpture would help put the place back on the map. They didn't much care what it was, but it had to be a big piece, in bronze.

I was interested. We had a couple of meetings and I ended up pitching him something on Proserpina and Pluto. Gerry didn't know the story, of course, but once we'd talked it through he agreed 'that whole regeneration thing' would do nicely for Porthzennan.

I said I'd cast the abduction, obviously. Dramatic, bold, but with a contemporary twist. Two figures, modern dress. Sixty feet high, twenty-five tonnes of bronze. My Proserpina would be young, just a little girl really. Pluto would be a middle-aged man, pulling her towards him. She'd not be a victim, though. She'd be a little bit knowing, a little bit *Lolita*. I wanted to hint that the old goat might've bitten off more than he could chew. As a private joke, I decided the girl would be holding a bunch of sea pinks—it amused me to think I'd be charging serious money for thrift.

I warned Gerry that it'd cost a packet, but he'd already managed to raise the money. He said he'd done it by 'reassigning' the coastal defence budget. The health and safety brigade kicked off when word got out, and as if on cue an accident involving a couple of locals added to the fuss. That made me feel a little queasy at first, but when all was said and done it wasn't my problem. As for Gerry, he was adamant there was no such thing as bad publicity. Looking at the size of the advance he was offering I wasn't going to disagree with him.

The day it happened I was down for the final commissioning meeting. I knew something was wrong the moment I rolled up to reception. The girl on the desk was red-eyed and wouldn't look me in the face. She said they'd been unable to contact me. When I looked I saw my phone was dead. Battery. The meeting had been cancelled 'because of the tragedy'. Apparently Gerry had gone sailing off Torknow Point the previous afternoon. His boat had drifted into the harbour empty a couple of hours later. A woman who'd been walking on the cliff top reported seeing him in difficulties. The body had been pulled from the rocks that morning.

I'd come a long way for the meeting and I didn't fancy heading back to London empty handed. I spent nearly half an hour at the front desk but no one could tell me what was going on or even whether the project was still on. Eventually I gave up and found myself standing on the steps outside. I was taking in the view and wondering what to do next when a small cold hand slipped into mine.

I looked down and there was this little girl. About ten or twelve, quite skinny. She had long dark hair, hanging lank, like she'd been swimming. Strands kept blowing about around her face, but she didn't seem to notice.

She was wearing a grubby pink beach dress and had those plastic shoes—jellies, I think they're called. There was sand stuck to her ankles and in little half moons just below her knees. She stared at me with big dark eyes. All of a sudden, she smiled and it was as if the sun had come out. I thought she was a pretty little thing.

"Now I've found you, I won't let go," she said. The smile faded and she looked grave. And she just stood there, holding my hand.

It was a sunny day and there were lots of people about. Children's voices were rising from the beach down below and there were a couple of gulls screaming at each other up on the roof. There was a stiff breeze blowing off the sea. The girl had to be cold.

"Hello," I said. She didn't reply. I tried to disengage my hand, but she tightened her grip.

"My name's Tom," I said. "What's yours? Have you lost someone?" I glanced around but couldn't see anyone that was obviously looking for her.

A dark haired woman in a green coat was passing on the other side of the road. She saw us, hesitated, then took a step forward. Her face was troubled. I thought she was about to say something but she turned and walked quickly away. The girl watched her go, then continued looking calmly out towards the headland.

"Do you live round here? Are you lost?" No reply. I thought maybe she was shy. Her clothes suggested she must have strayed from Trewardan. Well, I couldn't stand there all day and I couldn't just leave her, so I said, "Shall we see if we can find your family? Come on, let's go to the beach." She didn't speak but she didn't resist, so I took her down the steep path between the houses.

"Are you here on holiday?" She just trotted along beside me, not saying a word. A couple of times I made as if to free myself, but she didn't seem to take the hint. I was feeling a little bit uncomfortable by this time, walking along hand in hand with this pretty little girl, and I began to rehearse what I'd say if her family were to spot me first. I didn't want them accusing me of kidnapping her or something.

"I'm a sculptor," I said, to fill the silence as much as anything. "I'm going to make a great big statue for the harbour. There's a girl in my statue. She's called Proserpina. And this little girl, she was picking flowers one day when a bad man called Pluto came and dragged her down to hell."

I paused for a reaction, but none came. I ploughed on. "Proserpina's mummy wanted her back, but Pluto tricked the little girl so that forever afterwards she had to spend a part of each year in the underworld with him. While she was with Pluto, winter came and made everyone sad. But every time she escaped from Pluto, she brought the spring. My statue will show winter and spring having a tug of war."

The girl gave no sign she'd heard me.

We walked on in silence. When the slope levelled off the pavement grew sandier and I knew we were close to beach. We rounded a corner and found ourselves on the promenade. It was pretty busy—the narrow pavements were crowded with holidaymakers and lines of cars snaked past on their way up the coast. We crossed the road and went down the concrete steps.

Trewardan is the main beach at Porthzennan. It's big and wide and the tide goes out a long way, so most of the families go there. The dry sand fronting the prom was teeming— windbreaks and towels everywhere. There were couples playing bat and ball on the firm wet flats below the tideline. A knot of children and adults was in the water between the red and yellow flags away down the beach. If this was a place in need of regeneration, I couldn't see it.

"Can you spot them?" I said. "Is there anyone you recognise?"

Still she said nothing and I wondered whether she might be in shock. There was an old man nearby guarding a stack of deckchairs. I took her over to him. It was surprisingly hard work crossing the sand.

"This little girl seems to be lost," I said to him. "Is there a lifeguard or someone who looks after lost children on this beach?"

"There used to be all sorts here," he said, "but there isn't anymore. The lifeguard station closed down last season. Council said they didn't have the money, although they seem to have plenty when it suits them. Beach is only manned for a few hours each day now."

I didn't know what to do. I felt a flush of guilt, thinking maybe I'd led her away from where her family must be searching. I could hear the low hum of people's conversation as they enjoyed the sunshine. Somewhere a child was crying.

"You could try down there, but I wouldn't bank on it." The attendant pointed to the bathers. Next to one of the flags was a tall chair which seemed to be occupied. "You hold on tight, my love," he said to the girl. "This gentleman will see you safe."

Walking was easier once we were on the wet sand, but every now and then we'd have to skirt round shallow pools of water. The sensible thing to do would have been to take off my socks and shoes, but I wasn't there for a holiday. I just wanted to be rid of the damned child.

We walked a long way, out to where the sand was rippled by the tide. The lifeguard turned out to be a lad of about eighteen or nineteen. He was deep in conversation with a blonde girl in a swimsuit.

"Excuse me." I had to say it a couple of times to get his attention. "This little girl's lost."

"Can't help you, I'm afraid. I've got to stay here and watch the bathers." He grinned at the blonde. "I don't finish till four."

"Well is there a police station in the town? She won't say her name. Her parents must be frantic."

"The police station's not manned half the time these days," said the blonde. "You'd be better off taking her to the Tourist Information Office, to be honest. That's what I'd do. They're down by the harbour. They'll know what to do."

"Can't you call someone on the radio?" I said to the lifeguard. "She could wait here with you until they come."

I looked down, expecting the child to confirm what I was saying. Her hand felt cold on my fingers and the wind whipped round the hem of her little beach dress.

"Now I've found you, I won't let go," she smiled up at me.

The blonde looked at me suspiciously. The lifeguard frowned.

"This some kind of joke?" he said. He looked down at the girl. "I think your dad's had one too many."

"You should take her home, instead of teasing her," said the blonde. She bent down towards the girl, then saw something that seemed to change her mind. She straightened up and gave me a hard look. "You ought to be ashamed. She'll catch her death dressed like that. She doesn't look well now." It was true—her face did seem very pale.

"Look," I said. "I've had enough of this." But the blonde had waded off into the sea and the lifeguard was no longer listening. He'd picked up his loudhailer and was evicting a couple of surfers who'd strayed into the bathing area.

The red and yellow flags flapped in the wind and the bathers shrieked above the roar of the surf. I looked back towards the town and saw my footprints meandering across the sand. I didn't really think about that until afterwards. The girl didn't move. Just her long dark hair, whipping about her head.

I started marching her back up the beach. I stepped into a puddle that went over my shoe. There was no one near us apart from a couple picking their way down to the sea and a man flying one of those big stunt kites. I stopped and turned on her.

"I don't know what game you're playing, but I'm getting rather tired of it." I was even starting to sound like her father.

The sun seemed to blink as a shadow swept over us. There was a razzing overhead. I followed the girl's eyes and saw the pink and purple kite rise in the sky. It banked slowly and turned, swooping over us once more. As we watched, it began to spiral in ever tighter circles. The girl gripped my hand. Her upturned face was exultant, eyes bright.

I heard a shout away to our right, but I didn't catch the words. The shadow grew and I saw the kite come down. I tried to move but was held fast. She smiled and I saw those ridiculous plastic shoes planted firmly on the ground. I must have barged her out of the way, because the next thing I knew we were spattered with wet sand and the kite had smacked into the beach at our feet. The owner ran up.

"I shouted! I tried to warn you! I'm really sorry. Is she okay?" The girl was by my side, still holding tight. I opened my mouth to speak, but she beat me to it.

"Now I've found you, I won't let go," she said, smiling up at me. The sunlight made dark crescents under her eyes. There was the faintest trace of blue on her cheek, like you sometimes see on fine porcelain.

"Well that's a relief," said the man. He was gathering in the moorings of the kite. "She came down pretty hard. Look, how deep the nose has gone! Could've been a nasty accident."

I took the girl back to the top of the beach and we began picking our way towards the sea wall. It was more sheltered here and the breeze was less intense. The smell of suncream mingled with the fried onions from a hot dog stand further up the prom. There was a bin at the bottom of the steps and the wasps were zigzagging back and forth above a dropped ice cream. One buzzed close to my ear and I flinched away. The girl didn't seem to notice them. I took her up the steps and began walking along the seafront, making for the harbour on the other side of the headland.

We headed for a row of beach huts tucked under the cliff at the end of the prom. The road rises there and turns inland, and the arcades and shops give way to the holiday flats which lap at the edges of the old town. The headland's much more impressive from close up—like a great arm thrown across the beach, and Torknow Point a knuckled green fist surrounded by the sea.

I saw a flutter of blue and white tape among the rocks. There'd been a fall, quite a big one, and a fan of scree and boulders had spread out over the sand. A pair of gulls was wheeling over the cliffs. A wooden DANGER sign was lying half buried. I saw the words 'Coastal Defence Scheme' and the council logo. The girl stopped.

"What is it?" I said.

I could taste the salt on the wind. Suddenly I had the strongest image of poor Gerry Bateman being pulled from the sea under those great cliffs, the black water lifting and sucking between the rocks. I felt the girl shudder beside me. I thought it was because she was cold.

"Are you okay?" I said. She turned her face to me. Her eyes were as cold as the wind coming off the sea. As cold as her hand on mine. She held my gaze for a moment, then looked over at the line of tatty shops on the other side of the road. Heavily laden cars were still whizzing past, and I could hear the whine of a dustcart making its way along the shop fronts.

I was about to have another go at getting some information from the girl when suddenly she shot a gleeful look over her shoulder and launched herself into the traffic, pulling me into the road behind her.

"Now I've found you, I won't let go," she said. She was surprisingly strong for such a small child and she caught me off balance. I stumbled and saw the word STOP painted on the tarmac. The ground shook. A shadow fell across me. A great roar was drowned by a horn blast so deep and long that I was stunned. Someone screamed. Air brakes hissed and spat. I looked up. The naked pink dolly on the front of the dustcart stopped inches from my face.

For a second everything seemed to freeze. My ears were ringing. Then the driver launched himself halfway out of his cab shouting abuse. Passers by were staring from the pavement, some with their hands to their faces, others shaking their heads and grinning.

The girl just stood there holding my hand. A flock of seagulls wheeled sharply over the beach and settled back down on the sand.

I was pretty shaken up and I rounded on her. I started shouting about how stupid she'd been to run into the road like that. She waited for me to stop, her face impassive. Then she gave me that smile again and I saw red. I jerked my arm back to try and free myself, pulling her off balance so that she fell against me. It must have looked bad, because I heard someone yell, "Leave her alone, it wasn't her fault."

I stood there until the traffic began to move again and the onlookers had dispersed. Despite the breeze I was sweating. The girl stared quietly across at the headland until I started up the hill.

I heard a diesel engine behind us and moved in further from the edge of the kerb. An orange and cream bus was approaching on its way up into town. The bus slowed to take the turn and I saw the woman in the green coat at one of the windows. Her face was white, framed by her dark hair. She had the same troubled look. She looked frightened, to be honest. As the bus went by she put her hand to the window glass. It wasn't a wave. It looked more like an acknowledgement of the barrier between us. She seemed to give the tiniest shake of her head, but it didn't seem to be for me. Her eyes never left the girl.

The bus continued uphill without stopping. We trudged along after it. At the church, we left the main road and headed up into the old town and the skein of narrow streets that led to the harbour. There were no cars here. People were drifting about in ones and twos, window shopping or idly turning the postcard racks on the cobbles. It was strangely quiet after the bustle on the seafront. I needed to get out of this. I stopped.

"Look, I can't keep dragging you around all day. I think we should say goodbye here. Let go of me now. You'll be quite safe." I knew it wasn't going to work even as I said it. She just stood there dumbly, looking up at me with those dark, hungry eyes. I tried a different tack.

"Will you just let go of my bloody hand for five minutes? I don't know who the hell you are or where you came from, but you're nothing to do with me. Just go away, will you?"

A woman with a toddler stopped in the doorway of one of the shops.

"Aw, don't," she said. "We all feel like that some days, don't we?"

"Now I've found you, I won't let go." Again that smile.

"That's right, my love." The woman disappeared into the shop.

I looked helplessly at the girl, suddenly disgusted at my weakness, my inability to break free. There was something horrible in her pallor, in her lank hair and cold, skinny limbs. The permanent accusation of her presence. I realised I was frightened, but not for her.

I yanked my arm violently back and forth. The girl stumbled, but still she wouldn't let go. I pulled her roughly to her feet and in that moment I would have wrenched her arm from its socket if it meant I could escape.

"What do you want from me?" I shouted. Heads began to appear in doorways. I raised my hand and I would have hit her. One of the shopkeepers ran across, white with fury, and yelled at me to calm down. The girl hauled on my arm and began pulling me along the street. The shopkeeper called after us but didn't follow.

She set off confidently and at first I thought she'd recognised someone. Instead she just marched along, slightly ahead of me, dragging on my hand to make me keep up. The rigid beach shoes made her flat-footed on the cobbles. It was almost comical.

We reached the top of the old town. The wind freshened and I saw a strip of blue water between the buildings. There was a black metal signpost with a fan of pointers, the letters picked out in gold. To the left was the Coast Path and Torknow Point. Ahead lay the harbour and the Tourist Information Centre.

"This way." I started down the slope, but the girl planted her feet on the cobbles and wouldn't budge. I pulled hard and she took a half step, but I realised that if I wanted her to move I'd either have to drag her or carry her. There were still people about. I couldn't face another scene. She turned her face towards the coast path.

"Okay," I said. "But if we can't find them up there, we're going straight to the Tourist Info people."

The sign pointed to a narrow alleyway tunnelling between the buildings. It didn't look like much—a couple of those big green council bins pushed against the walls and sweet wrappers blowing about on the ground. The girl didn't hesitate. We plunged on into the darkness.

The alley opened out into a dusty track between the backyards of the houses. A few more yards and we emerged onto a wide shoulder of rough grass, climbing until the town was behind us. The footpath ran straight towards the trig point on a rocky outcrop about a quarter of a mile away.

There seemed to be no one else on the headland. The air was alive with the distant roar of the surf and the mewing of the gulls. The wind seemed to have sucked all the breath out of me but the girl kept toiling up the slope, dragging me onwards. My footsteps sounded hollow as we stumbled along between the tussocks of grass. There was a red mark on my hand where her fingers dug into the flesh.

I saw a woman silhouetted against the skyline. She was off the path and making her way slowly across the slope below the summit. She'd stop every few paces and bend down, then straighten up and move on. I couldn't see if there was a dog. Whatever she was doing, she was too preoccupied to notice us. I desperately wanted to call out to her but my voice wouldn't come. The girl forged on.

About a hundred yards from the summit, the path forked. A wide scar led up through the rocks to the trig point. The girl took the narrower track that skirted the summit and headed between clumps of sea pink towards the cliff. I glanced back over my shoulder at the long sweep of Trewardan Beach. Cars were crawling slowly along the road and hundreds of tiny dots speckled the wet sand. A lifetime away.

Ahead of us line after line of breakers swept in across Porthzennan Bay and the cliffs receded into the haze. The track veered to the left, running parallel to the cliff edge. Where the grass ended I saw another DANGER notice from the abandoned coastal protection scheme. A single strand of wire coiled from where the post was leaning and disappeared over the edge.

"What are we doing up here? Where are we going?" The fear lurched in me like a sickness.

I hung back, trying to slow her down. She pulled harder and shot me a look over her shoulder. Her eyes were bright and hard. Her mouth was open and I could see her teeth—small and white and sharp.

The track dipped to within a couple of feet of the cliff edge. The ground had sunk and long cracks had opened in the turf. Below us I could see the harbour wall and a scattering of small boats awaiting the tide.

"Stop! We must go back."

The girl turned on me. She smiled and I saw the blue about her lips. She opened her mouth and screamed.

"Now I've found you, I won't let go."

Her grip tightened and she threw her weight backwards. The cliff edge crumbled. I spun round and fell forward, clawing at the dust with my free hand. She'd gone over and was dragging me down. My legs kicked for purchase on the rock. Clods of earth bounced past me into the void.

"Amy! *No!*" A woman's voice somewhere above. The pressure on my hand relaxed and suddenly her weight was gone. I swung my arm up and heaved myself back onto the grass. Then I looked back down to where the sea was pounding, expecting to see her body smashed on the rocks.

There was no trace of the girl.

I scrambled to my feet. The woman in the green coat was standing on the track, holding the sea pinks she had been gathering. Then I saw the bronze plaque set into the rock beside her:

Amy Beckford, a beautiful girl, so full of life, and her father, Jonathan Beckford, who fell to their deaths in a landslip near this spot. This plaque is dedicated to their memory. "You are with us always."

"I saw you turn off the path," the woman said. "She was my daughter. Jonathan was my husband. She was picking flowers near the cliff edge—" She raised the bunch she was holding. "—it gave way. He died trying to save her."

She stooped and gently placed the flowers on a rock below the plaque, then stood and faced me.

"I saw his boat," she said. "I thought I saw—" She stopped and pushed a strand of dark hair from her face. "I thought I was losing my mind. But when they found him this morning I knew." For a moment her eyes hardened. "He got what he deserved."

She bowed her head. "She was with you on the steps and again in the town. I've seen your picture in the paper. I was afraid. I came up here. I tried to blot it out. Then I saw you on the track." She faltered, then gathered herself. "I couldn't let it happen again."

David Webb

She turned and slowly, carefully, picked her way back down the path towards the town. I watched her go, then stood for a long time while the breeze tugged at my clothes and hair and the long lines of breakers rolled in towards the shore. My hand hurt and I realised my fist was clenched. I opened it and saw what I had been holding. It was a handful of dust.

STELLA'S

SARAH PEPLOE

Isn't this what you came here for in the first place?
To be a star?

"AH," SHE SAID, LOOKING up at me. "There I am."
The johns at her sides laughed.

My first thought was, another lookalike. Stella had been a bit short with me lately, so maybe this was her way of firing me. *Get your coat sugar, your replacement's here.* The bitch. And she was better than me, this new one. My chin's a bit wrong, my eyebrows a bit light, my shoulders a bit wide, which you'd think would be impossible. She was perfect. She was unbelievable, she—

You know that dirty picture that you think is a man's face but look twice and it's a woman's body? It was like that. My eyes adjusted. I damn near turned an ankle.

Everyone was just yukking it up, except her, she was smirking and sucking down her martini like she was putting out a fire. I could feel my neck and ears getting red.

So I marched down the stairs right up to her and said, "Should I curtsey, or kneel?" which was her first line in *Iron Venus*.

There was a bit of spluttering from her arm candies. She ran her tongue across her teeth and chuckled, real deep down in her throat. Then she patted the seat opposite her.

"What's your poison, little honey?" she asked. Her voice plumed out soft like smoke. I could never entirely get the hang of it.

SO. I CAME OUT HERE to be in movies. Yeah, I was one of those. Half-escaped girls from Bumfuck Nowhere, dreaming of stardom, dreaming of revenge. It wasn't the airy business I make it sound, I worked like a dog. Auditions, screen tests, bit playing. Vamping like holy hell in the crowd scenes. Time passed. I read all the magazines. Clutched girl after girl to my heart and told myself, oh this one didn't get truly famous till she was twenty-two, that one didn't even get her first screen test till she was almost twenty-six. Time passed and passed. Money was tight. I slung hash for my hemhem respectable job and augmented my salary on evenings and Sundays.

I slipped back into that side of things like a cat under a gate. It was more lucrative and less trying than the hash house, less humiliating. It was easy. They don't want you to know. Specially not now, they couldn't have that, all us bitches rolling round the streets fat as geese instead of lining up outside St Vincent de Paul or whoever. Tootling along that tightrope between pity and disgust for their viewing pleasure. Heavens no.

Anyway I kicked the hash house and went to full time. Went from the street to houses. Each had their downsides and ups, but on the whole I preferred houses. They were comfier and felt safer, and usually had some arrangement with the law, whereas on the tiles you had to arrange that on a case-by-case basis, unless you had a pimp which… Jesus, I like the inside of my face where it is, thanks.

And I was happy. I wasn't feeling the lack of success like a hole blasted through me. It might not've looked it to Johnny Lunchpail, but my life was pretty well put together. I still did a little extra work here and there, not enough to live on, just to keep my hand in. I had a lot of friends. I wasn't on a breadline. I wasn't under the thumb of some hubby or daddy or Daddy. I could live and love as I liked. It was just a little twinge, sometimes. But nothing's ever perfect.

Then Cliff came knocking. I was so sure it was a put-up job at first.

"Bullshit," I'd said. "The studio wouldn't stand for it."

"Where d'you think I got the idea? They love it. They're bankrolling it! The Old Man'll wet his beak, course."

"Bit of a busman's holiday for him I woulda thought."

He slapped me on the back like I was choking.

"See? That's the kinda thing she'd say! They'll love you, toots. They all love a mouthy broad—"

"They do not—"

"A mouthy broad with a high set of tits then. Come and see," he said, like the voice in the Bible. Apart from the tits bit.

I PLUMPED FOR A boilermaker, partly to be sassy and partly because I was shaking like a shitting dog. She got a big kick out of that and had one herself.

I had heard tell of starlets going on a jolly to houses, like we were a petting zoo or something. This was different. For one, *we* were different—no one else offered the service that Stella's did. For another, there wasn't any tee-hee-aren't-I-naughty bullshit with her. She had a matter-of-fact manner. A knowingness, for all her questions. Course, that in itself could've been an act. She was a great actress, whatever she'd had to do to get anyone to notice. She was something else. For another another... well. I mean, Jesus. That face. That mile-high, black and white face, made of gin-flushed flesh and pointed at me.

Her boys drifted. It was her and me. She threw her whiskey back and sipped her beer and stared. We had the same make-up men they did. The studio sent them over on the QT. They had a tale or two to tell. Under the Max Factor so-and-so looks like she went ram-raiding on roller-skates, such-and-such has got pores like La Brea... Never her. They said other things about her. Close up, close-up, whatever, she was beautiful. I knew I looked like her. Academically. But right then I couldn't imagine anything less likely.

Some dink walked past stuck to Abilene and double-taked at the two of us.

"We're having tryouts," she said, cool as you like. His face. She twitched her head at Abilene.

"How's she make out?"

"Okay."

"As good as me? I mean you?"

"I never asked."

"Professional courtesy. Hah. You got an Iris here? Iris Caine?" Like there's another Iris.

"Nuh-uh."

She smiled like dawn over Avalon.

"That cunt'd give 'em frostbite," she said.

STELLA WAS LIKE NO madam I'd ever worked for, but every one you've ever read about. Feathers, fur and bug-orgy eyelashes. Mitsouko that entered the room five minutes before she did.

"Am I wrong," Cliff had said to her, tah-dahing his hands around me. "Am. I. Wrong?"

"Not bad," she said. "In a certain light."

"Christ, Stell, if I brung you Casafuckingnova you'd say his cock's an inch too long."

Stella gave me that mama bear look. That was rich. I had a hunch she was newer to the life than I was. Just a hunch.

"Whyncha give yourself a little tour, sugar. You can ask Wakey anything—" She pointed to the bar, "—or Jean," then to the sofa, occupied by a disturbingly young-looking redhead with her nose in a Gale Wilhelm. "See how you like us."

I retreated so Cliff could entreat. Him and Stella walked around with their heads together. Looked like he was really going to the bat for me, God bless him. I know he was getting a finder's fee but still.

The house was big and fancy, old-style but not old. The rooms were purple, red, pink. There were pictures on the walls. Vintage smut in big swirly frames with the gold leaf still sticky on them. Age being carefully scraped onto the chaise lounge. Pretend tradition. Pretend prestige. Pretend love goddesses of the silver screen. Everything looking like what it was meant to be.

I came back downstairs as the phrase "—like you got the Hope Diamond in your balls—" drifted across the room. She whapped him with her fan. Yeah, she had a fan.

They're putting on a show, I thought. One big dirty game of dress-up. I thought, I could go along with this.

Jean looked up and gave me a little wave. Turned out she was three months older than me.

Stella's

"WHAT ARE THEY LIKE?" she asked in this awful sweet-sticky whisper. "What do they want, when they want me, when they want you?"

"The usual." I'd stopped doing her voice. There didn't seem much point.

"I read somewhere that the fashion for rouge started up amongst ladies of the evening on account of they'd traded in their maidenly blushes. You must save a fortune."

"Whaddaya want, a biology class?"

"I want you to be specific."

"I'd have to charge—"

"You already have. Or she has." She pointed the cherry of her cigarette at Stella, at the middle of the bar doing her hail-well-met schtick to the guys. I caught her eye. I got nothing.

"Your dance card is all ticked for tonight. By me. See, reason I ask is, so few men *can*, worth writing home about. Like they think I'm made of glass or light or something. Like I'm precious. Hah. But you. They're safe with you. All the image, none of the responsibility. So. What are they like?"

I felt like a boil, red and lanced. *You want dirt, lady?*

So I started talking.

"Same again over here Wakey," she yelled, not taking her eyes off me.

AS A GENERAL RULE it's not a good idea to go drink-for-drink with a john. This right here? Not a general situation. I'd had a big dinner, which Stella always discouraged—*if they wanted some fat farting broad they'da stayed at home*—but tonight it probably worked in my favour. Kept me going.

It was so late it was early. She nearly dropped her bottle, then pretended she'd been dreamily twirling it around on the table.

"Well, she breathed. "Very illuminating. Most kind."

And slathered the table with a few more ten-spots.

"We haven't even sc-atched—scratched the surface, no doubt."

"We haven't drawn blood," I agreed. Drink for drink. You silly slut.

One of the boys came over to her ear and she got up, smoothly and steadily. Not in that try-hard-*good-evening-ossifer* way either. She could've been having herself a Caesar salad and a glass of water for lunch. She could've been acting drunk or acting sober.

"Au revoir," she said.

This point in the evening, I usually went for the Oscar. *You in town all weekend? Come back tomorrow! I'll get some good liquor in, we can have us a little party à deux.* That kind of thing.

This time I nodded.

I breathed in and felt like the air was going out the back of my head. I breathed out and my eye got caught and held by this pinkish flutter coming from the quiet end of the bar. There was a man there, raising his index finger at me in the manner of the occasional milquetoast asshole back when I was slinging hash who thought himself far too high-tone to whistle or bark or snap his fingers. I'd seen him around but we'd never spoken.

He did things for the studio. A film agent. You gotta put something on your business card.

"It's okay. C'mere."

It never is, have you noticed? Cliff was standing to one side of him like toilet roll on a stiletto.

"Shift your ass, Cliff. Let the lady have a seat."

The lady. At the hash house there were men who always made a point of calling me Miss. Brushing some of their sheer fucking class off the Formica and on to me. I sat down.

"Quite a night you've had," the agent said. "No doubt."

"No doubt!" Cliff chimed in. "And none of the other girls can say that. Coming toe-to-toe with your, ah, your original."

"Exciting, was it?" He took a final pull on his Old Gold and ground it in the ashtray by my wrist. "You look excited." The skin on his knuckles was new.

Cliff did more chiming. Christ, I thought, preserve me from this vaudeville shit. I never could handle this way of things. My pop, when he was around, if he was going to beat your ass it was always then and there, and then it was over. My mama went at a more leisurely pace. She'd think about it, put you in the cellar while she mulled it over. Sometimes she'd just chew you out. A lot of times she wouldn't do anything at all. But the waiting, the waiting.

"You did fine. From what I saw. You'da known about it if she wasn't happy."

I thought, *happy*?

"She sure did." Cliff again. If he'd laid belly-up at the guy's feet it might've injected a note of subtlety into the proceedings.

"She, she's fine, see. She's okay—"

"Yeah. You keep saying." He leaned towards me. He spoke quietly. "If, ah… if you were to ever mention this evening to anyone—"

"C'mon," Cliff said. "She knows what's good for her—"

The agent looked at Cliff. He didn't move his head. Just his eyes.

"I'm just saying is all, there's no nee—"

The agent's eyes went back to me. "You know what's good for you, he says. What is good for you?"

I hauled my voice up out of my throat. "Never mentioning this to anyone."

"Say one of those gossip-column coozes waves a few grand in your face. What would be good for you then?"

"I don't need their pin money."

"So it's quantity that's the determining factor? That's how you're wired I guess. But, see, the studio. They're some one-eyed jacks. There's a side of their face no one sees. Not so as they could ever tell about it. Know all those cheap cracks everyone makes about the Old Man having a big family? They don't know the half of it. Old Country boys, to a man. Things are very black and white with those guys. They don't have our nuanced modern attitudes about traitors and whores and such. They will hollow you out and dump what's left in the river. You ever seen stiffs pulled out of the river?"

He waited for me to answer that.

"Well then. You see what I'm saying. Your mother wouldn't know you after that. Not that you'd want her to." He jerked his head at Stella. "And then she'll get a new one."

He put his hat on and chucked me under the chin.

Stella's

"Be good."

Neither of us moved till he'd gone. Cliff went first.

"He didn't oughta, he… I told him you're okay—"

"Sure. Sweet of you, Cliff."

He flinched at *sweet*. I got changed and went home and went straight to bed.

I got woken up by the fishmonger next door heading out. My cheeks were tight and heavy. They crackled under my fingertips. I went to the bathroom and saw her face hovering over mine. Her lips bright and caked as a TB stiff's, her eyes panda-ed like the style when she was just starting out. I picked and scrubbed till it was me. Fuck you. Still here.

SHE DIDN'T COME BACK for weeks. When she did I felt—not happy to see her, but like I'd put a heavy bag down. I realised I had been waiting for her, all the time. Whatever else I'd been doing. I saw her there, in the same seat as before, just under the projector. That month's stag film was fluttering darkly across her face. I started to raise my hand in a wave, and she just looked at me like air. Air that was doing her a vague disservice. Stella gave a tiny little shake of her head. I went back upstairs.

It happened a few times. She'd sit downstairs with the guys and get stinko. I'd hear her laughing. Then she'd Go On Somewhere and I was allowed to creep out of my burrow.

Those were always quiet nights for me. I made up for it boodlewise the rest of the week but it still made me angry.

143

What was the percentage for her, screwing with my livelihood? Why? The other way round I could understand, but—

"What do they talk about?" I asked Jean. Jean was Dulcie Dickens. I shit you not. *Our Sooty Sweetheart, The Little Matchgirl, And Missy Makes Three!*...Yeah, that Dulcie Dickens. She made out like gangbusters.

"She acts like one of the guys. You know the kinda thing."

"Butch?"

"Nah. Desperate."

"What does she do if one of 'em's buying?"

"She got all her little gigolos round her like cellophane. And Stella probably gives out that—" Jean teetered between *she's* and *you're*. "—booked up. I dunno." She looked me smack in the eye, carefully. "I don't ask."

I'd followed her round the corner and to the top of the stairs without really noticing. The end of my tether. Her eyes were big and angry and sad. Her eyes always took some getting used to, because she'd come in of an evening in heaps of mascara, kohl, Ashes of Roses right up to those bullwhip eyebrows, then take it all off to go to work.

"Don't let it get to you."

She went downstairs, putting a skip in her step as soon as her feet became visible to anyone on the ground floor. She slid down the banister sometimes. They liked that.

When I got back in my room there was a box on the bed. I could plunge my hands in it up to the wrist. It had that smell. That smell that says this was life, not something farmed by man but something built and bred for itself, that ran and hunted and fucked all for itself, and now it's all for you, girlie. How do girls get minks? The same way minks get minks. Cliff's favourite joke. Favourite printable one.

A little card stuck under the ribbon on the lid. No message, just her first initial in swooping black. Of course. She wouldn't've risked an autograph.

I dashed back onto the landing and saw Bo heading for the second floor.

"You just—that was you right? The box on the bed?"

Bo had this funny way about him. Like, you all think all I am is some whorehouse muscle, I could be a secret agent on my days off, I could be a hairdresser, I could be a pastor with twelve kids. You'll never know.

"I put that box on the bed."

"Who gave it to you? Sh—they say anything?"

He tapped his nose.

"Don't—not about this. Please Bo, just tell me straight—"

He tapped his nose.

The next week, a dress. Sheer and blue-black. Perfect for me, for her. I hung it up carefully. I thought my hands were itching after I touched it but that passed.

The week after that, perfume. I couldn't tell which kind. I sprayed it onto the vanity to see if it would take the varnish off. It didn't.

The week after that, chocolates. A huge, heart-shaped, beribboned box straight out of the movies. The kind of thing she might pick at, reclining in kimono and mules, talking on the phone to a gal pal. A sunny blonde or a hot-head redhead, something to offset her. I popped one like a tick, half-expecting ground glass. It was caramel. I imagined her at home in slacks and curlers, methodically syringing them all full of laxative. Or would she have someone to do that for her? I put them under the bed.

The week after that. Gone midnight. In my room, all dolled up and nowhere to go. Sore as hell. I was trying to read but I kept dropping off. Just for a second or two, then the noise from downstairs or outside would drag me back. And one of those times I lifted my chin off my tits and just like that—

"You're not wearing it." She sniffed. "Any of it."

I stood. Like hell was I letting her shoulder in here, too.

"I—not tonight, but I have done. Thank you," I managed.

"For what?"

"The gifts."

"They're not gifts."

"What?"

"They're yours. They were always yours."

"*What*—"

"Lotta rooms in this joint. Almost like they want you to get lost."

"Why are you doing this?"

"This…?" she said, like she was being saintly patient with all my riddles.

"Stopping me working. I dunno if, if I offend you or—"

"You think *that's* why you're doing bad? Even if I wasn't here honey—"

Her lips drew back in this awful, angry laugh. She kept jerking her jaw forward like she'd been on the salt. I realised she was trying not to cry.

"You better learn to type or something because all this business—" She waved a vague hand up and down herself. "—is not the smart money. This is headed for the glue factory."

"But—"

"Ho yeah. It's coming. You can't see it yet. My contract's up in July and they're souring on me and I'm getting o—"

Her face held that panicked, silent *O* for a second. Then she hauled it back into the laugh.

"I can talk to you," she said. "Better than a diary. Ally Hirsch, my old meal ticket, taught me about Shakespeare and shit, he tried to get me to keep a diary. I never could get the hang of it. Probably for the fucking best, hah."

She walked towards me or I walked towards her. Her brows were drawn together, her head on one side. I caught on, all in a furious rush. She was *doing me*, the fucking bitch, she was—

She stopped. I guess. She touched my face, softly. I think I would've flinched less at a slap.

"God," she said. "I was something."

Our mouths met. Mine smeared, hers didn't.

Back at Euphemia's house I'd had a regular, this pencil-neck who'd decided I was a Real Bright Kid because I smiled and nodded at the right junctures in his monologues, he'd told me that women become dykes because they want to do it to themselves. It's the mirror stage of sexuality, he said. Masturbatory. Narcissistic and essentially immature.

(Smile, nod.) My ass. Every woman I've had, line 'em up if you have the room, you couldn't find a thing in common between me and them. Well. Maybe a couple things. But this, now. This was something else.

She kept saying *me, you, me*. As if she wasn't sure which of 'em made less sense. Kept muttering it and looking hungrily at the mirror like it was two extra girls, impatiently waiting their turn. She tilted my head back. Right back. I was a crystal ball, between her palms. I was a spell brewing. She lifted my hair from behind my ears. Thumbed my chin, pushed the tip of my nose up till my lips parted. I can stop this at any time, I thought, I can.

She said, "You ain't had any work done, have you?"

"No."

"Just the luck of the draw, ain't it? Looks. I favour my daddy. Allegedly. You know your daddy?"

"Yeah. He stuck around till I was ten."

She unpiggied my nose. I kept my eyes half closed. It seemed simpler. I couldn't see much of her through my lashes. Just her mouth, wide. She spat a laugh.

"Never know, huh."

Never know. We could fuck so hard we'd each come out the other side and would either of us know? There was such strength in her. Some real sinewy power, under the softness. She was always going on about callisthenics in the magazines. Shit I thought, is this like the mink, the dress? Another headgame, pull me close with one hand and push me away with the other? Both her hands were busy. She ran them over me like a boy. Not even like a boy: they would usually devote themselves to certain regions. She was on my neck, my elbows, my belly.

She stroked me with her fingertips and moaned. Then I realised it was the dress that she was stroking. Green as funny-pages poison, supple as birch. *Penelope Stark.* From her big scene at the governor's mansion, you know—"Your love, good sir, is the basest of coin." Stella had me watch it till my eyes near fell out.

"One from the vaults," she said softly. It was the real dress. The studio sent them over. The odd stitch busted, a little crispy under the arms with sweat. Good God I was thirteen before I wore anything that hadn't already been worn out by—at least— three other girls, and here I was doing it again. But this had only had one other occupant.

She smoothed it down my hips. Pulled me against her. Lifted my wrists with hers in a woozy waltz, pushed my back to arch under her hard palms. She was comparing. Does that sound like it would be a passionless thing? It wasn't. Affectionless, sure, but not passionless. I was Niagara Falls. That ain't entirely unprecedented but usually it's a bit of an assache—I mean, it always makes a man so damn smug. Not an issue in this case. A minxy urge took hold of me.

"What this old thing?" I said.

She laughed, that angry junkyard-dog of a laugh again.

"I just threw it on," I said.

She unpinned my hair and shoved me onto the bed.

AFTER, SHE ATE MOST of the chocolates. She seemed to expect them, under the bed and untouched.

"You want a drink?" I asked.

"None of whatever horse piss you got up here," she said, and handed me a hipflask.

"It'll be alright," I said. "You're something else, you ain't just a face. There's no one like you."

She said, "Sure, kid. Sure."

~~~

OUTSIDE GRAUMAN'S, someone was smashing my head against the sidewalk, over and over. It was daytime; people just stepped over us. I had little rag doll arms and I couldn't scream.

Sun. Midday burning me up on the bed and the smashing was still going on and it was knocking, knocking on the door. That real, almighty bastard's hammering. Shit. I hollered, "Just a second, sir!" and scrambled into something that wouldn't fall open. Be peachy wouldn't it, all this effort to put together the most picture-perfect, housiest house you ever did see and no one remembers to pay off the bulls—

"Grease us twice, you still in there?" That was another thing about Bo, he never properly cursed. Made him scarier.

"Yeah," I said, pointlessly. I made sure I was covered and unlocked the door. "What's with all the strong-arm, you scared the—"

"That was my asking," said the agent. He had a hand on Bo's bicep. "I was worried. Where's the girl?"

I did one hundred percent of nothing with my face and body and brain.

"She take a powder already?"

"Yes—"

"Well," he laughed softly, but kindly. "That'll happen. You put yourself together and we'll see you downstairs. No rush."

When the door was shut and locked I looked back at the room. I could've dreamed it. Except the chocolates were gone apart from the toffees, and I was raw inside and out, and the paddy wagon finery I'd thrown on was the dress she'd been wearing, and I smelt of her. Why were the curtains open?

I washed, and put her on. Not as good a job as Make-Up would've done, but good enough. It wasn't hard. Everyone wore her mouth these days, her eyes, her hair. And I had a head start, didn't I? Costume was a worry, but the shouldered and belted dress she'd worn to my room was the very thing. It was just the right side of severe and it didn't show too much skin. What it didn't hide could be handled with foundation and powder, more or less. The hickeys frightened me. I'd never seen myself so dark from someone's mouth. Like eggplant. Her nails had left welts all over me, dotted with red and violet. I was trying really hard not to think of the word *switched*.

IT WAS DEAD, downstairs. Everyone was asleep or had gone home. It was just the agent, sitting in one of the armchairs, and Bo, hovering.

"Ah," the agent said, "there she is. Your car's outside."

Or was it 'the' that he'd said?

We walked to the door, which he opened for me. He moved like he was going to lay a hand on the small of my back but he kept it at a distance, like my ass was a trashcan fire.

Why didn't I put my own duds on, or my own make-up? Why didn't I just say? Because he'd already made me for her, or acted like he had, so there was something afoot. But he couldn't: that was bunk. He *couldn't* think I *was*, really, so he was screwing with me to some purpose or other. If he could get me on the back fuck-me pump, raddled with terror and the need to please him, by the time we got wherever he was taking me I'd be a lamb. Like a more civilised version of putting me in the trunk. Perhaps he wanted to see how far I'd take it. The hothouse cultivation of a self. Perhaps it was professional curiosity.

Sure enough, at the mouth of Stella's little courtyard, a blue Rolls the size of a pleasure cruiser. It didn't look like the kind of car you'd take someone for a dirt nap in but what did that count for, with him? We took the long, sneaky way onto Sunset, then glided up the hill. Up, up, up. I thought, you're hanging onto the Hindenburg here sister. The seat went sticky under my back, my thighs. I could scream for help, I thought. Appeal to the driver. Sort of boiled-looking eyes in the rear-view. No suspicion, no contempt, no adoration. Nothing to work with there.

We stopped at the lights. People pointed and cooed. She was always so good to her fans.

He looked at me. Just looked, his face mildly expectant. I waved. I couldn't feel my hands but yeah, there they were, waving back at me in the not-too-tinted glass. She gave a lot with her hands. Draping out of a trunk in *Streets of Shame*, around the neck of a bottle in *A Kiss, A Curse!* I was good at her hands.

MY GUTS CLENCHED WITH the possibility they'd expect me to have a key for the gate, but the driver took care of that. It was definitely her place. You got the odd glimpse of it, in the magazines. It looked like you'd wanna lick it on a hot day. I'd tricked in some fancy joints in my time, other circumstances I wouldn't've felt a bit intimidated. The Rolls stopped. Offing me here, that'd raise some awkward questions, surely to God. A squeaky bit of me started to hope but I told it no. This could all be part of the prolonging. He could still spring the trap.

"Well." He slapped his hands down on his thighs in that way that preppy men use to mean goodbye. "You have a great day now. Any plans?"

I looked at her pool, covered over with a white tarp.

"Perhaps a swim," I said.

"Of course! Didn't I read that's your favourite pursuit?"

"Aw, yeah. When I was a kid they couldn't pull me out of the river."

Something faltered in his face, just for a second. Like we'd gone over a pothole.

I walked across the gravel, my shoulder blades waiting for a bullet every step. Her front door was open. It was cool and dark inside. And it was beautiful. There were two flights of stairs curving up to a landing and a set of double doors, all white and gold with a glow that light hadn't made.

She was stretched out on the left set of stairs, resting on her heels and elbows. It looked for a minute like she was asleep. Or lying down anyway. She lifted her head. She was wearing the biggest, darkest coat you ever saw but there were flashes of green when she straightened her legs and got up and walked towards me. The car sighed away down the drive on the edge of my hearing.

She looked *vital*. One time when I was a kid I saw a dog lying by the side of the road. Just a little dry blood on its snout. It was a podgy little pooch, which was unusual in itself. Hell, if you saw a dog with both its ears in our town it was there on vacation. It was sort of trembling and shifting so I thought it might be ok, so I went over and—

That was the sort of alive she looked. I felt the old anger at her, straight up, unadulterated by anything else.

"What," I said on the wings of what felt like the first full breath I'd taken since Bo'd woken me up, "was that?"

"She just needs to be consistent. She goes somewhere, she comes home, everyone sees."

"That guy, the film agent—"

"He's a gentleman."

"Aren't they all?"

"I wouldn't know."

"Kiss my ass, you sick old hag—"

"What are you getting sore for? You don't need to worry about anything. Enn-ee-thing. You're set for life, and so am I. Because the Old Man, he believes in me."

Her eyes were dinner plates.

"His faith has been reinforced. He knows. All those broads walking round lighting their smokes like me, shooting their mouth off to guys like me, dancing like me, covered in me, it's a glaze. All of you. No one can be me. I didn't get it but now I do. I was worried, hah. Worried! All you are is dress-up," she said, throwing back her head like when she'd played Hedda Gabler. Reviews were mixed. "I'm gonna last forever. But hell. I wouldn't begrudge you a bit of my dust."

She pulled a white silk scarf from her pocket and slung it around my head, the way she'd worn it in the courtroom after that typist from Decatur City accused her of bigamy.

"You did your piece, that's all you need to do. You can leave by the front," she said like she was offering me every wonder of the world, "if you're discreet—"

I jerked away from her, toppling the scarf, but that still left it round my neck. And her still holding it, in both hands.

"I don't want you near me again."

"Why would I want that? Did you think you thrilled me?"

"Sure," I spat. "All the image, none of the responsibility. Get to act like you're *so* wicked, but it's all fake. You get to run back to your palace and be a *nice lady* and no one says anything—"

"*Anything?*"

Her fists tightened on the scarf. We'd been further apart when we'd kissed. Her eyes did the same pothole thing the agent's had, but when she did it, oh God—

"They say *everything*. And it's true," she hissed. "You couldn't dream up the things I've done. I was bred to it. Soon as I could toddle, running all the errands, all the laundry. I hid in the coalhole when we got raided. I hauled buckets full of their babies out to the shithouse. There was pigs behind it."

She stretched her arms out and stepped back, her heels clacking on the marble.

"But now I'm here. And you're a cunt."

I MUMMIED MY HEAD IN the scarf and headed back to town on foot. She never came to Stella's again. That year she landed the lead in *Guadalajara*. It stayed in the first-run theatres till the following June. It was brilliant. She was brilliant. I'd go to the pictures again and again and she'd pour over me. Each time I saw it I'd go through a full pack of cigarettes. Each time I'd cry, but everyone did.

The johns changed. They seemed wary, feinting at the rough stuff, almost solemn when we got down to it. I put it down to her playing a nun. A nun in the throes of some pretty hefty crises of faith, but a nun nonetheless. Stella scared me up a habit from somewhere or other, not fancy dress, the real thing. Cliff bust a gut when he saw me in it.

Just one time, there was this guy. About my age. He seemed more into her older work, *Iron Venus, Dark Days and Bright Nights*, so I was playing those to the hilt. It was nice to be back in those skins.

"It's you," he panted.

I pretzelled my legs about his ass and cooed, "Yeah, baby it's me, it's me, and it's all for you—"

"No," he said. "No i-it's her—"

His dick did the salted slug inside me.

"It's her, you're *her*, *really*, Jesus—" Eyes bugging like a hammered bullock's. He broke out of the cage of my gams and backed off to the wall.

"Her," he squeaked.

When he'd gone I sat in front of the mirror, remembering her teeth and nails and her voice twining across my flesh saying *me, you, me*. Blood and hair and words. The man's face and the woman's body. But no, it was bullshit. My chin was still wrong, my shoulders still too wide. There is such a thing as being too good at your job. Still, he guilt-tipped like a champion, so I guess all's well that ends well.

FOCAL POINT

MICHAEL HITCHINS

I USUALLY WALK HOME from the station because to take a taxi, I believe, would be decadent and rather lazy. I'm determined not to become one of those enormously fat, old people, sitting there staring at the television or shuffling along the pavement. It's only a short walk to my house—a mile or so—but the exercise helps to counteract the effects of the flapjacks and pasties to which I'm partial. Sometimes I'll cycle, and occasionally Suzanne will pick me up, but generally, as I say, I walk. One evening though, as the train lurched across the Washburn valley, I resolved to break with routine since my legs were stiff and sore from pounding the canal towpath at lunchtime.

The taxis that snake around immediately outside the station are all from the same company and I make a point of not using them because this company is the station's *official provider*. It pays the railway company a premium for the privilege, which of course is reflected in the fare. Essentially, it's a monopoly. After disembarking, I strode, or rather hobbled, past the monopoly cars, each with its green trapezoid logo, and over the road to where taxis belonging to other firms were waiting. At the front of the queue, several yards ahead of the rest of the cars, was a large, box-shaped monstrosity. It was grey, perhaps, or beige or maybe brown—I couldn't tell exactly which under the harsh yellow street lights. It certainly wasn't black and white like all the other taxis—and it bore no logo at all. With its high-backed, utilitarian appearance, I took it to be a mobility vehicle and paused for a second, assuming the driver was waiting for a member of his family to arrive from the station. But then he wound down his window and said with a smile, "Where to, sir?"

I loaded my rucksack and sports bag onto the rear seat and jumped in the front. "I don't normally take taxis," I said, as we set off. "But I went running at lunchtime and my legs are killing me."

The driver nodded.

"I haven't been for ages but I've been asked to do a marathon so I need to put in the miles. It's a half marathon really but, you know—in fact, it's a corporate relay so I'm only doing two miles, ha ha, but, well, even so, I'm certainly out of practice."

It wasn't like me to be so chatty and I realised I was embarrassed about taking a cab for such a short distance. The driver, surely, would have preferred a longer, more valuable fare and must be cursing me for wasting his time. I even launched into the story of how I'd broken my ankle a few years previously and how I was still feeling pain from it, but then I stopped, suddenly aware I was prattling and that the driver, in fact, seemed benign and non-judgmental.

"This is a big car," I said, at last.

"A lot of people say that," said the taxi driver, "but if you look in the back—"

I looked round. A set of articulated rails lay folded up on the floor and a small ramp had been tucked down one side. It had evidently been adapted for wheelchair access.

"—you'll see it only takes three."

"Oh yes. So you carry… disabled people."

"Disabled. That's right. A few years ago I took early retirement. I sat around the house a bit, got bored, and decided to buy this because I wanted to, you know, give something back. So we take out disabled children—give the parents a break. It was my wife and me at first but she passed away, so my daughter helps now."

"You take them on outings?" I asked. "To urban farms and places?"

"No, nothing like that. It's not outings as such. Just little trips. We take them out two or three days a week. And look after them while the parents have a bit of respite."

"It's an actual service you advertise?"

"We don't advertise—it's just the same ones. But we do hospital trips as well for normal people—well, able-bodied people—because it's handy having the space for all the equipment, and getting them in and out. A lot of taxis aren't able to take the equipment—crutches and wheelchairs. So it's very nice getting to know people and having a laugh with them."

He had a quiet, plaintive voice and I pictured a white ray of sunlight streaming through trees on a cold morning. I imagined, from his accent, that he came from the Wirral, although I only have a vague idea of how they talk over there.

"I dropped off a lady today for an operation," he continued. "She's quite a character. A friend really—Dawn. She could barely walk. She's having one of her knees replaced. Terrible, seeing someone in so much pain, but that's the thing, you get to see the difference—before and after—so I've got my fingers crossed it goes well for her."

"Has she been waiting a long time?"

"Well, the waiting list wasn't too bad, but she was terrified of surgery because of what had happened in her family. Her mum and grandma both died on the operating table. Routine operations that went wrong."

We paused at a junction and the voice of the woman in the taxi office crackled from the two-way radio, arranging a pick-up elsewhere in town.

"How awful," I said. "Did they have weak hearts?"

"Probably, I don't know. But you can imagine she was worried sick about going under the anaesthetic."

"Hopefully things have improved since then."

"You'd think so, yes. But she was putting herself through all sorts of worry. She was still going out walking, but it was getting worse and worse and she was going through so much pain. She was down for the operation before. What was it? Six months ago. I took her to the hospital and she was alright to start with but as we got into the car park she started screaming and crying, saying, 'Take me home! Take me home!' And nothing I could say would calm her down so I had no choice but to take her home."

"But she's gone in today?"

"Yes. She was fine—quite happy about it."

"And how did they persuade her?"

"Well, it's a funny thing. You know Scarp Hill? She went up there and had a strange… well, the thing is, she's a very keen walker but she was actually saying she'd rather give up the walking completely than go through with the operation. I said, 'You can't go round cancelling operations—they cost a lot of money.' But her thinking was she wouldn't have the worry of the operation hanging over her and by giving up the long-distance walking, she wouldn't have to put herself through so much pain any more. She would just potter about indoors, read magazines and water her plants. So she was planning to walk up Scarp Hill and then that would be it, her last walk ever. She wasn't thinking straight, though. I mean to give up something you love and stay at home all the time. But anyway, last Saturday, she caught the bus to Fewby and started walking up the hill."

We slowed down to join a queue at some temporary traffic lights. After a treacherous winter the roads were in a sorry state and the council had chosen this week to start fixing them. My gaze flicked between the meter and the rheumy eyes of the driver, his face lit up every second by the strobing amber light of a colossal asphalt spreader.

Focal Point

According to the driver, Dawn had struggled along the footpath for about an hour when she saw a figure ahead of her, some way in the distance. At first, she couldn't tell whether it was a man or a woman or even whether it was moving away or coming towards her. For a full five minutes she was unable to work this out and stood transfixed by the strange phenomenon but, eventually, she discerned it was a woman in a quilted, lavender coloured jacket, walking towards her with a little dog scampering about her feet.

When they reached each other the dog ran up and Dawn bent down to stroke it but her bad knee gave way and she tumbled to the ground, writhing in agony. The woman took Dawn's hand and tried to pull her up but *she* fell over too and the pair of them lay there on the ground, laughing. Then Dawn burst into tears and told the woman all about the operation and why she was scared. "Oh, you've nothing to worry about," said the woman. "I've had *both* knees replaced and it's given me a new lease of life." From her jacket she produced a packet of tissues. "They do it one knee at a time," she went on. "After the first one I said I'd never go back for the other because I was in so much pain—your knee swells up to the size of a beach ball. I won't go into the gory details but it *would* swell up of course, because they hack your knee open and all the flesh is carved back and they're inserting these new knees. But I shouldn't be telling you all this."

"No, no, I'm not squeamish. I'd just like to know whether it's worth it," said Dawn.

"Oh yes, I can assure you on that score because I did go back and now I'm as right as rain. I'd definitely recommend it.

And if you're only having *one* done you'll be fine. After about a month you're seventy percent back to normal and you'll be able to do a short walk of a mile or so. Once it's all healed you'll be doing your long walks again with no pain whatsoever."

"No pain? I can't believe that."

"Well, there will be pain, of course, but it will pass."

Dawn had described to the driver a sense of calm that overcame her in this woman's presence. The woman exuded warmth and compassion, which manifested itself physically in a sort of golden glow, and this, evidently, affected Dawn more profoundly than the glib, professional assurances of her specialist.

With the woman's help, Dawn managed to stand up. The woman offered to escort her back down the hill, but Dawn said no, she was determined to reach the top. She thanked the woman and they hugged.

"Don't worry, Dawn," said the woman. "I know you're going to be alright."

The taxi driver cleared his throat and took a swig from a can of energy drink. "So, she carries on up the hill and when she gets to the top she turns round. She can see the woman far off down the bottom and she gets her camera out to… ah, but I didn't tell you about the camera, did I?"

By now, we had reached the front of the queue. The traffic lights changed to green and we started to move again.

"You see, Dawn always carries a camera with her, but she does this thing where she takes a photo of where she's going, and when she gets there she takes a photo of where she's been. If she sees a landmark like a church tower or a castle miles in the distance she takes a photo and then heads towards it and when she gets there she takes one of where she was when she set off."

"Sort of a visual diary," I said.

"Yes, I suppose so," said the driver. "She even does it on short trips to the shops. She's got a blog of them—with all the starts and finishes side by side. She calls them her *here* and *there* photographs. Like on that day she takes one of the hill, you know, with the big tree on it, and when she gets to the top she's about to take the *there* photo and she can see the woman and the dog down below. She takes the photo but when she looks at the camera she can't see them. She takes another photo and another and another, just to be sure, and in none of them can she see the woman with the little dog. There's a bit of glare from the sun, which makes it difficult, and when she was a kid she got some glass in her eye—her eyesight's never been 20/20—so, she decided to have a proper look at the photos when she got home and she'd probably see them then. But this thought gets in her head, 'What if the woman can't be photographed? What if she's an angel?'"

I stifled a laugh. "I'm sorry, it just seems—"

"Ridiculous, yes—but she's a very spiritual person is Dawn, and she was really affected by it. She felt all hot and dizzy and had to sit down beneath the tree and eat some chocolate because she was shaking so much. So when she got home... well, maybe I'd better stop there."

"Sorry?" I looked up and realised we'd arrived outside my house.

"I expect your dinner's ready."

"No, please go on."

"I'll turn the meter off though," he said. "Don't want you paying over the odds."

"Thank you."

"So, when she got home she uploaded the photos onto her computer but she still couldn't find the woman or the dog. And that's why she was sitting where you are this afternoon."

"You mean she's gone ahead with the operation because she believes that woman was an angel?"

"Exactly. Or a spirit or something that'd been sent to reassure her."

"Couldn't she just have been a nice person?"

"But what about the photographs?"

"Well, I haven't seen them—have you?"

"No, but Dawn wouldn't lie."

"You said yourself she had problems with her eyes."

Suzanne had pulled back our living room curtain and was peering out.

"Well, it's an interesting story," I said, trying to be pleasant. "Thank you." I handed over a tenner and opened the door.

"Thank *you*, sir," said the driver. "And thank you for, you know, listening."

I opened the door. "But wait," he added, tugging at my sleeve. "The dog."

"Pardon?"

"The dog was a Lhasa Apso. Dawn said, 'Isn't it cold for a little dog?' and the woman said, 'He's from Tibet. Or his ancestors were. He's a Lhasa Apso. They carry the spirits of the Dalai Lamas.'"

He nodded sagely, as though this was definitive proof of supernatural events.

"Well, there you go," I said. We both climbed out and he fetched my bags.

"And the other thing is, the woman knew her name. She said, 'Don't worry, *Dawn*. You're gonna to be alright.' But Dawn had never said her name. Which is odd, isn't it?"

"Yes," I said. "Very odd."

THE NEXT EVENING MY legs had recovered sufficiently for me to resume my customary stroll from the station. As I walked along, I thought about Dawn. Although I had never met her, and most likely never would, I hoped the operation had been a success. I imagined the taxi driver at her bedside with a bunch of flowers. There had been something in his tone that made me feel that he and Dawn were more than just friends. Perhaps the two of them would get married and go on long walks together, hand in hand.

As for the business about the golden woman and her spirit-bearing dog, I found it ludicrous that people had to resort to such fanciful notions to bolster their confidence. But that's not to say I wasn't intrigued. On the train, I had looked at Dawn's blog—there were many photos, charting walks all over the north of England, but it hadn't been updated for a couple of months. I also read about Lhasa Apsos. Apparently, it wasn't just the Dalai Lamas whose spirits the dogs carried; it was lamas in general. Laughably, I had imagined the Lhasa Apsos carrying the lamas along in their teeth but, of course (according to the belief), the souls of the dead gurus entered the bodies of the dogs and remained there until they were reincarnated into a new body—and that was what was meant by being *carried*. But really, what had this to do with a woman in the Yorkshire Dales?

When I turned the corner into my street I noticed a large car parked outside my house and, as I drew nearer, I recognised it as the taxi from the night before. I was puzzled. It was perfectly possible that one of my neighbours had hired the same taxi but why was the engine turned off and where was the driver? As I took off my coat in the hallway, I heard Suzanne talking in the living room and then, in response, the unmistakable, gentle tones of my friend from the Wirral. I opened the door. The driver was sitting on the sofa holding my favourite mug, staring into the fireplace. Suzanne turned towards me and said, "Jim's had some bad news."

The driver looked up and murmured, "She's dead."

Dawn, it transpired, had never come round after the operation. The doctors blamed some genetic defect. I stuttered platitudes—she was a very brave lady, it must have helped her to know you were there—but in my mind's eye was the image of Dawn sitting with the woman and the dog on Scarp Hill and I wondered if I dare broach the subject. It seemed callous to do so.

Then Suzanne announced that the driver—*Jim*—was staying for dinner.

"Of course," I said, but, I confess, my overriding thought was, what was this person doing in my house? Had I shown undue interest in his story? Had I, God forbid, come across as a patient, understanding listener? It transpired, however, that the poor man had been driving around at random for several hours and had ended up in our driveway. He found himself knocking on our door under some compulsion, it seemed, to tell me what had happened to Dawn.

Jim was appreciative of the meal but ate mainly in silence while Suzanne and I recounted the minutiae of our days. Eventually, it was he who said, "So, the angel was wrong."

"Hmm, well," I said. "To be honest, I don't think it was an angel. It was just a woman."

"If it was just a woman, I want to wring her bloody neck. She made Dawn have the operation."

"People are like that," said Suzanne. "They always say the things you want to hear. They always say, 'Oh, it'll be alright,' but what if it's not alright? It can't always be *alright*."

"Yes," I said, joining in. "And what happens then? Who's left to pick up the pieces?"

Jim didn't seem to listen. "Unless the angel wanted it to happen. Perhaps Dawn went into the body of the dog?"

"She died in hospital, didn't she? Not on Scarp Hill. Are you saying her spirit sailed out all the way to Fewbydale?"

"Perhaps. Or maybe the woman was at the hospital."

"With the dog?"

"Or maybe," said Jim, choking back tears, "maybe it was a *bad* angel."

"Oh Jim," said Suzanne, putting her arm round his shoulder. "You've had a shock, a bad shock, but it wasn't an angel at all. It was just a well-meaning woman who gave Dawn some advice. And at the end of the day it was really only Dawn who could make the decision. And who's to say it wasn't the right decision?"

"Well, she died, didn't she? But, anyway, what about the photographs?"

From his jacket pocket Jim produced what he said was Dawn's camera and handed it to me. It was a small, compact digital—on the cheap side but decent enough. The most recent picture was of a pretty house with jasmine winding up a trellis. The second was of Jim's taxi with Jim holding open the passenger door. The third was evidently taken from the top of Scarp Hill. The landscape was bleak but not without colour. Clumps of last year's ferns appeared orange against the vivid green sward. No human figure was apparent. As I zoomed in, the details became more ambiguous. Shapes melted into each other and flattened out, the vibrant colours reduced to washed-out blues and greys. Leafless thorn bushes, when magnified, resembled cobwebs or even shattered glass. Rocks in shadow became monstrous creatures and trees in the background transformed into human figures skulking in the undergrowth. It was quite possible the woman was in these photos, somewhere, but then again it was just as possible that she wasn't in them at all.

Focal Point

TWO DAYS LATER, I was sitting beside Jim again as he drove beyond Kettlewell and down into Fewbydale. Suzanne sat in the back with Jim's daughter, Jodie, and a young man called Nick. Suzanne and Jodie bonded immediately and launched into an improvised cross-talking double act, which kept Nick royally amused. This excitement contrasted with my sense of foreboding and I tried to work out exactly what we were hoping to achieve. Revenge? To make the woman feel bad? If we found her were we going to accuse her of being some sort of Tibetan ghost intent upon capturing the souls of elderly Englishwomen and inserting them into her dog? It was Suzanne who had suggested we go to Scarp Hill and find the woman. She thought it might help Jim come to terms with what happened and reasoned that since Dawn had met the woman last Saturday there was a chance she would be there again today. I anticipated taking a photo so I could prove to Jim it wasn't an angel, that she was just an ordinary woman who happened to give encouragement to someone. If it really was an angel, Jim, presumably, wanted reassurance that the woman was a messenger from a higher place to confirm that Dawn was taken deliberately. But the alternative that Jim had alluded to was preying on my mind—the possibility that the woman was somehow malevolent and that we were in danger.

We arrived at the visitor centre at about half past ten. Suzanne, Jodie and Nick headed inside to where art and craft activities were already going on, and, by the sound of it, some live folk music. There was no sign of the woman. I was keen to set out walking straightaway but Jim was content to mooch around the edge of the car park with a coffee and a cigarette. I stood with him for a while with my own coffee and we smiled and chatted. It seemed for a moment as if the focus of the expedition had nothing to do with Dawn and the golden lady and maybe all we needed was to get out here for some breathing space away from the town. And then I looked up towards Scarp Hill and saw the tree—a broad oak— magnificent on the otherwise bare summit, and started to walk.

From the car park, the path runs parallel with the Skirfare as it meanders along the valley, and I was surprised to see that the riverbed was dry. Millions of bone-coloured rocks lay exposed to the sun with just a few residual pools clinging on forlornly. As I rounded a bend, contemplating the unexpected silence and stillness of this ghost river, I was confronted by the rotting body of a sheep hanging from the branches of a hawthorn. I shivered with repulsion, imagining someone had hung it there as a sick joke but, as I wandered on, I reasoned the creature must have been swept downstream when the river was last in spate. I took a divergent path, which led me away from the river and up the hill to the oak silhouetted against the hazy sky.

When I finally reached the top I turned and looked out across the valley to the vast, slumbering slopes guarding the river and down to the grey houses clustered around the steeple at Fewby. I wished Jim had joined me—surely it would do him better to be up here instead of filling his lungs with tar in the car park. I still had Dawn's camera so I pulled it out and looked at the photo she'd taken from the hilltop. She was evidently sitting down when she took it, nestled in the roots of the tree, and I sat in the same place. Now that I was here I could make more sense of the landscape and I compared the image in the camera with the view in front of me, following the path down the hill, across a field, past an old barn, and then descending into a wood beside a ravaged plantation and on towards the village. Noticing some movement, I switched to shooting mode and tracked back along a moss-covered wall, and that's when I saw her—the woman in the lavender jacket. My hands trembled as I zoomed in and I watched as she opened a gate, walked through it and swung it shut behind her. I stood up. My view of the ground around her was obscured but I detected, from the tilt of her head, the presence of the little dog. I was about to press the shutter release when I noticed movement further to the left which I thought, at first, was a sheep clambering over the wall. But it wasn't a sheep; it was Jim, a plume of blue smoke rising above him. He must have decided to join me. He stepped into the path about ten yards further on from the woman. They were too far away for me to hear their conversation. Almost immediately, Jim started to gesticulate, jabbing his hands about in an angry manner, and the woman backed away. Jim stepped towards her, and then the woman lunged forward and seemed to strike him. I put the camera away and ran.

Hurtling down the path, while trying to avoid the fearsome rocks, I lost sight of the pair. I dashed through a sparse wood, my cheeks whipped by beech buds, and as I rounded a bend the yapping of the dog reached my ears, but then my weaker foot landed on a loose stone and I crashed to the ground, bashing my head on a rock. I tried to stand but must have lost consciousness. For how long I couldn't tell, perhaps just a few seconds, but when I came to I could feel blood. I touched the wound on my forehead and winced. For a few yards I could only crawl over large painful rocks and through puddles.

It must have taken me over twenty minutes to reach the spot where I had seen the altercation and when I did I found Jim prostrate and motionless. The woman had vanished. I tried to phone Suzanne but could get no signal. I attempted artificial respiration without success and then the whole hillside started vibrating. I was terrified—it felt like an earthquake or a hurricane—but then I saw the helicopter above me. It landed close by and two paramedics jumped out and took charge of Jim. At the same time, a four-by-four rolled up the hill bearing Jodie and a mountain rescue team. The paramedics carried on trying to revive Jim and then stretchered him into the helicopter, followed by Jodie. As the helicopter took off I heard Jodie yell my name and she threw something that fell onto the path—Jim's car keys. "Look after Nick!" she shouted.

After that I must have fainted again because the next thing I remember was being propped up in a corner of the café in the visitor centre and Suzanne asking if I wanted a cup of weak tea. I was confused and kept reliving the moment on the hill when Jim and the woman started fighting. I berated myself for not having taken a photo at that point and marvelled at my own inertia. I told Suzanne about the scene I'd witnessed, how Jim had been murdered by the golden woman, but Suzanne replied that it was the golden woman who had run down and raised the alarm about Jim. Her name was Ann Peachell and her dog was called Mollie. Ann had reported that she'd been confronted by a man who asked her if she was an angel and, when she said no, launched into a tirade, accusing her of devilry and witchcraft and of being the seed of Satan. He had then collapsed and Ann managed to break his fall before running for help.

The rescue team said I had broken my ankle and found me a wheelchair. I sat in the car park with Nick, who was very agitated. I told him Jim had gone for a nice ride in a helicopter but Suzanne snapped, "He's not a simpleton. Jim's been taken ill and he's gone to hospital." This calmed Nick down immediately. Suzanne discovered how to release the articulated rails in the taxi, wheeled Nick and me up, secured our chairs, and drove slowly out of the car park.

"Jim's going to be alright," Nick said, beaming. Looking back now I identify that moment as the beginning of a new chapter for Suzanne and me. The exuberance of the boy's smile gave me the sense that Nick was caring for us just as much as we were for him. In time, Jim *did* recover and the company the four of us founded has since given respite care to hundreds of people with muscular dystrophy and other degenerative conditions. I sometimes think about how much our lives have changed for the better simply because I happened to take a taxi one April evening.

As Suzanne negotiated the narrow lane out of Fewby in Jim's bulky taxi, we saw Ann Peachell walking along the pavement. Instinctively, I pulled the camera out of my pocket and turned it on. Ann saw us, picked up her dog and waved. Suzanne wound down the window and shouted goodbye. I smiled and nodded, turned off the camera and put it back in its bag.

FIRST BELL

PATRICK LACEY

NOBODY NEEDS TO ASK Eddie O'Hara why he gets up early each morning and heads to school one hour before homeroom. Not his parents or his friends and certainly not Dr Schmidt, who thinks he's improved leaps and bounds compared to where he was this time last year. *Everyone has different coping mechanisms,* she's told him time and time again during their visits.

Eddie opens his eyes. The sun is far in the distance, making things seem pink and dreamlike. Part of him wants the world to be like this all the time. He wishes he could live the rest of his life in this pre-dawn twilight.

He gets up and steps into the bathroom. After his morning piss and shower, he brushes his teeth and heads downstairs to eat peanut butter on dry toast. It's the five-grain kind his mother always buys. He keeps reminding her how much he hates the stuff but it always makes its way into the cupboard.

First Bell

His father sits at the kitchen table drinking black coffee and reading the newspaper. Eddie doesn't think his dad owns more than two suits and if he does, they're all the same charcoal shade of black. Even the ties all seem the same, so much so that for a moment he's back in his junior year and his father's heading to a normal day of work and Eddie's heading to a normal day of school and nothing has changed yet.

But the moment passes and he's back in the present, crunching the sandpaper toast and watching the pink skyline turn orange through the kitchen window.

"Morning," his father says.

"Morning," Eddie answers through a dry mouth. He grabs the orange juice from the fridge and takes a sip straight from the carton.

He can feel his father roll his eyes but he won't say anything. In fact, he rarely gives Eddie shit for anything anymore. He thinks his son has been through too much, that not even a year has toughened him up to simple things like being reprimanded.

In truth, Eddie wishes his mother or father would yell at him or ground him or at least tell him to shut up once in a while, like they did before everything changed. It wouldn't help him heal but it would make him feel just an inch more human.

His mother walks into the kitchen, as if she can hear his thoughts, and asks if he's feeling well. She holds his head and tells him he feels warm. She wants him to stay home, though she won't come out and say it.

He wants to stay home too but everyone in this kitchen knows that's not going to happen because it's been exactly one year to the day. Chrissy is waiting for him now more than ever.

"I'm fine," he says.

"You don't look fine."

"Leave him alone," his father chimes in, crumpling the paper as he turns to the sports section. "He's fine."

"I just—" She trails off though Eddie knows the path her words would've taken.

He puts a hand on her shoulder, gently, and smiles. "I'm fine. Really."

Her eyes glisten over with tears, though none fall down her cheek like they did that day. It's not the look of absolute panic from 365 days earlier when she got the call. It's the look of a mother who sees her son in pain every moment of his life, a boy who chases at ghosts because he refuses to let go. It's all he has anymore and they both know it.

Eddie finishes the last bit of dry toast, tells his parents he'll be home around seven, after his shift at the market. They tell him to keep his head up.

His Ford Taurus putters to life but just barely. The engine lets out a wailing, crying sound and he thinks how apt that is.

He backs out of the driveway and heads toward school. This early he always has his pick of the lot, so he parks close to the entrance and nods to Stefan, the maintenance man. He speaks mostly Spanish but they've shared a few words, mostly weather and sports.

"Beautiful day," Stefan says.

"Certainly is." Eddie locks the car and heads toward the front of the school. Though he doesn't turn around, he knows Stefan's eyes aren't following him. He's only been working at the school since the fall. He knows about what happened on this day last year but he doesn't know the details. To him, Eddie is just another kid.

Eddie walks toward the tree, a great big oak, its branches reaching across the street like pointing fingers. It was his favorite tree—Chrissy's too—but now it seems lifeless, a necessary evil.

The sun peeks from behind the clouds, shines through the spaces between the leaves. He throws his sweatshirt onto the ground and sits on it, trying to avoid grass stains. Birds chirp in the distance and a breeze rolls through the grass.

He looks at his watch, counting down the seconds, readying himself, though it's become routine. The first few times were a shock, enough so that he'd questioned his sanity. Now it's just part of his reality.

Seven seconds by his count. He looks up. No movement.

His eyes go back to his watch. Three. Two. One. Lift off.

The ghosts appear.

It's as if an unseen switch flips to the on position. One moment there's nothing, then there are pale forms going about their daily business, walking around and talking amongst each other like it's any other day. Their skin has a faint blue tinge like the ocean reflecting moonlight. There are twenty of them, always twenty, never more or less. They are the unlucky folks, the group that was in the wrong classroom at the wrong time.

The crowd seems to part like the Red Sea, Billy Anderson and Melissa Norton and James Wesley and Amanda Parker moving to the left and right, until Chrissy is revealed.

She smiles at him and blows a kiss and he can almost imagine half her skull isn't shattered, that her brain isn't in a warm dripping pile on the floor somewhere. He can almost see past the exit wound and imagine she's whole again and not just a walking memory.

She sits down next to him, leaning her back against the tree and leaning her head onto his shoulder. A drop of ghost blood drips from her injury and plops onto his jeans. It leaves behind a stain only they can see. His clothes are littered with them no matter how many times his mother puts them through the wash.

A jeep blaring talk radio drives by, slowing as they make eye contact with Eddie. He doesn't recognize the driver but he sees a look of concern and then sadness. Nothing new there.

Chrissy opens up her dead mouth but no words come out, only silence, like a film on mute. He's forced to remember their last conversation, to remind himself that they were going to the movies that night, going to see a slasher film. She always screamed just before the scary parts.

He smiles, telling her how much fun it's going to be. He can't wait. It's Friday. The whole weekend is ahead of them, filled with opportunity. She winks at him and nibbles her pale blue lip, their little code for getting laid, which they both planned on later that day one year ago. He winks back at her and she releases that lovely giggle, the one he'd give anything in the world to hear again. It comes out silent, unheard.

The rest of the unlucky busy themselves with muted conversation, though a few were outcasts who didn't have many friends. Manny Hernandez, for example, had just transferred in January. He was a loner but he seemed nice enough to Eddie. Manny leans against the railing, headphones on. He bobs his head and Eddie wonders what he's listening to, if it's the same song that was playing before the first bell—the *last* first bell—or if it's some ghostly music his own ears can't process.

Eddie's eyelids triple their weight, threatening to close. It would feel so good to just give in, to just sink back into blackness with Chrissy's head next to his. He shuts his eyes for a while. It could be seconds but something tells him it's longer.

Eventually, he opens them and his breath catches in his throat.

Eddie looks at his watch. It's almost ten past. He blinks and sees distinct figures bursting through the unlucky, real students on their way to class. None of the living notice the pale, slightly opaque forms as they pass through the ghostly bodies. The unlucky momentarily separate like clouds but they reform until each ghost is complete again. Complete but not whole. A few are missing ears. One or two have stubs and stumps in place of limbs. Duane Archer simply has a small hole in the middle of his forehead. Eddie can see clear through it.

Chrissy says she needs to get going. She has a math test and she needs to do some last-minute studying. She doesn't say it out loud of course but the words are burned into the inside of Eddie's skull.

He kisses her bloody mouth and he swears he feels skin instead of fog.

She walks away. Her jeans are skintight. He remembers admiring her curves as she walked away that day, toward homeroom. He wanted to follow her, to cop a feel and grab just another peck before the day started. He wanted to tell her not to worry about the math test. She would do just fine without her note cards. She was naturally smart. He wanted her all to himself no matter how selfish it seemed.

But his thoughts were cut off a few minutes later when he heard the loud bang. At first he thought it was a car crash but traffic was too congested, the latecomers trying to pull into the lot and get to class before the bell.

The second bang made him jump up from his spot by the tree and he knew then that it wasn't an accident or a muffler backfiring.

The third bang brought with it screaming, not like the slasher movie they'd planned on seeing that night. Real screams weren't like that. They were much more high-pitched and you could tell there was real pain behind them.

He ran toward the doors then but a sea of students and faculty came pouring out. From behind them came more bangs and more screams, until it was like a sickening symphony, the pleading and the crying making a distorted harmony.

There were bloody footprints, he noticed, stretching from the steps and onto the grass.

Eddie screamed her name but there was no answer, not over the chaos. His voice was lost in the panic and the shots, some louder than others, echoing through the halls and spilling outside into the warm spring day.

He mouths the words now, though this time last year he'd been sobbing them. *Chrissy. Chrissy, I love you.*

He'd said it before but he didn't know until that moment, 365 days ago to the minute, what exactly it meant.

First Bell

One last bang sounded before the police sirens wailed to life, before the two cop cars flew along the sidewalk. The men threw open their doors, guns raised, telling everyone to get down and remain calm.

A year later, Eddie wipes away a lone tear. The moisture tickles his cheek just like Chrissy used to tickle his stomach when he snuck into her house and into her bed, and then the first bell rings.

The unlucky look toward him, nod in their secret agreement, and dissipate. One moment they're ten feet away, ghostly images of another time, the next, they break apart like steam from a raging kettle just removed from the burner and they float into the sky toward some place he can't see from his spot against the tree.

They're gone until Monday morning, when Eddie wakes up an hour too early. Until he opens his eyes to the pink promise of sunlight in the distance, the moment he wishes he could grasp onto almost as much as watching Chrissy walk up the steps for the last time.

The bell seems eternal, a record skipping against an aging needle, and when Eddie shakes his head and comes to, students rush the doors like it's just another day. In the afternoon, at the end of the pep rally, there will be a moment of silence in remembrance. A few pricks in the back of the bleachers will whisper and snort with laughter, ruining the gesture, but most will bow their heads and close their eyes. And then the last bell will ring and school will be over for the week and most of them will forget for another year, and that's if they even have another service this time next June.

His knees are stiff from sitting Indian style. He stands slowly and waits for the pins and needles to wear off. He picks up his sweatshirt and drapes it over his shoulder. He heads toward homeroom, taking his time, not quite caring if he's a few minutes late. Mrs Anderson won't mark him tardy. Not today.

Halfway up the front steps, he freezes, convinced he heard something, a voice. But it can't be because they've already gone for the day. Rushing students go around him, the last of the stragglers. A few bump his shoulders and elbows.

What time are you going to pick me up?

He turns around. There is nothing, just the tree and the grass and the courtyard where there was once blood, though it's long since dried.

He turns back around and heads up the steps toward homeroom.

GHOST ESTATE, PHASE II

TRACY FAHEY

A FTER WHAT HAS happened, you don't cope too well. Things are ugly and strange. You live in a house full of loud voices and hot anger. Then a door slams. Silence. Nothing. The familiar things about you turn hard and hostile. Your head hurts. You forget things. You drift in an unhappy dream of wakefulness and weeping.

The only thing that makes sense is to leave. So you do. It's hard to remember *how*. There is a dim sense-memory somewhere of driving through the night, of seeing and not-seeing all at once, plastic bags jutting against your headrest, startled cars repeatedly flashing at you to dim your headlamps.

Your friend living in London offers you her house in the West of Ireland. "Don't expect anything," she warns. "It'll be awful. It's in the middle of nowhere. There's no one living there." The house is uninhabited. It is not-there. That is enough.

It's a ghost estate. An unfinished estate. The idea soothes you. It's nowhere. It runs on nevertime. It's like a strange forest, the streets all named for trees. You live at Number 5 Willow Drive. Behind you is Birch Road. To the left is Oaktree Gardens. And so on. You feel free to wander around it, filled with a horrible thistledown freedom to float away, unnoticed, unmissed.

You're free.

You're free to cry, free to eat cold toast, free to make and forget cups of tea, free to spend hours obsessively cleaning out cupboards or staring out the window. Free to wear the same dreadful house-uniform, day after leaden day, black pyjama bottoms with worn knees, bed-socks and a thin grey sweatshirt, bobbled and soft with age.

The nights are bad. Dry-eyed, mannequin-stiff, you lie in bed, brain crawling relentlessly over old conversations, decoding the nuances of voice and speech, searching for retrospective clues. Sometimes you close your eyes for long enough for patterns to form and dance in the blackness. It is as close as you come to dreams. Lying there you intone a mantra—*Soon it will be morning. Soon it will be morning. Soon it will be morning.* Eventually, the blind turns a paler grey, then streaks with orange, signalling the end of another night, the beginning of another day.

The days are better. Marginally. Sometimes they drag endlessly, seconds crawling, the hands of the kitchen clock stuck rigid, unmoving. Other days just slip by, morning into night, shockingly unmemorable. Sometimes you wonder—*Did I go into work?* You have a blurred memory of getting into the car, freeze-frame shots of yourself nodding hello at the receptionist, a drift of paper on a desk, a circle of blank faces around you at meetings. But *actual* memories, of feelings, thoughts, conversations? None.

There are the drives too, that eat up those lumpen hours between work and bed, long, aimless, crawling drives down grass-tufted country lanes, following the brown heritage signs to castles, old churches, ogham stones, sites of ancient battles. Arriving at your destination brings no sense of relief. You just sit in the car, unmoving. Sometimes you cry.

You like to walk around the estate. It requires no thinking. It's easier than work and somehow less depressing than the drives.

You live in Phase I, the first phase of the estate, the finished part. There are a few occupied houses. There's an old couple a few doors down, him quiet, white-haired, defeated, her pinch-faced, mouth twisted in a sneer of permanent disappointment at her neighbourhood. There's a small family in Birch Road, two children, one silent boy, one muted and strangely forlorn girl, cycling around on their tiny coloured bicycles, their wheels leaving a trail of echoes in their wake. No one ever talks to you, waves at you, acknowledges you. Everyone is trapped inside their private house of misery. Oh, and there's also a woman you see, in a red jumper. You don't know where she lives, but you see her, from time to time, wandering up and down the paths. She is the only other person who ever goes into Phase II of the estate.

Tracy Fahey

Phase II of the estate is very different. You like that part best. It is surrounded by a barricade. Leaning metal chicken-wire frames tilt against each other, balanced on half-built breeze-block walls. There are dusty security signs up—'24 HOUR SECURITY' they spell out, 'THIS AREA IS MONITORED NIGHT AND DAY'—and dirty white CCTV cameras, peeling with rusty scabs. You ignore all of them. There is a gap between the red-brown chicken-wire frames to slide through. Inside Phase II, the houses form a strange mirror image of your own street. The houses look normal at first, but the gardens are overgrown, nested with great drifts of purple weeds. There is the intense hum of bees, the dry ticking of insects, and the faraway dimmed buzz of a car winding a slow path down the main road. You walk down the grey, pitted walkway. Flowers crawl around your feet.

Phase II is ripe with strangeness. It is an uncanny mirror of your twinned Phase I. There is even a doppelganger of your own house. Number 5 Evergreen Drive. When you press your face close to the dirty window your shadow reveals a dark scar of a fireplace, a bare concrete floor, a broken plastic chair in the corner. In the tangled garden of Number 5, someone has dragged weather-pale planks on top of two large paint buckets to form a rough bench.

You like to sit there, the warm August sunshine gilding the hairs on your bare arms, the scent of wildflowers heavy in the thick air. Sometimes butterflies unfurl from the weeds, paper-white, fragile powder-blue or colourful explosions of yellow-orange-red-black. Once you saw a dragonfly, hovering, its long body a flash of peacock blue, hanging still and somehow sinister in the air. Sometimes you dream you live on Evergreen Drive, like Sleeping Beauty, roses growing over you, over your house, over the paths. Behind you, the completed houses of Phase I mirror their uncanny doubles. *Here*, you think, *here the outside matches my inside.* It is your place.

A few streets in, and the estate grows more feral, darker, more dangerous. Half-built house-skeletons press against the sky, some windows nailed up with faded boards, others open, black, blank. The only person you've ever seen here is the woman in the red jumper. She's always in the distance, drifting along in a zig-zag walk. Once your foot kicked a stone and you saw her start and disappear into the head-height weeds of an abandoned plot. She hides. Her erratic walk carries an undeniable whiff of madness. You like her, obscurely. You admire the persistence of her wardrobe. Her red jumper is the bright double of your own permanent home-uniform.

Some days you're convinced that there's another version of yourself, a better version, still living in your old life, still smiling, talking, walking, and enjoying life outside this bubble.

Some days you're almost happy.

Some days you think you'll never be happy again.

August drifts into September. The days compress, the nights swell into long, unbearable stretches of time. You buy books and fill the empty darkness with lamplight and stories, the more improbable the better.

Tracy Fahey

IT IS A HOT, MUGGY September night. Even if you could, it's too hot to sleep. You lie in bed, reading, your body prickling with perspiration, moving restlessly. Your knees slide against each other, damp with heat. You are queerly restless. Options flit through your mind—a cup of tea, a shower, some TV. No choices appeal. Abruptly, you stop reading, feeling feverish, querulous. You get up and look out the window. There is a full moon, almost hidden behind black trailing clouds. You stare at your reflection in the dark glass. You see your eyes, dark-ringed and weary, the slick of sweat on your collarbones. Portishead play softly on your stereo, a muffled sequence of dreamy, thrumming sonar notes sounding from some lost ghost ship. There is a flicker of movement at the corner of your eye, a flash of colour. *Red?* A red jumper? Is she outside, walking?

Suddenly, you know exactly what you want to do. You are filled with a strong desire to stand on dew-damp grass and to rotate slowly till you catch a faint after-breath of breeze. You don't even stop to think. Outside, there is almost perfect silence, broken only by the dim low throb of Portishead drifting from your window. You walk through the estate, in the darkness. There are streetlights dotted around the estate, puddling orange light on the footpaths. Other streetlights loom dark overhead, broken and not replaced. Silently, your bare feet tread cat-light on the cool concrete paths. As you walk silent and sure, down Birch Road, you see curtains move against a lighted window. For a few seconds you and the silent little boy look at each other, then with a twitch, the curtain falls.

You keep walking. At the fence to Phase II, you pause. Beyond the wire fence darkness lies like a blanket, only the

190

faintest shiver of moonlight glinting through the overcast sky. You stand, undecided. Then a cool breeze blows from the long grasses, as cold as if a fridge door had opened. *I know my way blindfolded*, you think, confident, as you slide between the barriers.

It is cooler in these dark not-streets. Damp air ruffles your hair and blows a chill little breath up your pyjama legs. You drift on, airy in darkness, like a dandelion clock. Abruptly, moonlight slants through an opening in the clouds. The light gleams palely on the windows of the houses. You see you are standing on Evergreen Drive. You thread your way through the weeds towards the bench in the garden of Number 5, then stop. It's not there! You turn around, bewildered. The bench has gone! And—even stranger—it looks like someone has cut the grass in the garden, inexpertly, unevenly. Is it the wrong street? The wrong house? But no, the moonlight softly illuminates the street sign, the house door. *The door!* The faded door you are used to seeing is open. It yawns ajar, dark, cool. You stand outside for a moment. The clouds peel off the moon. Suddenly it is bright as day. You feel exposed. The door stands open, inviting. The oddest thought springs up in your head. *If I could lie down in here*, you think, insistently, *I could sleep. I could sleep in this cool, silent house.*

And you step inside. The hallway is perfectly dark, but the door opening off it to the sitting room is outlined in light. You are finally inside the window. You look through it, the glass no longer dirty, the garden no longer unkempt. You feel a quick surge of vertigo—*which Number 5 am I in?*—then are reassured by the familiar broken plastic chair in the corner, the empty hole for the fireplace. The moonlight pours in, a limpid pool of pearly light. You tilt your face towards it, eyes closed.

There is a noise. Your eyes pop open. There it is again, a faraway sound. Something dropping? Then you hear it. A familiar pattern, repeated, the patter of footsteps. With a hiss, you draw in your breath. Clouds pull the moon back into shadow. You feel yourself wake completely, like a dazed sleepwalker. The shame of trespassing jolts through you. You slip out into the hall again, hand on the door. The footsteps are louder now, more insistent. You hear the unmistakable sound of bare feet slapping on concrete. And now, too, horribly, you hear the sound of ragged breathing. The footsteps are growing closer. You act entirely on instinct and pull the door closed, hands finding the bolt and sliding it to. You run into the living room, and stand flat against the wall, heart beating thick and fast in your throat.

The footsteps slap-crack up the path, louder, louder. There is a sound of a body falling against the door, hands scrabbling for the handles.

"Let me in! Oh please, let me in!" Then terrible, tearing sobs.

The hands clatter over the wooden door. There is a thud as they hit the wall, then the sharp scrabble of fingernails on glass as they find the window.

"Let me in! Oh please, let me in!" Fists beat against the glass.

Your heart is hammering in your throat. Your body feels dream-heavy, unable to run. Unbidden, the night-mantra words come back to you. *Soon it will be morning.* The wracking sobs grow louder. *Soon it will be morning.* You wrap your arms around yourself, cold hands clutching your elbows, feeling their points jut, impossibly real, into your palms.

The screams and thumps abruptly stop. You move slowly, cautiously towards the dark window. Outside all is black and still. Nothing. You place your hands lightly on the windowpane. Then it's bright. The sharp white of the moonlight pours in. In a moment of clear horror, you see her, the woman in the red jumper.

There was a time, as a child, when you insisted on sleeping with the curtains drawn tightly. You cried if the tiniest chink was left open. It was just a dream, your parents told you, over and over, softly, then crossly. You were too young to tell the difference. All you knew was that you were in bed and someone was outside your window, trying to get in. You heard the crunch of gravel under their feet, their hands beating the glass. Night after night this dream would come. You were too afraid to shout for help. All you could do was pull the blankets and pillows over your head, to muffle the sound, to hide. You hid, and shivered over all the different things that might be outside—giants, witches, monsters.

Now you stand, flooded with terror pure and stark as ice. You're falling, sinking, everything inside you drops vertiginously in a swoon of fear. Yet still you stand, hands splayed to the glass, feeling the vibrations of the pounding. In a dreamy, half-frozen sickness you watch the fists bang again and again against the windowpane.

"Let me in! Oh please, let me in!"

When you were a child you were always afraid to go to the window. That was wise. All of the imaginary intruders you dreamed of drop away.

What stands outside, face stretched and distorted in terror is worse than any imagining.

What stands outside is you.

A PLACE FOR EVERYONE

RUE KARNEY

D R SIMONE SONGER WAS a practical woman, so when the Beech Park Hospital for the Criminally Insane closed its doors as a consequence of the Liberation of Persons with Atypical Neural Wiring Act, she'd been first in line with her cheque book.

She was a strong advocate of the somewhat controversial act. Indeed, she'd composed a twenty-page submission to the Royal Commission into Atypical Neural Wiring, which had been widely quoted in the press, many of whom had described her as an enlightened and compassionate champion of the neurally misunderstood. (What the rabid pack of gutter press barbarians had called her does not bear repeating.)

'A place for everyone' was her personal motto. As she'd written in her submission: 'The victims of atypical neural wiring have their strengths and talents just like the rest of the population.' Many of these former 'patients', it had now been proven, were no more insane than nineteenth-century middle class women were hysterical. It was all about finding the right fit for their particular talents and urges. Dr Songer was determined to prove that, given the right surroundings and support, even the formerly criminally insane could make a positive contribution to society.

Dr Songer's inspection of the Beech Park Hospital grounds confirmed her conviction that it was perfect for her entrepreneurial aspirations. The hospital, set on two hectares of lush tropical gardens in Queensland's idyllic far north, had a practical concrete block building suitable for staff accommodation. A charming art deco inspired villa, with a spacious wood panelled office, original tiled bathroom and parquetry floored living area, was perfect for her private accommodation, and perhaps a few select guests interested in a more immersive tourist experience. The historic buildings of creaking tin and timber with wide wrap-around verandas and fourteen-foot-high plaster ceilings that dominated the front of the property were a heritage tourist's delight. The amusing collection of historic psychiatric paraphernalia—trolley beds framed with white metal cages; a large metal electroconvulsive therapy machine with oversized black headphones encasing electrodes; and several green armchairs with charming vintage leather restraints—was a bonus. The buildings would provide the perfect setting for tours, which she planned to offer day and night. The night tours, of course, would offer that something extra special.

A Place for Everyone

At the time of the hospital's closure there had been twenty remaining inmates: the usual collection of parent killers, flesh mutilators, animal dissectors and fire aficionados who made up the majority of such establishments. Of those twenty, four returned to live with family, two were quickly absorbed into the mainstream criminal justice system and one absconded into the rainforest where he remained at large. Dr Songer immediately offered the remaining thirteen—ten men and three women— jobs in her new establishment. With the help of a government subsidised societal reintegration scheme, she planned to retrain the former inmates in all aspects of hospitality to ensure future guests visiting Beech Park would enjoy the comfort of a unique five star tourist experience.

The local mayor was thrilled by Dr Songer's venture. The town had suffered a blow by missing out on one of the all-important exits in the Townsville to Cairns tunnel, and the upcoming tourist season for the township was looking dismal. No one was going to bother to take the thirty minute detour from the nearest tunnel exit to visit the Big Shell, which was less shell than ceramic encrusted concrete blob. It was old, tired and, compared to the high rises that lurched across the beachfront like broken teeth, not even remotely 'big'. For Mayor Graham Grimaldi, Dr Songer's personally guided tours of the Beech Park Hospital for the Criminally Insane were just the ticket. He intended to offer her all the support she required.

There were some who questioned his enthusiasm—several of his constituents had pointed out that Beech Park's rumoured head of housekeeping had burnt down the council's own Arts Hall—but Mayor Grimaldi stood his ground.

"After all," he said to a grumbling pensioner at the Saturday morning flea markets, "Dr Songer's a neuroscientist with more letters after her name than the Cyrillic alphabet."

"Letters don't put out fires," the pensioner retorted. He stalked off to sort through the bric-a-brac stall for a second-hand fire extinguisher, unaware that the multi-lettered doctor was herself browsing through the preloved wares.

Dr Songer was looking for shabby-chic cup and saucer sets to serve the Devonshire teas, and for a man with a distinctive tattoo. As a young woman, she had travelled through Queensland's far north while taking a break between university degrees. She had considered herself more at home in a laboratory than on the open road but travel broadened her mind, and her morals.

After a six month affair with a young man who showed her both the meaning of lust and his peculiarly provocative consequences of accidental brain trauma, she'd returned to university with an insatiable appetite for sex, tattoos and neuroscience. At the markets her eyes darted furtively around the various stalls in the hope that the man with the distinctive tattoo—a black crow with a blood red hibiscus flower blooming from one eye—would perhaps still be around.

The pensioner's nimble fingers scooted across the bric-a-brac table like picnic ants. Dr Songer's plump pink fingers plodded and probed alongside. Her shadow darkened the corner of the pensioner's vision. He shrank away from her bulk as she reached across him and grabbed a crystal sugar bowl.

Tattooed on the inside of her left arm was a variation of the caduceus. Two red-bellied black snakes entwined around a skeleton with delicate grey wings sprouting from its spine. The pensioner's own knobbled spine rattled as he scuttled away to the safety of the fresh veg stand, where he bought five bulbs of garlic, just in case.

Dr Songer remained blissfully unaware of the pensioner's fear and confusion (somewhat ignorant of paranormal lore, he thought the garlic would protect him from the tattooed skeleton) and continued shopping. And though she kept her eyes keen, she didn't see the man she was-but-wasn't looking for.

Back then, in the early 80s, everyone had called him Crow. She assumed it was because of his tattoo but it was, of course, because he came from South Australia. The nickname came long before the tattoo.

She'd met him when she was working as a barmaid in a pub frequented by cane cutters and truckies. He'd had thick black curly hair, long black eyelashes, tanned skin and a deep scar running from his right temple, around the front of his ear and down along the inside of his neck to the top of his collarbone. The scar was thick and fleshy. It rose out to meet her with the sweetness of ripe rosebuds. On her second shift at the pub she gave him free beers all afternoon, just so he'd let her touch that scar. She wondered if it had faded now, shrivelled into a thin wispy line like an octogenarian's dick. His hair would probably be gone. Definitely his eight pack stomach. But the tattoo would still be there.

Dr Songer paid for the crystal sugar bowl and wandered the markets one last time. She scanned the necks and forearms of tall middle-aged men, and took care to smile and nod at the small group of grumbling pensioners glaring in her direction. Then she got into her dusty four-wheel-drive and headed for the inaugural Beech Park Tourist Experience staff meeting.

THE THIRTEEN STAFF members sat in bright orange institutional-style plastic chairs, which were arranged in a wide semicircle around the fake wood-grain plastic table. Dr Songer rested her wide buttocks on the table's edge. Piled high next to her were their Beech Park patient files. According to the privacy section of the Atypical Neural Wiring Act, the files had been destroyed. But Dr Songer, though a firm believer in rehabilitation, was an even firmer believer in 'know what you're working with'.

"Let me start by saying how privileged I feel to be working with such a wonderfully diverse and creative group of people." She stood and patted her hand on top of the pile, and beamed out at her audience. "So much talent as yet undiscovered, waiting to blossom."

Her audience sat, some catatonically still, some fidgeting, others twisting their eyes inwards in an attempt to maintain control over their tics, as she swept around their semicircle.

She stopped in front of a male with untidy eyebrows and a closely shaved head.

"Glen, I believe you're handy with a spade and trowel?"

Glen's lips skewed like twisted rubber bands.

A Place for Everyone

She placed her hand on his shoulder and squeezed. "You're my head gardener."

She moved along to a woman with spiky red hair and wide, pale grey eyes. "Theresa, you enjoy working with knives, I believe?"

Theresa grinned and the corner of her left eye twitched.

"You'll be running the kitchen."

Two seats up from Theresa, a tall thin bald man with caved cheekbones and a rollercoaster nose sat straight-backed. His half-closed eyes turned up in the corners as if smiling at a secret. His file was the thickest of them all. A veteran Beech Park Hospital patient of some twenty-five years, his case had made headlines when it was discovered his uncanny knack for creating lifelike human sculptures was not so uncanny after all.

The man didn't flinch when Dr Songer leaned in close, her breath scraping like metal against his eardrums.

"Mr Victor Victor, such an honour to finally meet you." She eased back and smiled into his eyes. "You, my dear sir, will be leading the night tours."

Victor Victor breathed out a small hot peppermint breath and closed his eyes in assent.

"Those who have not been assigned leadership roles today, do not despair." Dr Songer's voice modelled bright confidence. "Although you will start in assistant roles each and every one of you has a vital part to play in the success of our venture.

"As extra incentive to do well, I am giving each of you five hundred shares in Songer Enterprises. If Beech Park is a success, so, my dear friends, shall all of you be."

✦

DR SONGER'S EMPLOYEES took to their new jobs enthusiastically. Under her watchful guidance, and that of the three trusted therapists on her staff, the former inmates of Beech Park transformed the place that had once labelled them as unfit for society into a beacon of enlightened science-based compassion and tourism excellence. The day tours were full almost every day; the Beech Park high teas had become a 'must-do' on several noted gastronomy-travel websites. But the biggest hit was, of course, the night tour.

Victor Victor proved a genius in the creation of the tours. From his careful selection of hand-held torches carried by each tourist, to the meticulous planning of the tour sequence, to the allure the rich timbre of his voice added to his telling of the former asylum's legends and lore, the Beech Park Night Tours were a spectacular success. Travel and lifestyle shows from across the globe had pencilled in the night tours to feature in their upcoming seasons.

Of course, Victor Victor's most genius stroke had been one that not even the entrepreneurial Dr Songer herself had considered.

The absconded inmate, whom local police had lost interest in trying to find, had not absconded far. Barry Arnott (or Biscuits, as he was more commonly known) had built himself a tidy and quite weatherproof shelter inside a hollowed-out trunk of an ancient fig tree deep within the rainforest. He lived off the rainforest plants and animals—he was a dab hand at roasting wildlife—and was careful to stay away from the main hiking paths. The rainforest gave him everything he needed: food, shelter, water, birdsong and beauty. He knew he should be happy. All those years locked up in the asylum, all he had wanted was to be alone and free. But now that he had what he thought he wanted, he realised something was missing. A purpose. A goal. A reason to slit the throat of an inquisitive pademelon or possum each day.

Victor Victor and Biscuits had been the two longest-serving inmates at Beech Park, but they had never been friends. Biscuits was too uncultured for Victor's liking. Nevertheless, even Victor had admired the lost-boy innocence that Biscuits exuded from his fine pores. Victor knew that aura would work well in creating just the right tension that was required for the part of soulful ghost that was to make the night tour an outstanding success. So, on his day off, Victor packed a backpack with water, fruit, muesli bars, flares, GPS and a light hooded rainproof jacket and set out into the rainforest.

The rainforest was endless and Biscuits was one thin man hiding within it, but in his post-institutional malaise he had been creeping closer and closer to his former jail. Victor had barely made it past the obligatory National Park warning signs when he spotted Biscuits crouched behind a tree fern.

The two men looked at each other. Above them, birds trilled and squawked. Beneath their feet, leaves rustled. The damp rainforest floor had the comforting smell of rot. Biscuits breathed it in and straightened out his knees. He nodded at Victor.

"I sense," said Victor in his sombre voice, "that we are both in a position where our needs can be met by some mutually satisfying arrangement."

Biscuits scratched his neck at the itchy spot behind the fleshiest part of his scar.

"I can give you a job," said Victor. "I think you'll like it."

Biscuits looked up at the sky. He'd never had a real job, not since the accident. Even at the hospital he wasn't allowed to do anything besides fold clean sheets, and that had to be done with two supervisors looking on. A job would give him a purpose. He angled his head towards the east and dragged his lower lip up into the curve of a smile.

DR SONGER DIDN'T find out about the inclusion of a ghost on the night tour until the day after his first appearance, when the bookings phone rang off the hook and the website crashed from an overload of enquiries. As she attempted to manoeuvre her way through the administrative mess to get her website back online, Victor hovered outside her office.

"What is it, Victor?"

Victor sidled in. The sun slanting through the window made diamond patterns on his nose. He ran his pianist's fingers across his dull, mottled scalp. The corners of his eyes lifted as he lowered his lids in a play of submission.

"Spit it out."

"Ma'am, I think you will find that the flood of enquiries is due to the new feature added to last night's tour."

Dr Songer's eyes narrowed.

"The wraith, Dr Songer. Forgive my impertinence but I saw a niche to be filled and I found a body to fill it."

The doctor sat back in her chair. "Go on."

"I recently made contact with the former patient who had absconded into the rainforest. As his erstwhile roommate I was aware of his particular personal qualities that made him an eminently suitable ghost figure to add that extra touch of authenticity to the night tour. He was, as they say in the popular media, quite a hit."

"I see." Dr Songer steepled her fingers under her chin. The glossy ink of her latest tattoo shone brightly from the pale skin of her exposed forearm. "Bring him in this afternoon and have Valerie sort out his paperwork."

Victor looked down and studied the antique patterned rug on the floor. "Biscuits prefers not to be seen in public, Dr Songer. It might be best to keep him off the books until your solicitor looks into his current legal status."

"Biscuits?" Dr Songer slopped the name around the inside of her mouth. She pursed her lips and swallowed. "You're right, as always. You'll look after him in the meantime?"

"Of course, Doctor." Victor dropped his chin in a bow. He left to find Biscuits and give him the good news.

Rue Karney

MAYOR GRIMALDI'S eyeballs were aflower with bursting blood vessels. The Queens's Birthday weekend was a highlight of the tourist season and, riding on the phenomenal success of Dr Songer's Beech Park Asylum Experience, the weekend promised to break all former tourism records. But instead of sipping champagne and updating his online profile to account for his latest achievements he was behind closed doors with Dr Songer, her solicitor Lyle Vo and Detective Morton Breece, the highest ranking police officer in the district.

"You understand how this looks, Dr Songer." Detective Breece's belly oozed over his belt like overheated yeast.

"No, I don't." Dr Songer sat straight-backed in her chair. The shifting patterns of her tattooed forearms rolled under the light of her authentic art deco period lamp.

"A woman is missing after taking your night tour," said Breece.

"Exactly," said Vo. "A missing woman who probably ran off into the rainforest to make a bit of whoopee with a good-looking Swedish backpacker."

"All the other tour guests are accounted for," snapped Breece. "And the woman was last seen on the night tour."

"I'm sure this is just a misunderstanding, Detective." Grimaldi clenched his teeth. "We don't want to frighten people off with rumours before our biggest weekend."

"On the contrary," said Dr Songer. "Rumour has already spread and our bookings for the night tour have filled up until the end of the year."

"You can't run the tours while there's a missing person investigation going on," said Breece.

"Don't be ridiculous." Dr Songer, Mayor Grimaldi and Lyle Vo spoke as one.

"We cannot be held responsible if a guest wanders off after the tour has finished," said Dr Songer. "The woman signed the guest book at the tour's close. What she did after that is not our responsibility."

"If anything, you should be reopening your investigation into the former patient who disappeared into the rainforest and was never seen again." Grimaldi pushed out his chest and his chin.

Dr Songer's lips tightened a millimetre. "Yes." She gave a clipped nod. "Mayor Grimaldi is correct. If your police do their job correctly and find the absconded individual you may well find the missing woman."

Detective Breece pushed himself up out of the orange plastic chair and balanced on his too small feet. He glared at the solicitor, the mayor and the doctor in turn as he ran his fingers through the tufts of ginger hair on his head. He emitted a low grunt then slouched out of the office.

Mayor Grimaldi soaked up the sweat of his brow with the thick hairs of his forearm. "Bloody hell, Simone, I—"

"Don't worry about a thing, Graham." Dr Songer pressed her lips into a thin smile. "Everything is under control."

BISCUITS WAS NERVOUS. He loved his job too much to lose it. For the first time in his forty-eight years he was finally living the dream, as his old surfing mates used to say. At first he hadn't fully grasped what Victor Victor expected from him but his boss had been patient, encouraging Biscuits, performance after performance, to greater heights of artistic integrity and truthfulness. It had even been Victor's idea to follow the woman after the end of the tour, give her a bit of extra attention so she'd spread the word to her friends about what a thrillingly terrifying and authentic experience she'd had with the ghost of Beech Park.

Biscuits had tackled his extended assignment with enthusiasm. He'd tracked the woman quietly, so she was unaware of his presence until his breath was almost on her neck. She'd turned, stared, screamed. He'd reached for her, his eyes wide, mouth slack and nostrils flared.

And, in that moment, he understood what it meant to become truly lost in what Victor called 'the creative flow'.

There was the woman, frozen in terror and fascination, the thick shadows of the rainforest, the yellowish glow of the half moon and the sultry scent of mud, rotting leaves and jasmine swirling through his head. She swooned before his spectral terror.

Next thing he knew, she was lying at his feet with an extra smile, located a few inches below her mouth, grinning up at him.

Biscuits hadn't meant to slit her throat. He wasn't even sure how the razor sharp, ten inch blade knife had slipped from his hands to the soft underside of her chin. But what was done was done. And now he had to face the big boss, Dr Songer, and explain himself.

A Place for Everyone

DR SONGER PRIDED herself on her ability to keep emotions in check. So when Victor Victor walked in with the man he called Biscuits, she gripped clawed hands into the edges of her silky oak desk to steady herself. The tall, thin man with dark curly hair who followed Victor into the room stood with his head drooped and his arms hanging loose by his sides. And there it was. The tattoo she'd been looking for.

It had faded. The crow was now more sailor-tattoo blue than black and the hibiscus had faded to a pale imitation of blood red. But the scar on his neck, although brown rather than fleshy pink, was as thick and luscious as ever.

"Sit down." Dr Songer kept her words clipped and tone curt while her heart raged against her ribs. She remained standing, not trusting her body's ability to move with authority.

In the corner of the room, hidden by shadows, Lyle Vo sat discreetly in his off-the-record presence. He noted the peculiar inward curl of Dr Songer's toes as she stood behind her desk, but, as usual, kept his counsel.

Victor Victor sat on the edge of his hard plastic seat. Beside him, Biscuits rubbed at the itchy part of his scar while his eyes darted around the room.

Dr Songer's intestines twisted. *He doesn't recognise me,* she thought. She fell into her sea green leather chair as her knees gave way.

But then the man called Biscuits looked into her eyes and down at her chest.

"Bloody hell," he said. "I remember those tits."

Dr Songer smiled as her own personal hibiscus unfurled into a magnificent bloom.

"Hello Crow," she said.

After the initial disconcertion caused by Biscuits' opening statement, the decision-makers in the room quickly organised a list of what needed to be done. Dr Songer had at her disposal some human remains that would suffice as those of absconded former patient Barry Arnott and could be placed in an area even Detective Breece couldn't miss. She was saddened to order the alteration of Biscuits' distinctive tattoo and correction of his neck scar by a discreet colleague who specialised in plastic surgery. But as always her emotions were overridden by practical necessities. No visible trace of Barry Arnott could remain.

Biscuits, too, was a little sorry to lose those parts of him that had seen him reunited with the lost love of his life but considered himself more than compensated by his new employment arrangements. Not only was his role as night tour ghost to continue, he was allocated extra-special duties in deference to his particular talents.

Mayor Grimaldi, as the ever-vigilant Lyle Vo had discovered, had some indiscretions of his own that he'd rather not let see the light of day. It didn't take long for Vo to convince Grimaldi that a side line in contract killing would benefit them all. The only thing Grimaldi had to do was alert a few people in circles outside the law that unwanted persons could be discreetly disposed of for a reasonable fee; he could leave the rest to the team at Beech Park.

The rainforest is a big place. A body, once lost in the forest's depths, is almost impossible to find, particularly if the disposal has been meticulously planned.

DR SONGER GAZED through the casement window. With the thin body of her lover curled by her side, she knew she should be a satisfied woman. She ran her plump fingers along Crow's ribcage, counting his bones one by one, and considered how her life had changed since she'd made Beech Park her own.

Business was booming. Occasional mysterious disappearances from the Beech Park tours served only to enhance the venture's reputation. She'd had to hire two more staff (both former patients of Tasmanian institutions) just to deal with administration. The exclusive immersive experience, now handled by the extraordinarily talented Theresa, was booked out two years in advance. Victor Victor had continued to shine and was a surprise recipient of the local council's recent Citizenship (Services to the Community) Award. Everyone was doing well.

And yet.

Dr Simone Songer was a practical woman. She knew it was not good people management to allow the atypically neurally wired to become bored. They needed goals, challenges to stretch their special strengths and talents.

She slipped off the bed and padded on plump feet to the corner of the room where Detective Breece lay prone in the green antique hospital chair. The vintage leather restraints drawn tight across his paunch gave him, she thought, an almost authoritative demeanour, despite the rabbit fear that lit his eyes.

She brushed her fingers across the gaffer tape that sealed his lips.

"Tomorrow," she whispered in his ear. "Tomorrow, I promise, we'll find a place for you."

UNDER HIS WING, POOR THING

KERIS MCDONALD

T HE YEAR I TURNED TEN my mother had to go into hospital and I was sent to live with my Gran and Granda in their end-terrace house at the top of the Whitley Bank road for, I was told, "just a few weeks love, until your Mam's better." The year I turned ten I lived in the room under the North Wind. The year I turned ten I saw something no ten-year-old should.

This was in the days before Social Services were expected to come into every home at the drop of a hat: the days of chopper bikes and space-hoppers and flares, of horrible long haircuts on impossibly skinny boys and interminable industrial strikes—and provided you weren't actually caught begging on the street it wasn't likely that anyone in authority would take much notice of what went on in your family. Although my mother was driven away in an ambulance leaving the three of us—I was the eldest and the only girl—without an adult at home, it would have caused the most terrible shame in the neighbourhood for us to be taken into care; a real offence against the family dignity that would have been. So Auntie Cath, Mam's younger sister, accepted responsibility for Robbie my littlest brother: she said he was small enough to share a bedroom with her own Keith, and she supposed she could manage with two little lads in the house though there wasn't room for more. Andrew, who was about seven at the time, stayed with his best mate Tim who lived over the road. And I went to Gran and Granda's, which wasn't even in Leeds but in one of the outlying towns up in the Pennine hills. I don't suppose anyone in authority, except maybe our school, was even told about the splintering of our family. It was only supposed to be for a few weeks anyway, and that mostly over the Easter break.

Granda picked me up from the local station, where the stationmaster'd had a good shout at me because I'd managed to get my ticket (a floppy grey rag from too much handling on the journey) stuck in the exit turnstile.

"Now then," said Granda, dropping his tab-end on the floor and rubbing his tobacco-stained fingers down his coat. He was a little bloke, not that much taller than me, though he'd been in the navy when younger and had the blurred tattoos to prove it. We walked up Whitley Bank with him carrying my suitcase and me hauling the big carton of soap powder he'd bought on the way. The soap smell oozed out onto my hands and the rough cardboard etched lines into my fingers. We didn't talk much at all while we walked.

Under His Wing, Poor Thing

I'd met both him and Gran before of course, on trips with Mam, but I knew she didn't get on with them and I had no particular fondness for them for various reasons, some of which seem trivial and cruel now. We used to sit in a row on the end of Gran's bed, watching the distant TV in the far corner, wishing we could turn up the volume or change the channel, writhing in agonies of boredom such as only children can feel. My legs would twitch and tic with inaction. We never went upstairs, though we were sometimes shooed out in fine weather to wander around on the fields. I know that those visits almost always used to end up with Mam and Gran yelling at each other, and the three of us kids would go out round the side of the house and sit on the coal bunker until our mother came out and thrust our coats at us as a sign we were leaving.

Whitley Bank was right at the edge of town and was the steepest street I'd ever seen in my short life. For decades whenever I heard the phrase 'it's the start of a slippery slope', I used to picture Whitley Bank, its square stone sets shiny in the rain. I never saw it tarmacked in my time, though I suppose nowadays it must be and probably it's a popular route out up onto the moors. In those days lorries would come over the top of the hills and make their way down the street with a great squealing of brakes, and men would toil up on foot with their dogs to go rabbiting, but there wasn't much other passing traffic. Granda's house was right at the very top of the row; higher up was only the winding road and the rough verges, neglected fields punctuated by the odd rusty shed, all the way up to where the moorland proper began. Behind their terrace the heath rose in a sheer cliff, so close to the buildings that the back rooms were all but underground. In front, over the road, the hill fell away nearly as steeply, so that you could stand in the gutter and see the whole town below you: rank upon rank of old terraces and the sprawl of the new council estates, the soot-blackened spires of churches and the grey slabs of the high-rises already defeatist in their modernity. The most impressive buildings were the enormous cloth mills—cotton mostly, I think; we were just on the edge of the wet West Pennines, any further east and you were into the rain-shadow of the hills and in wool country. With their angled roofs and clustered chimneys the mills were bigger than anything else in town, bigger than churches, bigger than God. The painted lettering of the factory names was still legible right across the town. But there was never any smoke from those chimneys, nor any lights behind the blackened windows now.

Our door was green, and as Granda pushed it open he yelled, "It's us. I've got her." He did it, I later realised, to allay any fears Gran might feel upon hearing us enter. It wasn't as if she could come trotting out and see who had walked into her home.

It was a tall narrow house, the rooms stacked up on each other, but Gran lived only on the ground floor. All the houses in the row were tall, three floors to the slate roof and an attic. Maybe they were quite posh dwellings once, not being what you'd describe as cramped workmen's cottages at all, but now they were all grimy and weather-blackened and the net curtains in the front room windows were sagging and yellow like they'd got the jaundice. Out of all in the row, ours was the most ill-kept; Gran couldn't really manage housework and Granda, though he'd been trained to tidiness by his stint in the navy, wouldn't stoop to what he called Women's Work, like washing the coal dust out of the curtains. We had open fires in all the rooms, though I rarely saw any burning except the one in Gran's room, which had been the parlour once upon a time. Of course, Granda's policy of laissez-faire extended to structural matters too, though I didn't find that out until later.

Gran was in her armchair by the fire, a big black cat curled in her lap. Two skinny grey kittens were playing on the candlewick bedspread behind her. She was actually capable of tottering through to the kitchen, with the aid of her two sticks and a bit of a hand up from her husband, but she didn't attempt the journey unless she could help it. Her entire world consisted of that front room, where she slept, or watched the TV that was never turned off until the test-pattern was transmitted, or read the Mills & Boon novels that Granda fetched her from the town library. The front room, plus the kitchen behind it and the toilet in the under-stairs cupboard. Being at the end of the terrace, the house could have had side windows easily enough to let more natural light in, but that had not entered the architect's head, and the electric lights were sparse and equipped only with 40 Watt bulbs, so the interior was in perpetual half-darkness.

"Ella!" she cried when she saw me, holding out her arms so that I had to embrace her and kiss the soft cheek that smelt of carbolic and cats. I was very careful not to lean against her legs, of course. From the waist up Gran looked normal, in a shapeless old-woman way, but her legs were swollen out of all proportion to the rest of her. I'm not sure what it was that was actually wrong: something related to her hips, I think. It's too late to check up on those details now. I used to sneak uncomfortable looks at those turgid legs, especially when I was younger, wondering how they could be attached to the rest of her. They were just about cylindrical and the feet beneath looked spherical in their slippers. She always wore stockings that wrinkled around her ankles and were far too dark a shade of bronze for her pallid English skin. "You're looking grand, lass."

"She's getting taller," Granda commented as he seated himself in the other armchair. "Come on over here onto my knee, Lilabet; let's have a look at you."

He was the only one who ever called me that. I was Liz to brothers and friends, Ella to Gran—and Mam when she was in a good mood—and even Lizard to the bullying lads at school, but Lilabet only to Granda. I didn't go over to him though; when I sat on his knee he used to put his hand up my skirt and I'd decided not to fall for that one again. It was the reason I'd packed only jeans, for my stay. I sat on the edge of the unmade bed instead, stroking the kittens and cooing at their cuteness.

"Blackie's latest litter," Gran said. "Probably her last, I'm thinking; she's getting on a bit now."

"Aren't we all?" said Granda, rolling a cigarette.

"Where's Nipper?" I asked, referring to Granda's little skewbald terrier with the unblinking stare and the hair-trigger temper.

He lit the roll-up from the fire. "Eh. Silly beggar went and got hisself stuck down a rat-hole. I couldn't dig him out, he were that deep."

Under His Wing, Poor Thing

I said nothing, though I saw Gran frowning. I'd always been nervous of Nipper, but I didn't want to imagine what sort of a fate getting wedged in a rat-hole might entail. A kitten pounced on my hand.

"Heard him howling for days."

"You daft sod," Gran said. "Fancy saying that in front of the child. What's wrong with you?"

Granda looked surprised.

"Why don't you go and get her a cuppa? You can do something useful, for a change."

I blinked as tiny needle-teeth explored the limits of what I would tolerate at my wrist. "I don't need a drink," I said. "I'm not thirsty."

"Well it's a ways to teatime. You sure you don't want something to put you on?"

"I had a drink on the train, Gran."

"Fair enough. But you can still put the pot on, our Granda." She called him that when I was around; his real name was Charlie, as hers was Edith. "I'm perishing for a brew. And you'd better take our lass's suitcase up to her room so she can get settled in."

Granda grunted in acquiescence and left me and Gran and the cats to our mysterious feminine business. Gran patted the arm of her chair until I came over and could look right into her grey face.

"You're going to be alright here, Ella, don't you fret. You're not worried about your mam, are you?"

I shook my head.

"She's going to be fine, you'll see. Right as rain again in a few weeks."

"I know," I said. She was never right as rain, not really, but we'd been through similar episodes before and at least I knew she would be back to normal eventually. I was trying to take it in my stride. It had been me who'd phoned Auntie Cath in the first place.

"She's a fighter, that lass; you'll see. Even as a child she were a fighter. Now you'll be a good girl for your Granda and me, won't you Ella?"

I nodded.

"Right. Now you're going to be sleeping up on the second floor. If you go and unpack now you'll be in time to help me get the tea ready."

I trailed up the stairs, in no hurry, fixing my bearings. There was brown lino underfoot and the balusters were painted white, but the thick gloss was chipped back to the wood like cavities in tooth enamel. On the back landing between the ground and the first floor was a door; edging it open revealed a cupboard filled with cardboard boxes, bottles of turps, tins of paint and a folded ladder. I couldn't imagine the last time anyone had tried their hand at decorating here. The first floor, like all the others, consisted of two rooms, one where my Granda slept—within earshot, but out of Gran's direct control—and the other his workshop. That room was full of incomprehensible junk: lathes and workbenches, boxes of tools and bolts and fixings, and the disembowelled carcasses of several machines including a television and a vacuum cleaner. Granda had worked on ships' engines long ago and in a printworks after being demobbed so he loved tinkering with machines, 'keeping his hand in' as he said. There were photos on the walls of men in naval uniform posing in bars and on decks, posters of gunships that looked like they'd been cut out of boys' magazines, and a model of an aircraft carrier constructed from balsawood. I got only the most cursory impression of this from my first glance around the door, filling in most of the details on subsequent visits. I quite liked the smell of oil and WD40 and Granda never minded me taking an interest in the workshop, though he did lock the top drawer that held his magazines.

The second between-floors landing hosted a cupboard-sized room with a bath though no sink or toilet. There was actually a window over the bath, my first glimpse out of the back of the house. A couple of feet beyond the glass was a wall of rock half-clothed in tussocky upland grass.

At last I reached my own floor, and that was where Granda caught up with me. "This is yours, Lilabet," he said, holding the door open for me. I looked into a room much bigger than any we had at home—certainly bigger than my bedroom, because being the lone girl I got the smallest and my brothers shared the largest—with a high ceiling and almost no furniture to fill it, only a Utility wardrobe and a bed with an iron frame. The floorboards were bare, though several rugs had been laid around the area of the bed. The window had a rather deep sill, good for sitting on, but no curtain except for a drape of nylon netting. One abandoned Elvis poster clung forlornly to the colourless walls.

"This used to be your mam's room," Granda told me. There were liver spots on his hands, I noticed.

"What's in there?" I asked, pointing at the door along the landing. It was imperative that I knew straight away, because if I didn't I would only lie awake at night wondering what was going to open the door and creep out. Already I'd realised how isolated I was going to be up here.

"Nothing." Obligingly, he led the way over and turned the key left in the lock. The room revealed, the one at the back of the house, was as large as mine but much darker, facing as it did onto the hillside and not helped at all by a morbid orange wallpaper. There was nothing in here at all, except a newspaper spilled across the floorboards.

"We don't use this room," Granda explained, pointing up at the ceiling. I saw that the plaster was sagging and discoloured, with great blooms of black and green mildew blossoming on the white field. The wallpaper was hanging off in swathes in that corner and the smell of wet bread was pungent. "Damp, you see. There's a leak in the roof and it rains in."

"Why don't you fix it?" I asked, confident in his ability to mend anything.

He looked uncomfortable. "I'm too old for a night out on the tiles," he joked.

Satisfied, I led the retreat back to the landing. The stairs ascended still further, but they were noticeably narrower here and the top flight was boxed in rather than banistered. I squinted up into the gloom. "Is that the attic?"

"Aye. You're not to go up there, Lilabet. It's not safe."

My curiosity was stung. "Why not? What's up there?"

"Only the North Wind." He twisted his mouth wryly, but it didn't quite look like a smile. "He comes to stay sometimes, and he brings his mate the Rain with him on occasion. They've made a right mess of the roof and the woodwork." He put his hand on my shoulder and leaned in to look me in the eye. "You'll have to promise me you won't be going up there, lass. If he sees a pretty little girl like you he'll steal you away and we'll never hear from you again."

If I'd been any older I'd have known he was talking metaphorically. If Mam had been there she would have given a derisive laugh and I'd have known he was just lying. But standing on the ill-lit stairs in the depths of that dark and half-derelict house I just accepted the strangeness of it all along with everything else I'd had to assimilate.

"Okay."

"Good lass." He chucked me under my chin and I flinched away a little, but felt his hand tighten on my shoulder. "It'll be good to have you living here," he said. "The old house is the better for having more womenfolk in it, and I'm not the sort to complain about being outnumbered by the lasses."

Twisting, I pulled firmly out from under his hand and retreated to my new bedroom door. "I'm going to get my stuff ready," I told him, "and then I'll go down and see Gran." With that I shut the door between us. He took the hint, at any rate. I heard his footsteps descending the long flights while I unpacked my little tartan suitcase.

Those were the days before certain factors loomed so large in the public mind, before 'paedophiles' existed, when there were just 'dirty old men'. I have no memory of feeling any fear of my Granda, just a resigned wariness. It was one of the reasons I had for not wanting to live with them, alright, but it was pretty much on a par with the distaste that I felt for her swollen legs or the nicotine stains on his teeth or the smell of cat pee in the downstairs rooms; they were all part and parcel of the same burden.

Pushing my suitcase under the bed, I felt a sudden wave of loss come rolling over and soak me, leaving me gasping for Mam, my face wet. When I licked the corner of my mouth I could taste the salt.

That night, huddled under my inadequate blankets, I couldn't get to sleep because the window rattled ceaselessly in its frame and the netting did nothing to keep the moon out. I watched the grey light crawl across the walls, chasing the shadows into corners. Sometime after midnight by the glowing hands on my Mickey Mouse watch, I heard Granda's footsteps ascending the stairs from the floor below, very slowly and quietly. I held my breath and stared at the window. He reached my landing and paused there for a long moment, then shuffled across to my door. I heard the handle turn and the door open, then the thump as it struck the bedframe. After retiring for the night I'd dragged the bed inch by patient inch across the floorboards until it wedged the door closed.

"Lilabet!" came Granda's hoarse whisper.

I faked a snore. I don't suppose it was convincing. After another pause I heard his footsteps retreat across the landing and start on the stairs. It took me a while to realise that he was going further *up*, not returning downstairs, and I frowned to myself. I listened to the creak of the joists overhead and, much fainter, the rumble of his voice. It came intermittently, as if he were conversing with someone inaudible. I was puzzled to think what he was doing talking to himself in the darkened attic, but I'd fallen asleep before he came back down again.

It wasn't the last time I heard him go up to the attic for a chat, though.

In the days that followed I spent a lot of time out of the house, whatever the weather. I'd take every opportunity to walk down into town on shopping errands and I spent hours in the library where I was supposed to be picking out new books for Gran; even just wandering the streets I felt warmer and happier than I did in that house up on Whitley Bank. There was always a wind gusting up the valley-side there, rattling the windows and muttering in the chimney. I wore my coat nearly all the time indoors there, even in bed. When I wasn't down in town I wandered around on the open hillside, clogging up my trainers with sheep-dung and staining my jeans with mud. I made friends with the youngest daughter on a farm two fields away and would help her gather the eggs in their new battery house, grateful for the stinking warmth inside the shed and not really sensible, as I would be now, of the hens' cramped and insanitary conditions.

Maisie said my Granda was a bit daft in the head, everyone knew, and I didn't argue.

I discovered that if you climbed the slope behind the houses you could stand on a level with the guttering and look straight across at the hole in Granda's roof. Where the slates were missing I could make out the laths and a shredded piece of felt and a shadowy space beyond that was the interior of the attic. The hole looked big enough to step through for a kid my size and seemed temptingly close, almost close enough to reach. I'd sit on the grass and eye the distance like I'd eye a particularly revolting scab, fascinated and a bit nauseated. The problem and the source of the fascination was that black drop of three storeys between rock-face and house. I couldn't stop picturing what would happen to anyone jumping short and tumbling down that slot into the dank shadows below. There would be no second chance. And yet that gap was so narrow!—on the ground a quite feasible distance. It was just the horrible depth of the drop that made it impossible to attempt.

I think now that it was my first real inkling of mortality, of the terrible, narrow-mouthed, non-negotiable abyss of death. I dreamt about that jump many times while I stayed in that house; dreamt that I was girding myself for the leap. Always I woke up mid-jump, not knowing if I'd made it.

Of course there was an easier route into the forbidden attic and it was just a matter of time before I found an excuse to try. One night I was just beginning to nod off when I heard a thump overhead that jolted me wide awake. It was followed by a scratching that ran from one side of the ceiling to the other and a faint flapping, and then more thumps. I knew the sound: we'd had a starling fall down the chimney at home once and it was the same frantic, restless noise. Only this was much, much louder.

I pulled the bed away from my door and crept out onto the landing. It was nearly pitch black out there but I didn't want to turn the light on and alert Granda, so I fetched the box of matches from my unlit fireplace and struck them one at a time as I climbed, as quietly as I could on the bare stairs. The shadows jumped around me. I was twitchy with nerves and my eyes itched from staring. At the top of the last flight was no landing but a plain wooden door. I put my ear to it. Once again I heard the fluttering, the soft thumps, the scrabbling of sharp claws on a wooden surface. It sounded much louder than a starling.

"Lilabet?" Granda's voice was harsh. I jumped. "What are you doing up here?"

I spun to face him down the steps, my heart pounding beneath my brushed-cotton pyjamas. He had a big car torch in his hand and was shining it up into my face.

"What did I tell you? I said you don't come up here!"

"There's an owl," I stammered. "Trapped in the attic, like. I heard it."

"Not an owl." His voice dropped to a whisper. He came up the stairs to compensate for the loss of volume, and I squashed myself against the wall. I was glad to see he had both hands full, though I didn't understand why the one not clutching the torch was holding a dead rabbit from the pantry. "Not an owl, though he'd got the eyes. Great orange eyes. He never took them off me." There was something about my Granda's expression that really alarmed me, something not right. His own pupils were enormously dilated. "Nine days," he whispered, looking straight through me as if I wasn't there, "sat hunched up on the bow, staring at me. Nine bloody days. Sea like glass. What was I supposed to do?"

"Dunno," I breathed.

"He won't leave me alone." Granda inhaled sharply though his nose. "Followed me home. What am I supposed to do about it?" I slid past him, and all of a sudden his eyes seemed to focus on my face. "Get yourself back down there," he snapped. "All the way. Go wait with your Gran till I tell you."

I'd have much rather barricaded myself back in my room, but I obeyed him. By the time I crashed into Gran's room, my fright was already transmuted to high dudgeon.

"What's up, our Ella?" Gran was propped up in bed by a mound of yellowing pillows.

"Granda sent me down."

"Where is he?"

"In the attic," I said as nastily as I could, "feeding dead rabbits to the North Wind."

She stared at me for a long time. I flopped down in her armchair, and then wished I hadn't: her greasy warmth seemed to cling to the cushions. Her watery gaze rested on me without sympathy. "You think your Granda's a daft old git, then, do you lass?"

I grunted. That wasn't the half of it.

"I can see you've no patience for him. Do you know what happened to him in the war, Ella?"

I shook my head sulkily.

"He was on a run across the Atlantic when his ship was sunk by a U-boat. Him and twelve others piled into this open lifeboat, and then the rest of the convoy sailed off and left them, like they had to; couldn't risk hanging around to pick up survivors in case they got torpedoed themselves. Left the little lifeboats bobbing around on the open ocean as dark fell. Nine days they drifted, Ella. Nine days in the North Atlantic in the middle of January. All the lifeboats got split up in a heavy swell. By the time a Sunderland spotted him he was the only one left alive in his boat; all the others had froze to death. Inches of ice all across the woodwork and the bodies, he said."

I shivered despite myself.

"So he's had a lot to deal with, lass. You don't go judging what you don't understand."

But what I still didn't understand was his talk of orange eyes. And what it was he kept in the attic. If it was an owl, I reasoned to Maisie the next day, then that would explain the rabbit. But it couldn't be loose in the room because then it could escape through the roof. It must be tied to a stand. Maybe it had fallen off and hung from its traces, accounting for the scrabbling claws and the flapping I'd heard.

Maisie told me slyly that my Granda sometimes took a sack of dead hens off her dad, fallen birds, not fit for eating. He'd said they were for the dog. I knew Nipper was dead months back.

I decided I had to get a look in the attic.

It wasn't easy. Granda didn't leave the house that often during the day, and I didn't want to try it again at night; it had been too spooky. I resorted to lying, telling Gran as I returned to the house one afternoon that I'd not been able to get her cigarettes because the man at the corner shop wasn't selling them to underage kids any more. Grumbling under his breath, Granda stumped off down the hill, and I headed for the attic stairs. In a paper bag in my coat pocket were the soft yellow bodies of two little chicks Maisie had swiped for me. If there was an owl I wanted to feed it. Maisie would have come with me, but the weeks had piled up now and she, like all normal kids, was back at school for the new term.

By the time I reached the top stairs I was half wishing that I'd left this until the weekend, so that at least I wouldn't be on my own. It was a grey day with the clouds pressed low down over the roofs of Whitley Bank and wisps of fog smudging the moor-tops, so there wasn't much light in the stairwell. As I got to the attic door I could only just make out the bolt fixed to the woodwork; I was certain it hadn't been there the other night. My fingers found the heavy padlock and tugged at it, but it was secure. For a moment I was baffled. Then I had an idea and I turned and pattered down the stairs to Granda's workshop.

He was nothing if not an orderly man. Even the drawers and boxes of incomprehensible metal fittings were sorted and graded and kept in an order that made sense to him. And on one wall was a green pin-board on which hung scores of keys in all shapes and sizes. I dragged a stool over and climbed up on the bench to reach them. His orderliness had stopped short of labelling, so I took a handful of those that seemed the most likely and retraced my path to the attic door.

None of the keys fit. It took a second trip—and a deliberate effort to re-gather my determination—before I found one that did. Kneeling in the half-dark, a dim grey line of light from under the door my only comfort, fitting metal to metal by touch more than by sight, I had to fight my own impulse to give up. I wanted it all to be over, to be back downstairs again in Gran's smelly parlour playing with the cats. But I wanted to know; I wanted to know. There was no sound from beyond the door, no sound at all but my own shallow breathing.

Finally the key turned and I slipped the bolt and stepped into the attic.

Under His Wing, Poor Thing

It was a big room, twice the size of my bedroom because it ran right from front to back of the house, but—except in the middle under the peak of the roof—the sloping ceiling was almost too low for an adult to stand upright. The whole space was filled with the sweet-sour smell of rotting wood. The only light source was the rent in the tiles; there were no windows or skylights, and the electric socket hanging from the ridge was as empty as that of a lost tooth. The bare floorboards were grey and scratched, though under the hole they were stained with red and black moulds and blotched with furry white patches, and there were drifts of dead leaves in every corner.

There was no owl. I walked right into the room to check. There wasn't anything that I'd been expecting: no stand and chain, no droppings splotched on the floor, not even any bones. The only smell was that of damp, and the only furniture was an iron-framed bed with a thin mattress covered in a rumpled sheet. I walked round the foot and there on the floor behind it was a big book. That was all.

I stood quietly for a moment. Out on the moor a crow was cawing but that was the only sound in the grey and desolate world. I looked up at the thick clouds. Then, because there was nothing else, I went over to the book and knelt to open it. It turned out to be a photo album. The first few pages held really small black and white photos of men in sailors' uniforms. They mostly looked like they'd been taken on land; one was definitely in Trafalgar Square, even I recognised that. The rest of the album was blank, but tucked into the back cover was a big newspaper which I took out and spread on the floor. It called itself the *Daily Express*, though it didn't look much like the

Express I was familiar with, and it was dated to January 1942. There was a piece on the front page about the sinking of an allied shipping convoy. I flipped it open and started looking through the other pages, finding funny-looking adverts for mothballs and thermal underwear and dodgy-sounding medicines, then a page of strip cartoons. I became so engrossed that I lost track of time; what jerked me back to alertness was the sound of heavy feet on the stair.

"Lilabet!" roared my Granda's voice.

This was much worse than being caught on the stairs. I jumped up and fled instinctively for the only exit: the hole in the tiles. Squeezing between two horizontal laths I got my head and torso out into the open air. Below me a short slope led down to the gutter; it would be easy enough to climb out and slide down, and from there it was only a leap to the side of the hill. The mist was scudding along, driven by a freshening wind. I was so close to the bank that I could see droplets of water hanging from individual blades of grass. I pictured that wet grass sliding between my clutching fingers, my feet kicking in the empty air, the sickening lurch as I slipped down over the edge. And I knew I couldn't do it.

"Lilabet! Are you up there?"

I pulled in again, feeling sick, and backed across the mildewed boards to stand against the far wall, pressing my shoulder to the plaster. That was where Granda found me when he burst in through the door, red-faced and breathless from the climb. He cast his gaze around the room; I could see the whites of his eyes.

"Lilabet," he hissed. "What does it take? What does it bloody take to make you listen to me, you stupid girl? Come here!"

I didn't move. For the first time I was really scared of him; I had no idea what he would do to me.

"Come here!" he groaned, then fumbled for his belt buckle. "God help me that I should have to leather a girl—"

I flattened my back to the wall, rigid with denial. My throat, dry as sand, had closed up. Nothing on earth could have persuaded me to walk toward him just then.

"You stupid bloody child, I'm going to tan you to within an inch of your life!" He took a few steps into the room, his leather belt folded double in his fist.

Then the room went dark, just for a moment. Something had filled the hole in the roof, blocking the light. I felt the air sucked out of my lungs. Then the temperature plummeted. As the grey light of day filtered back I turned my head, gasping, and my exhalation lay like a plume of smoke on the frosty air.

It stood, hunched, under the highest part of the roof. Whatever it was, it shouldn't have been able to get through that hole, which was a squeeze even for a child my size. And this thing was bigger than Granda—bigger than most men. I looked at it, but my eyes did not understand what they were seeing. Feathers made of smoke. Wings. From the inchoate shadows great orange eyes like an owl's—luminous and perfectly round and completely insane—were the only things clear to me.

"Oh no," said Granda weakly.

The orange eyes flicked as it blinked. It was looking straight at me through the wreathes of my frozen breath.

233

"Lilabet," whispered Granda. "Get behind me."

I started to sidle backward into the angle of the roof, away from the thing. It reached out a hand toward me; despite its wings it had human hands, but the talons on the fingers were those of a bird of prey.

I've seen its likeness twice since that day—or something like it. Once was an illustration in a children's book, quite a famous story. When I saw that I walked out of the library and I've never been back in one or picked up a novel since that day. The second time was many years later, when the air travel company I was working for launched onto the stock market and we held a publicity bash at the British Museum. I saw it then, depicted in stone, in the Ancient Sculpture wing: a hall filled with vast pieces of artwork pillaged from Egypt and Assyria and Greece. When I saw it then I put down my martini and ran out of the museum and threw up down my new Gucci dress and the marble steps.

"No you don't," said Granda, stepping between it and me. His little, rumpled, wiry body looked tiny under its bulk. "Not my granddaughter."

The thing hesitated.

"Lilabet," he said through gritted teeth, "get out."

I scuttled sideways toward the door. The thing turned, its attention fixed on me, and lurched forward.

"No!" shouted Granda, raising his arms and stepping toward it. It was as if something in it snapped. Its hands shot out. Granda screamed. I saw a beak stoop to rend at him. The room filled with beating wings. And then it stepped back through the hole and took Granda with it; the laths snapped and slates were smashed as his body was jerked through. For a moment there was darkness and then the light was streaming in again with the wet mild air of spring, and my Granda and the winged thing were gone from view. But I heard him fall because he screamed all the way.

I ran down the stairs, my hands over my ears.

THEY FOUND HIS BODY in the damp gap between house and hill.

That was more than forty years ago. My life has changed beyond recognition. I'm a successful businesswoman now, with grandchildren of my own. I'm considered hard-headed and practical. I don't believe in God or Santa Claus or the North Wind.

I don't believe that that was what happened in the attic.

I've talked to a number of therapists and we all agree. I believe that what took place up there was something completely different, something terrible and traumatic but that I shouldn't have to feel guilty about. I believe what happened to Granda was his own fault. Not mine.

The trouble is that's not how I remember it. No matter how much therapy I sit through. No matter how much regression hypnotism I undergo. The trauma, the psychiatrists say, is so deeply rooted that I still can't bring myself to fully accept it. I'm a bit of a puzzle to them.

The trouble is that yesterday I saw it again. In New York.

I was in Central Park, by the skating rink. It was late afternoon, already dark, and the snow was thick on the ground and my breath was white on the air. As I moved through the crowds under the coloured lights I saw a big bulky figure, indistinct in the gloom and the press: a tall man in a big coat with a deep hood, perhaps. He turned toward me only briefly, but I caught the flash of luminous owl-eyes, orange and inhuman, under the cowl.

"Lilabet," his voice came to me, softly. Then he slipped away, a shadow among other shadows.

I sit in my hotel room surrounded by hothouse flowers and I drink my way steadily through the mini-bar and I look out at the thick thick snow on the streets. Steam creeps from the pavement vents, filling the air with mist. It's been another bad winter, the latest in a string, and it's brought the city to a near standstill. People are blaming climate change. People are blaming the federal government. People are blaming the Chinese for burning too much coal.

CNN says more snow is on the way, carried down by winds from the north.

I can't get warm.

THE FOOLISH LIGHT

GUY BURTENSHAW

CRONEHAM FERRY WAS once a windswept and desolate place on a stretch of the river Yare, and many would say that little has changed.

At the place where the ferry crosses, other than the geese, there is little more than an inn, an old windmill—now devoid of its sails—and the tiny chain-powered ferry that takes travellers across the thirty foot of water to the other side of the river.

Mark Forester had never been to Croneham Ferry before. He had never been to Norfolk before, but his father had loved the county and his dying wish had been that his ashes be scattered at Croneham Ferry.

It had been dark when Mark arrived. It was mid December and there was a bitter frost in the air carried uncomfortably on a northerly wind. The cold bit at his hands and face, but that was all pushed away by a dram of whisky in the Croneham Ferry Inn.

"You travelled far?" the barmaid asked him, as he returned to the bar for a second whisky.

"Westerham in Kent," Mark said. "It's been a long drive."

"But worth it," she said. "Peace and quiet is what we have up here in bucketloads."

"A little too quiet for me, but I'll get used to it."

"There's a ferry goes down river to Yarmouth twice a day if you get bored."

Marvellous, Mark thought. *And if I get really depressed I could drown myself.*

"Is there much in the town?" he asked. "I only passed the edge when I drove in."

"There's a few cafés facing the river. The quickest way to get there is along the bank. It's about a mile as the crow flies, give or take."

Mark couldn't figure out why his father had chosen such a godforsaken place to have his remains scattered. He couldn't think of a worse place to spend eternity. His only consolation was that he would only need to spend the one night in Croneham Ferry before heading back south first thing in the morning.

From his father's description, the place that he was looking for would be found by walking along a raised causeway that ran parallel to the river. He assumed that was the bank the barmaid had mentioned. It would have been impossible to locate if the river had flooded but thankfully—or not—the water level was unseasonably low, which should make it easy to find the location of the scattering site.

"Do you know of a circle of wooden pillars around here?" Mark asked, uneasiness creeping over him. His father had been particular about his not mentioning the site to anyone, in case they became suspicious about why he wanted to find it. He assumed his father wanted his last resting place to remain a secret from locals who might object to the scattering of ashes in their community. He assumed there would be a law against such activities.

The barmaid looked confused. "Wooden pillars?" she asked.

"Never mind," Mark said. "I'm heading back home in the morning."

"We scared you off already?"

Mark laughed, hoping it didn't sound too forced, and the barmaid smiled in return.

"My father used to stay up here sometimes. I thought I'd stop by and see the place for myself."

"Your father," the barmaid said. "What was his name?"

"Robert. Robert Forester."

"Not old Professor Forester?"

"Yes." Mark was surprised she knew his father. "He died six months ago."

"I'm sad to hear it. He used to arrive here the first Saturday in December every year without fail. We'll all miss him this year. He was a very intelligent man. Knew all sorts of things. Used to tell us the most amazing tales. He loved walking by the river to Croneham and back. Dozer used to rush off to meet him every day at four o'clock."

"Dozer?"

"He's my dog. Old now, but still fit as a fiddle. Used to have an instinct for it. Asleep one minute, up and alert the next, bounding off to the stile to meet him. He's around somewhere. Shaggy looking foxhound. Can't miss him."

"I'll keep an eye out."

Mark didn't like to tell her that his father had actually made the journey one last time and was at that very moment in a small box in the boot of his car, especially considering that he would be staying the night at the inn.

"He loved his folklore and myths," Mark said. "Used to scare me senseless at Halloween with his creepy tales of ancient Celtic and Saxon myths."

"That he did," she said, as though remembering some of the stories he had told her. "Makes you look at those broads and marshes in a whole different light. By the way, my name's Jenny."

Mark desperately wanted to bring up the subject of the wooden circle again, but he restrained himself. He didn't think it could be that difficult to locate, especially if he knew what he was looking for, and his father's description had been quite specific. It had been his father's wish, and he doubted his father would have left his last resting place to confusion and chance.

Mark picked up his glass and downed the contents, the liquid warming his stomach. "I better get some sleep. Early start tomorrow."

"You never know," Jenny said. "You might change your mind and decide to stay a few days when you experience dawn in Croneham. The Christmas spirit comes early to Croneham."

"You never know." Mark had no intention of staying any longer than was necessary. He didn't tell Jenny just how early a start it would be.

MARK'S ALARM CLOCK beeped on the bedside table. It was one o'clock in the morning. A faint silvery light illuminated a long rectangle across the floor from the window. He was still wearing the clothes he'd arrived in. There'd been no point changing when he'd be traipsing along the bank in the dark looking for a wooden circle. He might look a bit dishevelled, even pong a bit, but he doubted there'd be anyone about to notice.

He went to the window and looked up at the moon. Just as his father had said, the moon was full and appeared larger than normal. He knew that was due to the moon being closer to the earth than its usual orbit, and with the cloudless sky the whole countryside was bathed in a silver light.

He put on a pair of sturdy leather walking boots and went to the door. If all went to plan, he'd be back again within a couple of hours, and might even catch a few hours sleep before breakfast and the long drive back south. No one would even know that he'd been out.

Guy Burtenshaw

MARK CLOSED THE BOOT of his car and picked the wooden box up. It felt heavy, but he supposed it should be. His father had been a large man. He hoped the final place wouldn't be too far away. The raised bank went for about a mile separating the marshland from the river, so it couldn't be more than a mile away, but he knew that a mile in the moonlight would seem a lot further, especially when carrying a box that was heavier with every passing minute.

He looked up at the full moon again. "Shine well on me Selene," he said. His father had always called the moon Selene after the goddess.

"Here goes," he said and headed towards the quayside where he could reach the start of the bank.

The way ahead was unlit, so he was grateful that the moon was providing some light. The journey would have been treacherous on any other night, and he would've probably ended up either falling down the bank and breaking his leg or going headfirst into the freezing river.

The paving of the quayside gave way to the muddy path that ran along the top of the bank, reaching a stile just before the derelict windmill. There was a sign attached to the stile warning ramblers that the path was closed for the winter, but as the water level in the river was so low, he couldn't see what danger there would be in walking along it. He carefully made his way over the stile and continued, unease spreading through him as he passed the dark hulk of the windmill.

The sails were missing, and had probably been so for a long time. He tried not to look towards the mill, not to give into the fear that someone was watching him from the darkness, but he

242

couldn't help himself. He glanced briefly, but it only made the sensation worse.

He told himself that even if there was someone watching him from the shadows it didn't matter. He was in the countryside, in the middle of nowhere. He was not in the city with a drug addict or discharged psychiatric patient waiting in every darkened doorway to stab him to death.

He continued along the bank leaving the mill behind, the box firmly held in his hands. The night was still, not even a slight breeze. The surface of the river was as still as a millpond. His father couldn't have chosen a more perfect night if he'd tried.

His father had told him many tales over the years, but the one that came to mind as he made his way across the marshland was that of the lantern man. He remembered being told the story one Halloween night many years ago, and it had terrified his adolescent mind. In previous centuries people had believed that lights seen over the marshes were the lantern man, luring people to their deaths in the mud.

He'd read that if you were carrying a lamp, the lantern man always ran to the light, so the way to escape was to put the lamp down and run as fast as you could. A treacherous task when surrounded by marshland. He'd also read that the lantern man always headed towards the sound of a whistle, but that wasn't a lot of use when you were alone.

Mark knew that the lantern man was nothing more than a myth built up by people seeing bright lights in the marshes at night, the same as stories from all over the country about Will-o'-the-wisp, the Corpse Candle or Jack-o-lantern, but he also knew that the lights were nothing more than gas escaping from the earth and igniting. No one really believed they were anything else these days. No more dangerous than a firefly.

In the distance he could see light coming from the houses on the edge of the town on the other side of the marshland. He wished his father had chosen a different site for his ashes. He wished his father had chosen a more decent hour. He couldn't imagine that he would ever visit the area ever again, so there would be no visits. The journey from Kent was long, and he had no plans to move.

He looked across the piece of land between the bank and the river, searching for anything that stood out. He didn't think he would see a perfect circle of wooden bollards waiting for his arrival. That would be far too easy. His only real concern was what to do if he actually reached the houses on the edge of the town. He'd have to turn around and walk back again. If that happened, the chances of finding the final place wouldn't be good, and he really didn't want to let his father down. His father had even left instructions on what was to be said as he scattered the ashes. Mark had the words on a piece of paper in his pocket. He'd read them, but he didn't know what they meant. He guessed they were some ancient Celtic dialect written out phonetically for the uninitiated.

A small white bird sat by the river. It was sitting very still as though asleep. Mark stopped to look at it, waiting to see if it moved. A fox dashed along the riverbank and grabbed the bird between its jaws. The bird flapped in a desperate attempt to escape, but the fox dashed away in the direction from which it had come, heading towards the ferry. In its way the country was just as violent as the city. There was death waiting at every turn, but as his father had once said, where there is death, life always follows.

He noticed a dark shape close to the riverbank. In the moonlight he couldn't make out what it was, but he supposed he had to get a closer look. He hoped that he wouldn't have to investigate every dark shape along the entire length of the bank. If he did, it would take him through to dawn.

He made his way down the bank and gingerly started towards the river, pressing carefully down with his foot. He worried that the ground would be so waterlogged he'd simply sink without trace.

The ground was very springy, but he didn't sink more than a couple of inches, although he didn't stand still for more than a couple of seconds to test this. When he reached the river he smiled. The dark shape was circular, about six feet across. It looked like a round pool of dark water with the tops of wooden posts around its edge. The wood looked ancient, like the ends of eroded breakwaters on a beach, but it was clearly the place his father had described.

He crouched down and placed the box on the ground. A coldness passed through him as he raised the lid. He missed his father, and to think that what was in the box was all that remained of him made him feel sad. It felt almost disrespectful throwing his ashes into the dirty looking pool.

He picked the box up and, remaining crouched, he held it out over the water and started to tip. Panic filled him as the box fell from his hands and into the water. It sank. Mark's heart was hammering. He hadn't had any plans to keep the box, but it felt like an electric shock as it hit the water and disappeared. He supposed it was like having a near miss: you were fine but still shaken.

He stood and retrieved the paper from his pocket. His hands trembled as he unfolded it and saw his father's handwriting. He looked up at the moon, then back at the paper, and he slowly read, being careful to pronounce the words exactly how they were spelt.

MARK SAT AT THE TABLE staring blankly at a car waiting to drive onto the ferry. Nothing much seemed to be happening.

It had been a little after two by the time he'd got back to the inn, and he'd slept soundly, but since waking at dawn he'd been feeling a deep sense of anxiety. He wanted to get away from the river and the inn.

"Earth calling Mark."

Mark turned and saw Jenny standing by the table.

"Sorry," he said.

"You were a million miles away," she said. "Somewhere nice I hope."

"What?" He didn't have a clue what she was talking about.

"Tea or coffee?"

"Coffee please, and some toast. Wholemeal."

"We do a great full English breakfast."

"Toast will be fine," he said, trying not to sound too irritated. He wanted to be left alone. "Just toast."

"Be right back," she said and headed off to the kitchen.

The car had driven onto the ferry leaving him with a view of the river. There were geese waddling about, but not a lot else was happening. The day-trippers had not yet arrived, and it was hardly a through road. The road ended at the river, the only way to continue being on the small chain ferry. He didn't know the area at all, but he guessed there were easier and quicker ways to get across, probably via a bridge further up or down the river. The ferry was more of a relic for tourists.

The controller checked the back of the ferry, then started to get back onboard. As he stepped onto the deck he turned his head and stared straight at Mark. It felt as though their eyes locked for a moment, then Mark broke the hold and quickly turned his head.

"Your coffee and toast," Jenny said, as she put a cup and plate in front of him and a rack of toast in the middle of the table. "Bon appétit." She smiled and walked away.

He had anything but a bon appétit, but he forced himself to eat a slice of heavily buttered toast and washed it down with a cup of strong black coffee. The last thing he felt like doing was driving the hundred and twenty miles back to Kent, especially along the inadequate roads that Norfolk offered, but he was determined to be gone before nine and home before midday. There were service stations on the route back, so he could stop for coffee if his eyelids starting feeling heavy.

Coffee finished, he turned his attention back to the river. A fog was drifting in from the reed beds on the opposite side, slowly moving towards the inn. It looked as though it was going to be dense and unpleasant to drive in, but he knew that as soon as he left the marshes the fog would disappear. The road across the marsh to Croneham would take no more than ten minutes, less if he put his foot down. He hadn't seen a single speed camera since entering Norfolk, and he doubted whether the police would set up a speed trap on a road that didn't lead anywhere other than a time warp.

As he started to look away something flashed in the fog across the river. He glanced back. He stared for what felt like several minutes, but there was nothing there.

"More coffee?" Jenny asked.

"No thanks." She started to walk away. "Jenny?"

"Yes?"

"Has anyone ever seen lights out over the marshes around here, at night?"

"You mean Jack?"

"Jack?"

"Jack-o-lantern. The lantern man. Yes, all the time."

"Marsh gasses," he said.

"I wouldn't let Jack hear that. If you see the lantern you have to lay flat on the ground as quickly as you can and hold your breath, or he'll suck the air right out of your lungs."

"No one actually believes in the lantern man anymore do they?"

"Outsiders always belittle the old ways. You might not believe in Jack, but he believes in you."

She smirked as she turned away, and Mark got the feeling she was making fun of him.

The Foolish Light

MARK WALKED THROUGH the fog that surrounded the inn in a dense blanket, and found his way to the small parking area. He stopped dead in his tracks when he saw two of his tyres were flat. He walked around the car to discover that the other two tyres were also flat.

He only had one spare and there was no point replacing one tyre. He needed to find a garage. His father has belonged to the RAC, but he had never felt the need to join, something he now regretted. Even a tiny town like Croneham would have a garage with four tyres that they would part with for a price.

Getting back to Kent by midday was out of the question, but he was determined that he'd get back before dark. He knew going back into the inn to ask Jenny would have been the sensible thing to do, but he did not want to be a nuisance, and his head felt heavy and his body exhausted. The quickest way to Croneham was along the bank, and that was the route he would be taking. He felt that the walk would clear his head for what would be a long drive home.

The fog was denser than the darkness he'd walked through during the night. He couldn't see the river, and visibility had reduced to about ten feet. One wrong foot and he'd tumble off the bank. He couldn't imagine anyone would be taking a walk across the marshes until the fog cleared, and the fog didn't look as though it would be clearing anytime soon.

A light flashed to his right and he stopped dead in his tracks, but when he looked right again, there was nothing there.

He had never seen the marsh lights before, but he couldn't think of any other explanation. It occurred to him that perhaps Jenny and some locals were playing a trick on him, but it seemed unlikely. Unless his father had also left instructions for them to play a final joke on him.

"Hello," he called out, his voice muffled as though the fog was swallowing the sound. "Jenny?"

Off to his right a dark shadow moved. He thought of the fox he saw the night before, but dismissed it. The shadow was taller like a person running. His father would've told him that it was the ghost of some poor soul following the lantern man to his doom.

"I know you're there," he shouted, though it was probably nothing more than a bird flying through the fog. "Very funny."

There was no response. He was in no mood for games. He turned back to the track and started forward. A dark shadow dashed across the track about fifteen feet in front of him and disappeared into the fog.

"Okay," he shouted. "You got me. Never deny the lantern man."

There was still no response from the fog. He stepped forward, his ankle twisting on the side of the bank and, before he could even attempt to balance, his feet slipped out from beneath him and he rolled down onto the marsh. He expected someone to rush to his aid, but all remained still.

Mark lay still for a moment wishing that he had chosen to walk along the road to the town. The damp from the sodden ground started to soak through his clothes. He shuddered at the cold and sat up, his back hurting from the tumble.

He looked around at the fog. It felt as though he was the only person left on Earth. He listened, but couldn't hear anything. He wanted to shout for help, but what would he do if anyone actually came? He'd taken a walk along a closed path and fallen in the fog. They'd be laughing about him before he even made it back to the inn.

He got to his feet and turned to make his way back up to the path. A shape threw itself towards him from the top of the bank. He raised his arms in front of his face to defend himself, but nothing happened. Heart beating ferociously he lowered his arms. He was alone.

A shape moved off to his right. He spun around almost falling again.

"Stop this," he shouted. "It's gone beyond a joke now. Leave me be and let me be on my way."

He was starting to wonder whether perhaps the people that were taunting him in the fog were the same people that had slashed the tyres on his car. They were probably local youths playing games with an outsider. He was surprised that anyone ever visited their tiny town if that was the way they treated visitors.

He clambered up the bank, determined not to let anyone slow him down further. All he wanted to do was find a garage and get his tyres fixed so that he could get as far away from Croneham Ferry as he could, as quickly as he could. If anyone wanted to come running out of the mist then he wouldn't stop them. He'd simply ignore them.

He made it back up the bank to the path more easily than he thought he would. For a brief moment he felt disorientated, unsure of which way he was heading. He'd fallen to his right, so he knew in which direction the river was. He started walking, picking up speed as he went.

The fog had become so dense that he was having trouble even seeing the ground about his feet. He slowed. There was a light in front. It looked like a torch. He headed towards it, realising his error too late and once more tumbled, this time hitting the ground more forcefully. He tried to sit up, a pain shooting up his neck and into his head. He fell back, the brilliance of the foggy shroud giving way to darkness.

MARK FELT PAIN. HIS head felt as though someone had forced a red-hot needle through his skull. He opened his eyes. He was lying on a sofa in a small lounge that he didn't recognise.

"You were very lucky," a woman said.

He turned his head and saw Jenny sitting on a sofa with the man he'd seen earlier manning the ferry.

"Where am I?" Mark asked.

"The inn," Jenny said. "Joe saw you wandering along the bank. He told me and I told him to go see if you're okay. Lucky for you he did."

"Don't know what you're thinking trying that way in this fog," Joe said. "Madness. Could have died your death out there."

"My tyres are flat," Mark said. "I need to find a garage."

"All four?" Joe asked.

"Someone slashed them. I need to get back home."

"Should have said," Jenny said. "Could have given you a lift over to Latham's Garage, although you'd have to be mad to drive in this weather. End up in the marsh."

Mark's head was starting to spin. He wanted to get away from the inn, and he felt trapped. He started to get up.

"Where do you think you're going?" Jenny asked. "You're lucky you didn't get hypothermia."

"I have to get back to Kent today."

"Don't worry. You can stay here tonight and go back tomorrow morning. One day won't kill you."

Mark didn't think it would kill him, but he was pretty sure it might drive him insane. He was still determined that he'd be gone before midday.

He sat up.

"At least have some lunch inside you before you leave," Jenny said. "Then I'll give old Latham a call and see if he can drive you over some tyres. Save travelling over."

Mark looked at his watch. It said eleven-thirty.

"What time is it?" he asked.

"Half eleven," said Jenny.

"I left here before nine."

"It was after ten by the time you got back here," Joe said.

"You need rest," Jenny insisted. "Even if Latham came over and put new tyres on your car, it would be madness to drive across the marsh in this fog. You'd end up crashing. Look what happened to you already."

Mark tried to stand, but fell back into the sofa as a wave of dizziness hit him like vertigo. He knew that they were right. He was in no fit state to drive. He didn't have anything back in Kent that couldn't wait another day. He could have an early night, get a good ten hours sleep and head off as soon as it got light, fog or no fog.

MARK TOOK UP THE offer of lunch, but he could barely manage to swallow more than a few mouthfuls of the steak and ale pie. It wasn't that he wasn't hungry, or that the pie wasn't good. His mind was elsewhere. Memories of his father. Memories of his childhood. Memories of his past, but not quite. There was always something just out of sight, just out of his vision. But always there. Always watching him. However hard he struggled to remember, to see, he could not. He felt tense. There was a nauseous feeling in the pit of his stomach that felt as though someone had reached inside and taken hold of his intestines, squeezing them tight.

No one else had taken the room that he'd vacated, so he'd been given the same room. If he'd been feeling himself he would've taken a few drams of whisky to knock himself out, but as it was he'd have to rely on pure tiredness to drag him into sleep.

Jenny seemed to know Latham, the owner of the garage, and had arranged for someone to come and replace the tyres, but they wouldn't be able to get out to the inn until late afternoon.

The Foolish Light

The unease that Mark had felt since waking had not waned and, if anything, had worsened. The atmosphere inside the inn was stifling, and there'd been no relief when he'd stepped outside. He'd sat in his room looking out of the window, watching the ferry as it made its way across to the other side and back again. At first it'd helped him relax, but then he'd started thinking about the stories his father had told him, and he remembered the story of Charon taking the dead across the River Styx in a ferry to the Underworld. He didn't need much imagination to see Joe as Charon drifting slowly into the fog.

Mark tried sleeping, but every time he closed his eyes he saw the dark pool of water and the eroded stumps forming the circle, the stumps looking like severed arms reaching up from the earth. He saw the box hitting the water. The fox grabbing the white bird in its jaws, blood dripping into the pool.

He decided to sit in the bar and have a brandy. Brandy always helped to calm his nerves. He considered walking along the road to the station in Croneham and trying to get to Norwich, where he'd be able to get a train to London. He'd pay someone to drive his car back. He just wanted to get away.

MARK HADN'T EXPECTED to find many people in the bar, and he wasn't disappointed. Jenny was behind the bar polishing glasses, and Joe had come in from the cold and was sitting at a table by the window reading a local newspaper with Dozer asleep on the floor beneath the table.

Mark ordered a brandy and Jenny poured a double, letting him have the drink on the house.

"I was thinking of getting a train back to London," Mark said. "I have some urgent business to attend to."

"Must be urgent," she said. "What about your car?"

"Would Latham be able to arrange for my car to be driven back to my home address in Kent? I know it's a long way."

Jenny laughed, then said, "Old man Latham would be able to arrange anything for a price, as long as you're not in any hurry."

"No hurry."

"*You* seem to be in a hurry to get away though," she said. "Not to your liking up here?"

"No no," he said quickly feeling awkward. "I love it up here, but I have urgent business back in London."

Jenny smiled. "No worries. It's very quiet here. I went to London once and I hated it. Couldn't wait to get out of the place. Too noisy. Too smelly. Too unfriendly."

"You're not wrong," he agreed.

"But you're still determined to rush back?"

"No choice." He looked out of the window at the fog and shivered. It felt as though he was being smothered. "It's a very lonely place out here."

"We like to call it solitude, and that's usually why people drive here from the city. It's why your father used to drive up here."

"It's very eerie at night with the shadows and the marsh lights, and with the fog it's just plain creepy."

"It's not the shadows you need to worry about. It's the lights. The shadows are warnings to keep away. The unfortunate souls. The lights are lures to lead you in."

"I'm not a superstitious man," he said. "There are rational explanations for everything."

"I was thinking yesterday," she said. "About what you said about a circle of wooden bollards."

"I recall."

"You weren't talking about the Devil's Jaw were you?"

"What's the Devil's Jaw?"

"The bits of wood that stick out of the ground down by the river. They're in a sort of circle."

"Satan's Yawn," Joe said as he approached.

"Possibly," Mark said. "And why is it named after the devil?" He wasn't sure he really wanted to know.

"It's been there far longer than any devil," said Jenny. "The demons associated with that place are much older. The legend has it that the site was a place where sacrificial rituals took place. The victims were eviscerated and thrown into a pit between the stakes. On the winter solstice their souls come back. But of course, it's only folklore. An old story to scare people. The people that put it there disappeared over two thousand years ago."

"I would never go near that place at night, let alone on the solstice," Joe said.

"That's why someone closes the path around the solstice," Jenny said. "Some people like to keep the superstitions alive. And then some people like to ignore signposts and go wandering around the marshes in the fog."

"I've learnt my lesson," Mark said.

"The Romans used to call the marsh lights *ignis fatuus*."

"I know," Mark said. "It means 'the foolish fire'."

"'Foolish light', and if you should find yourself too close to the light, you best throw yourself to the earth and hold your breath for as long as you dare."

"Because of the gas."

"Because it could save your life."

Mark finished his brandy and was tempted to ask for another, but stopped himself. He needed to try to keep his head clear.

MARK LOOKED ALONG the road. It curved around disappearing into the fog. He didn't relish having to walk along that road to the station. It would take longer than walking along the bank, but now he knew there was no real reason why the bank was closed to pedestrians. The sign had been put up by an overly superstitious local warning outsiders to keep away.

"There are no such things as good and evil spirits," he said to himself. "The lantern man is a joke."

Dozer dashed out from the shadows behind the inn and ran towards the river.

"Dozer," Mark called out.

Dozer stopped and looked back. Mark thought he was going to run towards him, but instead he turned back and started running along the riverbank heading for the path that led to the stile.

"Dozer," he called out again, but the dog ignored him and continued.

Jenny's words filled his head. "Dozer used to go bounding along the bank at four o'clock every evening when your father stayed."

Mark looked at his watch. It was four o'clock. He looked towards the stile just in time to see Dozer leaping straight over and disappearing from view.

He looked back along the darkened road, and then towards the stile. In his head he could see Dozer bounding up to his father and the two of them walking back to the inn together.

"What the hell," he said. "If my father could go that way, then so can I."

Mark made his way to the stile and looked over. Dozer was sitting on his haunches about fifty feet away looking at him.

"Here boy," Mark called, holding out his hand.

Dozer barked once, then turned and started walking along the bank, wagging his tail as he went.

Mark climbed over the stile and headed along the bank, disappearing into the fog as he followed Dozer.

JOE HAD SEEN DOZER standing on the riverbank as he'd crossed the river. Dozer had been standing proud, legs rigid, shoulders raised, nose pointing towards the sky.

He fetched Jenny from the inn, knowing that she was worried about the dog, and they made their way along the bank together. Dozer made no signs of movement as they approached.

"Dozer?" Jenny called as they drew level.

"He looks as though he's standing guard," Joe said.

"Over what?" Jenny asked. "The river?"

"The mouth. He's standing right next to it."

Jenny carefully clambered down the bank, and made her way towards where Dozer was standing.

"Dozer," she said as she reached him, and gently patted him on the head.

Dozer tilted his head and stared up at her.

Joe joined them. "This is where my great grandfather was found," he said. "Right here by the bank."

"I know," she said. "He belittled the lantern man."

"What time did Mark get back from town? His car's still in the car park."

"He must have taken the train back like he said. He never came back."

They turned and looked down at the circle of ancient wooden posts. Steam rose from the earth inside the circle like escaping spirits. The mud bubbled as pockets of gas broke the surface.

THE PHILOSOPHER'S WAY

B. E. SCULLY

T HE GRANDFATHER CLOCK struck eight o'clock. Stephen Berg knew that before it struck nine, he would be dead. This realization didn't frighten him though. In fact, he had been looking forward to it for some time.

Only a few more lines and the pact would be complete. All he had to do then was to wait for Stilts to appear just like the little shaman or sorcerer or whatever bewitched creature he was. For almost fifty years, Stephen had avoided including 'demon' or 'devil' in this list of considerations. If Stilts's magic was of the black variety, it was too late to do anything about that now.

If Stilts had a proper name, he'd never mentioned it, and Stephen had never asked. He'd taken to calling him Rumpelstiltskin after a fairy tale in one of his childhood books, and through the years he'd shortened it to Stilts. Unlike the

Brothers Grimm imp of Stephen's memory, however, Stilts didn't have a snowy white beard and pointy ears. It was rather the overall effect that called to mind the fairy tale rogue: the lithe little frame that always looked set to break into a jig; the sly, crooked smile ready with a riddle and a sprinkle of menace.

He certainly had been a riddle all those years ago when he'd materialized out of nowhere in the university library. In that lifetime ago, Stephen had been a fourth year undergraduate student in philosophy. He had intellect, drive, and the monk-like dedication of the fanatical—in other words, all the necessary ingredients for a brilliant academic career. Yet he was missing the most essential one: money. A hard-earned scholarship had gotten him this far, but it wouldn't get him through the long years of graduate school.

His father, of course, couldn't offer any help even if he'd wanted to. "Fine work sittin' on your duff all night with them books while your poor old dad is out scraping to put the food in front of your face," he'd say; or, "Try puttin' in a real day's work and you'll see how far all them fancy words will get you." And lest Stephen should ever forget his favorite: "Your mother, God rest her soul, always did say you were somethin' special. Let's both hope for her sake *and* mine you prove her right."

Stephen had more than proven her right, even if his father had been too ignorant to see it. He'd graduated first in his class at the private school his father, honoring a last promise to his dying wife, had slaved away to pay for. Now he was ready to graduate from an Ivy League school, his place in its doctoral program already secured. But scholarships weren't as plentiful for graduate students. If he couldn't find funding to continue his studies, his degree wouldn't be worth the piece of paper it was printed on.

As graduation day loomed nearer, Stephen spent more and more time sequestered in the most deserted corners of the library he could find. That day he'd chosen the Rare Map Archives. The stillness was broken only by the steam that occasionally hammered the radiator back to life, so the intrusion of the nasal, high-pitched lisp was all the more startling.

"A ssss-splendid day for working the brain, no?"

Stephen looked up at an odd little man carrying a black bowler hat and a cane with a handle in the shape of a cat's head. The overhead lights illuminated the man's scrupulously bald head in an unforgiving phosphorescent glow. He made himself comfortable in the chair across from Stephen as if settling in for some time.

Stephen ignored his question with a tight-lipped smile. He didn't enjoy making small talk with strangers on a good day, and this was not a good day.

The man's eyes were layered in wrinkles that scrunched up when he smiled like crumpled pieces of paper. Drawing the word out so that it produced an unsettling sing-song effect, he said, "You are a student of philos-o-*phee*, I see."

He gestured toward the book Stephen was reading, a dense volume about the role of animal consciousness in higher order thought processes. "Ah, fiddling with riddles! My favorite way to pass the time."

"I'd hardly call some of the most complex issues of philosophical enquiry 'fiddling with riddles'." Stephen closed the book and stood up to leave. He had far better things to do with his time than waste it on some half-wit whose idea of philosophical contemplation was which shoe to put on first in the morning.

"As you say—if I may?" The little man extended his hand toward the book.

Stephen wanted nothing more than to get rid of this irritating creature with his crooked clown smile and bizarre penchant for speaking in rhymes, but he never could resist the temptation to show a fool his foolishness. He handed over the book without bothering to contain a smirk. "Be my guest."

The little man scanned through the pages, stopping occasionally to study a passage and utter, "Indeed, I see!" or, "Just so, just so!" or some other such inanity. Stephen kept quiet, smirk firmly in place, until the half-witted fool proceeded not only to dismantle the book's entire philosophical premise, but to propose an astonishingly clear and original counter-thesis of his own.

Stephen picked his no-longer-smirking jaw up off the floor and sat back down. "I'm Stephen Berg," he said, extending his hand. "I assume you've come to teach a course at the university?"

The little man frowned down at Stephen's hand without offering his own in return. "I am not a scholar like yourself," he said, the half-smile returning when Stephen's hand departed. "Just a seeker of knowledge however it comes, and so, you see, thus master of none!"

"Well, you seem to be a master by my standards. Then again, in a few more months that assessment may not be worth all that much."

"Oh, no, why so?"

And then Stephen, who as a rule didn't even discuss the weather with strangers, proceeded to tell this man he'd just met the story of his soon to be short-circuited academic career.

When he finished, the little man let him sit in gloomy silence a while before saying, "And yet, I'll bet, there's more to life than *know*-ledge, no?"

Youth's arrogance answered for him. "In a world full of empty illusions, nothing matters except knowledge."

The half-smile collapsed into a thin line and then reasserted itself. The little man leaned closer, and Stephen caught a whiff of something sharp-edged and cool hiding beneath the sickly sweet surface. A memory came back to him of the pink wintergreen candies his grandmother always kept stowed in her purse. No matter how many he ate, the sugar never failed to seduce his senses into forgetting the menthol kick to come.

"The real-deal question is: are you willing to sacrifice everything—everything!—for *knowledge?*"

"Y-yes—" The word stuck in Stephen's throat before he cleared it of any doubt. "*Yes.*"

"*Ev—ery—thing?*"

"Yes!"

"Ah ha! I see. Then so it shall be!" The little man donned his hat, tipped it in Stephen's direction, and without another word vanished just as suddenly as he'd come.

Disoriented by the strange encounter, Stephen trudged back to his cold, equally dispirited room. He stopped in the lobby to check his usually empty mailbox. Today, though, it contained one long white envelope with no return address. He tore it open and then, as if this strangest of days couldn't get any stranger, there it was: a letter informing him that he'd been awarded a graduate scholarship he couldn't even remember applying for. Apparently, the scholarship was funded by anonymous donations to a private organization unaffiliated with any university.

Stephen stood in the lobby holding the letter. He was certain he'd never applied for a scholarship he hadn't known existed from an organization he'd never heard of. The money from the scholarship would be enough to get him through graduate school—just barely, but enough. And yet where had it come from? Stephen suddenly recalled the strange little man with the cat's head cane. A faint odor of sickly sweet-sharp wintergreen candy floated through the stale lobby air.

Stephen shook himself back to reality with the reminder that he'd just gotten what he wanted more than anything else in the world—he could finish graduate school and become the scholar he had always known he could be. What difference did it make how he got there?

Just then a sing-song voice seemed to whisper in his ear. "Are you willing to sacrifice everything—*ev—ery—thing*—for knowledge?"

"Yes!" Stephen shouted, but only the empty echo of the lobby answered back.

The Philosopher's Way

IT WASN'T EASY EVEN with the scholarship money. Stephen took a job serving food in the university cafeteria just to keep the electricity turned on and the fridge somewhat filled. Every time he flopped a lump of mashed potatoes or Swiss steak onto the plate of some empty-headed fool bragging about how many beers he'd slammed at the last frat party, or how *everyone* plagiarizes essays these days, or how unfair it was to have to read an entire *chapter* a week, he fought down the black bile of bitterness. Time, he knew, was on his side.

Unlike his peers, Stephen wasted none of that time socializing. On weekends, when the bars and clubs surrounding the university spilled crowds of young revelers into the streets, he stayed home and studied. His only trips were to philosophy conferences. When his father died a month before his comprehensive exams, it was a great sacrifice to fly home and arrange the funeral.

By the time he graduated, Stephen was fluent in five languages, including Latin and Ancient Greek. He had published four major articles in top scholarly journals and had a publishing offer to expand his dissertation into a book. Offers were already rolling in for fast-track tenure positions at some of the best universities in the country; all of which made it even more inexplicable when Stephen turned them all down.

"A *high school?*" his advisor had raged. "You're set to become one of the top scholars in the field and you're throwing it away on a *high school?*"

"One of the most rigorous private boys' high schools in New York City, if not the country," Stephen corrected, but of course it was no use. His advisor never spoke to him again, and Stephen didn't really blame him. If it had been his student, he'd have felt the same way.

What his advisor didn't know, however, was that Stephen had no interest in fine-tuning young adult minds already cementing into their own trivial opinions, self-serving biases, and pedestrian world views. No, what he wanted was to get hold of minds right at that elusive, still flexible moment between the fluidity of childhood and the certainty of adulthood. He wanted the clay most pliable beneath the master's hands.

On the first day of class Stephen drew a line high up on the chalkboard. "This," he told his students, "is Plato, Aristotle, Socrates, St Thomas Aquinas."

He then drew another line in the middle of the board. "This is Descartes, Hegel, Rousseau, Kant."

Next he held up the piece of chalk, threw it down to the hard marble floor, and ground it into bits beneath the heel of his boot. "And this, gentlemen," he finished with a sardonic smile, "is you."

He made lists for his students to memorize: The 50 Greatest Pieces of Literature (or Works of Art, Philosophical Arguments, or any other subject that he felt formed the essential elements of life). In the classroom, he could rupture a student's ego with one dismissive wave of the hand or slash of his notoriously bloody red correction pen. He quickly became known as the school's most difficult, demanding teacher, and so naturally, he was either despised or adored by students and colleagues alike. Indeed, it was difficult to tell which group was more intimidated by his eccentric, chilly charisma and formidable intellect.

His hair had started receding as far back as his twenties, so he shaved it down to a gleaming dome. He had seven exact copies of a custom-made black suit which he wore every day with a waistcoat, fob watch, and black silk bowtie. One day he passed an old-style haberdashery shop that drew him back to its rows of hats, cravat-clad mannequins, and especially, canes. On impulse he ordered an ebony model with a handle in the shape of a black cat's head.

Stephen had never forgotten the odd little man who by now he thought of as 'Stilts'. Sometimes, though, he convinced himself that he had imagined or invented the entire encounter. As for the money that had allowed him to finish his studies, maybe he *had* applied for some obscure scholarship and simply forgotten about it. Only in the raw, unflinching hours when sleep would not come did Stephen allow the truth to creep in. But what was the truth, anyway? That some eccentric had provided financial assistance to a promising young scholar? There was nothing suspect or remarkable in that, and yet the formless worry gnawing at the edges of his consciousness persisted. After all, Rumpelstiltskin had eventually demanded a very high price for *his* gold.

"One must be willing to sacrifice *everything*," Stephen would remind himself in the still, whispering hours before dawn. And he had already made that promise long ago.

At school he inspired a group of students the other boys called 'Bergites' in honor of their intellectual and corporeal inspiration. Dressed in black jackets and bowties, they kept themselves apart from the other boys, heads bent together in discussion over a book of poetry or philosophical argument. A few of them even shaved those deep-thinking heads. Among this group, Stephen singled out a select few for special attention—not just those with intellectual promise, but those who were just a little lost, who couldn't quite crack the code of the mundane, mindless world around them. Stephen kept an eye out for the ones who were looking for something more.

"Are you prepared to sacrifice *everything* for knowledge?" he would ask. If a boy hesitated or said, "Maybe," or, "I'm not sure," he would say, "You are apparently not the person I thought you were," before striking the misguided soul off of his list.

"You must cut away all unworthy influences," he often reminded his students. "Television, girlfriends, rock and roll music. If you surround yourself with garbage, you will eventually become a part of the garbage."

Like other teachers, Stephen took his students on field trips and engaged in extracurricular activities. Unlike other teachers, he would also invite his favorites over to his apartment for more 'individual instruction'. If there were occasional whispers of 'inappropriate contact' or concerns about Mr Berg's 'excessive control' over some of his students, his impeccable credentials quickly silenced them.

The Philosopher's Way

"We're lucky to have him," some smiling principal would always reassure an anxious parent. "Quite a genius, really, and sometimes genius makes its own rules, you know."

Stephen paid no attention to his critics. These little smart-ass rich kids had been born with a guaranteed ticket in their hands to some of the most powerful, privileged positions in the world. It was his job to teach them that there were bigger, better places that even their tickets couldn't take them unless they were willing to sacrifice *everything* to get there.

Looking back, he couldn't quite put his finger on when things began to change. All of a sudden there were fresh-faced administrators visiting his classroom, burdening him with mindless review processes and tedious new protocols. The younger teachers used terms like 'cooperative learning' and 'student-based instruction' as if they were in a playgroup instead of a classroom. Those same teachers no longer wished to be called by the long-standing address 'Sir', preferring 'Mister' or even, in some horrifying cases, first names. A steady trickle of them weren't Sirs at all; the first women appeared in front of the classroom and then multiplied throughout the school when it finally went fully co-ed.

Stephen might have endured these erosions of the old order if it hadn't been for Jeremy Denk. A shy, nervous boy with a penchant for Greek poetry, he'd been one of the hopeful Bergites eventually exiled from Stephen's inner circle. Two years after graduation, he'd jumped to his death off the Manhattan Bridge. In a suicide note to his family, he'd explained that life was no longer worth living for those who had 'lost the philosopher's way'. Of course no one could directly link Stephen to his death—the boy had always been a delusional fool, a mediocre middling striving for greatness! Even so, Stephen was neither surprised nor particularly disappointed when the principal called him in for a meeting one day to discuss certain 'complaints and concerns' with regard to his teaching.

He retired early without protest. Through the years, his apartment had become a gathering place for former students who remained devoted to him after graduation. One day a group of them informed him that they had combined their resources to buy him a restored Victorian cottage an hour or so upstate. Members of this group of supporters often used the cottage for extended visits, so Stephen's life continued much the same as it always had, surrounded by his books and acolytes.

Eventually, though, they drifted away. One would get married and start having children; another would move across the country or begin putting in more time at work. Stephen often found himself alone in his study with an increasingly refilled snifter of brandy. With the grandfather clock seeming to tick down the very moments of his life, the doubts began to creep in between the chiming intervals. Of all the students through all of those years, how many had slipped into mediocrity and commonplace pursuits? How many had forsaken art and literature and philosophy for the hollow, straw-man promise of money and status? And what of the Jeremy Denks? And yet he *had* succeeded with most of them! Among his former students were some of the leading scholars and innovators in their fields, and more than a few had written to tell him that *he* had been one of their biggest influences! Why, just look at Darrel Gaines! The most loyal of Stephen's former students, Darrel had become one of the world's foremost art appraisers; just last year he had discovered and authenticated a lost Rembrandt that sold for over a hundred million dollars at auction.

And yet the doubts continued to tick away as steady as the grandfather clock.

One evening a *tap-tap-tapping* and the faint smell of wintergreen candy drifted into the study from the hallway. When the unmistakable cat's head cane and black bowler hat appeared in the doorway, Stephen didn't bother to ask how Stilts had gotten into the locked house. He didn't bother to wonder why, despite the decades that had turned Stephen into a wrinkled, gray old man, Stilts looked exactly the same. Stephen had known even in that long-ago library that this was no ordinary man. And he hadn't reappeared now for any ordinary purpose.

"I've been wondering when you would show up to collect the interest on your loan," Stephen said.

Stilts removed the bowler hat from his gleaming bald head and held the hat out in front of him in an elaborate bow. "No need to repay the philosopher's way."

Stephen started at the words—Jeremy Denk's words—

Stilts tap-tapped his way over to the books lining the far wall of the study. "Lifetimes and ages within these pages, no?"

Maybe Stephen's third glass of brandy answered for him, or maybe the doubts finally wished to speak for themselves. "And yet in the end what does any of it matter?"

Stilts closed his eyes as if recalling some long-ago words. "In a world full of empty illusions, nothing matters except knowledge."

Stephen failed to recognize his own youthful claim. "Yes, but it would be nice to know that it all meant something more than just… *this*," he said, gesturing vaguely around the study.

"What more to be—what more to mean?" Stilts asked.

"Oh, I don't know. Maybe for some of that hard-won knowledge to survive after I'm through with it. Or after it's through with me, as the case may be."

"Ah, I see, and do agree!" Stilts said, clapping his hands. "Not just to teach, but something with a deeper reach." He pointed his finger at his head and then pointed it at Stephen's, firing his hand as if it were a gun. Turning back to the books, he ran one silk-gloved finger along their spines. "A fair trade for the philosopher's way—to add one's own to the lofty tomes."

He whirled around to face Stephen, the crooked smile widening into something even more unsettling. "And so you should, and so you shall! Write down every last insight and intent; write down a lifetime of wisdom and all it has meant! Write and write to the very last page, the very last line—and then you shall die!"

Stephen suddenly felt a brush of red heat, as if he'd edged too close to a blazing fire. "I'm sorry, I don't understand."

"It is as I said, but I'll say it again. Compose your magnum opus, your life's masterpiece! And once you have finished, that life will cease."

274

The image of the fairy tale imp danced to life in Stephen's mind, only he wasn't spinning sheaves of gold but writing in page after page of an enormous book. "You'll forgive me if I say that doesn't sound like much of a bargain," Stephen whispered beneath ash-dry lips.

"Oh, you see, *you* will die, but the book shall live! And one will have all you have given it!"

Stephen put his hands against the side of his head and pressed as hard as he could. "I'm sorry, I still don't understand."

Stilts tapped his foot and scowled as if dealing with a particularly dull-witted child. "Put into one book all you have learned and bequeath it to the one who most deserves. When this lucky scholar reads the words, he will then own all that was yours—not simply the *words* written there, but the lifetime behind them, transferred to your heir!"

Stephen remembered a conversation he had once overheard between the ever-loyal Darrel and another of his less enthusiastic supporters, a young man who had eventually broken off all ties with the group. "You need to start thinking for yourself in this world," the young man had said. "I mean, how will you ever deal with life after he dies?"

"That's easy," Darrel had answered. "I'll just ask myself, 'What would Stephen do?'"

Now, if he hadn't lost his mind entirely and Stilts and his promise were real—and what evidence was there to doubt it? —Darrel would never have to ask himself that question. He would know *exactly* what Stephen would do and think and believe; he would have a lifetime of experience and insight and knowledge as if it had been uploaded straight out of Stephen's brain and into his. The masterpiece book would be like a sacred talisman in defiance of death itself...

Stilts's lilting sing-song broke into his thoughts. "Say the word and it shall be so—that is what you wanted, no?"

"Yes—"

"Then so it shall be, cross my heart and hope to die—but remember the *one* condition that must apply!"

Rumpelstiltskin, Rumpelstiltskin! an ancient child's voice suddenly sounded in Stephen's ear. "When I finish writing the book, I die."

Stilts jumped up and clapped his hands. Then as if out of some long-delayed nightmare, he began to dance around—first a little hip-hop from one foot to the other, then a sprightly little jig around the room with his cane tap-tap-tapping out an accompaniment.

"Stop!" Stephen shouted. The light in the room seemed painfully bright, the air stiflingly hot.

Stilts froze in place like a child playing a game of tag. Then he straightened up, tipped his black bowler hat in Stephen's direction, and was gone as suddenly as he'd arrived.

FROM THEN ON STEPHEN rarely left the cottage. He had known without asking that his masterpiece had to be produced in the old way, by hand. A former student who ran a publishing house arranged a one-of-a-kind, leather bound portfolio for him, so thick and wide that Stephen needed both hands to lift it. Day after day and night after night he sat filling page after page with an encyclopedic volume of literary, artistic, and philosophical references interwoven with his thoughts, theories, insights, experiences—everything he could manage to cram in with handwriting so small it left his hands aching with cramps. By the end of the evening he was often exhausted, but luckily Darrel was there to help.

Despite the protests of his family, Darrel had moved into the cottage permanently. He cooked all of the meals, massaged Stephen's arthritic hands, and kept him company whenever Stephen's eyes grew too tired to write. Sometimes Darrel asked about the 'project' that occupied so much of his mentor's time and attention, and Stephen had often been keenly tempted to share his extraordinary secret. In the end, though, he kept it to himself, saying only that he was working on his 'masterpiece', his 'lifetime's inheritance' to Darrel, his one true disciple. How Stephen relished the idea of Darrel, grief-stricken and inconsolable after his death, discovering the book and its lifetime of treasures—it would almost be like coming back from the grave, immortally preserved within its pages! What amount of sacrifice was too great for that?

THE CLOCK BONGED Stephen back to the present, and he was astonished when it struck ten times. Where had the time gone?

There must be no further delay—the time was now. He bent over the page, finished the last line, and closed the book.

Now that it was done, the old finger of doubt searched out the tender places in Stephen's belief. Maybe he had been a fool to believe in Stilts's magic; maybe 'the pact' was nothing more than the fanciful hopes of an old man gazing into the dwindling flame of his own extinction.

"Alright, I've done my part," Stephen shouted to the empty room. "Now where are you, you old trickster?"

Right on cue, Stilts ducked his bald head into the room as if he'd been waiting in the hallway all along. Stephen wouldn't have been surprised to learn that he had. Stilts twirled the cat cane like a baton, rapped it against the floor three times, and performed an elaborate bow. "At your service!"

"Actually, it's your service I've been waiting for. I've finished; I'm ready." As soon as the words left his mouth, a painful spasm wracked his chest. He forced himself not to cry out in pain.

Stilts picked up the book and began leafing gingerly through the pages. His grin was so widely stretched it looked like a reflection in a funhouse mirror. "Yes, indeed—the masterpiece. Shall I hold it up for you to see? One last look, before you leave?"

The pain tore loose and ran a paralyzing pathway down Stephen's left arm. Stilts held the book up and turned through the pages like a magician exhibiting a trick. For his part, Stephen was as astonished as any magic show audience.

"You cheated me!" he gasped.

Stilts collapsed his face into the exaggerated pantomime of a scolded child. He stamped his foot and banged the cane. "I never cheat a game that can't be won; I never steal a thing that can't be owned!"

Stephen fell to his knees and clutched his chest. Stilts knelt beside him and gazed at him as if he were a curious specimen in a zoo. He tilted his head as if considering some matter of tremendous importance, then said, "The real-deal question is: are you willing to sacrifice everything—everything!—for *knowledge*?"

DARREL GAINES WANDERED in and out of each room of the cottage, remembering. It had been exactly one year since his beloved mentor had died, and he supposed things had gotten easier; as easy as they were ever going to get, that is. He paused in the doorway of the last, most important room—the study, the place where the late, great Stephen Berg had spent so many hours of so many days and years. All gone now, and Stephen gone with them.

He crossed the room and sat down at the antique desk where he once again considered the book that had meant so much to the man who had meant so much to him—his 'inheritance', as Stephen had called it, his masterpiece. Darrel would sit with that masterpiece for many of his own hours and days and years yet to come; sometimes he thought he understood, that the book's meaning was right within his grasp;

other times he only understood that he'd never really understand why his mentor had devoted so much time and attached so much importance to an enormous volume filled with page after page of entirely blank, empty space.

DREAMING A DREAM TO PRIZE

MARK FORSHAW

A BOVE THE TOWN THE bare hills rise like vast *memento mori*: *Remember,* they seem to say, *we were here long before you came to this place, and we will be here long after your bodies burn up, or burst open in the ground, long after your buildings have turned to rubble.*

Death is in the faces of an ageing population. Many young people leave. Those that stay find their flesh runs to fat or melts off their bones. No one is a healthy shape or weight. At night the streets are empty, so are the pubs. By day the people I see are mostly old. They lack mobility, their gaits are distorted by an assortment of pains. They cough a great deal and expectorate without inhibition or shame. Their faces are grey, the skin papery. It is impossible to imagine anyone I see biting with relish into an apple.

I grew up here and left, and went far away, as soon as I was able. Now I'm back.

MUCH HAS HAPPENED since I wrote the vignette above, late one night in the house.

It started with a video, a short film I found late one night posted on YouTube.

In those days we didn't have digital cameras, mobile phones. If I want to catch a sight of my younger self then I find him in snatches of music, fragments of video made for mass consumption in the 1980s. The few family snapshots that survive, the fewer still that feature me, I find wholly unconvincing.

Putting the name of my high school into YouTube, then, was not meant to yield such startling results. I merely wanted a glimpse of the grim old place after years of being away. I was drinking; earlier in the evening I'd been listening to Hüsker Dü. Perhaps these are reasons why, on what was a warm and fragrant night in Santa Monica, I started to think about damp green English playing fields and the corridors and classrooms of distant beige buildings. But I expected to see them, if at all, entirely through a younger generation's eyes.

To my mild surprise—this was before YouTube had become quite so vastly comprehensive—there were a handful of videos posted by pupils and alumni of my former school. The results were mixed in with videos posted by kids from schools with similar names. I was scrolling through the pages, already losing interest, when I saw a muted image, a still of a girl tinted in pastel shades, and it filled me with a feeling for which there is no simple name. I remember I made some kind of noise, a noise that should've been soft but seemed to sound loudly in the quiet of my rooms. A moment of paralysis followed when I couldn't click the image. But then I saw the name of the person who had uploaded the film and my mind regained some perspective. I'd known this individual once, though he had never been a friend, and I remembered that occasionally he'd brought a camcorder into school. In fact, I'd seen him on television not many months earlier. He'd become—a rare success for a fellow former pupil—a professor of film at King's College London and I'd recognised him in a documentary on Antonioni, though he was much changed from his youthful incarnation.

I tapped my mouse and, tinged with pale purple, Anna Wray tilted her head and smiled, reluctantly, slantwise. Stephen Miller, the professor to be, panned the camera away from her and a line of my friends came into shot. In the 1980s I used to watch American films and lament inwardly that the kids at my school didn't look like the kids in bratty teen movies. Now it seemed the differences were non-existent. I saw that we *had* been living in the 1980s all along, and that I'd wasted them wishing I lived in an elsewhere that was more intense. It was hardly coincidental, I thought, that I was experiencing my present pangs sat in a big house in California.

And yet, about Anna, my girlfriend back then, the only girl I was interested in, there was nothing of the Molly Ringwald. She stood apart, and even more so now, on this video, as classically English. If she resembled anyone from the 1980s then it was perhaps Sarah Patterson, uncanny and utterly forbidden in *The*

Company of Wolves. Anna was several years older, of course, than red-cloaked Rosaleen. Now, with the passing of many years, all I could see was how young she was—how young they all were, all of my friends. Starkly so.

They capered for the camera, as people do, or did, when there was no real point to their being filmed. As ever, Anna distinctly kept her distance, an essential but mysterious presence, too beautiful to be a loner, too aloof to belong. It seemed to me that the camera kept returning to her, almost as a point of reference: *look, here is troubling beauty*—the camera sweeps from her face—*and here are the seductions of the banal*. Already, the future professor of film possessed a keen eye.

The video was short, just a couple of minutes long. I watched it again and again. For me it was an artefact of infinite melancholy. Anna, my friends, an English autumn day in the 1980s, and, glimpsed in the far background, the sombre hills. Despite its brevity, its grainy quality, its strange tints, the video helped me to remember many things. Chief among these was the curious paradox of Anna's features. Her white face, framed by dark hair, seemed at first glance to glow in its lucidity. Her eyes, when they rested on you, were wide and clear. Yet who could tell what Anna was thinking? No one that I ever met. I remembered a number of schoolyard comments to this effect, and many such comments a few years later. Always Anna was suspected of secrets, of profundity. Her face exhibited unhidden depths.

Over the following days and weeks and months I returned to the video many times. Eventually a handful of comments were posted, none of them by me. The top comment was short and sickly: 'Anna Wray. Forever beautiful! R.I.P.'

Steadily I began to divest myself of responsibilities, disregarding all protests, and to simplify, to the degree that it was feasible, my financial affairs. I contacted a solicitor in the UK and asked her to approach the current owners of Anna's former family home. They proved to be practical, unsentimental types and a persuasive price, with certain stipulations, was swiftly agreed. Within a few months, I had acquired the house.

The final night at my place on Alta I took a walk along Ocean Avenue and down to the beach. A voice in my head said: *Why isn't there a voice in your head saying: What the devil are you doing?* Only the waves of the Pacific answered. The next day I took a plane to Heathrow.

On the plane to London, in the hotel, and then later on the train to the north, I read a big book by that supremely American novelist, Thomas Wolfe. Anna had always thought I would become a professor of English. But then Anna had no gift for deciphering destinies. *You Can't Go Home Again.* You can't go home again. Why shouldn't a self-aware person also be haunted? Not every phantom signifies the return of the repressed. Later, quite deliberately, I read some Edgar Allan Poe.

In Manchester I met the solicitor and collected the keys. Then I took a black cab twenty-five miles north and saw, surrounded by darkening hills, the town for the first time in eighteen years. I'd been prepared for a deterioration, but what I found was sheer civic abasement. If an actual miasmic haze had hung over the place I doubt it could have looked any more mournful. The cab slowed dramatically as we passed through the centre, the driver perhaps sharing my disbelief. I thought of educated friends in California who had visited London, Oxford, the Cotswolds. They had no idea that places like this existed in England.

Striking, then, to find so impressive an edifice (indeed a series of such edifices) on the outskirts of town. Anna's family hadn't been wealthy, at least not according to my adult understanding of the word. A timely inheritance had boosted her parents' purchasing power and, of course, in the late 1970s housing costs in England weren't what they are today. Mr and Mrs Wray had found themselves a rundown villa, four bedrooms, built of grey stone, set in spacious grounds with oak and ash. They'd renovated it and lived in it with Anna and her sister until a few months after Anna's death.

With the cab receding down the driveway and my bags at my feet, I stood before the house. *My* house. Ivy ran rampant around the heavy front door, up the walls and even over the chimney stacks. The large bay windows of the lower floor revealed little of the dim interior through their leaded panes. About me was a melancholy English quiet. I approached the door and let myself inside.

The electricity was connected, but I spent a farcical forty minutes locating the internal stop tap. Only when I had successfully brought the house to some semblance of life, with lights on and the central heating running, did I ascend the stairs and enter the room which had once been Anna's. This had been her retreat, the room in which we had spent so much time together. Later, it was the room in which she had died.

It was utterly bare, as was the whole house. I had issued strict instructions that the vacating vendors should remove every last trace of themselves before handing over the keys.

In London, in Muswell Hill, I had visited a storage unit that I'd held there for many years. From it I'd retrieved a number of items relating to my pre-American life. They were a startling mixture of the familiar and the entirely forgotten. Now I sat cross-legged on the stripped floorboards of the silent room and took from my bag a photograph of Anna sitting in exactly the same spot more than two decades earlier. I suppose I stared at it for several minutes, hunting out every detail, not of Anna's face, but of the furnishings in the room. At last, a little stiffly, I rose and went to lie down in the corner of the room. From my bag I took another picture of Anna, taken on the same day, lying on her bed. I repeated my procedure, and then repeated it again, four times in four further parts of the room. When I was finished I went downstairs, searched through the takeaway menus that had piled up behind the front door, and ordered some particularly spicy Indian food.

THE HOUSE HAD THREE large reception rooms. These I ignored. Instead, I established my simple base of operations in the kitchen. A big table, a comfy chair, my MacBook Pro— these were all I needed on the lower floor of the house.

Slowly, upstairs, Anna's room took shape. I worked from photographs mainly, also from letters and fragmentary diaries of the period—all of these retrieved from storage in London. I worked, too, from memory, disciplining myself to hold my mind in the past for longer and longer, to scrutinise scenes and to rotate various tableaux. I bought a divan bed and placed it exactly where Anna's had been. I located a company that made bespoke bedding in an 80s style and ordered several sets, buying curtains from the same people. Almost immediately, I'd begun to think about music. I remembered certain sections of Anna's record collection very well, and found helpful references to its obscurer niches in material I'd written at the time. Online, I tracked down what I believed was exactly the right Pioneer mini hi-fi, fully serviced, including all new belts, and had it shipped overnight from Norfolk. It worked perfectly. By this time I'd also ordered paint, rollers and brushes. During the day, I decorated; at night I roamed the web snapping up original pressings of Anna's favourite albums. I found this to be a supremely relaxing activity and determined to take my time, setting higher and higher standards for condition. When the painting was done I began trawling the web for items of furniture that seemed to match what I saw in the photographs. I discovered that it was only when they arrived that I could judge if they were truly right, especially in their proportions. I began to buy multiple versions of each piece and store the unused ones in the empty rooms. Meanwhile, in the evenings, I continued to win vintage vinyl auctions.

What had seemed a simple enough task revealed itself steadily to be exhausting, not least because—as I should have realised from the start—it was *exhaustive*: the resurrection from memory, and scant notes, of a dead person's living space. When I finally settled on a wardrobe for Anna's room it occurred to me that it needed to be filled with clothes. So it was back to the photographs, back to meditation and memory, and back onto eBay, to do the best I could to reconstruct yet another part of Anna's outward life.

It's true that I was obsessed, but not helplessly so. I was acting from conscious, not unconscious, motives. I knew what it was I was doing.

As the room moved closer to completion I allowed myself more extended physical and mental breaks from my work. I bought myself a car. I bought myself boots and a decent warm, waterproof coat and began to take long walks out on the West Pennine Moors, often in gales and heavy autumn downpours. I discovered, wholly for myself, the music of Richard Skelton and listened to nothing else as I strode through the hills.

Out one afternoon, under a vast, fast-changing sky of various greys, I had an encounter, a conversation, which I will not record verbatim, but which I will describe. I was stood amid the stone ruins of an eighteenth-century farmstead, looking over the dull, corrugated waters of a large reservoir, when I saw I was being hailed by an approaching figure. He reached me, and as I removed my earphones, he extended his hand. We shook, and as we did so I recognised him, just about—a contemporary at school—and spoke his name. He smiled still more broadly and grasped my shoulder and professed his delight, and we left the ruins and began to walk together in the direction of the moor top road.

As we went, I stole several sidelong glances at my companion. He was, inevitably, already sharing with me the vicissitudes of an unadventurous grown-up life, gesturing expansively to indicate small changes. His misfortunes were minor, yet he had aged badly and my initial irritation at meeting him turned to disquiet at his physical downturn. I waited for my moment, wondering all the while about how Anna might have matured had she lived. At last, I managed to interject and expressed surprise that he'd recognised me at a distance after so many years.

Oh, you needn't be surprised, he replied, you've hardly changed a bit, still boyish even—must be all that healthy living over in LA.

Nevertheless, I pressed, I remained a little taken aback. I hadn't stepped foot in the north for more than a decade and a half. Wasn't it was something of an improbable meeting between he and I?

Oh, but I knew you were back, he said.

I made it plain that I was startled by this.

Yes, a few of us are still in regular touch, what with Facebook and everything. You've been seen, down at the gates of Anna's old place, taking deliveries day after day. News like that gets around, eventually, I'm afraid.

His eyes were still friendly, if unabashedly enquiring. I felt, however, not the faintest flush of shame or embarrassment, nor any desire to confide in my former friend, and fended off his questions with ease.

Dreaming a Dream to Prize

IT OCCURRED TO ME that, although I was slender, and indeed had lost a few pounds since entering the house, I was still too heavy. And so I began to restrict my diet and to fast intermittently. I wanted to get back to the weight I'd been at around eighteen.

For the room was now prepared, more or less. I'd acquired the correct lamp, rug, posters, books. I'd sought out copies of long discontinued music magazines and was immensely gratified to discover that I remembered individual sentences from articles I must have read twenty years ago lying on her bed. I'd set up a Phillips VCR and obtained VHS copies of certain films, everything I recollected that Anna loved, from the early work of Savage Steve Holland to *The Exterminating Angel* of Luis Buñuel.

The wardrobe and chests of drawers were filled with clothes; the floor was home to various pairs of trainers, boots and shoes. On eBay I'd acquired a vintage bottle of the Coty perfume that Anna received as a Christmas gift in 1989, though I recalled she wore it only rarely; sadly, its degraded scent prompted no sudden rush of memories.

I had long exhausted the photographs as a source of information about Anna's room and Anna's possessions. During extended periods of concentrated recollection particular objects suggested themselves, and when this happened I sought them out online. One night, in the grip of inspiration, I was heading downstairs to the kitchen to begin yet another of these searches. At the staircase window I happened to pause and glance out into the darkened grounds. Beneath the bare branches of an oak I saw, unmistakably, human movement, the recoil of someone who had been watching the house. Running down the remainder of the stairs, I opened the front door and darted barefoot into the night. Some distance ahead of me, through thinly falling snow, I saw a female figure, dressed in a winter coat, fleeing down the driveway. I didn't pursue the woman, but returned immediately to the house, more than a little unsettled by the intrusion.

For a while I paced in the kitchen, my feet growing colder and colder. I remember thinking I couldn't spare the few moments I needed to find some footwear to warm them up. Repeatedly I turned to the MacBook, each time intending to begin my search for that next burningly important item. Each time I turned away. It was, eventually, a presentiment of my success that sent me running back up the stairs and into the room. Somehow, I saw it with fresh eyes. For the first time the room convinced me of its accuracy. More than this, I felt enfolded by it. Anna's room was at last restored to life.

I'D BEEN SLEEPING ON a futon in an upstairs room that was otherwise more or less empty. Now, finally, I began to sleep in Anna's bed.

I slept a great deal. I was tired after the intensity of my endeavours, but I wanted also to put myself in a certain receptive state. Each night, each afternoon, before going to sleep, I incubated dreams of Anna. I had a photograph, a simple, very true portrait of her that I had taken twenty years earlier. It was housed in a silver frame that she'd given to me as a gift one birthday. This picture I'd wrapped in tissue paper and placed in storage when I left for America. For the first time since returning to England, I brought it out. Before sleep, I spent time looking at it. I never gazed at it to excess. Gradually, through sleep and dreams and memory, I reoriented my mind, away from the practicalities of resurrecting the room, away from my seemingly endless search for objects. From the moment I'd entered the house I had thought of Anna herself only obliquely. Throughout those months I'd never been trying to summon up the once-living person, merely her environment. Now everything changed.

My dreams were obedient, as I knew they would be. They came to me through the gates of burnished horn. Night after night, day after day, my dreams were only of Anna. I had dreamt of her before of course, over the years, but nothing like this. These dreams were radiant. She came to me as she was at seventeen and eighteen... as she was up until her death. For the first time in two decades I heard her voice, in my sleep, and when I woke I could remember how it sounded. In the dream room, where we met, she showed me possessions of hers I had forgotten to buy, and, as fast as I was able, I sought them out online. For now, in my waking hours, I rarely and only briefly visited the other parts of the house. I hated to do so. I lived in Anna's room. I belonged there. I slept there and I ate there, snacking at odd hours as we had once done together. I listened to her music. I watched her films. Over and over, I read certain of her letters to me aloud.

And I slept and slept. In sleep, I was truly young again, and Anna's living face was video vivid.

It was curious to do so little after doing so much my whole adult life. My weight was dropping, but so was my level of fitness. My heartbeat was erratic at times and my blood felt sluggish. I lay on the floor, I lay on the bed. I dozed, I dreamed, I lost myself in reverie and private rituals. I seemed to be forever peeling off and pulling on the same pair of black Levi 501s.

Late one afternoon, with the light already fading and darkness returning to the room, I heard, unmistakably, the sound of someone entering the house.

I was lying on the rug. The room was silent. The album I'd been listening to had finished playing some time ago. Mildly, I started. The front door had been pushed open. It was heavy and had always stuck a little. I heard noises, someone was moving about; there were footsteps—those, I thought, of a single individual—on tiled and wooden floors. This was no hypnagogia or lucid dream. There could be no doubt. A visitor was ascending the stairs.

I didn't move. I merely waited. Certain images, for me almost religious, played out in my mind, though they did so with no special intensity. The steps were slow, but not exactly stealthy. I tried to visualise the upper hallway. I suspected every door was hanging open but that of the room.

The unseen person had, presumably, reached the top of the stairs. There was a lengthy pause and then creaks on the landing. The creaking continued for some time, growing now closer, now more distant; when it stopped I thought I knew exactly where my guest was standing. I watched the door handle but it didn't turn.

Anna? I called at last from the floor, and for some reason I laughed as I said it.

On the other side of the door someone let out a breath, or perhaps it was a soft, short cry. There was a moment when nothing happened at all, and then the person moved away, rather clumsily it seemed, and retreated down the stairs. Eventually I rose from my spot and ventured out of the room. The intruder had left nothing of themselves behind, only the front door agape. I wandered around the house, checking that I was truly alone, and eventually pushed the door closed again.

In the kitchen I wrote and sent two emails, each to a different associate in London. Both of these men had done very well from their relationship with me and my businesses. What they owed me was far more than a favour or two. The emails contained explicit instructions and an injunction to refrain from asking questions. Within minutes both had replied to say that they understood.

Back upstairs, I clipped my finger and toe nails, shaved, and choppily cut my hair. Then I took a long hot bath and, after getting dry, rubbed myself with a quantity of sweet almond oil. I was feeling good.

From a bag in my former bedroom I took out a brand new pair of 501s and an appropriate t-shirt. I dressed and went downstairs. I ate a fruit salad and drank a glass of wine.

With every food order I'd placed since arriving at the house I had included two bottles of my favourite single malt. These bottles were standing, untouched, in a utility room just beyond the kitchen. Now I brought them through and poured the contents down the sink, littering the worktops and table with the empties. One bottle I threw into a corner where it smashed to bits on the tiles. Taking the last remaining unopened bottle and a package, recently delivered, from Swann Morton, I returned to Anna's room.

Inside the room, I flung open the windows to admit fresh air and changed the bedding from one retro set to another. Invigorated, I stretched and performed push ups and sit ups, listening all the while to *Fire of Love*. With the windows closed once more, I lit candles, a mixture of tealights and pillars and votives. The room was ready—and so was I.

Sitting cross-legged on the bed, I opened the whisky and took a mouthful. Then I unwrapped my package and, using tweezers, connected blade to handle. Chugging intermittently on the bottle of Scotch, I read aloud, for the first time, the most intense letter that Anna ever wrote me. Finally, I took up her photograph and spoke to it some words that will remain wholly private, even from the eyes of the self that now taps this out on his Mac.

More whisky and it was time—the clock on the cabinet said so. I brought my left leg out of the Levis and made a deep incision. Then I lay back on the bed.

Everything in the house was quiet. Blood was seeping into the fabrics of the bed. I did my best to control my breathing and remain calm. One breath, then another, trying not to think about the beating of my heart. I waited. I waited. I was feeling exceptionally strange.

Finally, I heard a slamming sound and the room seemed to shift out of focus. From the staircase there came an energetic thumping. The door opened, and into the room ran Anna, switching on the light. She looked hassled. Her hair was damp from a rain that was not falling. She yanked off her bag and flung her coat onto the floor. As in my dreams, and yet so much more so, Anna was clear and bright before me. The room, however—or, rather, the objects it contained—had grown ghostly and confusing, full of competing solidities, partial doublings. The effect was of a three-dimensional palimpsest. My reconstruction had not been perfect.

Anna went to the hi-fi and dropped the needle on the record, but it was *Dragnet* and not *Fire of Love* that came from the speakers. Hurriedly, she undressed and changed, pulling on black clothes that emerged from the twofold darkness of the wardrobe. This was Anna aged eighteen, going through one of her happier stages and determined not to show it. I remembered the period well.

At the chest of drawers, which also served as her dressing table, Anna bent to examine herself in the mirror. Amidst overlapping lines and the twin silvered surfaces I could see her steady pale reflection, her eyes wide and cryptic; of course, I, lying on the bed behind her, was not there for those eyes to perceive. Swiftly, Anna brushed her hair. From a basket, she picked up a pencil and touched up her eyeliner. Then, from a clip at the mirror's edge, she plucked a photo of herself. She gazed at it a moment and let it fall amidst the cosmetic clutter that I had failed to convincingly reproduce. Pausing, she regarded herself still. And then she said, *sotto voce*:

> He falls to such perusal of my face
> As he would draw it.

Turning, she scooped up her coat and bag. The needle came off the LP and she rushed out of the room, slapping the light switch as she left. As she pounded down the stairs I heard her shout: Mum, I'll be back later. I'm going to meet... She ended with my name. And then, at the banging of door, she was gone.

I HAVE THE HAZIEST recollection of being carried downstairs and later of a paramedic bending over me in the ambulance. When I awoke on the ward my leg was heavily bandaged and I was attached to a saline drip. I'd received a blood transfusion and my wound had been stitched.

Of course, it was necessary for me to be psychiatrically assessed. I blamed overwork, alcohol abuse and a belated release of grief over Anna's death. Most of all, I blamed the house and my foolish idea of buying it as an English getaway. I stated, truthfully enough, that the house would be going onto the market as soon as I was well. I promised to take a proper holiday and only then to ease back into the life of business. My actions—and with this, eventually, they had to agree—had been wholly out of character. I was, simply, drunk, and cut off from the place I now called home.

In London, walking with the aid of a stick, I called upon a very surprised Professor Stephen Miller at King's. We talked in his office and, several days later, lunched together. I explained to him about my love of Antonioni, Buñuel, Bergman and many others. I outlined my intention to donate a substantial sum to his institution to create a dedicated bursary fund for students who shared our love of film. I deplored, from an American perspective, the lack of cinematic knowledge among the young.

I ordered a second bottle of wine and the conversation turned to our personal circumstances. He was married, I was not. I did most of the talking. Eventually, I touched upon my past, certain portions of which he had glimpsed from afar when we were young. I mentioned Anna and the short film he had posted online. Amidst the tables of an emptying restaurant, I spoke of an enduring grief that was akin to a private cult. I fear I rather embarrassed myself.

The evening of the same day, the video of Anna and my friends was taken down from YouTube. Two days later, at my hotel, I received a small package of tapes and a short letter of reassurance regarding the fate of all digital copies. And with that I took out my Mac and booked my flight home, to California.

PROFESSOR DONALDSON'S SÉANCE

STEWART PRINGLE

D R KNOCK HAD BARELY stepped into the hallway when he suspected he'd made a mistake. By the time the maid entered, feeling her way from the dimly lit staircase with a bolt of black silk wrapped around her eyes, he was quite certain.

"Professor Donaldson is almost ready for you, sir. It is…?"

"Dr Knock."

"That's right, sir. If you could just wait here for a moment—"

She fumbled for his coat and hat, colliding with a Japanese vase which Dr Knock's companion hastily steadied, and cautiously exited into the gloom.

"Wonderful, isn't it?" George offered hopefully. "Real cloak and dagger stuff."

Professor Donaldson's Séance

Dr Knock pursed his lips. The scent of lavender and cheap incense. The hoodwinked maidservant. The low-burning lamps. The black serge tacked haphazardly over the windows. He'd seen this all before, in a dozen narrow town houses up and down Conduit Street. This dilettante humbug that peppered the affluent squares of Holborn and Chelsea.

"They found her selling matches outside the Aldwych." Knock's companion continued, "She's the very soul of discretion, and Alphonse believes that with the proper instruction she may even prove to be sensitive herself. They're hoping to bring her on, though of course the blindfold is absolutely essential until she's been properly inducted."

A glassy chime forestalled Knock's reply, and he turned to see an absurd spectre of a woman gliding down the hallway in a rustle of bombazine.

"Mr Peterson! I sensed it at once, didn't I Florence?" She clutched the maid's wrist in one chalky hand. "I did! And who is this with you... it must... it must be... the elusive Dr Knock! What a pleasure it is to have you among us!"

Bedecked in a confusion of pendants and lace, drifting in a cloud of pungent floral scents, Madame Caroline was a sallow woman, with cloudy eyes and a face framed by a halo of frizettes worked through with wisps of lilac ribbons.

"Madame!" George took her free hand and kissed one of the thick rings that squeezed round her fingers. "And how was your trip? I had been told not to expect you this evening."

"Harrogate? Never arrived! Never departed, dear boy. Florence had the most dreadful premonition regarding the two-thirty from King's Cross and so the entire outing was abandoned. Tolly instructed her that the correct course of action would be a weekend at the coast, and so we relocated our party to the Grand in Brighton, the better to take advantage of the electromagnetic properties of the salt-infused air."

Observing the ghost of a smile on the pretty, tanned features beneath her blindfold, Dr Knock made an instant reappraisal of the young maid's ingenuity. Madame Caroline tugged her wrist sharply and led the way up a wide staircase.

"I'm very glad, for my own sake," George burbled as he followed. "I cannot imagine we could expect the same success without you, and I'm anxious that the doctor should have something truly extraordinary to report."

A snort from Madame Caroline. "I fear you overestimate my continued usefulness to Donald. Window-dressing, my dear. Little more. We are moving beyond the age of the medium. We are looking to a future far beyond my powers."

"Impossible!" spluttered George.

"I will say no more, Mr Peterson. It is not my part to explain. All will become clear."

She stopped at the head of the staircase, and rotating awkwardly she addressed the group with a sudden gravity. "The things that have occurred in this house since you were last a guest... they are quite—" Her eyes were now quite sharp and sincere, and they fell solidly on the stern face of Dr Knock. "—improbable."

It was an unusual choice of word for a woman whose reputation amongst London society rested firmly on making the improbable palatable and the impossible practically fashionable. It would be an exaggeration to suggest that Dr

Professor Donaldson's Séance

Knock's interest was piqued, but it was with fractionally revitalised patience that he followed Madame Caroline, maid attached, and his friend and erstwhile colleague down a short corridor into the drawing room of Professor Donald Donaldson.

He saw the mirror first. Saw his own neatly moustachioed face above his collar and his one tenacious streak of hair plastered slickly over his crown. Then he noticed the smell, and recognised it at once. The sharp tang of oxidising metals as the acid slowly worked its way through their coils was the same smell that he had encountered in countless laboratories and lecture halls: it was the smell of a galvanic battery. Its presence in this dark panelled drawing room, with familiar long table and shaded gas lamps, was a surprise, and he saw George lift a handkerchief to his mouth, coughing slightly.

"What's the matter with him?" Madame Caroline asked nobody in particular. "Oh, of course! Florence, the censers!"

For her own sake, the elderly medium seemed unconcerned, wafting the air in front of her and inhaling deeply, as one might in front of a perfumer's sample.

"The professor and I have come to find the presence of the batteries rather invigorating. It is refreshing, is it not, to feel their charge work over the senses?"

Watching the maid stumble to the fireplace, extract a red-hot coal from the embers with a pair of tongs and begin to shakily transport it to a censer hanging precariously close to the curtains, Dr Knock rapidly stepped forward and relieved her of the duty. The coal fizzed on contact with the pastille, sending a tongue of bittersweet incense into the close atmosphere.

Repeating this operation with each of the censers in turn, Dr Knock noted that each contained a different scent, the effect no doubt calculated to fuddle and overwhelm the senses of this 'professor's' clientele. Indeed, he began to feel drowsy himself, as the room filled with fine smoke and Madame Caroline prattled airily away about an article that had appeared in *The Banner of Light*, about subscriptions and petitions, quarrels with rivals and with conjurers—all the squalid and inadequate controversies that until recently had swallowed so much of Knock's time and attention.

He was so drowsy, in fact, that it took him several moments to notice the patterning of fine copper tubes inlaid across the oak panelling of the walls. He followed it now, as it led from what he had at first taken to be a bookcase, but now saw as a cabinet laden with the familiar glass galvanic jars, and worked its way across every surface of the room. It twisted this way and that, like the dead fingers of ivy that lattice a wall when the stem has been severed, eventually finding the floor and snaking towards the mirror that had first caught his eye on entering the room. The mirror sat propped at one end of the long table. The height and breadth of a sheet of writing paper, its frame was inlaid with obscure Hellenic designs that glinted in the light of a single candle roughly a foot in front of it. Moving to inspect it, Knock observed that the mass of copper tubing led into a series of sockets in its back. Unusual though the mirror appeared, its adornments were refreshingly evident and resolutely worldly. Dr Knock smiled, in spite of himself, but could not resist bending to peek under the table, idly conducting his customary elimination of tricks, trap doors, pedal-operated table rappers and other spiritualist shams.

"She's not under there," spoke a quiet voice in his ear, causing Knock to jerk upwards slightly and come within an inch of cracking his head on the underside of the table. "At least, she is not there yet." The man who had spoken was a good deal shorter than Knock had anticipated, though every bit as hirsute as he appeared in *The Zoist*'s sketches, where he was regularly portrayed holding court over a room of revolving furniture and swooning gentry. The professor's fecund sideburns leant outward when he smiled, as he did now, offering his hand to Knock, who reddened slightly as he returned the gesture.

"Dr Knock, is it not?" The professor bowed his head. "It is an honour to have you at our little gathering. I have made a great study of your work in the *Proceedings*. You are a man of great talent and," with the smallest of pauses, "perspicacity."

Knock reddened further, failing to supress a nervous flicker of his moustached lip. Since his resignation of the editorship of the *London Psychical Proceedings* his articles had taken a pronounced swing towards the sceptical, and he was certain that his host had made at least as great a study of those.

"Please, sit." The professor gestured and Knock took a seat at the long table, facing George whose twinkling eyes remained locked on him.

Madame Caroline had now taken her place at the foot of the table, which Knock observed with relief was free of crystal, planchette or writing slate. A solitary glass of brandy took their place by her jewelled right hand. The professor guided Florence from the room and locked the door behind her, depositing the key in the pocket of his waistcoat.

"Welcome, my friends. I must begin by thanking you both, and in particular our distinguished guest Dr Knock, in taking the time to attend my little demonstration. I ask you here, Doctor, because I know well that you believe me to be a fraud. No! Please, do not take offence at my honesty. We are all friends here, and I would ask for no less than the most acute scientific scrutiny to be applied to what you are to witness here tonight, nor the harshest condemnation should you, after viewing the proceedings, demonstrate without margin for doubt that they have been a hoax."

It was in that 'margin for doubt' that most of these men operate, observed Dr Knock, silently.

"I ask you here Mr Peterson—"

"George, please."

"George. I ask you here George because I believe a man of your talents and sensitivity to be the most capable of announcing my discoveries to the world, should you and your old colleague agree between you that it does warrant it."

For the first time Knock noticed the odd placement of words in the professor's speech. His English was almost perfect, but it was clear that his Christian name was more than simply a performer's affectation.

"You are both of you, I know, familiar with many of the marvellous scientific achievements which have taken place over the past century in the field of the 'animal magnetism'. You have followed in your work, Dr Knock, the countless variations on the theory and practice since Franz Mesmer made his first discoveries almost fifty years ago."

Knock shifted awkwardly in his chair.

"You have yourself attended on many occasions the experiments of Dr Elliotson at the University College Hospital. You have seen his manipulation of the 'mesmeric currents' in the bodies of the sisters Okey, their trance states and impossible pronouncements, the traversing of their memories and personalities from our world to one above it or below it."

Below it? This Donaldson was beginning to sound more like a papist than a scientist. Knock had indeed visited the University Hospital on many occasions. He'd made the Okey sisters and Elliotson's experiments in mesmeric trances a focus of his time with the *Proceedings*. He'd felt that tightening of his chest, that breathless feeling like a sharp inhalation of ether, as he allowed himself to wonder if he was indeed witness to a new era of science, of medicine, of theology. Then came the deflation, time and time again, as the results failed to be reproduced. As the shadow of that new world had been blasted away by the sodium glare of thorough scientific examination. Knock was lost in this gloomy reverie when he felt two hands grasp suddenly at his shoulders.

"How close they were! And yet how far! With their wild theories of magnetic energies flowing through the human body!" Donaldson was gripping Knock rather tightly as he warmed to his theme. "Not so wild!" Donaldson swept towards Madame Caroline, whose half-shuttered eyes cast upwards at the ceiling gave her the appearance of an elderly dog begging at table.

"How close too were our friends the spiritualists! Who beckoned the departed to take residence once more in flesh, in sensitive flesh like that of our esteemed Madame Caroline! I have dwelled long in their marvellous world of spirit guides and elemental emanations. I have learned much from them. But I have travelled further." Sweeping around the room he gestured at the galvanic cabinet, then upwards to three great metal globes that Knock now saw hung pendulous above each of the seated guests. He frowned at the sphere above his own head, and for the first time entertained a slight concern for his own safety. There was, Knock reminded himself, every reason to believe that this Professor Donaldson was quite mad. He noticed George nervously inspecting his chair, and guessed that he was assessing its conductivity. For his own part he was grateful that he had chosen the thickest soled of his shoes.

"Mesmer's first instincts were in many ways absolutely correct," the host continued. "There is indeed a substance in existence that modern science has failed to take into account. It is a substance akin to Mesmer's fluid, one that has the properties of the magnet or the electrical current, and yet is truthfully neither. Mesmer was wrong in one respect, one key respect, which has fatally twisted the inquiries of great minds for five decades. This fluid, this field if you will, does not emanate from within the human body but from *without it!*" These last words spoken with such vehemence that the flame of the candle sputtered, its fluctuation aped by its twin in the mirror's reflection.

"We are in it now, all of us. We are in it when we wake and when we sleep. It flows through the streets of London and in the air above it. It spreads like a miasma, like a swarm of tiny insects through the houses of London and Paris, through the jungles of Africa and the ancient temples of India. It is the medium of every living soul. As the human lungs need air, as those of the fish must have water, so must the soul forever bathe in this substance. It is, if you wish, the emanation of the creator in our physical world."

Knock did not wish it, and his eyes narrowed on Donaldson. George let out a "Hah!" and clapped his hands together. This was very much his kind of thinking.

"I see you are all anxious for my demonstration, and so I will be brief. When the great Mesmer manipulated his magnetic wand and placed it upon the location of a physical wound on his patient he was merely focussing the transmission of this field to the location of the harm, where its natural benevolence encouraged the healing process. When we engage the services of a 'sensitive' such as Madame Caroline—"

At the mention of her name the medium suddenly jerked into life, as if awoken from an entirely earthly bout of somnambulism.

"It is because her remarkable talents and natural physiological make up have rendered her a particularly effective lodestone, if you will, for its powers. Madame Caroline feels, I know, that she is becoming redundant in the face of my equipment," and here he moved to a bank of levers located to the left of his galvanic batteries, "but the reverse is true. We are all of us now seated inside what you might compare to a lightning conductor. The room has been lined with metals chosen for their peculiar conductivity for the living field around us, channelled here into a looking glass. But metal alone is not sufficient for developing the field. Not to the extent that we can expect... visitations."

"You will have observed, no doubt, the galvanic bank which will supply the electrical charge for my device, but it is to be you yourselves who will provide the essential physical charge. You may feel a slight tingling in your fingertips and perhaps on the ends of your nose. Please, do not allow these to alarm you."

With that Donaldson swung the largest of the levers downward and it sparked as it made contact. The walls began to emit a low hum, climbing rapidly to a steady and undulating throb that provoked a niggling pain in Knock's molars. George was grinning like a lunatic as Donaldson swiftly moved around the room and extinguished the gaslights, until the gently swaying candle flame and its reflection were the only illumination. Madame Caroline had begun to mutter under her breath, her eyelids flickering and her hands spread tightly on the table top.

"All I ask of you now is to look into the mirror glass. I ask that you clear your minds as far as is possible, and to look into the mirror. Watch the flame of this candle in its depths. It is here that we will hope to make contact. It is here that we will hope to see them."

"The ghosts?" offered George.

"Perhaps." Donaldson's smile could barely be seen in the candlelight.

Knock's teeth continued to ache as he gazed dispassionately at the candle flames. He was aware that Donaldson had continued to speak, his low voice slipping in and out of alignment with the humming of his ridiculous stage machinery. Something about 'phantasms of the living', about images from the present as well as from the past.

"—ghosts of those who have lived, are yet living still, or who may even be yet to live—"

Flickering this way and that as Donaldson spoke. Like two eyes of flame, or a dancer rehearsing against a great glass, observing her own movements and delighting in the reciprocity of her reflection. If it wasn't for the pain in his jaw, the feeling that his back teeth were swelling in size to force out his others, Knock felt this ballet of twinned flames would be almost soothing.

"—the veil of years or the miles of physical distances collapsed by the field… the field… the field—"

Something shifted. Knock noticed it at once but could not at first be sure quite what it was. When he realised, a trickle of sweat squeezed itself from the pores on the nape of his neck and inched down his spine. His eyes widened as he stared at the candle. The candle! One single candle flame. Its twin in the mirror had vanished, as if it had been abruptly snuffed out. Nothing could have induced Knock to take his eyes away from the uncanny spectacle, but he felt certain that George had noticed it too. The professor was no longer speaking. The room had taken a sharp intake of breath, and was in no hurry to release it.

The flame itself had stilled, as if it too was observing the curious departure of its dancing partner. Knock looked beyond it now, at the surface of the professor's looking glass. It reflected nothing, yet its sudden oily blackness retained a reflective appearance. As Knock stared, the surface, which had looked like nothing so much as a pool of spilled ink, seemed to float backwards. Gain depth. Until without a perceptible change having taken place, Knock suddenly seemed to be squinting into a chasm, or into a wardrobe with an infinite shadowy recess at its back.

"It is beginning."

It was. The pain in his teeth had subsided, and the room now seemed to hum with a frequency that was perfectly in tune with that of Knock's own breathing, or with the minute vibrations of his own nervous system. Madame Caroline was burbling again, but her voice sounded terribly distant, a quiet descant to the room's simple tune.

"It is not unusual at this stage to see shapes, patterns or even pictures forming in the glass." Donaldson almost whispered.

Knock let his mind play in the empty space where the mirror had been. He imagined that the candle was still there, or his own reflection as he had seen it earlier, but found he could not sustain the thought. He fancifully attempted to hang a Turner seascape in its frame, only to have it fall away into the dark. He tried something simpler. A box of matches. A cube. A ball. Again and again the blackness swallowed his imagining. A sphere. A disc. A circle. A circle! There it was, a faint circle, an outline, a dream of a circle, suspended in the centre of the looking glass. It too seemed terribly far away, and further and fainter every second. Then with a shock he saw that it was not a circle: it was a fruit, an apple or a pear, as if hanging from a branch. Its colours were still muted but it was there, hung in

312

the black distance. As if one would only have to reach out, reach out terribly far into the frame, and pluck it.

"Hands on the table, Doctor."

Knock saw that he was indeed reaching out, his fingers stretching towards the mirror, and tugged his hand away, slamming it firmly against the table top.

"Do not be alarmed. It is normal. We are making a connection."

Knock shook his head, squeezing his eyes shut before allowing them to open and refocus on the glass. It was as if he had awoken from a trance. How had he allowed himself to be taken in so completely? The trick was simple. An ingeniously presented but technically facile variation on the Proteus illusion of Professor Pepper. The correct angling of light and reflection to create the illusion of spectral objects on a glass pane. He had seen it performed a dozen times, at first in scientific demonstrations, then time and time again in the theatre where he and George would afterwards dissect the merit of its application and technical accomplishment. The oldest trick in the book. All done with mirrors. As if affronted by Knock's sudden relapse into scepticism the spectral fruit had vanished altogether. And how tawdry it all appeared now! The gilded frame and elaborate séance room. Knock stood to leave.

"Sit." The tone was imperious. "Sit down, Dr Knock and watch."

Knock sat, taken aback by this little man's sudden change of tone. His eyes were flaming and his brow knit tight.

"Watch."

Knock watched, and as he did he saw something that, if not quite miraculous, was far beyond the powers of any Pepper's illusion he had yet seen. The mirror fogged suddenly, as if a line of tapers had been lighted beneath it. Then the fog cleared, and the face of a girl popped suddenly into existence in the centre of the frame. Not merely a face, but a neck, and not floating in its centre but occupying a space that looked as real as the room around them. As if the mirror was reflecting another room entirely. One that was brightly lit and cluttered with strange objects. But it was the face that Knock stared at. Not ashen like the objects that had appeared at first, but full and blooming with colours. At first Knock thought it was the head of a dummy, perhaps a waxwork like those at Madame Tussaud's, though one of astounding verisimilitude. Its lips were painted like a waxwork, and its face powdered like that of the Marie Antoinette which Knock had greatly admired on his last visit. Then the eyes began to move, flicking back and forth, never catching Knock's, nor seeming to attempt to. Its lip moved too, quivering slightly.

"She is with us," Donaldson declared. "We have made the connection. The field is strong with us today."

The eyes continued to move, as if the figure they belonged to was itself in a trance state. Then they stopped, fixing very definitely on the flame of the candle, as if gazing through a mirror into a light suspended in another room. The eyebrows, which were thin and painted in the French style, bent into a frown. Her face suggested the first bloom of womanhood, but her hair fell loose and free like that of a child. Two large hoops of inlaid gold hung from her earlobes. The mouth opened and

314

closed several times, almost as if the figure was speaking, but no sound was heard beside the throb of the room.

"Remarkable."

It was George.

"Just remarkable! Who is she?"

Professor Donaldson made no reply at first. George bent down from his seat to glance under the table. He shook his head in amazement. There was no sign of a clever arrangement of mirrors, no suspiciously angled lamps, no shivering feet of a complicit maid concealed behind the tablecloth.

At last Donaldson answered, "I believe her to be a young gypsy girl. Perhaps one who has recently died, or perhaps one still living. Though where she has reached us from, I cannot say. The field stretches far in all directions. It is omnipresent. It is total. Who can say from where it snares its emanations?"

Knock wasn't really listening. He had that feeling again, for the first time in many, many years. That breathless feeling, that tensing of the abdomen, that rush of pure wonder.

And then something happened. A hand appeared. It was the girl's hand and she held it out in front of her face, as if she was pushing on the pane of glass. As if she was pushing outward from inside the mirror. It was just a finger at first, and Knock saw the tip of it flatten as it reached the dividing line between her world and his own. The figure removed it, and he saw her face twisting further into a scowl. Again the hand was lifted, and again it pushed against the surface. Harder now, jabbing at it, almost scratching at it. Obscuring the face which Knock now saw only in glimpses, furious and twisted. The smile fell from his face.

Stewart Pringle

"What is she doing?" It was the first time Knock had spoken since he first entered the house, and Donaldson seemed thrown.

"She is… she is making a contact. She is making a contact with our world."

Knock's eyes remained fixed on the scratching fingers, the hand that pawed again and again at the surface. Somehow its soundlessness made it all the more terrible, accompanied only by a steady rise in the humming noise, which now began to dip and crest unevenly. She was trying to do something, she was trying to get out. With a terrible shudder Knock shouted his thought as soon as it had formed:

"She's trying to get through!"

Madame Caroline gave a shriek as a galvanic battery shattered within the cabinet. The humming had broken into a lolling gallop, and sparks flew from the bank of levers. George pushed his chair away from the table. Donaldson strode to the galvanic cabinet, his sweat twinkling in the candlelight. Still the hand clawed at the glass, still the fingers pressed with ever increasing desperation. The pain had returned to Knock's jaw, so hot and fierce that he could barely open it to cry:

"Switch it off, man! Send her back!"

Donaldson reached for the lever but his hand recoiled as a snake of blue fire whipped from the panel. Madame Caroline's mumbled nonsense had become a torrent. George had backed against the wooden panels. The hand pulled back, and the furious face of the girl, her red lips caught in a snarl, her powdered face a mask of rage seemed to stare straight out into the séance room, as the hand reached out once more, a single finger extended as if to pierce the looking glass and shiver into Knock's world.

"Send her—!"

Lurching forwards, Knock threw his body across the table towards the looking glass, sending the candle flying from its holder and extinguishing itself on the table top, as the doctor's hand caught the mirror and brought it crashing downwards, where it broke into fragments in the silent dark.

"IT'S GONE."

"What's gone?"

"Everything. It's just gone. Just... gone."

"Have you lost the connection?"

"Maybe. How can you tell?"

"Give it here."

Lucy's brother grabbed the tablet from her and prodded it. Nothing.

"You've fucked it."

"No I haven't."

"Yes you have, you've fucked it. It's fucked."

"I don't see what it was supposed to do anyway."

"Nothing. It's just a candle and you just sort of stare at it. It's spooky."

"Is it?"

"It was."

"Before I fucked it?"

He threw himself on her bed with a half yawn.

"You didn't really. It's probably just the router being shit again. The candle only shows when you've got wi-fi."

"Why?"

"Don't know, don't care. It's stupid."

He held down the home key until the black screen folded away. Then pressed his finger to the gem-like square with its single candle flame until it shivered and a small cross appeared in its corner. He pressed it again and the box titled 'Professor Donaldson's Séance' blinked out of existence.

Do you want to rate this app?

He pressed **Okay**.

"Who's that bloke supposed to be?" Lucy asked as she tied her shoes.

"Hmm?"

"The bloke with the moustache. He popped up just before the candle went out."

"Don't know—"

"Don't care, fine. Maybe he's supposed to be scary. Like a ghost."

"With a moustache?"

"Good point. You coming?" she asked from the doorway.

"Give me a sec. Okay, with you."

Lucy's brother threw the tablet back onto the bed, picked up his jacket, and followed her down the stairs and out into a warm summer's day. The tablet glowed for a moment before the screen flicked automatically into a thick inky black.

SHIFTING SANDS

DAISY BLACK

1946

THERE IS SOMETHING rotten about the coast at Covehithe. At low tide, the sea draws back from the pebbles, and the white sands become a daily museum of dead things. Broken branches, bleached and rubbed smooth, lie littered among empty crab shells and stinking seaweed. Occasionally, far worse things are thrown up, and then quickly forgotten. The narrow strip of coast decays and crumbles into the water, only to be consumed and eventually regurgitated onto the beach, odd-shaped and reeking.

Today, there is the carcass of a dead dolphin. The ragged tail flaps pointlessly in the wind and its mottled skin has already lost the gleam of the water. A small boy stands over it, holding a stick. He stares at the dolphin, marvelling at how its mouth lies bared in a savage grin at the sky. He slides the stick into the long gash along its side. The stick comes out clean.

Already bored, the boy moves on. He picks a pocketful of stones, scrambles to the edge of the grey surf and starts to skim them, flush against the surface. One, two, three. As each stone hits the waves, it is accompanied by a shouted buzz… BOOM. For the boy is playing at soldiers. He's heard the stories about bombs that skip across water, smashing down dams. Choosing each stone with care, he curves his fingers around it, flexes his back and snaps his arm forward: launching the stone into flight until it crashes into the surface, spinning.

Where the sands end the shore begins, shallow at first, then giving way to higher cliffs and a wood of spindly birch, beech and ash. When the boy's arm becomes tired, he scrambles up the muddy bank, avoiding the scraps of barbed wire and the warning notices that cleave, half-buried, to the soil. He wanders towards the wood, his stick transformed under his hands into a gun, bang, bang. Under the cover of the trees, all sounds shift. The trees deaden the noise of the waves and replace it with their own, of branches clicking anxiously together in the low wind. It's as if they already know that they too will one day fall over the cliff and add to the mess of driftwood on the sands below. The boy's voice, as he takes aim at his imaginary enemies, is flat, muted, his bullets shooting through a silencer. The dead leaves rasp underfoot, and suddenly he realises that, though his voice is muffled, his breath has become too loud. He stops what he's doing and stands very still, listening to the trees. Slowly, he peels a thick strip of bark from his stick, exposing the pale wood underneath.

Shifting Sands

He doesn't see the old man, at first.

When he does, he stops dead, angry and afraid. This is *his* wood; *his* secret place. Nobody else comes up here, not even the other children from the village. He doesn't like the idea that anyone else might be here. He also doesn't like the thought that the man has probably been watching him playing for some time. He lowers the stick, feeling rather foolish.

"What do you want?" His voice sounds ruder than he meant it to.

"Hello, Wilf," the old man says.

The boy doesn't bother asking how the old man knows his name. It's a small place; everybody knows everybody else, and all their business. So even though he has no idea who the man is, he reckons he must know his father, and must therefore also know that he, Wilf, is trespassing. So he tries to sound a bit more polite with his answer.

"Can I help you?"

"Yes."

The old man moves out of the mottled light of the trees, so that the boy can see him properly. What he sees causes him to jump. The man's entire body looks as though it has been washed out by the sea. The skin on his hands folds, loose and papery, like the bark of the silver birches surrounding him. His face, eyes, lips, hair, all of the same greenish-beige, cast only the briefest shadows, as if flattened out by the grinding waves. And his head and hands seem to be caught in a cage of flexible glass tubes. Tubes running from each nostril, over his ears and behind his head, disappearing below the collar of his shirt. The boy takes a tentative step backwards. Seeing this, the old man speaks again.

"You are going to kill me, Wilf."

"W-what?" The boy's voice vibrates among the clicking trees, and is swiftly borne away by the wind.

"You with your sticks and stones, your bullets and bombs. You are going to kill me."

Tensing to run, the boy's hand closes around one of the stones in his pocket. The old man raises his voice and advances on him, speaking clearly and slowly, as if to someone rather deaf.

"You are going to kill me. And I'd rather you didn't."

"What are you talking about?" A stone lies smooth and comforting, hidden in the boy's palm. "Keep away from me. I'll… I'll hit you."

But the old man doesn't seem to understand his threat, and continues to step closer, and closer, until the boy can see his pale eyes, the iris and pupil only defined by faint grey specks that refuse to reflect light. He is now only a couple of metres away, his gaze fixed earnestly on the boy's face.

"Please. I don't want to die."

The boy's hand is ready, and with the speed and agility of his earlier sport he launches the stone at the man's chest and runs, expecting to hear the thump of rock striking flesh. But that noise doesn't come. As he runs, he can hear only the clicking of bark against bark, then the nearer rush of shingle on the beach far below. And when he stops to look back, expecting to see the man either chasing him or hunched over in pain among the leaves, he sees nothing. Only trees.

Shifting Sands

So he runs again, hard, down to the beach, back along the dirt track, past the church and into the village, not stopping until he reaches the door of his house. There, he throws his stick away. He's had enough of guns. When his mother asks how he's got his clothes in such a mess he tells her, but his father beats him for making up stories.

That was the first time he saw him.

1954

TWO TEENAGE BOYS ARE crouching down behind the back of the school. Both of them wear grass-stained trousers and crooked ties, their shirts spilling untidily from underneath their pullovers. Wilf is holding the short stub of a cigarette, which he takes a long drag from before passing it across. Reaching across to take it, Mike notices how cold Wilf's hands are.

"What's up?" he asks. Wilf is looking out across the playground.

"Nothing."

"Yeah, right." Mike glances at Wilf, his look shrewd and calculating. "Why'd you skive biology, then? You never skive."

"Dissection."

Mike is incredulous. "What, you're squeamish about cutting stuff up?"

"Nope. Just don't like knives, that's all."

Mike takes a long draw on the cigarette, pulling the red embers up the last fraction of an inch of crinkled paper until it burns his fingers. He stubs it out, roughly, in the dirt. The boys sit for a while in silence. Wilf starts to pick at the frayed edge of his shirt sleeves. Mike remembers how, at primary school, Wilf used to run away whenever the local children played at soldiers.

"You don't like guns, either, do you?"

"Nope."

"Why not?"

Wilf thinks about it, briefly. "Dunno."

"You must have some idea."

"Well, yeah, okay, I do know why, but I don't want to talk about it."

"How come?" Mike is being too curious, and Wilf feels a surge of anger.

"Because last time I told someone I got a walloping, alright?"

"Oh."

A bell jangles. Wilf stands quickly.

"We'd better go." But Mike remains sitting.

"You can tell me. I won't pass it on."

In the distance, Wilf can hear the rumble of several hundred chairs being pushed away from desks and the hubbub of shrieking voices as the classrooms start to empty into the corridors. He thinks, he has known Mike long enough now, and he's always been decent. So he decides to explain.

"Okay then. It started when I was six, right? I... I saw this old man on the beach. Except he wasn't really a man, I don't know what he was. He was bloody scary. He said I was going to kill him. Kept on and on about it, wouldn't shut up. So I threw a stone at him, and ran away."

Now Wilf has finally begun to tell someone, the words rush out, unguarded.

"I got worried that there'd be a report or something, that an old man had been hit with a stone, and that I'd get into trouble, but there was nothing. He'd just vanished. So I thought that was the end of it. But after a few months I saw him again, somewhere else. Still saying I was going to kill him. Now I've started seeing him everywhere. In the park, in the school corridors, in the woods, at home. Always when I'm alone. Sometimes he looks alive, sometimes he looks dead. And he keeps talking to me. Keeps saying I'm going to kill him."

He falters. Mike's face has become closed and shuttered. Wilf is not even sure if he's still listening. The sound of the students inside the building is growing louder.

"And that—that's why I hate knives, and guns, and anything else that might be used to kill someone, okay?"

The double doors to their right split open, spilling a noisy, violent mass of teenagers out onto the tarmac. Mike stands awkwardly. Glancing at those around them, he moves closer to Wilf, his whisper low and fierce. "You're bloody crazy. You keep away from me, alright?"

And then he's gone, pulled into the torrent of bodies. Wilf stares after him. Then, expressionless, he rests his back against the wall and sinks down until his backside rests on his heels. And very quietly, in a voice unlike his own, he mutters to himself, "You're still going to do it, you know. You are going to kill me. Please don't. Please don't. Please."

Daisy Black

1971

THE SMALL FLAT IS full of people when Wilf arrives. Men and women, talking, drinking, laughing, the colours of their clothes made drab by the heavily scented fug that fills the place. Wilf hovers in the doorway, feeling hot and uncomfortable. Somewhere in the huddle of bodies, a record is playing. There are too many people here, far more than he has become used to. He turns to go, but someone has already managed to work his way through the crowd towards him.

"Hey!" Wilf stops and recognises the stringy, blonde-haired man in front of him. He is dressed in an oversized, offensively purple jumper, and somehow manages to radiate a sense of being always on the brink of an adventure. A look passes between them.

"Mike."

Already Mike has realised that Wilf wants to bolt. He steps out into the hallway, pulling the door closed behind him. The noise of the people, and of the record player, becomes quieter.

"You're out, then," Mike says.

"Yes." They stand there in the corridor, listening to the party going on without them. Then Mike takes a step forward, and they embrace clumsily.

"Sorry," he says. "I should've known. That you wouldn't want too many people about."

"It's alright."

"I can ask them to leave, if you like?" But Wilf is beginning to smile for the first time in months.

"No, don't. I'll cope. Can't deny you the honour of showing off your 'crazy' friend."

Mike's face cracks into a smile too, and he kicks open the door.

"In that case, after you."

Later that evening, when everyone else has gone and the house is quiet, Wilf and Mike sit at the kitchen table, mugs of stewed brown tea in front of them. Wilf is concentrating hard, trying to roll a small amount of tobacco into thin paper. His hands keep shaking and a few shreds spill onto the floor. Mike holds out his hand, and Wilf places the sorry mess in his palm. A few deft twists later, and it's passed back, neatly rolled and ready to smoke.

"Thank you."

"No problem."

"Not for that. I mean... thank you. For tonight. For visiting. For the stuff you sent me. All the books and letters. They kept me going."

Mike waves away Wilf's thanks. "Least I could do."

But Wilf's eyes are shining, and he pulls a scruffy piece of paper out of his wallet.

"This one. This... made me want to get out. Get better. It gave me something to go for." Mike squints down at the paper, recognising his own writing, something he'd copied out many months ago.

"*I saw the best minds of my generation destroyed by madness, starving hysterical naked...*"

As Mike reads, Wilf starts to feel embarrassed. A flush begins to rise from the back of his neck, up under his messily cropped hair, where it lingers, making him warm and fidgety. It's one thing, he thinks, to read those words on his own, to keep the shadows at bay, to keep his mind too busy to conjure up all the things it should not. It's another to hear the same words in the mouth of a friend, in a badly lit kitchen with mugs of lukewarm tea and a dirty Formica table top and the stale smells of beer and weed muddling in the air. So as soon as Mike finishes, Wilf snatches up the poem, and fumbles it back into his wallet, spilling several more scraps of paper and a few coins as he does so. They pick them up together, their arms crossing as they reach over the table. Wilf feels his embarrassment rise.

"It's the… the drugs they give me. Make me clumsy."

Mike smiles sympathetically. "Are they any good? Should I get some?"

"Nope. Just make you sleep. A lot. And drop things."

Wilf fumbles with his cigarette lighter. He notices that Mike is drumming his fingers on the table top. He clearly wants to ask something, but is weighing up how he should do it.

"I still see him, Mike. If that's what you want to know."

"I wasn't going to—"

"It's okay. You can ask." A spark; the paper flares as Wilf's cigarette glows into life.

"I told them it had stopped, of course," he says. "They took some convincing. But it was obvious their treatment wasn't working. Couldn't see the point in hanging around there for months for no reason. Waste of time." Wilf glances down at the wallet lying between them.

"I'm not sane, man. I never will be."

Mike shifts in his seat. "So what do you do when you see him?"

"Close my eyes. Wait until he's gone. Run. Shit, I don't know. He shows up everywhere. I don't want to die… I don't want to die—" Wilf sees the tension in his friend's shoulders, and tries to lighten his voice. "But I'm coming to terms with it. I wouldn't even mind it so much, but he always says the same things. It's boring. You'd think after all these years he'd have developed some different conversation, eh?"

He has finally coaxed a smile out of Mike.

"Well, at least it's predictable. What if he asked you to explain the meaning of the universe? Then you'd be stuck."

Wilf looks serious again.

"No I wouldn't. I'd direct him to you."

They finish their tea. After a while, Mike goes out to the bathroom. He is just wiping his hands when he hears a crash and rushes back to the kitchen.

Both mugs are on the floor, the ceramic spinning out in lethal shards across the lino, and the knife holder beside the draining board is upset, reflecting beams of light that stripe Wilf's face. Wilf is huddled, shaking, against the kitchen sink, eyes shut, hands clutched close to his body, out of the way of the knives, willing himself not to vomit.

"Every time." Wilf says. "Every time."

Stepping across the debris, Mike pulls his friend into his arms until the shaking has stopped.

Daisy Black

2002

WILF SITS OUTSIDE the Bell Inn. The sea air ruffles his grey hair and fills the crevices of his lips with salt, and he can hear, beyond the sand dunes, the distant sound of the breakers against the shore. He smiles. He knows that being here is a victory.

The pub door opens, and Mike emerges, backwards, his hands full with two pints. Wilf goes to help, propping open the stiff oak door with his foot. After years of reading in odd places and under bad lighting, Mike's eyesight is worse than it once was.

"What took you so long?" Wilf asks as he takes his pint. Mike grunts.

"Got chatting."

"These old boys," says Wilf, "will spin you all colours of yarn if you let them." Mike doesn't answer. He is staring down at his glass as if he can't remember how it got there.

"What is it?" Wilf asks. Mike wets his lips.

"Well… it was just something one of them was saying. Local nonsense."

"What?"

"A bit of an old story. Something that happened during the war."

"Oh?" Wilf leans forward. "You know, you can't just say that and then stop."

Shifting Sands

"I just don't want to—" Mike leans across the table and lowers his voice. "—set you off, you know."

"It's fine," Wilf says. "I'm managing, aren't I? I mean, we're here, aren't we? By the sea." Wilf leans back, looking more carefree than he has been in years. And so Mike relents.

"This old man in the pub—"

"*We* are old men."

"Yes, I know. This man was saying how his friend's dad said that something pretty nasty happened along this coast. During the war."

"Did it? I never heard anything."

"Well, you wouldn't have. Because you know how the government held that the Germans never landed here?"

"Yes."

"Well, that might not be true. So this guy lived a few miles from here, not far from the air base at Bawdsey. One night they heard a volley of explosions further down the coast. Near Shingle Street. He went outside, and saw the sky was all red and black. The sea was on fire, and he could smell burning oil coming in on the wind. And where the smoke had cleared, he also thought he could see ships, out there in the flames."

Will feels a prickling rush of adrenaline. "So what had happened?" he asks.

"Well, this old boy got up early the next morning, and went down to the beach. He saw a bunch of soldiers in the distance, and a truck, but didn't pay it much heed; they'd been using that area for training for months. As he got closer, he saw they were shifting these black oily objects into the truck and covering them with tarps. They were awkward, heavy things. As he

331

walked, this blackened old bit of twill blew towards him and wrapped around his boot. A bit further on, he saw a sodden field cap had been washed up in the surf. And then... then he turned back pretty sharp, because he now knew what the objects were that the soldiers were loading into the truck. Some lieutenant ran after him. Told him he hadn't seen anything— that the soldiers hadn't been there that day—and reminded him that there was a war on. Told him to take his walks somewhere else for a few weeks. So he did, and that was that."

Wilf is sitting back in his chair with a faraway expression. Mike nudges him with his foot.

"You alright?" Then, uncertainly, "I did tell you it was nonsense."

But Wilf's feet have started to tap with nervous energy, juddering the table and threatening to spill their drinks.

"Wilf? Say something."

"It's a good story," Wilf says at last. "But mine is worse. Because in mine, I can't walk away and pretend it never happened." The head of Mike's pint falls over the rim of the glass, causing a cascade of froth to hit the table. Mike lifts his glass quickly out of harm's way.

"It's okay," he says softly. "It's okay." But he knows he's trying to stop the tide from coming in.

"Because he doesn't sound German." Wilf's voice is getting higher, becoming childlike, pleading. "He doesn't... hasn't... ever. He sounds English. Local, even. Like me. And you. He speaks like... like he's from around here."

"I know, I know." Mike stands and fumbles for Wilf's hand. "I'm sorry. I shouldn't have told you. Bad idea on my part."

"No, no! It *is* a good idea. I mean…" Wilf stands up and begins to pace, trying to work things out. "That might be why… why he's… why he looks like… like that. Even if… his voice is definitely wrong, Mike, though."

Mike looks pained. "It's just a story," he says quietly.

"But it could explain what's happening to me!" Wilf's voice has risen to a shriek.

Mike sighs. "Well, maybe it does, and maybe it doesn't. How the hell should I know anything about this stuff? It was a mistake to come here. I said so before."

Faced with his friend's concern, Wilf stops pacing and tries to calm himself down. "It's alright." He takes a deep breath, and, with a colossal effort, manages to master himself. "It's alright."

"Come on," Mike says, firmly. "Let's go home."

"No." Wilf sits down carefully. "I'm fine. Who cares if he doesn't speak German, eh? He's only in my head. He can speak broad Suffolk, or Cornish, or Dutch, or Elvish, for all I care. Let's finish our beer."

Mike looks sceptical.

"Seriously, I'll be fine."

"Alright then." Mike relents. "We'll finish up here." He retrieves his soggy glass from the window ledge where he'd placed it. "You owe me at least half a pint, by the way."

And so they sit and talk, two men outside a pub, and the sea breeze continues to rummage its way through Wilf's hair, and the distant shingle rumbles beneath the waves, and the autumn evening falls in a dark cloud that gradually draws across the redness of the sun, and, for the first time in many years, Wilf feels something lift inside him.

~~~

2011

THE CARE HOME IS a broad, sunny place. The residents' rooms are a fair size, each with flocked papered walls, a nondescript picture and a brown paisley armchair several sizes too small for anyone of adult size. "Because," as Mike often says, "when you get to our age, you learn to love brown paisley."

Wilf walks down the home corridors, muffled in an outdoor coat and holding a small stack of large-print books. He finds the door to Mike's room slightly ajar, and lingers briefly, listening to Mike's ragged, slow breathing and the faint clicking buzz of machinery. When he enters, Mike is propped up in bed as usual, hunched awkwardly over a book. His lips move silently, trying to read, though his eyes now struggle to make out even the enlarged words.

"What are you reading, old man?" Mike glances up, and his look of frustrated concentration is immediately replaced with joy. He turns the book over so that Wilf can see the front cover: *On the Road.*

"Still wasting your eyesight on a book we both know inside out?"

"Well, an old bugger like me can still dream of seeing the world, can't he?"

"We've already seen a lot of it. But you dream away." Wilf lowers himself gracelessly into the chair. Mike gives a dry, hacking laugh.

"Your arse is too big," he says.

Even as he grins in response, Wilf doesn't miss the spasm of pain that crosses Mike's face when he twists to place the book on the bedside table. In the last few weeks, Mike seems to have shrunk, somehow, to a papery thinness.

"It breaks me up, seeing you like this," Wilf says quietly.

"It's not so bad."

"We both know that's bullshit." Mike looks at him sternly. "How many times have I visited you in various hospitals or institutions over the years?"

Wilf considers this.

"Five or six times?" he ventures.

"Twenty-five."

"Well, it doesn't count if you include the multiple visits to the same place."

"Twenty-five times, Wilf. So don't you try worming your way out of your visiting duties now. You know the drill. You come to visit, bring me things to read, and moan about the furnishings. In return, I don't give up until I walk back out that paisley-curtained front door with you."

Wilf nods, admiring his friend's determination to fight on, fighting as he fought for Wilf's own sanity in those early days, now still fighting, on, and on, and on, for his own life, regardless of the pain it brought to himself and others. He nods, knowing that Mike knows he will never walk out the front door with him, paisley-curtained or otherwise. He nods, knowing that his appearance of agreement is a lie, that it's the first lie in their long relationship, that he has never lied before, not about the voices in his head, or his phobias of sharp objects and bullets and bombs and broken glass and poison and the sea. But he also knows that Mike depends on this lie, and so he nods even as he hates himself for doing it.

They chat for a while, both resolutely ignoring the beeping and clicking of the machine, until eventually and unapologetically Mike drifts into a doze. Wilf sits quietly in the small room for a while, aimlessly finding patterns in the horrible flocked wallpaper. He picks up Mike's copy of *On the Road*, turning it over in his lined, dry hands. It is full of ticket stubs – from concerts, gigs, trains, cinemas, aeroplanes. On page forty-five a piece of marram grass acts as a bookmark.

Eventually, the carer comes in to check Mike is ready for bed, and Wilf shuffles out of the room, planning to make his way home. He's halfway to the main exit when he realises that the book is still in his hands. Frustrated with himself, he turns back, hoping to slip the book onto Mike's bedside table where he can find it when he wakes. On the way, he meets the carer, who has just finished looking after his friend and has turned off the main light in the room. He nods to her, before gently pushing open the door and stepping inside.

The room is now dimly lit by a corner lamp, but the machine the sleeper is hooked up to emits a slowly pulsing green LED that casts small shadows on the crinkled bed sheets. One hand lies prone on top of the sheets, stretched out in unconscious supplication. Click-click, goes the machine at irregular intervals. Wilf edges his way around it, suddenly gripped with an urgent desire to see his friend's face.

As he does so, the light from the machine flashes on, illuminating the top of the bed. Overriding the yellow glow of the corner lamp, the sterile green bleaches out the sleeper's features, flattening his eyes, lips and hair and drawing attention to the flexible tubes—the many, many tubes that seem to be flowing out from the face and across the pillow to where the machine pulses. And, after all these years, Wilf finally recognises him. The green light flashes off.

"No," he says quietly. Then, "No, no, no!"

The sea rushes chaotically into Wilf's ears, and he takes a step back from the bed. The light flashes on again, once more bleaching the face in front of him. And now Wilf is angry, angrier than he's ever been in his life before. Angry that, after all these years, he has been trapped so easily. Angry that it's the person he has most loved who is the one who'd poisoned his life. Angry that, after all that fighting—through his own pain and, in the last two years, through Mike's—it only comes to this.

But now, it *will* end, and Wilf knows what he must do. Listening carefully for the approach of a nurse, he gently tugs the oxygen tubes from Mike's bleached face, returning something of its familiarity. Then he bends down and switches the machine off at the wall. The green light stops. The clicking stops. The sound of the sea stops.

And now he can see, in the kinder colours of the lamplight, the face of the man in front of him. After the first few minutes, death comes swiftly, gently, in an undramatic fashion, until Wilf is left sitting there alone. And just as he had done in the hospitals, he staves off the darkness by reading the final pages of the book in his hands. And, he thinks, how strange that it wasn't the knives, or the guns, that did it. In the end, it was only the flick of a switch.

And, on a beach somewhere, a boy is skipping stones and playing at soldiers.

MOON CHILD

MERE JOYCE

WARNING: DEAD GIRL AHEAD.

I read the graffitied note sprayed a bloody red over the attic stairway. It makes my stomach pinch, and I grimace as I duck low and head upwards. The steep, narrow staircase creaks under my weight as I ascend into the dark space, my mind picking through the stringy tangles of my memory. The attic isn't exactly creepy, but it does remind me of something, only I can't think of what.

Forgetting makes me nervous. I pull at the edge of my sweater, and at the edges of my mind. The sooner I remember, the more at ease I will be.

I look behind me to make sure Dalvin hasn't started up yet. We had strict instructions to only come up here one at a time, since the staircase is so old it might actually collapse with the weight of two grown people. But Dalvin is impatient. He is still at the bottom of the stairs now, though I can see wide muddy eyes peering at me through the mane of unkempt hair he thinks is so fashionable. I know he's jittery, so I hurry my pace.

Even though it's late, the attic is not very dark, and once I am fully onto the uneven floor, I understand why. A section of the old roof has rotted through, and the bright moon shines in, illuminating the attic in a greyish light. This is the perfect setting for us. We aren't supposed to use artificial light since it makes it harder to see our targets. But falling into a ditch or tripping over a misplaced footstool in the darkness can lead to horrible—and horribly ironic—demises.

"How's it looking up there?" Dalvin calls up to me as I move away from the stairs, careful to get my footing on a sturdy part of the floor.

"Utterly unoriginal," I reply. "As if we're really in an attic. Only a basement could be more stereotypical, and even that's not a guarantee."

"She's young, she doesn't know any better," Dalvin laughs, taking the stairs two at a time and appearing beside me before I even realize he's started up. I smile weakly, but my attention is devoted to my surrounding space. It's a big attic; it sprawls openly across the entire width of the building, and I can see in the shadows what looks to be several half-walls, possibly from an unfinished renovation or perhaps left over from an old expansion.

Good hiding spaces, at any rate.

It's cold up here, which is hardly surprising given that it's late November and the frost is growing thicker every night. Nevertheless, I am shivering as I move towards the centre of the large room. Moriana trained us to wear sweaters on our missions, so sudden changes in temperature won't affect our concentration. It seems logical enough, but our mistress has failed to see the basic problem with her teachings. I am wearing my sweater now, yet I am still cold; no one ever trained me how to deal with that.

I turn back to survey the progress of the group, trying to distract my limbs from their trembling dance. Leanne's not watching where she's going, and her frizzled braid gets caught on the splintered wood of a low-hanging beam as she reaches the top of the staircase.

"Dammit!" She tugs her hair free, and lets out a long breath as she looks around. "Alright, let's make this quick. I've got a date when this is over."

"Leanne, it's already ten," Jace says as he comes up behind her, the last member of our strange quartet. "By the time we release, it'll be well after midnight." Leanne rolls her eyes, and moves to help Dalvin set up. Even in the faint light of the moon, it's easy to see my teammates; the orange peel shaded suits Moriana makes us wear are great for spotting each other in the darkness. Which is the point, of course, though that doesn't mean we look any less ridiculous in them. In the daylight, we seem like alien tourists, or a really sad family band. At night, we're like safety cones, dim spots of neon brightness in the dark.

I'm kicking up dust as I walk around the room, and it's starting to make me feel like I need to sneeze. Strictly speaking we're not supposed to do this, move around the area and all. But no one really follows that rule. It's not like it's a crime scene here, not now anyways. So I walk while the others get settled, trying to figure out what this place reminds me of. It's not somewhere I've ever been before, and I'm pretty sure I've never dreamt of it either. But it's familiar.

I wonder if maybe that has something to do with Keiria.

A soft bubble of movement floats to my left and my head jerks towards it, but then I realize that it's only a broken mirror against a far wall reflecting Leanne as she sets out her candles.

"Any sightings yet?" Dalvin asks me as he draws a twisting spiral on the floorboards with his yellow chalk. I shake my head, turning back to watch his deft hands as they arc over the dust-encased wood, drawing the symbol he knows so well. I used to draw like Dalvin, but his skills far exceed mine. My creations are skittish sketches next to his smooth renditions, and I get more enjoyment out of watching him than I ever did out of drawing myself. When his hands glide, his hideous attempts to be fashionable trickle off, leaving only the true Dalvin: his eyes slow to blink, his hair pushed back out of the way, his lips tight in concentration.

I feel relaxed and focused watching him work, until Leanne lights the first of her seven candles, and the jolt of air that rises from nowhere develops into a queasiness low in my stomach. I wanted to come here, but now that I am actually standing in this old attic, I'm starting to wish I'd turned the opportunity down.

I smell something, a perfume of copper, green apples, and dead flowers. They are a cluster of scents I know far too well, and with their caress my heart staggers in its beating, halting my breath. I step away from the others to compose myself, hoping no one has noticed my strange behaviour. If they find out, I'll be in big trouble, so I get myself under control and continue further into the attic.

There is a rustling behind one of the half-walls ahead to the right, which may just be a mouse, or which may be something else entirely. I don't say anything to the others. If they knew about this case, really knew, I'd be kicked off the team. It'd be a Conflict of Interest, and Moriana would have me detained for days.

So I keep my mouth shut.

I pass by a stack of moulding gym mats, and suddenly I realize what this attic reminds me of. *The Neverending Story*. It was my favourite book when I was younger, and now I wonder how this attic looks in the day. Does it have any magic? Has it ever? I hope so. For Keiria's sake, I truly hope so.

The rustling grows louder, and I realize it's not a rustling at all but rather a dragging sound, like fingernails scraping against the floor.

I glance over my shoulder to see if my teammates have caught the noise. Dalvin is bent over his drawing, trying to get the edges smudged just right for a proper effect. Leanne has finished lighting her candles, and as I watch she carefully places them at points along Dalvin's creation. Jace waits, ready to start the incantation, ready to use his voice to ignite the power of this ritual.

And I, as always, do nothing. As always, I am only here to attract, only here as the all-important bait. It took me a few years to fully grasp how bloodthirsty spirits can be, and it took even longer for me to accept that my blood is like honey for them.

It took no time, however, for me to understand why.

"Okay, we're up," Dalvin calls out a moment later, his voice too harsh for the fragility of this space.

"Let's get this done then," Jace says, and I can tell he's nervous. He, too, plays a role in this ritual that is not always pleasant. The power he incites can cause him great pleasure, or great pain. The trouble is, he can never tell which until it's too late to do anything about it.

"What's the matter, Jacey? Afraid?" Leanne replies with a smirk, and Jace sneers at her.

"You said yourself you wanted to get this over with quickly," he says, and she laughs. I don't blame Jace for being nervous. These missions are dangerous, and I don't think Leanne has ever fully understood that. And why should she? She's never been on an unsuccessful team before, never seen what can happen when things go wrong. But Jace has, and so have I. It's not just energy and mist we're dealing with, but for the girl who lights the candles, the girl who only started with us because she is Moriana's niece and she had nothing better to do with her time, the whole mission is just a game.

"Leanne, give us a rundown of the case," Dalvin says, and I'm glad his attention is on her because a frigid cold has swept over me in a fierce gust. I twist back to face the shadows of the room as a prickling starts over my skin. This cold makes my earlier discomfort seem trivial, as if I had been standing in a sunny spring meadow compared to the frozen tundra I find myself in now.

In *The Neverending Story*, there is a land of everlasting ice, where the Old Man of Wandering Mountain lives. Whenever I

344

used to read that part of the story, I always felt cold, and now, thinking of it, I have to work to keep my teeth from chattering. Is this what the Arctic feels like? Only, it's not that type of cold; it's freezing me from the inside. My core is cold, my organs numb, my blood slowed to an aching crawl through my veins.

"Case #26492," Leanne recites, her strong memory her only valuable asset to the team. "Female. She was ten when she died, and she was brought to my aunt's attention four months ago. The principal of this school wants her gone so the school can get funding for a new expansion."

"How much would that suck, dying at school?" Jace says, and I can imagine Leanne glowering at his interruption.

"Violent tendencies have likely always been present, but a record has been kept for a couple of years now. Students and teachers have reported loud noises, and about seven months ago the front window of the attic was smashed open from the inside. When the man came up to repair it, he got scratches down his face, some requiring stitches. So the principal's had enough, and now it's time for us to send this little pest to Purgatory."

Dalvin clicks his tongue against the roof of his mouth. "Still, you've got to feel bad for her, dying in a place like this, and so young too," he says, and I shake my head. Dying in a place like this is only half of it. Case files are always vague; we're here to deal with spirits, not people, and Moriana doesn't want us feeling any connection to the ghosts we release. But I can't help the fact that I know this story, and I can't help the fact that there's much more to it than a little girl dying.

The truth is gruesome, but simple. This attic once held the school's Phys. Ed. equipment. Nearly twenty years ago, a little girl was asked by her teacher to return the skipping ropes to the attic after school one day. The little girl, however, asked her sister to return the ropes instead, and that sister was the one who came up here with her teacher.

A teacher who proceeded to brutally rape her and then leave her to die a slow, agonizingly lonely death.

Keiria.

I am almost paralyzed from the cold, and yet my head tilts upwards, until I can see through the hole in the ceiling, see the almost-full moon amazingly bright against the dark sky and the dark wood of the roof.

Moon Child.

The thought comes unexpectedly, but it hits me hard, like someone has thrown it at my body and I've taken the full blow. I want to laugh, but instead tears sting at the corners of my eyes. I always loved the adventure of our favourite story; the bravery of Atreyu was what set my blood on fire. But not Keiria. Keiria loved Moon Child, the mystery of her, the beauty, the unquestionable wisdom that not even my warrior hero could comprehend.

We loved to pretend we were a part of that world. I remember how much we bothered our mother to let us up into our attic so that we could have a truer experience, and I remember how much she resisted, although in the end we prevailed. And yet, we hated the attic at school, where all the Phys. Ed. equipment was kept. I hated it the most, but the funny part is, I never even saw it. I knew it was there, and for some reason it scared me. So when my teacher asked me to put the skipping ropes away after school one day, I begged Keiria to do it instead.

"It'll be just like Bastian," I remember saying, and now that it's so clear to me, I can't believe the memory ever faded at all. "It'll be just like when he gives Moon Child her name." The glistening in her eyes, the bright spark of imagination just waiting for its chance to shine. Keiria didn't like the attic either, but I knew she couldn't resist the idea of having such a pure experience, such a marvellous connection to the thing she loved most in the world. I had her on the edge, and all I needed was to push her over. "Maybe, if you go up there, you'll see Moon Child too," I whispered in her ear. It was a temptation impossible to ignore, and as I knew she would, Keiria agreed. She was like that; she always agreed.

"I owe you one," I said to her, and then I ran off in the selfish way children have of forgetting what is not happening in the very instant of their minds.

I never went back to this school after that day, and I never went into the attic at home again.

I never opened *The Neverending Story* again either.

The others don't know how I am involved in the murder that took place here so many years ago, and if they find out, I'll be helpless to save her. There are others who could be here for her release, but no one attracts the spirits like I do, because no one has been so responsible for the creation of a spirit as me. And I have to see her again, anyways. I want to be here when she finally gets the peace she deserves.

347

I lower my gaze back to where the noises issue from the depths of the attic, and I slink forward while Jace begins Moriana's ritual.

His words sink beneath my pores, buzzing against my skin like an insect drowning in my blood. My gaze blurs, my vision obscured by the indecipherable language spreading through my ears and along my eyes. I blink, red and black, and only when the ritual claims my heart and slows its pulse do I begin to see shape and colour again. My legs tingle, my fingers cramp, and I force my eyes open wide.

And I see her.

It's hard to miss the greyish mass of shadow, but even if she were invisible I would know where she was. She sways before me, her gaze rippling through my entire body like rough water after the wave of the ritual. She is only a shade of a person, but I can still make out vague details of her face. I am certain she knows who I am too, though I look different now than I did when I was ten. I think perhaps she has been waiting for me, and this thought is both comforting and horrific.

The smell of her is overwhelming. The copper of the necklace she always wore, the apples she ate every day at lunch, and the dried flowers she braided into her wheat-blonde hair.

"Keiria," I whisper. I don't mean to, but I can't resist her pull.

It's enough to get her going. She moves towards me, and for an instant I am filled with an emotional swelling, like someone who sees a long-forgotten friend getting off of a plane. I see her and I want to hold her, to tell her how much I've missed her, to laugh and thank the universe for giving me this second chance. But then she touches me, and all those happy thoughts drop from my mind like dying sparsile stars falling from the sky, freezing my smile in a deep grimace.

Her hand, the energy where her hand once was, folds around my neck, and I gasp. It is not as if she is strangling me; rather, it is like my throat is suddenly smaller than it used to be, and I haven't yet had the time to adapt my breathing. But I can't adapt, because it grows smaller still, and the air I do manage to take in begins to dwindle.

I gaze up at Keiria with confusion, though no terror or hurt at what she is doing actually grips at me. She stares down. I am sure she is staring down at me, and a hand of shadow splashes across my face, burning my cheeks. I sink to the ground, unable to withstand the dizzying pain.

The others hear me fall. They call my name, foregoing the ritual as they move towards me in the darkness. When they see what's happening, they pull back. They are behind me, but I know they pull back; it's almost as if I am seeing things double, seeing from my spot on the floor, and seeing from Keiria's floating mass at the same time.

They don't stop her, don't extinguish the open ritual or attempt to pry me away. And for some reason, I'm glad. Their fear is obvious, though, and it does send a snaking sliver of alarm through me. Why are they so surprised? We release violent spirits. That's what we do. So why are they so baffled by this now?

But then I realize what it is. It's her. I focus my hazy sights on Keiria, and I see the grey mass that looks a little beige in places, that appears a little more solid than it probably should. Is the shadow fading?

It is.

My desire to survive propels me to reach my hands up in an effort to push Keiria away. My hand closes around her wrist, but its grip is flimsy, like it's been asleep and is now unable to tighten its hold. I study my hands, and panic when I stare directly through them. They are solid, yet I can see Keiria's shape beyond the skin, skin which now has a distinctly grey quality to it. Grey. I look up at Keiria and see that her eyes are now clearly defined within her ghastly face, all while my own senses lose focus.

I see double because my sight is flicking back and forth between us, between seeing Keiria and seeing me, between seeing an old dusty attic and seeing a sunny attic in its place, with a tall man who is so familiar it hurts. My colleagues are before me, horrified faces and shaking limbs, and then there is only him. My throat closes in, and I feel myself being beaten and used, until every inch of my body is on the verge of ripping apart. I see myself as a girl, looking at my sister, and I see her looking at me as I tell her, "I owe you one."

It shouldn't be possible for spirits to switch bodies like this. I wonder if we are special because we are sisters. Or perhaps we are special because we are twins. And maybe we're not special at all, only other ghosts haven't discovered this talent yet. And maybe they have, only no one else has bothered to notice.

I wonder what living in this attic will be like. I wonder how long I will be here until they come back and release me. Will I be like Bastian in Fantastica, lost in a world of imagination without ever knowing what he's missing back at home? Or will it be like Bastian's trip to the City of the Old Emperors, a place where humans don't belong, a place where memory fails until only misery remains? Will I even remember *The Neverending Story* when I'm only a spirit, when I'm doomed to suffer in Keiria's place?

I force myself to smile at my sister, to show her that I understand, that I am willing to make amends for stealing her life those years ago.

As I crumple to the floor, I have an overwhelming sensation of being swallowed by The Nothing. That part of the story used to scare Keiria, and I'm happy that I finally have the chance to take some of her fears away, to give life back to my own Moon Child, my eternally Childlike Empress.

THE EIGHT PANE SASH

JEANETTE GREAVES

FRANK AND MELISSA WERE new together, in a rose tinted world where life was fine, and the spin of the planet was enough to make them giddy.

They both had history; they'd both struggled, with some success, to get from the bottom of the heap. They had a long list of past addresses behind them, scattered across the country. It was natural, Frank said, that the memories of those houses would creep into his dreams. Perhaps it was the artist in him. He talked about the dreams a lot, and was surprised that Lissa didn't have similar ones. He dreamed about houses, he dreamed about the roads and pathways to those houses, and about the neighbourhoods that the houses were in. He told her that there were all kinds of houses, some of them could have doubled for homes he'd had. Some were new to his dreams. All of them, he said, led to all the others.

The Eight Pane Sash

Lissa pretended to be interested in these dreams. At first they seemed to be a way to his past, his confidence, his life. She would ask him if she was in any of the houses. He would smile and shake his head. "It's maybe too soon for that."

He loved her, and he picked up on her unease at her absence from his dreams. He said that, maybe, the way for her to get into his dreams was to move in with him.

She'd refused; she'd been down that path before. She loved her Victorian detached house, her deep and narrow back garden, the attics and cellars. In many ways, Frank said, it could have been a dream house. It was just waiting for something.

His home was a gleaming glass and steel apartment, new, spacious, and city central. He loved the light, for his paintings, and he enjoyed being close to so many galleries. It was a place that he'd never visited in his dreams.

He couldn't resist the urge to talk about his dreams. In them, the houses were not central. Things happened, dream life went on, and the houses were just background. He told her about an interwar council estate semi-detached house, a normal enough house, except that the steps from the coal shed led down to a cellar, and then a subcellar. There was a block of student flats with a room that opened up into a luxury hotel suite. There was a Victorian house, much like her own home, with a fire escape that led back on itself to a third floor, inaccessible from the rest of the house. His recurring favourite, for several weeks, was a row of terraced houses built into a steeply sloping Pennine hillside. The cellar of the house at the north end of the row had a tiny door that led straight onto the roof of the house at the south end of the row. Frankie loved the idea of it. Every one of those houses, he said, called out to him and welcomed him. He was at home in his dreams.

As their relationship grew, Frank sensed that Lissa's interest in his night world had waned, and he talked about the dream houses less and less. He was quiet in the mornings, and she learnt that it was best to leave early. He wasn't a morning person; he didn't want to chat. He was elsewhere, and she knew that he was struggling to break free from a dream, from a house and a place that had no space for her. She didn't mind: he was an affectionate, witty man who was generous with his time and happy to share her interests.

He asked her again to move in with him, and she asked him, in return, to move into her house. There was room, in the apartment and the house, for a couple, but both sensed that it was the wrong move. A year after their first date, Frank proposed that they look for a home for the two of them. He also proposed that they get married. After a little thought, Lissa agreed to both. They had savings, good incomes, they owned their homes, and they had the leeway to consider building a home that suited them both. She joked that Frank, the house dreamer, should run the project. With a speed that she found slightly insulting, he agreed.

She had her own ideas—she wanted to live away from the city centre. She wanted a private garden, with trees. She wanted to be close enough to a road to hear the hum of traffic, to know that life went on away from the house. Frank agreed to everything. He registered with estate agents, saying that he was looking for a building plot, or a house that needed to be worked on, or even a home that was already perfect for him and his love. He threw himself into the project, and Lissa found him less upset than she'd thought he would be when she told him that she had to go away for work. She had to go to the States for six months. Of course, she'd come back for long weekends, once or twice, but that was probably all she'd be able to manage. He reassured her that yes, it was fine, they'd be okay, they could talk every day anyway. It wasn't going to be a problem. Besides, he had commissions to work on, and he had the house project, so he would be too busy to mope. She kissed him on the nose, and said that she hoped that he would mope, just a little bit, just for her.

The job in the States was demanding, and although she faithfully found time to talk to Frank at least once a day, she had to cancel her first weekend back home. She was apologetic, and promised to add a couple of days to the next planned visit. Frank put on a disappointed face, and made all the right noises, but what he really wanted to talk about was the plot of land that he'd found up for auction.

"Do you trust me? To buy this place? It's perfect. Look, I'll send you all the details. We can easily afford it, with savings and just selling my place, so if—"

"If what? If it doesn't work out?" Lissa smiled. "It'll work out. I'll be selling my place, go wild. Okay, send me the details."

She was surprised at first. It wasn't a house, it was a job lot parcel of land—quite a large parcel. There was a farm track leading to an outbuilding that was described as a barn with potential. There was a big old Georgian detached house with a big front garden, facing onto an A road, that had no connection with the barn other than locality, and backing onto that, somewhat uphill of the big house, there was a row of weavers' cottages facing onto a narrow lane. Frank was at pains to reassure her that his interest was in the big house, although the barn had potential as a studio for him and an office for her. The cottages could be renovated and rented out, although he was considering demolishing one of them in order to build a driveway to the lane from the main house. He loved the idea of having three separate exits from the estate. She admitted that the project had a lot of potential, and gave him free rein to pursue his ideas.

The updates came in, and before long the house was all he was talking about. The sale went through, and she put her own house on the market, ready to invest in a joint future. They made plans for a wedding, with a grand reception at the new place. Frank sent photographs and videos of the work as it proceeded. The farm track was prepared for site traffic, and materials and workers moved in.

Finally, Lissa managed to get a break from her project and arrived at the site. The project manager directed her to the main house, where she found Frank poring over plans and layouts.

"I think we should have a tunnel, from the house cellar to the barn—it's three hundred yards from the back door to the barn, and a tunnel would be a great way of avoiding the weather. I thought about a covered walkway, but that's maybe too intrusive. What do you think?" He sounded abstracted.

"Hiya Frank." Lissa waited.

"And the cottages—it would be useful to have access from the back, even if we're renting them out—I thought we could build a path to the back, and build a new wall for their gardens, something in red brick, with matching back gates—it would look great. After all, they'll be visible from the bedroom window, and we want them to be stylish. Oh, come and take a look at the loft ladders, the action on them is incredible—push a button, the hatch goes up and the stairs come down. Amazing."

"Frankie." Lissa said, with an edge of impatience in her voice.

He turned round. "Oh. Yes. Oh." He shook his head. "It's good to see you. When did you get back? Where are you staying? Here? I mean, it's possible, but you'd be more comfortable in a B&B."

"Where are you staying?" Lissa asked.

"Here. Upstairs, the back bedroom is liveable, but there's just an airbed… I've not moved in… it's just so I can supervise and come up with ideas—"

"That's fine. We'll share the airbed," Lissa said firmly. "Now, let's get something to eat in town, then we can come back and you can give me the tour."

He looked at the plans. "Lissa, look, there's a cellar door here. It's been covered over, but it leads outside… we should look at opening it up."

She took his hand. "Dinner, talk—not house talk—then bed. Okay?"

He blinked and nodded, then slowly smiled and nodded again. "Sure. Sorry. I'm an idiot. I kinda got wrapped up in this project but now—you're back. How long for?"

"Five days. Shall we stay here and work on the house, or shall we do something else?"

Frank looked at her for a long time. "I think," he said, "we'll take some time together. London? Lakes?"

"Lakes," she said. "I'll book. We'll drive up tomorrow."

He was chatty over dinner, showing interest in her job, in the people she was working with. He talked about having the house 'liveable' by the time she was home permanently, although it would take time to get things exactly right. He wasn't painting—no time, he said; he was too busy with the house, and the barn, and the cottages. He was taking a lot of photographs of the place, of how it was changing as the workers moved in. He was pleased with the photographs, and was thinking of putting them into a book, or a film, or an exhibition.

"So, how's the flat? Is it for sale?" she asked.

"Oh, that place? Sold. You had a few bits and bobs there, so I've packed them up and sent them to your house," he said. "Speaking of your place, I think the wardrobes in your spare bedroom would look just perfect in one of the guest rooms in the new place. Would that be okay?"

"Sure, I suppose we should be thinking about what we're keeping, and what we're selling. What about your stuff?" She had a soft spot for his grandmother's dinner service; she'd already told him that.

"Oh, all gone. Except books, art, music, that's in storage."

"Your nan's Wedgwood?"

"Gone, sold. I got a good price. I tried and tried, but I couldn't see it in the dining room here. It doesn't fit. I've got my eye on some early Denby, but we can talk about that later."

The Eight Pane Sash

Later was bedtime, and the soothing of an ache that had been too long unassuaged. Afterwards, bathed by the moonlight from the uncurtained window, Frank drifted into sleep. Lissa lay on the airbed, taking in the details of the room, part familiar from photographs and descriptions. Something jarred, and she stared at the window for several minutes, until the day caught up with her and she fell asleep.

The next morning, as they prepared breakfast together, she touched Frank's shoulder. "The window, in the bedroom, did you replace it?"

"Replace? Um?" He looked confused. "I put it right."

"Put it right? I remember, in the photos, it was a four-by-four pane double sash... now it's an eight-by-eight pane."

"Yes, the four-by-four was wrong. I put it right." Frank looked puzzled.

"But you told me the windows were all original to the house, how could it be wrong?"

Frank bit his lower lip. "In my head, this one, the eight-by-eight, that's the right one."

Lissa spoke carefully. "You mean, in your dream?"

Frank nodded.

"So, the bedroom is part of one of your dream houses? And the window didn't match? So you changed the window? Who did it?"

"I did it."

Lissa turned away. She knew that however gifted an artist Frank was, and however clear his plans for the house, he didn't have the skills to replace a Georgian double sash window. She cleared her throat. "I think a few days away from here would do you good. I've booked the hotel, and we can check in early, so I thought we'd set off after breakfast."

"Can't be done. Lunchtime, at the earliest. I have to do the sketches for the crazy paving path to the cottages. It has to be right—"

"How can crazy paving be wrong?" Lissa asked.

"Well, you know, the curve, the colours, the… the pattern? I've got a clear idea of what it should look like."

Lunchtime came and went, and mid-afternoon found Frank comparing colour charts with a decorator. Lissa overheard him saying, "Would it be possible to age the dining room doors a bit? After they've been painted? I'm not looking for the newly decorated look. I want something a bit lived in."

He ordered takeaway for the evening meal, then seemed to remember that they'd had plans. "Oh hell, I'm sorry Lissa. We'll set out after this."

"Too late. I'll ring and tell them we'll arrive tomorrow." Lissa looked at the curry in its plastic boxes and shrugged. "I'm off out. I'm going to the Ancient Oak for a proper meal. I'll see you later."

The next morning, she couldn't find Frank at all. A contractor told her that he'd been seen heading for the cottages, but Lissa couldn't find him. She'd been searching the cottages for half an hour when he emerged from a back door.

"Where were you?"

"In the cottage, checking out the floors. Two of them are right, the others will need work."

"I was just in there. I didn't see you."

"I was in the box room."

The Eight Pane Sash

Lissa fought against a tide of irritation. "There is no box room."

"Third bedroom?" Frank tried a smile.

"It's a two bedroom cottage," Lissa said. "Honestly, you're going gaga. Come on, I've packed a case for you. We can leave now and be in the Lakes by lunchtime."

"Ah—"

"What?" she snapped.

"It's the barn conversion, I've realised it needs a veranda. I was going to measure it out today."

She shook her head. "I'm flying back to New York the day after tomorrow. I want a break, just us, away from the house. I've taken time off work, why can't you?"

"Oh, it's not work... look, I thought this place was for us?" Frank pleaded.

"So did I. I was obviously mistaken," Lissa said. She stalked to her car, threw Frank's suitcase onto the drive, and left.

Days later, back in New York, she took his call.

"You just left." He sounded plaintive.

"I came back for a break, not to watch you indulge your whims over the house."

"It's our house." Now he really sounded hurt.

"It's our lives, together. I took time off work. I expected you to take time away from the house project. We agreed that's what we'd do... we'd spend some time together. What went wrong?" She kept her voice even.

"I don't know." His voice came from very far away. "I don't know Lissa. I don't understand. I lost focus. Sometimes, I don't quite know where I am."

She paused. "Frankie, honey, are you okay?"

There was a silence. Then, "Yes. I'm okay. Just a bit vague at times. Don't worry, I get like this sometimes, when there's a big project. When are you home again?"

"Seven weeks, then I'm home for good. I'm looking forward to it."

"Seven weeks? Oh, the house will be ready by then, and the barn and cottages will be well on their way. Will you be moving in with me at the new house?"

"Sure, hon. My place is still on the market, and there have been some bites already." She changed the subject, and they talked about her work, then about films, TV, books. He didn't seem to be up to date with the latest episodes of their favourite series, but after all, there was no cable or satellite yet at the new place.

Two or three times, he wasn't there for their regular calls. It was late, for him, in England, and she knew it was unreasonable to expect him to work on the house and stay up till late every night. She changed the time of the calls, fitting them in at lunchtime when she could. Her project was stressful, close to completion, and she didn't really mind if a call or two went unanswered. When Frank did reply, the connection was often dodgy, and he kept promising to improve the wi-fi at the new house. In the rush of trying to complete the project on time, she barely noticed the run of missed calls until it had been five days since she'd heard from him. Worried, she emailed, texted, rang every number she had for him. Nothing.

She rang his friends and colleagues. They were vague about his whereabouts; he'd been in contact less and less over the last six months; they'd assumed he was working on the house, seeing Lissa, making wedding plans. She got in touch with the contractors on the house. They'd all seen him recently, they said, but couldn't say when they'd spoken to him last.

Lissa flew home, leaving the project, desperate for news. She went straight to the new house, and found only contractors finishing the last few jobs. She sent them away, and wandered from barn to cottages to house. There were paths connecting the buildings. There was a tunnel, complete, that ran between them. There were verandas and balconies, out of character with everything, that gave views of the estate, of the paths and roads that surrounded it. There was a wooden bridge, or at least half a bridge, that rose from the side of the barn and reached towards the back of the cottages. She stood on the veranda of the barn and looked towards the house. She saw a shadow, behind the sash window in the main bedroom. She ran to the house, and upstairs. The bedroom was not as she remembered it. The window was the replacement that she remembered, but the only door that was familiar was the one she'd entered through. Every wall was packed with door frames, so many styles and sizes, she couldn't grasp how there could be room for all of them. She opened a door, a modern, cheap, crimson painted door with an anodised steel handle, mock brass. There was nothing behind it but brick. She shut it gently and sat on the bed, reaching for her phone.

Frank had gone. There was no trace of him, infrared detectors found no trace of the heat of decay, and sniffer dogs found no scent of a corpse. The police and his friends concluded that he was missing. Some told her that he'd be back, that the artistic temperament was prone to such absences. Lissa walked away from the estate, and back to her own home, the house she loved, the familiar garden and walls, the colours that she knew so well. She offered rewards for any information that would help her to find Frank. She travelled the country, talking to his friends, searching for clues. She slept and she dreamt, and hoped for a dream of him.

She dreamt of a motorway junction, vast concrete sweeps and curves that joined together in a baffling maze. She dreamt of finding a single exit, one car wide, that led from the grey concrete edifice to green lanes. She woke, frustrated, and it was a full day later that sleep came again and led her down the green lane to her own home. She followed the dream, up the stairs, and up the stairs again, to the attic room that wasn't there, through the red door that swung in the breeze of another place, and into the house that needed her so much, the house that hungered to inhabit her, the house that was ready now, to tell her what it wanted to be.

THE ANATOMY OF MERMAIDS

ELISABETH BRANDER

VIVIEN SLEPT WITH THE seashells. She'd amassed quite a collection over the past several months, most of them acquired during her long rambles on the beach while a few were gifts from farther afield; and now her bed was littered with gracefully curved gastropod shells, bivalve shells with delicate ridges, and even a rare nautilus shell whose interior shone with the colors of the rainbow. It should have been awkward and uncomfortable, sleeping in a bed strewn with so many pieces of the ocean, but she'd grown accustomed to it. Her limbs had learned how to curve in just the right way so they brushed up against the calcified ridges and whorls without encountering any sharp or jagged edges, and she fell asleep each night brushing her fingers over their familiar contours.

She dreamed of the mermaids, terrifying and seductive with their sharp white teeth and razor-edged fins, and when she woke up she could taste blood on her tongue.

VIVIEN USED TO LOVE the water unequivocally. She'd grown up in Nebraska, which was practically as far from the ocean as you could get, but her mom had taken her to the public pool every Saturday morning once she was old enough to start toddling, and so she took to swimming as easily as walking. She used to splash around in the chlorinated water with her goggles hanging around her neck like a necklace of seashells, heedless of the stinging in her eyes and happily pretending she had a graceful tail instead of chubby little legs. Mom looked at her and shook her head, told her that she knew about little girls who were so taken with the water that their skin started to sprout scales and their hair became thick and green, like strands of seaweed. She just laughed, and asked Mom when it would happen to her.

The Christmas she turned ten her parents gave her a conch shell. It was a beautiful specimen, the rich ivory exterior giving way to a soft, sunrise-pink interior, and so large it took both of her tiny hands to hold it. Mom smiled as she watched Vivien explore the dips and ridges with her fingers, then told her to hold it against her ear.

The Anatomy of Mermaids

Do you hear that? she said. *It's what the ocean sounds like. Now you can listen to it wherever you are.* She leaned down and kissed the top of Vivien's head. *My little mermaid.*

That night was the first time Vivien dreamed of the ocean, of blue water and endless skies, and when she woke up the next morning the first thing she did was press the conch against her head to listen to the sound of the waves.

From that point on she always wanted to see the ocean, but she saw Lake Michigan first. She was a teenager, and her family spent two weeks vacationing in the Leelanau Peninsula just a stone's throw from Sleeping Bear Dunes. They went in early June just after school let out to avoid the large groups of tourists that started to show up in late July and August, and while Lake Michigan was probably still too cold for most people's tastes, Vivien thought it was perfect. The trick was that you had to run headlong into the waves without stopping, then plunge quickly underwater. The first minute or so was like a shock to the system, but then it felt wonderful, cool without being freezing. The rest of the family preferred hiking the sand dunes or going into town for hot pasties followed by cones of Superman ice cream, but she was in the water every day, even when the northern Michigan breeze turned chilly and the sun hid behind the clouds.

She cried when they left to go back to the flat, dry cornfields of the Great Plains, hiding her tears behind the time-honored excuse of a sudden allergy attack. When they got back she'd sit on the wraparound porch of their house and close her eyes, summoning up the memory of how she'd dive underwater and then look up at the water above. It had been beautiful, the

367

surface shimmering like the liquid face of a mirror. Then she opened her eyes and the image was gone, leaving nothing before her but the dusty earth of the American Midwest.

SHE LEFT THE NEBRASKA plains when she was eighteen and graduated from high school, trading its flat, dun-colored landscapes for the stern Gothic beauty of the University of Chicago. Her parents had wanted her to go to Nebraska, mainly for the free tuition, but she'd been adamant. The loans would work themselves out, she said, and besides, she wanted a challenge. She wanted the hours spent hunched over books in the ugly brutalist shell of Regenstein Library, wanted the stress that came with working on five research papers at once and feeling the cranial ache that came from trying to cram in too much information all at once. She wanted to be at U of C, and that was that. In the end, her parents capitulated, and she won.

It only took a month for her to fall in love with Chicago. She'd never been one for small town America, and had always felt cramped and uncomfortable in her tiny hometown, but Chicago—Chicago was the city of her heart. She loved walking down Michigan Avenue being surrounded by crowds of people, and loved the beauty of downtown's skyscrapers at night. A group of freshman went to the bar on the top of the Hancock building right after midterms for celebratory drinks, and Vivien had looked down at the brightly lit cityscape laid out beneath her and thought that it was one of the most beautiful things she'd ever seen. Life and energy and endless potential: that was what Chicago was to her.

And then there was the lake.

Vivien had never forgotten that trip to the dunes. That experience had been enough to tell her that when she left the Heartland she needed to be close to water, close to an *immense* body of water, not some small swimming hole or filthy brown river. That was something Chicago gave her. Vivien adored the city, adored its noise and glitter and throbbing pulse of life, but her favorite thing was to go alone to the beach and look at Lake Michigan. It was remarkably changeable. One day it would be a rich royal blue, deep and inviting; the next a clear, crisp jade; and finally dull slate gray, threatening and ominous. She liked to think of it as an ever-changing chimera, with her as its faithful guardian.

Vivien swam in it as often as she could. She had never lost the love of being immersed in water, of letting it surround and support her. Being in the water was the only time when she felt graceful and comfortable in her body. She'd inherited her mother's knobby knees and awkward gait, making running a decidedly unpleasant experience, and gym class had always been a special kind of torment. Swimming, however, was different. When she swam her legs and arms worked in harmony, turning her from a gangly kid into something powerful. She liked to think that being in water was her natural state; it was walking on two legs that felt strange and wrong.

Swimming off of the Chicago lakefront wasn't as transcendent as swimming up north, where there were no manmade structures in sight, but it was still the same Lake

Michigan water, clear and sweet, and so Vivien loved it. In the last warm days of summer she went to North Avenue Beach, swimming past the crowds who played in the surf until she had enough space to roll over onto her back and let her gaze trail over the panorama of the city's skyscrapers. In autumn, when the weather cooled and the trees in the quadrangle turned into blazes of red and orange, she contented herself with kneeling close to the surf and letting the water run over the tips of her fingers: *Hello, I'm still here.*

She went to her parents' house in Nebraska for Christmas, back to achingly empty snowfields and dull, never-ending horizons, and hated almost every minute of it. She was back in Chicago right after Boxing Day, just in time for her first experience with the New Year's Day Polar Plunge. And *that* had been something extraordinary: running across the ice on the beach to get to the dark, frigid water and then jumping in, letting the waves close over her head and feeling the chill penetrate her bones before coming up sputtering and *cold*, colder than she'd ever been in her life.

It felt almost like being born again.

THEN SHE MET FINALLY met the ocean in person, and her relationship to water changed irrevocably.

She was twenty-one. Her sophomore year roommate—Penelope, like Odysseus' pining wife—was from Miami, and she insisted that Vivien spend Thanksgiving vacation with her.

The Anatomy of Mermaids

Penelope claimed that going to Nebraska in November was the epitome of depression, and that she really didn't want to find someone new to live with if it drove Vivien to desperate measures. Vivien couldn't really argue with that logic, and, figuring that Thanksgiving in Florida sounded considerably more fun than either spending it in Nebraska with her family or in Chicago alone, put down the money for a plane ticket.

Vivien didn't care for the city of Miami itself—it was cacophonous and had an underlying layer of tackiness that she found irritating at best—but seeing the ocean for the first time was one of those rare occasions that merited the word *transcendent*. Penelope drove the two of them out to Virginia Key beach just a few hours after their plane landed, insisting that she couldn't wait to get her feet wet, and Vivien had been more than happy to go along with that plan. They stopped at Penelope's parents' house just long enough to drop off their suitcases and then they were back in the car, heading to the water.

They arrived at sunset, when the water was a rich dark blue set against a sky that was painted in shades of pink and gold. Vivien stared out across that endless expanse and listened to the sound of the waves pounding against the shore. She'd heard it before, with her conch pressed against her ear, but now she could also taste the salt air and feel the sea run across her skin. Looking at the ocean gave her a feeling of belonging that she'd never quite had before, and she had to blink back a sudden rush of tears.

Home, she thought, *I've come home.*

The day after Thanksgiving Penelope went to her aunt's house and Vivien went to the beach. Seventy-five was on the cooler side for the Florida natives, but she was a northerner, and the air was perfect for her blood. She spent the day flopped out on the sand, basking in the bright Florida sunlight until her skin cried out for relief, then running out into the blue waves. The waters of the Atlantic were different from those of the Great Lakes—they were thicker, more languid to move through, and left the taste of salt in her mouth—but they welcomed her in the same way, supporting her body and washing away all of its landlocked awkwardness.

She splashed back out onto the beach when her fingers were pruned and she desperately wanted a drink of fresh water, then dropped down onto her towel and kept her eyes fixed on the waves. They were hypnotic. The water began to swell somewhere in the middle horizon, white lace appearing on its crest as it gathered height and speed, then finally crashed and bubbled against the sand with a low roar. Vivien closed her eyes and listened to the ceaseless pounding of water against land. It was almost enough to lull her to sleep.

She opened her eyes and looked at the woman sitting next to her. At first glance she looked like a typical Florida native in her early twenties: cut-off jean shorts paired with a bright pink tank top, toenails sparkling with purple glitter polish, long brown hair streaked gold by the sun. Her face, though—her face was at odds with the rest of her appearance. The features were young but the expression behind them looked old, older than anything Vivien could imagine. She looked more like the statues of Isis that Vivien had seen in the Oriental Institute than a woman of flesh and blood, and Vivien felt a sudden, almost overpowering urge to press her forehead to the ground in obeisance.

Then the woman smiled, and Vivien's eyes widened in horrified awe. All she could see were those *teeth*, jutting out of the woman's pink gums like needles fashioned out of nacre. It was as if some cruel god had mistakenly given a human the mouth of an anglerfish. It was grotesque. An abomination.

The woman's smile grew wider. Vivien started to back away, wanting to put some distance between herself and that ungodly grin, but the woman was fast. She managed to clamber on top of Vivien in the space of a second, trapping her in a cage of bony limbs. Vivien could smell blood on the woman's breath, and she opened her mouth to scream—

The woman began to sing, and Vivien forgot everything else.

It was like nothing Vivien had ever heard before. When she remembered it later, she would think it had sounded something like water transmuted into music; in the moment, her only thought was that she never wanted it to end. It was sweet and wild, and so achingly beautiful that it could almost make Vivien forget the sheer *wrongness* of the singer's face.

She felt a shadow fall over her face and opened her eyes to see Penelope looking down at her. *You're well on your way to getting burned*, she said, her eyes crinkling up with laughter, and tossed a tube of sunscreen at Vivien.

Vivien stared blankly up at her roommate, feeling numb. There was no trace of the woman (*mermaid*, her mind whispered, *it was a mermaid*), and Vivien might have thought that she'd dreamed the entire encounter if it weren't for the cowry shell on the sand next to her. She picked it up and cradled it between her palms. It was beautiful, its smooth surface speckled with spots of amber and brown. She remembered that hideous mouth and wanted to fling it far away from her, all the way back into the depths. Then she remembered the singing, and hesitated. Her fingers closed around it, holding it tight.

VIVIEN COULD acknowledge that she'd seen something ugly that day on Virginia Key Beach. She'd seen something dark and twisted and most definitely dangerous (but also beautiful and seductive and utterly fantastical). She knew she'd be better off if she could just forget the ocean. That proved to be impossible. The memory of the woman and her song took up residence in Vivien's brain and haunted her dreams, stealing her concentration and leaving her pale and wan. Her grades started to slip. She became withdrawn. Her advisor pulled her to the side and recommended counseling. Her friends asked her what was wrong, but she had no real answer.

She went back to the beach and looked out at Lake Michigan, trying to find the peace that it had always brought her before, but the lake turned away from her. It was beautiful but remote, and when she pulled off her glove to dip her fingers into the surf, she felt none of the connection that used to bring her so much joy. It was as though the lake could sense the taint of saltwater in her veins, and rejected her for it.

The Anatomy of Mermaids

She went back to her room and pretended to be sick, crawling under the covers and crying very quietly into her pillow so that Penelope couldn't hear. The ocean hovered in the darkness behind her closed eyelids, a beautiful canvas of shifting blues and greens that promised both freedom and eternity. The sight made her sick with longing. Vivien didn't know if it was because she had always been a part of the sea or if the woman's song had corrupted (or awakened) something within her, but the one thing she felt sure of was that she needed the ocean to survive. Staying on dry land would kill her.

And that aching discontent was bad enough in and of itself, but then the physical hunger kicked in. And that was worse.

Vivien had been a vegetarian ever since she was twelve. Her family had gone to a party at Dad's friend's cattle ranch, held in honor of the eldest daughter's graduation from high school. There had been a lot of food: tables full of potato salad and gelatin molds, carrot sticks and bowls of ranch dressing, and, of course, steaks and hamburgers sizzling away on the large Webster grill. It was a typical Midwestern summer barbecue, like dozens upon dozens of others Vivien had been to by that point in her life.

Except this time she and the other kids spent the morning running around the barns and petting the warm, smooth hide of the cows, and letting the little calves thrust their damp noses into their hands. They scratched at velvety soft ears and looked into warm brown eyes that were gentle and trusting, and then when their parents called them back to eat they were presented with bloody chunks of seared flesh. Vivien had looked at them and started to bawl. She was inconsolable. There was no way she could bring herself to eat meat after that day, much to her mother's consternation.

It was therefore a little disconcerting to come back from Florida with an insistent, undeniable craving for flesh. She couldn't deny it. The more she tried to ignore it, the worse the craving got, and she finally decided to screw it all and give in. She was going to do it *properly* though—she wasn't going to end almost a decade of vegetarianism by going to McDonald's and getting a cheap, chemical-filled Big Mac. No. Vivien did her research. She looked into which Chicago butchers were sourcing local, grass-fed organic beef, and then went out and bought a nice thick rib-eye that was dark red and marbled with fat.

She pan seared her prize in the tiny dorm room. It smelled amazing. When it was ready Vivien took a moment to just stare at the cooked flesh, with its dark brown crispy crust and rivulets of juice running out of it, then devoured the entire thing in about fifteen minutes flat. It was arguably the most delicious thing she had ever eaten.

Five minutes after that she was on her knees in the dorm bathroom throwing it all back up, her body violently rejecting the sudden influx of meat after so many years of abstinence. By the time she was done emptying her stomach she was trembling and exhausted, and her mouth tasted like bile. She felt miserable, but at the same time she wanted more. She wanted to use her teeth to tear and rend, and to feel hot blood run down the throat.

That night she curled up around her pillow with the cowry shell clenched in her fist. When she closed her eyes, the mermaids came to her. They swam up out of the ocean's depths to circle around her in a swirl of pale white arms and shimmering tails, singing their haunting melody. They were hideous and beautiful and alluring, and even though they repulsed one part of her, another part wanted nothing more than to join them.

When she woke up, she felt the rhythm of the surf throbbing in her veins and knew there was only one road she could take.

SIX MONTHS AFTER SHE saw the mermaid, Vivien left Chicago. There wasn't much keeping her there at that point—she'd fallen off on her studies, to the point that she was facing academic suspension, and she no longer had it in her to care. Her friends' attempts to cheer her up by dragging her downtown to concerts and museums and coffee shops just left her feeling even more disconnected and miserable, and after a while they stopped trying. Her counselor talked about maybe going back to Nebraska, staying with her parents while she 'found her footing again,' and when Vivien heard *that* she wanted to throw up. Being surrounded by cornfields would kill her. No, if she had to leave Chicago she'd go back to ground zero, to the place where everything had started to fall apart. She'd go back to Miami, and the ocean.

Vivien packed a single duffel bag with all the worldly possessions she deemed worth keeping, and bought a one-way ticket on a Greyhound bus headed to Florida. Her parents were inconsolable. They yelled at first, then wept, then yelled some more, and finally watched her go with bewildered sadness. Vivien ignored them. She was beyond caring. All she knew was that she was sick, being hollowed out from the inside, and the only thing that could fix her was the ocean.

Finding her footing in Miami was easier than she thought it would be. It helped that she didn't care about a career, or finding love, or anything else long-term—all she needed was to make enough money for a roof and food. She settled into a combination of waitressing and bartending, and split the rent on an apartment close to the beach with two other girls. She told them she'd finally had enough of living up north and wanted to do the sand and sun Florida thing. They all smiled and told her they got it. They didn't, but there was no point in trying to explain.

She visited the Atlantic the way she used to visit Lake Michigan. It was still as beautiful and alluring as ever, and when she plunged into the briny waves the ache that had taken root somewhere deep inside her started to fade. She didn't see the mermaid, or any of her sisters, but she knew they were there. She could hear their song every time she dove under the waves. It grew clearer and clearer every time she heard it, until it sounded like it was coming from within her own head rather than the dark blue depths. She eventually caught herself humming the melody from time to time, the notes and cadences coming to her as naturally as breathing, and she knew she was almost ready.

She kept eating meat. Her body had gotten used to it, and she no longer threw up afterward. She started preferring her steaks rarer and rarer until she was barely cooking them at all, just lightly warming them up before tearing into the pink muscle with her incisors.

The irrevocable change finally happened three months after she came to Florida. She was eating dinner—more meat, red and bloody—when she accidentally bit her lip, the tooth sliding into flesh as smooth and easy as a hot knife going into butter. She reached up and ran her finger over her canines. Their form had changed. They were no longer mostly flat and dull the way human teeth were, but instead tapered into a sharp, well-defined point. As recently as a few months ago, she would have been horrified. As things stood now, all she felt was calm acceptance.

She swept her tongue over the small wound, swallowing the droplets of blood that had gathered there, and stared down at her plate. It was empty except for a small pool of bloody meat juice and a few scraps of pale fat. The question of what it would be like to taste human flesh floated up from the darker recesses of her brain, and she didn't immediately push it away. She was more curious than anything else.

She pressed her finger to the plate and swept up the last traces of juice, popped it into her mouth, and licked it clean.

SHE WENT DOWN TO THE beach just after two o'clock in the morning, when no one was awake to see her go. Her roommates wouldn't notice her absence until tomorrow night, when they would knock tentatively on her bedroom door and slip inside. They'd look at the collection of seashells strewn across Vivien's bed and wonder, but not know what to make of it, and when she failed to reappear the day after that the police would be called. The investigation would, of course, prove fruitless, and Vivien would ultimately become just another name on the missing persons list.

Vivien would never know that, but it wouldn't have mattered if she did. She made her way to the most isolated stretch of beach she could find and stripped off her clothes, leaving them in a pile beside her. The night air felt good on her skin, and she took a moment to savor it before stepping into the surf. The water splashed playfully at her ankles as if in greeting. She waded deeper until the waves were pushing against her knees, then her chest, and then she finally had to lift her feet off the sandy bottom and start kicking her way forward.

She swam farther than she had ever dared go before, far enough to leave the lights of the city behind. There was no moon, but the stars were almost terrifying in their intensity. Vivien had never seen them so big and close, close enough that she could almost reach up and touch them. Or perhaps some of them had fallen into the ocean itself, and if she swam down far enough she would find them resting on seafloor like luminescent pearls. She wanted to find out. She took one last deep breath and dove down under the waves, letting the endless Atlantic embrace and overwhelm her until every other sensation faded away.

The change didn't hurt. It was easy and organic, her legs fusing together and sprouting shimmering green and blue scales while her hair grew green and long. She opened her mouth and let the sea rush into her, as natural as breathing air had been. She flipped her powerful fins once, then twice, propelling herself deeper into the black depths. Her sisters were lurking below with their long white arms stretched outward in greeting and their voices lifted in song. Vivien spiraled down deeper to join them, bubbles trailing in her wake. For the first time in months, there was no ache in her chest. She was complete.

Her sister mermaids swirled around her, and Vivien joined her voice with theirs. She felt calm and at peace, and when the others took her arms and guided her back toward the surface she went willingly. They emerged far from land, somewhere in the middle of the ocean's endless expanse, and there was nothing to break the horizon but the lonely lights of a small fishing boat.

Vivien ran her tongue over her sharp, deadly teeth, and sang.

AUTHOR BIOS

ALLEN ASHLEY is an award-winning writer, editor, poet, tutor and event host. His most recent book is as editor of *Astrologica: Stories of the Zodiac* (Alchemy Press, 2013). His next two books will be: *Dreaming Spheres—Poems of the Solar System*, a collaboration written with poet Sarah Doyle due from PS Publishing's Stanza imprint in Autumn 2014; and as editor of *Sensorama: Stories of the Senses*, due from Eibonvale Press in late 2014 or early 2015. Allen runs five creative writing groups including the hugely successful Clockhouse London Writers. He also co-hosts, along with Sarah Doyle, Rhyme & Rhythm Jazz-Poetry Club at the Dugdale Centre, Enfield. Allen is well-known as a champion of the short story form, particularly in the SF/F/H genres. He writes a regular column for the British Fantasy Society Email Newsletter and is the judge of the annual British Fantasy Society Short Story Competition. His website is www.allenashley.com.

A Sheffield-based medievalist, writer, folkie and theatre practitioner, **DAISY BLACK** has recently completed a PhD on the workings of time in the medieval mystery plays. Daisy grew up in East Anglia, and, although she often walks on the beach where her story is set, she has not yet seen anything strange there. This is her third published story, following 'A Life in Six Umbrellas' (2012) and 'The Carrier' (2013). She has had several plays performed at theatres, folk festivals and on streets around the UK (most recently 'Passion Tree' for Manchester Histories Festival), and has had poetry published and TV pilots filmed. Her academic publications examine medieval plays dealing with Joseph's sceptical reaction to his pregnant virgin wife, spiritual cannibalism, and time travelling trees. She is currently working on a book of modern mystery drama, and can occasionally be spotted teaching ceilidh dances and playing a blue-faced fool at folk festivals. Daisy enjoys dark fiction, tea and cake and heavy metal morris dancing.

ELISABETH BRANDER has on-going love affairs with science fiction, fantasy, fairy tales (proper fairy tales, not the watered down and sanitized versions), and all things macabre. She studied Japanese language and literature as an undergraduate, then did an about-face and decided to get her Masters in early modern European history, focusing on witchcraft in the Holy Roman Empire. She picked up her Masters of Library Science at the same time, which now lets her work as the rare book librarian at a medical library in Saint Louis, Missouri. Being surrounded by several centuries worth of medical books means that a source of inspiration is never too far away, whether it comes from a seventeenth-century cure for epilepsy that calls for the brain of a man who died a violent death, or smiling

384

skeletons displaying their innards. She lives with a cat named Malefica, who is supposed to be her familiar. In reality, the cat is the one calling the shots. If she were a mythical creature she would, perhaps unsurprisingly, be a mermaid.

GUY BURTENSHAW lives in a small town in southern England and has been writing horror stories for many years. He has self-published several horror novels and his short stories can be found in various magazines and anthologies. He also writes murder mystery novels under the pseudonym G.D. Shaw.

JAMES EVERINGTON mainly writes dark supernatural fiction, although he occasionally takes a break and writes dark non-supernatural fiction. His second collection of such tales, *Falling Over*, is out now from Infinity Plus, and he has had work published in *Supernatural Tales*, *Dark Moon Digest*, *Morpheus Tales* and the *Little Visible Delight* anthology, amongst others. He has a black cat and cream carpets, which shows how much thought he puts into those parts of his life that aren't book-related. Oh and he drinks Guinness, if anyone's asking. You can find out what James is currently up to at his Scattershot Writing site (www.jameseverington.blogspot.com).

TRACY FAHEY is a Gothic devotee whose research interests lie chiefly in uncanny domestic space and its various interactions and intersections with literature, art, design and folktales. She works as Head of Department of Fine Art at Limerick School of Art and Design where she runs a research centre in fine art, design and curatorial studies. She also runs a fine art collaborative practice, Gothicise (www.gothicise.weebly.com), who have carried out a number of site-specific projects in Ireland. She has given papers on the Gothic in New Zealand, California, Denmark, Scotland, Wales and England on topics including Irish castles, liminal landscapes, suburban terror, dark folklore, fairy-tale architecture, medical abnormality and werewolves. Her short story in this edited collection, 'Ghost Estate, Phase II', ties in the traditional trope of the haunted house with the contemporary Irish landscape of ghost estates, and suggests how these mournful never-houses can be construed as an uncanny mirror of economic and cultural ruin.

MARK FORSHAW grew up in the wilds of the Rossendale Valley, a place where the weird is woven into everyday life. His own Fortean encounters include two daylight UFO sightings and, on Christmas Eve 1984, an absurdly classic ghost, complete with spectral horse. A cheerful friend he trusts implicitly once saw Death standing in a farmer's field. Mark's debut publication, in the year 2000, was an academic article criticising Douglas Coupland's insufficient irony in his use of millennial and supernatural imagery. After years spent reading too much and writing too little, except about other people's fiction, Mark is now working on his own stories. They are full of hints of the coming apocalypse and appearances by desirable ghosts. On personality tests, Mark scores highly for rationality and critical thinking. He divides his time between the past and the present versions of himself, and Santa Monica and Stockport. He is an occasionally published poet.

JEANETTE GREAVES prefers dusk to dawn, and winter to summer. She wanted to be a goth, but her hair was too floppy and she was allergic to make-up. She has had a wide variety of jobs, and has found that being a writer has given her the perfect excuse for never having stuck with one thing. It was all 'research', obviously. Jeanette has had stories published in two previous Hic Dragones anthologies and is delighted to have completed a hat trick with 'The Eight Pane Sash'. She's old enough to know better, and blogs at www.bloginbasket.com.

RACHEL HALSALL is a nineteen-year-old alternative model, who has been writing short stories ever since she learned to read and has been published several times in various Young Writers anthologies from the age of twelve onwards. She has always been fascinated by the macabre, arranging ghost circles and hiding makeshift Ouija boards from her parents long before she began reading horror in earnest. Her introduction to classic Hammer horror films and the works of Stephen King set her love of the genre in stone and she has rarely strayed from it since. After winning an award for her short story 'The Erlking' in a competition for Waterstone's in collaboration with the feminist and alternative lifestyle website Mookychick, Rachel decided to further pursue her passion for writing by enrolling in an undergraduate course in English Language and Creative Writing at Manchester Metropolitan University and is continuing to write articles and short stories for publication.

MICHAEL HITCHINS is a writer of plays and short stories that often have a fantastical or peculiar bent, exploring the manifestation of natural and supernatural phenomena within urban environments, the effects of human activity on the natural world, and the imprint of the past (both physical and mental) on our lives today. He loves walking and cycling in the Yorkshire Dales, photographing trees and rivers, and engaging (with limited ability) in various art and craft activities, such as making mosaics and marbling. He is a member of his local theatre-writing group, a story-writing workshop and a poetry reading group. He studied English at Lancaster University and lives in Harrogate, North Yorkshire with his wife, two sons and dog, Maddox.

MERE JOYCE holds a bachelor's degree in English from York University, Toronto, and a Master of Library and Information Science from the University of Western Ontario. As both a writer and a librarian, she understands the importance of a good read, and the impact the right story can have. Mere has always found something inherently dark in many cherished children's stories, and often something unexpectedly deep in even the goriest of horror. One day she decided to try her hand at mingling the light of innocence with the shadows of fear, and she has been delighting in the possibilities ever since. When she's not reading, writing or recommending books, Mere is usually at home with her husband and her own luck dragon (also known as her dog) Falkor. You can visit her online at http://merejoyce.blogspot.com.

RUE KARNEY is a horror writer and amateur neuroscientist with a not-so-secret love of the bizarre and gruesome. Kicked out of high school for allegedly blaspheming in front of a nun, she chose to explore her peripatetic leanings by boarding a bus with a one-way ticket and a dog-eared copy of *Frankenstein*. She has worked as an artists' model, barmaid and frozen food packer but (apart from writing horror) her most interesting job has been cleaning toilets in a pub in the middle of the Australian desert. When not creating malicious characters and evil scenarios designed to make readers squirm, Rue enjoys baking bread, learning French and reading about psychopaths.

HANNAH KATE is an editor, writer and aspiring novelist based in North Manchester. She is currently the editor-in-chief at Hic Dragones, and has had stories published in anthologies by Fox Spirit Books and CFZ Press. Her poetry has appeared in a number of magazines and anthologies, and her debut collection, *Variant Spelling*, was published in 2011. Hannah also reviews books for a number of websites, including Monster Librarian. Under the name Hannah Priest, she is an academic writer and researcher, and has published numerous articles and reviews about medieval and contemporary popular culture, including pieces on twelfth-century knights, twenty-first-century werewolves, and *Resident Evil*. Hannah likes cats, hates sleep, and doesn't play well with others.

PATRICK LACEY is an Editorial Assistant in the healthcare industry. When he's not reading about blood clots and infectious diseases, he writes about things that make the general public uncomfortable. He lives in Massachusetts with his wife, his pomeranian, and his muse, who he's pretty sure is trying to kill him. Follow him on Twitter (@patlacey).

KERIS MCDONALD lives in the not-very-grim north of England and has seen her horror short stories published in *All Hallows* magazine and anthologies by Ashtree Press. Her story 'Nepenthes' appeared in the Hic Dragones anthology *Impossible Spaces*. She spends most of her writing time under the pen name 'Janine Ashbless' though, spinning tales of supernatural erotica and passionate romantic adventure for publishers such as HarperCollins and Virgin. Her ninth novel, *Cover Him with Darkness*, a dark story of fallen angels and religious conspiracy, was published in October 2014 by Cleis Press. 'Under His Wing, Poor Thing' is set in West Yorkshire, and is inspired by the landscape around Elland where her husband used to live, memories of creepy 1970s children's TV shows, and a particular illustration by Pauline Baynes in C.S. Lewis's *The Last Battle*.

SARAH PEPLOE was born and raised in Norwich (all attempts to count her fingers gratefully received). She has since headed West/North, working as a student, a librarian, a life model and various breeds of office and retail monkey in the process. Her writing has appeared in *Cassiopeia Magazine*, *Murky Depths*, *Flash* and *330 Words*. She illustrated the poetry chapbooks *Ghosts at the Dinner Table* and *He is in the Stars,* and the anthology *Livid Among the Ghostings* for Manchester-based performance poet Anna Percy. She also produces comics as part of Mindstain Comics co-operative, including *Celeriac:*

Vegetable Spawn of Cthulhu, Wanker's Tan, Convention (with George Joy) and *Grunt8790* (with Steven Burton). She lives in York. Sundry yatterings @peplovna.

STEWART PRINGLE is a writer, producer and critic based in London. His plays for the stage include *As Ye Sow, The Ghost Hunter* and *The Horror! The Horror!* (with Tom Richards and Jeffrey Mayhew) and have been performed at venues across the UK. He co-founded Theatre of the Damned in 2010 and co-created and produced the London Horror Festival between 2011 and 2013. He is a regular theatre critic for Time Out London and has also written for publications including *Headpress, Culture Wars* and *The Guardian*. His first film, *Whisper*, is currently in production by BreakNeck Films. Stewart is the artistic director of the Old Red Lion Theatre, Islington.

Author, historian, and adventurer at the intersection, **BRANDY SCHILLACE** is managing editor of *Culture, Medicine, and Psychiatry* and Research Associate/public engagement for the Dittrick Museum of Medical History. Brandy has written fiction, non-fiction and blogs for *Inside Higher Ed, Huffington Post, Belt Magazine* and the *Centre for Medical Humanities,* Durham (UK). In addition to academic articles, she is co-editor of a collection titled *Unnatural Reproductions and Monstrosity* (Cambria, 2014) and a cultural history of grief ritual, *Death's Summer Coat* (Elliott and Thompson, 2015). Taking a cue from Edward Gorey and John Bellairs, she writes fantasy gothic and YA fiction, but with a medical twist. Her first series, *The Jacob Maresheth Chronicles*, is published with Cooperative Trade. She is also working on a second series, *The Witchwood at Nob's End*, plus a mystery series and a novel about rogue scholarship and nefarious goats. As part of her further adventures in history, medicine and literature, she created the fictionreboot-dailydose.com blog. When she isn't researching arsenic poisoning for the Dittrick Museum, writing fiction, taking over the world or herding cats, Brandy teaches for Case Western Reserve University and develops medical humanities curricula for the Cleveland Clinic Lerner College of Medicine.

B.E. SCULLY lives in a haunted red house that lacks a foundation, in the misty woods of Oregon, with a variety of human and animal companions. Scully is the author of the critically acclaimed gothic thriller *Verland: the Transformation*, the short story collection *The Knife and the Wound It Deals*, and numerous short stories, poems and articles. Her latest novella, *The Eye That Blinds*, will be released by DarkFuse Publishing in 2015. Published work, interviews, and odd scribblings can be found at bescully.com.

DAVID WEBB writes stories and poems. Some of them have been published; others have been abandoned as beyond saving. Having renounced a Civil Service career in 2008, David now restores and maintains gardens. He lives in Barnet, is married and has two talented daughters. He is curmudgeonly and cynical as well as being a loving husband and father, which is confusing for friends and family alike. He has strong views about many things, some of which are probably wrong. David was born in 1960 and increasingly feels that whatever it is he'd better get on with it. He has yet to master the art of writing a short biography without it appearing either embarrassingly needy or hopelessly arrogant. While happy with his lot and proud of his achievements, he struggles with the notion that anyone would want to hear him blowing his own trumpet. He hopes you like the story.

AUDREY WILLIAMS earned her MFA from Chicago State University. She has published short stories and poetry. Her work has appeared in *African American Review*, *Verse/Chorus: an Anthology*, *The Alchemist Review*, *Bewildering Stories* and *Torrid Literature*. She received an Honorable Mention for a novel excerpt from *ByLine Magazine* and has a YA story forthcoming from Sleepytown Press. She also loves photography. Audrey lives in Chicago, Illinois with Danielle, Chris, Jeremy and Malik.

ACKNOWLEDGEMENTS

'Ghost Pine Lake' by Brandy Schillace was originally published in the *Winona Daily News* (October 25, 2012). 'Haunting Melody' by Allen Ashley was originally published in *Unspoken Water* 3 (2012), edited by Ian Hunter.

Hannah Kate would like to thank two websites: www.manchesterhistory.net and www.theskyliner.org, for inspiration and information that helped with the writing of 'Lever's Row'.